PARADOX LOST

PARADOX LOST

Adrian L. Youseman

Matador
5 Weir Road
Kibworth Beauchamp
Leicester LE8 0LQ, UK
Tel: (+44) 116 279 2299
Fax: (+44) 116 279 2277
Email: books@troubador.co.uk
Web: www.troubador.co.uk/matador

ISBN 978 1780880 150

British Library Cataloguing in Publication Data.
A catalogue record for this book is available from the British Library.

Typeset in 10.5pt Aldine401 BT Roman by Troubador Publishing Ltd, Leicester, UK

Matador is an imprint of Troubador Publishing Ltd

Printed and bound in the UK by TJ International, Padstow, Cornwall

*This book would not have been possible
without the loving support of my wife and the
editorial work of Alice McVeigh*

1

The Awakening (2006)

He awoke in complete blackness, without even the slightest hint of pearl suggesting dawn. His lids flickered in that first rush of consciousness, confirming the inky veil of instinct: he was in darkness, though not blind. The weight of gravity assured him that he was lying down, but everything else felt strange… the pillow was tight; the mattress firm: this instantly struck him as being unnervingly unfamiliar. His hands sought in vain the padded counterpane of his own bed; instead he located some silken fabric with just a few harder points of contact. This initial rush of information frustratingly refused to combine and form a picture in his head; nothing registered as he had expected.

His mind raced as he realized he had no recollection at all where he was: the flashing images in his mind felt separated from reality. His conflicting sensations set one part of his brain against another and drew him almost into a scream, but his mouth felt clammy, like half-set glue, and yielded little more than a groan.

Bizarrely, as if his punishment had been self-inflicted, the more he relaxed, the freer his body became. Sensing release, he gradually eased onto his elbow, half-upright. There he raised his hand and rubbed it across his eyes, as if that alone could remove the darkness.

Andrew felt for his watch, yet it had been removed. Increasingly curious, he padded his body with his hands, to see what else he could learn from his attire. His clothing was strange, smooth and almost silky to the touch – perhaps some kind of tunic. His feet were also bare and the surface was smooth as liquid.

What had happened yesterday? His memories seemed distant as if it had been days or weeks since he was last awake. Still worse, it occurred to him that someone could be imposing them upon him: it was almost mind-splittingly nerve-racking not knowing for sure if his thoughts were even his own. He had to accept the possibility that someone had been – or was still – playing with his mind in some way. Or even that he had been drugged.

'Basics,' he said aloud. 'My name is Andrew Marshall.' He could have doubted even this memory, but the first reassuring thoughts were coming together. 'I'm married to Alison. Our children are Mary, Harry and James.' The names helped, summoning up the casual atmosphere of their Surrey house, along with the strange mix of village life and busy traffic of southeast England... Then, just as suddenly, the comfort evaporated, leaving him with a strange feeling about the children, even about Alison.

They were unmistakably recent memories, but at the same time felt weirdly distanced. This conflict between the sequence of memory and the feeling of being separated from his family was startling. Such a flood of visions – if not reassuring – might well drive him back into the horrible confusion he had just left... he contented himself with summoning his children in his head; they were playing in the sun-filled back garden while Alison brought out a tray of drinks from the kitchen. Surely the image of his children was real... he felt as if he was now burrowing dangerously near layers of panic but the longer the darkness went on the more he conjectured the worst.

'Is anybody there?' he cried, feeling rather foolish. The lack of response seemed a deafening weight in this darkness. Not even his own voice echoed to greet him.

Ignored, Andrew forced himself to focus on the environment, much like a prison cell. Any normal cell would have a monitoring system, he reasoned; if so, somebody would come soon, unless they were intent on observing his reactions. Or unless he was on an infrared monitoring system. He stirred, uneasy at the thought - cellblocks were normally noisy with walls and corridors, unless the walls were soundproofed, or the other inhabitants afraid to respond.

Andrew's imagination – always vivid – flashbacked to various news stories: hostages, kidnaps, crop circles, the lunatic fringe. Yet he wasn't the type of person to travel riskily, nor did he possess wealth enough to be ransomed. Besides, his surroundings seemed a bit too clinical to fit any such scenario. He shoved the soles of his feet against the floor to reassure himself of the smooth cool surface beneath. He would have given a lot for the feeblest light.

He clung to the end of each second, until the strain of listening evaporated into hopelessness. Perhaps he would simply have to accept his situation until someone was prepared to impart some explanation – even light – into the room. His intuition was that he would be interrogated in some way, as there seemed nothing wrong with him, apart from a groggy sensation in his head. As he speculated, it struck him that he was just feeding his fears to no useful purpose, and determined to distract himself by finding out more about his surroundings.

The bed felt reassuringly solid and, unable to tell the extent of his surroundings, he decided to count and measure his steps. He longed for some cord or rope as a guide, suddenly and almost guiltily realising how tough life must be, day-in and day-out for the blind. Again he rubbed his eyes, but this time took care to note every detail of his skin, lashes and lids. There seemed no obvious wound or sensitivity, so he still felt reasonably sure that they were still seeking into the inky blackness around him.

His hands brushed across the bed, but it seemed very standard, almost sterile with its crisp pillow and laundered sheets. As his hand ran across the top, he felt the change from the cotton of the fold to the thicker blanket on top. He recalled that he had awoken on top of the blankets, as if not intended to be there that for long (from somewhere, he remembered the last time he had awoken displaced, but lovingly tucked in, as a small boy). Yet his environment still gave him a comforting sense of order, with his change of clothes and precisely made bed.

Standing, he carefully positioned his calves evenly against the side of the bed in order to square his direction. He ventured into the darkness, using small, calculated paces, his hands gently circling the space directly before him. Six or seven feet onwards, his thigh hit a horizontal strip of contact like a solid bar. His fingers flickered over the obstacle. Hard and rectangular, it resembled a table, but he was disappointed to find nothing resembling a lamp on its surface – or, indeed, any object at all. Working his hands around the outside edges he discovered a chair-back, tight to the far side edge. It was positioned as if to observe the bed, rather than to be used by its inhabitant, which felt unsettling.

He decided to risk a turn and had explored at least twenty feet without encountering anything before he decided to head back to the table. Miscalculating with his increased confidence heading back, his toes cracked into the table a full step before he expected. He put his weight on to the table, testing his toes gingerly to reassure himself that the damage was slight.

Waiting for the pain to subside, he worked his way along the table to stand behind the chair, as if to face the bed in this mire of blindness, though this too was unsettling, as he kept imagining infrared cameras blinking towards him… where would the door be? Roused to stubbornness, he set off again, determined to set his position and map it in his head. He was almost prepared to give up as before when his left fingers touched a plain smooth wall, something strangely comforting in this dark dream-like place… he felt his way along until his right hand suddenly slid into thin air, and he halted as if the wall had slipped out from under his hand.

Just a metre from the corner, the tip of his fingers hit a new flat surface, with an outline quickly confirmed as the size and shape of a doorway. He covered every inch in methodical detail in search of a handle without locating one. However, the mere fact that there was a door eased his mind. With renewed hope, he felt all round the walls either side of the door, in full expectation there must be – somewhere – a light switch, or else a control for the door. Several times he searched, in growing disbelief that there was nothing there. With every movement of his hands the warmth of finding the door was eroded, until the smooth blank recess in the wall became an object of frustration that he irrationally longed to kick, to injure.

Taking a long step back, he threw his full weight on to the door, the sides of his fists thumping hard into it. He had expected it to flex at least, or hear an echo of impact on the other side. Instead, there was a thud as if it was made of brick or concrete, with an accompanying ache in his flesh and bones.

Pausing for a few seconds, he clutched at the prospect that perhaps it was a disused doorway and that on that principle there would be another, most probably at the other end. This time he had a reference point, so returning to the corner of the doorway, he reset his confidence and returned his position so as to bisect desk and bed. Sure enough, this time he allowed more for his confidence in returning, and soon touched the bed.

In the end he gave up. 'A waiting game,' he thought. 'I can do that.' Staring into the darkness, he battled with his eyelids as they tried to close, repeatedly shaking his head to force them open, but it was weariness that eventually prevailed.

His mind was now laced with dream-like flashes: fragments of real memory or simply dreams echoing in his head? Picture upon picture scanned past as if lit by sheet lightning, but one continually recurred: a hospital bed surrounded by surgical equipment, but he couldn't see the patient. The frustration of not knowing needled him into wakefulness.

When his eyelids flashed open, the first thing he noticed was a soft creamy light coming from the doorway. Then he shot bolt upright as he took in his surroundings.

'What the bloody –' Not that the walls around him were unexpected, but he felt sure that he had felt and walked much further – at least six or seven metres further – than could have been possible. The room was almost empty, its walls, ceiling and floor strangely metallic; it was impossible to tell whether it might even be some type of granite by its sheen. The door looked like frosted glass and was improbably thin, compared to the memory of its impact against his fists, while the light – from some distant source – enabled the faintest outline of a long corridor to be distinguishable. As he peered into the blurred distance, he could sense something emerging from the centre of the light. With every movement towards the door, the light in the room also gathered strength, warming from a dull moony colour into warm clarity, and he realised that the shape of a person was walking quietly towards him.

2

Awakening (1990)

As Caittie turned over in bed for the umpteenth time, she knew that the despairing trend of her thoughts must have permeated her dreams; waking stressed was now a habit.

The red glare of the clock indicated 5.05 and only the faintest glimmer of dawn showed through the gap in the curtains. It wouldn't be light for some time and she knew how annoyed Keith would get if disturbed. These rules (which he set and she inevitably followed) meant that her whole life sometimes felt like nothing more than some small sub-clause of his. It wasn't that anything he expected was unreasonable so much as rigid and unnecessary. Any change of routine ranked as a mortal sin, springing from his deep need for control. Then there were the meltdowns: hopeless of resolution, because, no matter how long she spent explaining the needless hurtfulness of his actions, he was unrepentant. His attitude towards her, which had long since lost any justification of being born of concern, was every day scorching away the love she had once felt for him, as it showed such a total lack of respect and regard for her.

For the hundredth time, Caittie asked herself what she had seen in him in the first place – yet, in those early days, Keith had been very different. It was only once they became a couple when his abruptness assumed priority, as if by right. She had become, metaphorically, his comfy pair of slippers – which his dark arts had turned into cast-iron fetters.

Of course, they had met when she was still running away from her past. Yet she still seemed addicted to repeating the negatives, as if trapped in her own perpetual groundhog day. Cocooned in a life of seeming security, courted by Dr Jekyll yet living with Mr. Hyde, her heart felt heavier by the day. How gradually Keith had chipped away at every corner of their lives! Like a child with scissors sharper than he could handle, the pleasure of the cut seemed more important than the very fabric of her life. Each week his comments sliced deeper, as if tailoring her into the shape he wanted. The years she had spent trying to make these things better – only to find new barriers always erected, so that she could never feel the complete person she longed to be! Had she not suffered from a naturally affectionate disposition, she would surely have hated him by this time.

He had stolen her life and her freedom, but because she knew he couldn't help himself she still felt something like pity for him. Though, whatever this feeling really was, it was ebbing fast. Like grains of sand, the more she tried to grasp them, the swifter they seemed to slip through the fingers. And then, whenever he realised she was unhappy, there was always the sex card, which she would fall for every time. Because the sex worked, she invariably hoped it would prove a new beginning... even though it always ended in emptiness.

And yet. If Keith was never to be the one to fill this space, was it too daunting to consider an alternative? Though the very prospect of escaping from Keith would surely turn his verbal butchery into wholesale slaughter... this question nagged her like desire, especially in the dead of night.

She felt a dark slouch of a cat near the bottom of the bed. Keith's precious cat, always taking pride of place! Yet Caittie eased her leg back, frightened to wake Tinkerbelle, as the first thing the cat would be likely to do would be to reclaim Keith, awakening him. How pathetic, she thought, always letting the cat win! She liked animals, but not on beds; and if at any time the cat got pushed off, however accidentally, she had committed yet another sin. In the house, Tinkerbelle reigned: the supreme being, electing to sleep on Caittie's half of the bed as by divine right.

The irony was that it was Caittie's flat, and Caittie's bed, and that Keith had brought Tinkerbelle with him when he moved in: a move rather too premature for her liking. She had to laugh at the length of time it had taken her to realize that when Keith came home, it was Tinkerbelle he greeted first, virtually every time. In fact, it had taken her absurdly long to work out that the ideals of equality that Keith had so enthused about when they first met bore no resemblance to the actual reality.

It was now 6.45, and fresh air and a cleared head seemed still more alluring. Slipping out of bed, Caittie swiftly gathered up her clothes. It had been ages since she had gone for an early morning jog, as Keith hated anything that disturbed his routine. In the hall, throwing her clothes on, she flicked back her dark blonde hair and gathered up it in her hand, fixing it in a loose ponytail. She crossed the hall with caution and the click of the latch provided a starting pistol to set her dashing down the stairs. She had reached the bottom and hardly drawn breath before making any attempt to put her shoes on.

The crisp morning air struck her bed-warm face pleasantly as her breathing started to catch up with the stressed pace she had first set. She soon slipped into a jog, relaxing after shaking off a predator. All this, and for what? Just to avoid some ear bashing from Keith? Still, the thought of causing pain – her guilt doubled by the subsequent pain of confrontation.

With the flow of endorphins in her veins, she remembered again why she loved to run. The situation with Keith, the issues with her father, her being in-between jobs, all these stresses loosened with the regular thudding of her trainers on the ground.

The trust fund her father had left her mother and Caittie meant that neither would have to work again unless they chose to – and her mother at least did not intend to. The combination of her salary and the trust income had allowed her to save a considerable amount since university – something which seemed to grate on Keith. He had a well-paid position working for a government research department, but she still paid all the household expenses. He was only spending a minute portion of his salary on living expense, yet always claimed to be short for his next big expenditure, most recently an Italian sports car.

She was just starting to feel the incline biting into her thighs as her doubts made her pace quicken. 'Here I am,' she thought: 'a mentally and physically strong person reduced to feeling fearful, because I'm trying to hold on to a destructive relationship. Why?' Her feet beat out a crisp 'no more, no more, no more', but her breathing became heavier as she ploughed through the steepest part of the hill. Reaching the brow, she suddenly remembered.

'The box!' she cried, unaware that a man in a business suit on the other side of the road was staring at her, almost offended, before deciding that she was a lunatic. The downward jar through her legs vibrated through her body as she tried to control her downhill pace. The box: of course. Why hadn't she thought of it before?

The box had been left to her by her father – something she'd always subconsciously rebelled against – but suddenly it alone seemed to fulfill her need to rid herself of ghosts, both past and present. Her determination to access its secrets made more and more sense with every stride. Venting these issues would set her free to be herself. It would provide distance from Keith, further her understanding of her still-shadowy father and just might prove a strong enough motive to overcome her mother's desire that Caittie would succumb to their wishes in the end, as she had always done before.

Luckily, after reading her father's letter on her twenty-first, she had summoned up sufficient commonsense to do as he had said and left the box wrapped. No one – not even Mother – knew what was inside the parcel or where she had hidden it, as the letter had suggested that anyone with such knowledge might be mysteriously at risk. Her mother's house had been burgled a couple of times since then, but the key to the safety deposit box was well hidden and remained undisturbed. Interestingly, her mother took such invasions well in her stride, as they had happened still more frequently while Caittie's father was still alive (as a renowned archeologist, her father's home seemed irresistible to those wondering whether he had ever succeeded in capturing treasure trove, whether illicit or not).

As for the box, occasionally at family gatherings the question would arise – half joking, half serious *'Well, haven't you opened it yet?'* – a query which had commanded Keith's attention. So much so that, upon moving in, he had immediately asked Caittie about it. His insistence that there should be no secrets between them was met by an equal determination on her side that he would have to trust her, as she would betray her father's words to no one. In short: this was one battle of wills she was never going to lose.

Suddenly, the weight of her life seemed self-inflicted: she had so little to tie her down. Plus, as much as she was grateful for her father's money, it had proved a bitter pill to swallow, coming from the world that had kept her father away for so much of the time, ensuring that she never truly knew him... nor had the lustre of his reputation generally been to her advantage. When after university she assisted on expeditions to different parts of the world, just the mention of his name sent the principal archeologists into huddled conversations, after which she was never quite treated with the same casualness again. The question always remained, in the back of her mind, as to what had happened to her father – and why.

She knew where the answers lay – in the box, the box left to her, which had been presented on her twenty-first birthday by the family's solicitor. How well she recalled her anger upon reading his accompanying letter and trying to not let it show as the family watched, attempting to appear casual and unconcerned.

'*By the time you read this, you will be well towards finishing your degree – if I am right, it will be in History or Archeology,*' it had begun and 'How dare you!' had trembled on her lips. The anger and frustration she felt that he could think he would know what she would do, when he didn't know her at all!

'*Dearest Caittie, I don't know what you're thinking right now, but all I can assume is that you have decided it is time to follow my work. First and most crucially, I have to warn you that you're being followed. No matter how careful you have been or cautious with my earlier warnings, you are being watched and followed. I know this because I have been followed myself the last few years and the fact they have not yet gotten hold of this information suggests that they will without doubt be after you similarly. In fact, almost as soon as they know you've accessed this box, they will be on to you.*

And so: who are these people? I wish that I could say for sure, but they're certainly government sponsored, whether of one government or from several.

And now for your instructions: do not take this information out of the safety deposit box room for any reason. Instead, memorise what you need to and destroy everything you make notes on as soon as you have used it.

Draw out as much cash as you can: other transactions are far too traceable. If you must use the phone, never use one where you are staying and try not to use it until you are about to leave any place for good. In addition: keep it short, calls become traceable faster with each passing year. Mobiles – believe me – are still more dangerous.

And now I should fill you in on what this is all about, in hopes that you might succeed where I must have failed.

At university, I met up with several men, who – though from rather different fields – shared a common interest in unexplained phenomena. If you remember, they used to come to the house when you were small, as we created and built up our post-university business, which was to prove surprisingly lucrative. If you can't recall them: Frank is American, Michael rather exotic, of Greek extraction, and George the very apologetically overweight Englishman. It seems a bit childish now, but we used to conduct all our notes under the acronym of GAMF (our initials). Yet still, as we began to investigate one subject in particular, strange things started to happen, and we began to realise that we were being watched.

Naturally, we'd suspected that we might be rooting about the edge of government secrets, but I still can't imagine why our research could be of any more special interest than that of many other such groups.

At any rate, George (to be honest, probably our least effective member) suddenly disappeared. Frank, who had connections – never really explained – immediately warned Michael that he was likely to be framed on a murder charge, and advised that he go into hiding. I still doubt whether Frank ever told us all he knew, but he was always trying to impress, so it was hard to know what to believe sometimes. In short, what you have in your hands – rather than being the whole facts – is truly only all that I know. But first you might wonder why I didn't choose to confide in the others completely.

My disappearance – your possession of this letter – is proof that I must not have been careful enough. Knowing that I might not live to see you grow up was – and indeed is – very hard for me, but as you will discover, in the end I discovered that I had no choice.

In this box, you will find two more envelopes and inside them the key to what has consumed me. The envelope marked 2 shouldn't be opened until you're sure you're ready to start. The package is sealed in your last birthday wrapping paper, which you might remember as a one-off: my strange wrapping style should make it very evident if anyone tampers with it.

The letter and her father's words had filled her with anger – so much so that, for many years, she couldn't contemplate venturing further with it and the recollection torched inside of her, unforgotten, just under the edge of her consciousness. Also, being so many years since his disappearance, the warnings seemed ridiculous within the normality of her life and the temper of that day had initially resolved her not to believe until something showed itself.

Although furious at her abandonment, she had secured the box safely, feeling that she could never grieve completely for her father until this task (his last?) had been completed. Perhaps it was now time to find out – perhaps she had kept him waiting long enough. It was more than nerves that gave her pause: it was the risk of finding out whether she could believe her father's actions justified. After all, in terms of his memory, she still had a lot to lose.

She had completed the hill and jogged through the small local park. By half-seven, the traffic was picking up with retail workers and those early Saturday morning shoppers desperate to claim the first bargain… the bustle made it hard to concentrate on working out a plan in her head. How to get at the box without arousing Keith's suspicions – and then what? Suddenly, Caittie remembered: Monday. Keith would be at work and she could arrange to go to her mum's. Her decision formed, it seemed sensible to steel herself against Keith for the next two days.

First, and most crucially, she knew the box must be kept out of the way from everyone close to her – she might need a safe house or hotel to work from, in case her father's warnings proved well-founded. She might need to fabricate some cover stories and even some means to enable her to travel, if necessary, without exciting too much worry or suspicion. She summoned to mind colleagues who had once offered her positions on 'digs', old university friends, ex-flatmates continually proposing that she drop everything and visit them.

The strangest part was the excitement of what she was contemplating, mixed with the heady endorphins rushing through her from the exercise. She was startled to recognise the prospect of danger as a life-giving force. Perhaps her father understood that this quality would eventually make the challenge irresistible. Her current life, especially her life with Keith, was beginning to remind her of suffering in a pair of shoes too small for a time, and she began to long for the comfort of her old friendly, worn-in boots… surely there comes a point where one changes simply because there is no other choice?

Nearing the apartment block, however, reality started hitting home. ('Must keep cool. Keith must not know; Mum must not know. I need to keep everything normal – although Keith will get possessive, just as he always does when I least need it.') Although she was still sparking with energy, she found the need to pull herself up the stairs via the handrail, as if her legs were affected by the trepidation starting to well up inside of her.

There were noises in the kitchen. Caittie shut the door quietly behind her.

'Where the bloody hell have you been?' came from the kitchen, in tight tones.

'I was just – running!'

'You never said anything about going out at this sort of time, did you?'

'You know how you loathe it when I wake you up.'

There was a dark line underscored between his eyes. 'I needed to know where you were! You might at least have left a note!'

He wanted her to give way. Yet she was still holding onto that firm and determined Caittie that had been allowed to surface whilst she was running.

'What do you mean by "needed"?'

'It would just be nice to be kept informed.'

'That's not what you said – *needed* is what you said. I could understand your being worried for my safety, but *needed* means something else. That's all about you and your needs.'

He was visibly discomfited by her new assurance. 'Bollocks! You sneak out, knowing would upset me and now, hey, it's *my* fault?'

'We're two adults sharing a flat – which I happen to own, incidentally – and I took an adult decision about leaving quietly in order to have a run – but either way, I didn't want to disturb you.'

'Two adults sharing a flat, what kind of crap is that? We're meant to be partners!' Keith had switched from sarcasm to defence: the emotion card.

Caittie could see that she'd pushed him into unfamiliar territory. 'Perhaps because you treat me as a possession.'

'Oh Caittie! You know how much I love and care for you.' Keith's voice had changed again, and yet this hurt tone seemed as false as it was unfamiliar.

'No, you need me. You need me to be in certain places at certain times. You need me to live around your life. Anything you love is – is the *idea* of me, you have no concept of me personally, or of what I might need.' Sensing that this was getting bitter, too near the bone, she lightened the tone. 'You see, if you were tuned into my needs, you'd have poured me a coffee by now, instead of standing there enjoying your own.'

The rest of the weekend was a game of avoidance, with them both dancing round each other, each sensing that any further discussion of this topic could spill over and end everything. She phoned her mum later that morning and all was set – even a meal in the freezer for Keith's tea with the taped-on heating instruction. How the time dragged, but how the thoughts and hopes of what might lay ahead swirled round her head in the weekend's long silences!

13

3

Interview

Andrew watched the door slide into the wall with a sibilant hiss that (to him at least) failed to match its tested solidity. Stepping into the room was a man, perhaps forty, perhaps fifty, tall and grey-haired yet broad-shouldered and possessed of an enviable assurance. He could be no one's notion of a terrorist, still less of an alien, or not as Andrew had imagined them, at any rate. Yet there was something very sci-fi about the way he merely lifted his hand, causing the door to swish back into its place. No handle, no buttons, no key; just the bizarre way this door and man were connected with neither thought nor effort.

The man's wrinkles around his eyes deepened as he looked intently at Andrew: a quizzical look, as if he was trying to read Andrew's face and from that distance would have preferred a larger print. At length Andrew felt obliged to drop his gaze, though this annoyed him.

'Hello, Andrew,' said the stranger, moving towards the chair behind the desk. Andrew felt at an instant disadvantage – a sudden worry that he was ill, and that the stranger, so at ease and confident, was in command: a surgeon, a consultant, a psychiatrist. (That was it, he'd gone quietly mad.) The man exuded an aura both powerful and passive, the last trait Andrew had expected, riddling the shell of his resolve with renewed self-doubt. Andrew had felt this before when an important person entered a room, their reputation preceding them, but here there was no explanation beyond instinct.

In silence, the man eased himself into the chair and leaned back, while a neat folder materialised squarely on the desk. The silence took on an edgy quality: yet the longer it lasted, the more stubborn Andrew felt, and the more determined not to respond, though there were a thousand words trying to escape.

'Reluctant to speak, Andrew?' There was an air of grave

disappointment – along with a force that suggested that silence was not an option.

'Depends.'

Andrew felt relieved, as if the game of chess had begun, but was not about to cooperate without a full explanation.

'Upon what?'

'On why I am here.'

'You have no idea then?' The man's hand rubbed his chin, as if he had suspected as much.

'Maybe that's why I am asking!' Andrew knew he sounded terse but his head still felt fuzzy and he ached for clarity.

'You have nothing to fear. We need you to answer some questions and the more you cooperate, the easier it will be for both of us.'

'*We* need! *Both* of us! What do you mean?'

'Are you going to try and read into everything?' The man sighed as if this process was likely to take longer than he had hoped.

'That depends on what you say, and how soon I feel sure what this is all about.'

Immediately Andrew regretted his brashness, but the stranger had gifted him the chance.

'I know you long for answers – and you will learn all, in time. How much and how soon depends upon your cooperation. However, rest assured, I cannot lie to you. At times I might *appear* a bit evasive, but I'm sure you understand this is all part of the process. It will all make sense later.'

'Does that mean I get to know who the – we – or the you for that matter – is? Or are you too much the politician for that?'

'For this phase of this interview I am willing to tell you that my name is Pierre.'

'Right, Pierre, nice to meet you – and I'd like to know what the hell you mean by "phase"?'

Quietly he replied, 'I'm sure you understand the word and exactly what it means.'

'And where the fuck did those walls come from?' Andrew spat out the expletive like a gambit, though it tasted horrible in his mouth. He felt like a child, needing to thrust in a verbal spike in order to test his boundaries.

'The walls – well, you'll just have to accept them.'

'But they weren't there before!'

Smoothly: 'And they may not be there later. Now I know you wouldn't want to do yourself scant justice. What I hope is that you learn to trust me: I can assure you everything will make sense in time.'

Andrew, dangerously: 'In time? In how long, exactly?'

'A time that will only be extended if you lose your temper as I will then be obliged to terminate the session.' And with this, Pierre picked up the folder from the table as if resigned to his expulsion.

Andrew felt flattened: he had certainly located a boundary, but what sort of forced interrogation maintained a level of moral integrity?

He said, more mildly: 'Odd: I always thought trust was earned rather than demanded.'

Pierre replaced the folder, saying: 'Sometimes one discovers that one has no choice other than to trust. This will be initially frustrating for you, in that for most this is a simple process, but for you, well, there are certain things I cannot yet tell you.'

'Why not? Or can't you tell me that, either?'

Pierre made a reserved gesture. 'Some reactions can still change the outcome for the worst.'

'But listen: last night I walked *metres* past those walls, and believe me, they weren't there. So what am I supposed to think? That I've gone mad?'

'I can't answer that.'

'Why not? You're the one in control, what can *you* have to lose?'

Pierre half-smiled, which Andrew found bizarrely reassuring. 'Only by taking things in the right order can we achieve the purpose of these discussions. Trust me, you will never go mad if you cooperate. Instead, you'll understand everything.'

A surge of energy swelled up inside Andrew. Half sulky, half belligerent, he sprang from the bed to his feet in a single movement… Launching himself across the room, he thrust his fist towards the wall.

'Stop!' came from Pierre too late as Andrew's hand smashed against the wall, an instant pain shooting up his arm. Staggering backwards, Andrew was now very confused. The wall that he thought imaginary had dealt him a painful blow. He found himself bent forward clamping his hand between his legs as if to hold it together, glaring furiously towards Pierre, who appeared unmoved. Tentatively, Andrew withdrew his hand to inspect the damage. The pain remained intense, but knowing how hard he had hit the wall it was surprising that there was no broken skin where he expected it. No blood, no obvious wound: his fingers traced an intact series of interwoven bones.

Pierre said evenly, 'Perhaps now even you of all people will see there is an easy way and a hard way of doing things, and trust me – I am trying to make it easy for you.'

Arrogant bastard. 'Hang on, I might be hurting here, but you don't have to be so bloody sarcastic. You used those words – easy way, hard way – as if you *knew* it was something that I – that I always say.'

Again Andrew stopped and waited for a reaction, but none came. 'If you carry on like this without giving me any answers to my questions, you are going to drive me mad very quickly. I suppose that's your nasty little game, to drive me mad and break me down! Well, I'm onto you.'

These first few experiences and exchanges were forming a puzzle in his head, which needed some retrenchment until he could make sense of it. He could see little choice now than to remain guarded and then push to get those reactions or information that would enable him to see the bigger picture. It was an auto reflex response he had had all his life – analyze a failing or defeat and turn it into knowledge or victory. So much part of his persona, it was often turned into obsession, often an unexplained thirst, but a response which restored him some sense of control.

'What have I said that upset you?' Pierre was now obviously enjoying the exchange and as his knowing tone again tried to force Andrew into dialogue.

'You said "the easy way or the hard way" as if you knew I use it with my kids. You're – you're almost teasing me with my own advice. You've been watching me!'

'Ah, that. Yes, perhaps. I must have picked up on it in your notes.' Pierre placed his broad hand on the folder which had remained shut.

'Notes? What notes? I suppose you're not going to tell me that either!' It was cheap but he couldn't resist.

Pierre hesitated for just a few seconds. 'Sorry.'

'Sorry?' It was the last word he was expecting from Pierre and he could not hide the confusion from his voice.

'Sorry I cannot tell you more now. Sorry I seemed sarcastic. Sorry we have started the hard way.' Pierre's words struck Andrew, for there was no pride or loss of pride, just sincerity.

'Well, then – thanks.' Although grudgingly grateful, he was suddenly conscious of a complete lack of pain in his hand, as if it had been turned off at the switch, a hallucinatory feeling. Had he been drugged? Would that explain the muddy feeling in his brain? He wished Pierre would leave, give him time to regain his sense of reality and get a grasp of what kind of interrogation he was to undergo.

Under his breath: 'Perhaps you can explain the easy way now?'

'All you need to do is trust that I am not here to harm you. Trust me when I say that you will only be kept here until you answer my questions honestly and openly. Trust me to do no harm.'

Back to shrink-speak, thought Andrew, but stayed silent.

'We will need to explore some aspects of your answers before we decide what to do with you. Only this will determine how long this takes and how long it will be before I can answer the questions you ask. At the end of these phases, you will be released from here. And now, I'm afraid, I can tell you no more.'

4

Mum's the word

On Sunday morning, Keith had made a couple of phonecalls and announced that he was going for lunchtime drink with Dave-from-work, as he usually did after a biggish argument. Apart from a distant wave or the occasional phone message, Caittie had never met Dave. Whenever she attempted to engage him in conversation, the replies were monosyllabic: not shy, never rude, just politely evasive, as if Keith had painted her as someone not to be trusted. Any attempt to break the ice with a get-together – perhaps with Mrs. Dave – was met with Keith's assurance that it was 'men's stuff', to such a degree that she had begun to doubt whether Mrs. Dave even existed. It always struck Caittie as strange that they could keep a conversation going for a whole lunchtime, but Keith always returned with a new string of justifications for his actions – and, anyway, she found it convenient. Perhaps she had even subconsciously created the argument the other day to get him out the way.

As soon as Keith left for the pub, she began to pack as many clothes as she could into some canvas shopping bags, artfully rearranging the remaining clothes so the wardrobe didn't appear emptied. All Keith knew was that she was going to her mother's for the day and would be back late, which was all he needed to know, for if he sensed anything of the truth he would certainly try to put obstacles in her way. After putting the bags in her car boot, she was able to relax and make things appear as normal as possible for when he returned.

It was not a long drive from her flat in Uxbridge to Stratford, so it was easier to just lie in bed on Monday morning until Keith left for work. He tried to engage her in conversation a few times, but her muttered responses were clear to him that it was pointless. Eventually she managed a muttered, 'See you later,' which he accepted. There followed a few remaining sounds from different rooms, until his customary 'Bye' as he opened the front door.

The instant the door clicked shut, Caittie sat up, nervy but purposeful. She longed to make sure Keith had gone, but wanted to make the most of every second before her own departure. It seemed like ages, but it was actually only a few minutes as she waited to be sure. Each second passed as a heavy, imaginary footstep, just in case he got to his car and for some reason walked back again. When she could breathe again, the first thing she did was to make a quick list of everything she needed, as it had swirled round her head all weekend. A few moments in the kitchen writing this list was an easy option just in case Keith came back. She knew he would be scheming and wondering how he could get her back into his routine as he always had done before. It was not like him to come back after forgetting things; but the last few days had showed he was increasingly suspicious – just when she so needed to be free! She was aware that the list became a double comfort in that lists were always a crutch, as well as something easily hidden were he to suddenly return.

First she wrote: 'Recover box from the safety deposit'. And then she wondered how she could feel so sure that what she would find in the box would involve taking her any further than London. There was no reason but the subconscious assumption that, as her father's work had taken him away so often, the box would now offer her the same opportunity. Or perhaps it was sheer longing. Certainly, as each item was added – covering every eventuality – she soon realised she had far too much. Keith would surely notice the disappearance of even half the list. As the only essentials were her passport and cash, she was about to start crossing off most of the other items, when it dawned on her there was a good compromise. There were lots of bits of old make up and toiletries in her chest of drawers and cupboards, so with careful juggling she took the time to pick out her few basic favourites from the shelves and replace them with spares. Each time she had to stand back and look as if it was a piece of art, to be sure that it looked like her usual chaos of things. The essentials she put in a shoulder satchel and the rest went in a plastic bag. She was about to leave when it dawned on her she usually left Keith a reminder about his dinner in the freezer whenever she was late home or staying over. Going back to the kitchen, her heart raced as she saw her absurdly long list still there, like a wedding list after the bride had absconded. Such a simple error! But it would betray everything. Tearing the list, she pocketed it, taking no chances of his finding it in the rubbish. It was then relief to scribble his dinner instructions, finishing as always with the traitorous 'XCaittie.'

Caittie slipped into her bank on the high street, feeling strangely light-headed as she withdrew the maximum each of her accounts allowed without fuss. Not knowing what places her father would need her to go, she could only feel prepared with plenty of money in her pocket. She remembered what he had written ('Take cash… You will be watched… ') The only person behind her was a square-cut woman with a dachshund – anyone less likely to be any sort of a watcher would be hard to imagine.

It struck her suddenly as delicious, the thought of spending her carefully guarded savings, the taste of adventure. She'd lived for so long without spending anything unnecessarily, trying to keep her distance from the trust money – it had become a habit at university, and one she had never consciously challenged. Driving up the M40 seemed almost a blur, her mind was so distracted by the strange mix of excitement and relaxation, the relaxation born from the relief of leaving Keith behind and the sense that she was in control at last. The familiar landmarks reminded her of the different eras in which she used to make these journeys. When she gained access to the first part of her trust fund for university, she had bought the Uxbridge flat. Her original idea was to do something ground-breaking in this thrilling new age of science, leading to hours spent poring over various courses at Brunel University, but at the last minute she had switched to Archaeology at Kings, something even at the time that she recognised as a defeat.

The fact was that her avid interest in any news or article remotely connected to her father's work had remained, despite all her inner resistance, resulting in frustration and even self-loathing. When not being able to decide on her subject at Brunel, it suddenly just seemed logical to remove this conflict – and more practical still to complete the purchase of her flat, as Uxbridge allowed easy underground access to London and was on the way to her mother's house in Stratford. The tube journey each day boosted her heavy study reading and made it simpler to pick and choose the occasions to join in with university social life. It was easier most weekends to take the tube back to the flat, shower and change while the Friday traffic subsided and then drive up to her mum's for the weekend. Sometimes with a friend, most often Wendy, but towards the end of her last year it was Keith. It was only when she finished university that it became clear to her this whole process was a ritual: a ritual as necessary as her change of career. It was the process of being absorbed in archaeology just as her father was, each weekend bringing home all the week's new things to her mother, who always listened intently. Perhaps they both needed it, to still feel connected to her father by connecting with the work he loved. And, just as there was no 'right time' to let go of such feelings, neither could disappoint the other by even approaching the subject of stopping. The possibility – however far-fetched – in those early days that he might still return meant this was the best way to keep hope alive.

Wendy had become a close friend at university, though the memory of how it had ended still caused Caittie's cheeks to flush. She had never had a serious boyfriend before university, largely due to the fact she would dump them very quickly. Attractive as Caittie was, there was always a steady interest, but the fear of being abandoned again, as she perceived her father to have abandoned her, remained. She vowed no man would ever get close enough to have such power to hurt her again. It was some time before she realised that her behaviour was more about her own anger and that she would someday have to take the risk. In fact, she began each new attempt with hope, and ended it with disappointment, reaching the same panic point with the same result. All this made her feel like a predatory spider, luring in a mate only to destroy them.

By contrast, her friendships with girls seemed genuine and unstressed, causing her to doubt during her teens whether she could ever have a successful heterosexual relationship. It seemed refreshing, then, that in her first week at university, Wendy had made a point of sitting next to her several times for lunch. Conversation, more in-depth conversation and friendship soon followed, which was new ground for Caittie; she had always been popular, but had mixed in a large group. After a few weeks, they seemed to be doing everything together, so the invitation for Wendy to come visit Stratford for the weekend seemed natural. In fact, after a few months, Wendy seemed part of the ritual. She too could also spend hours talking and listening to Caittie's mother. Though not a natural scholar, she also seemed capable of immersing herself in archeological data. Everything seemed to evolve effortlessly until Wendy seemed like the sister she'd never had: the degree course, the ritual visits to her mother and the common acquaintance they shared meant that their life seemed more and more like a single entity, until Caittie's old doubts about her sexuality began to intrude in her dreams. Her curiosity was tinged with excitement, and even rebellion, which was even more tempting as she knew her dad would have hated her to have been a lesbian.

More than once, she had even contemplated experimenting with Wendy in hopes of at once removing doubt and further punishing her father for his desertion – a strange logic, which, once considered, had defeated any action, as any decision or blame would then be hers. After a time she dismissed the idea – whispering secrets under the covers at her mother's house, heads huddled like little girls was all Caittie needed, as if to replace something friendly and sisterly she had missed as a child. It was more than a friendship; they became inseparable. On the next term's change of accommodation Wendy had moved into Caittie's flat and enjoyed about a year, before the kiss that destroyed this peaceful oasis in Caittie's life. Lip on lip: untender, neither friendly nor sisterly – a demand more than a request, the kind of kiss that could have moved her profoundly from a man. Later, she wondered at herself how so short a moment could have implications so profound, as there was instantly no other choice than to confront her fears and fantasies. Still worse was Wendy's reaction, still intense, as if Caittie's issues were only secondary. As if she had been within touching distance of something owed her, only to have it ripped away.

In just those few seconds the relationship dissolved, with both aware that there was no going back. It was not so much the gender problem but Wendy's naked aggression that repulsed her. But when she had dreamed of someone capable of connecting with her soul, it was a man – even as she kept pushing any chance away.

During their friendship, Caittie had often admired Wendy's fearless attitude towards sex, though never imitated it. Wendy's sexual feelings were very predatory and she loved to manipulate men, but doubted she could ever love them. At the end of the day she planned to find a man who could give her everything she wanted, someone whose desires she could use. She used to tell Caittie, with a little smile, that the baseness of male sexuality was so profound it would be a shame not to take advantage of it. At the peak of their closeness, Wendy had used peoples' assumptions, deliberately caressing Caittie's hair or stroking her soft arm, almost as a provocation, something her friend endured rather than encouraged.

Soon after the fateful kiss, and without discussion, Wendy moved out. Caittie thought it would be difficult meeting on the same course, but without Caittie's help Wendy struggled and eventually dropped out. A friend soon heard she had gone on a dig in France with another old friend and shortly after got a letter from her to that effect. They still wrote to each other occasionally, never referring to the occasion that had demolished their friendship.

This whole period with Wendy had taken Caittie from the start of her degree to well into her second year. She had felt lonely when it ended and tended to avoid social events, rebuffing overtures from several men, including Keith. It was a mixture of his persistence and her sorrow that eventually made her weaken and agree to date him. He was a postgraduate student which seemed to give him an enviable amount of free time – he'd seemed constantly available to come around. Perhaps this was how Caittie found herself passively drifting, from his staying over the odd night, to the point when half of his clothes seemed to be at her flat to the moment when he had moved in. It was not a conscious invitation, except to Keith's cat, harshly threatened with eviction from Keith's own place, which he had manoeuvred into an offer of something far more committed than she had intended.

Just as Wendy had, Keith enjoyed talking to Caittie's mum, not in conjunction with any shared interest but instead as fellow members of the self-elected society for the purpose of 'sorting Caittie out for her own good'. The endorsement of Caittie's mum ('so attractive, and such lovely manners') gave Keith the confidence to morph his subtle controlling behaviour into direct methods, while her conscientious attempts to make the relationship work blinded Caittie to the power of the alliance against her. Initially a matter of proving her sexuality to herself, her relationship with Keith had long since drifted into disastrous waters.

During this review, Caittie had left the M40, sped through Stratford and was approaching a turn of the road about a mile from her mother's. Many miles, movements and traffic decisions must have claimed some of her attention in the meantime, yet she felt a shiver of shock from not being able to actually remember the larger part of her journey. Quaint little cottages manifested themselves in and beyond the high street: her mother had chosen the village, at least partly, for that reason. It was in many ways a time-warp and her mother's age and situation made losing herself in the local Women's Institute and Amateur Dramatics almost too easy, although perhaps she had every excuse.

As she turned her neat little car into the drive, Caittie decided that perhaps losing oneself in village life was a very reasonable reaction to having a husband of many years who suddenly tells you he is being followed, admits that what he is about to do is likely to make the danger worse and then disappears. The alternative would have involved wondering fruitlessly what could possibly have made someone leave their loved ones so mysteriously.

It had taken Caittie some time to recognise her mother's behaviour as defensive, because of her continued fascination with her husband's work, a fascination that surfaced every time she had the chance to talk archaeology with Caittie and Wendy, beneath every layer of fury, anger and denial. Today, she was clearly on the alert. The front door opened the instant Caittie pulled in the drive.

'Hi!'

'Caittie, darling,' Caittie got out the car to give her a hug and a kiss, though the urgency behind the hug rather alarmed her.

'You all right, Mum?'

'I've been so worried about you!'

'I'm not late. I'm almost exactly on time.'

'But your call on Saturday made it all sound so urgent, and you've never come down mid-week before. And you haven't brought Keith for a while, have you?'

Her mother turned and walked indoors, her haircut impeccable, her outfit elegant, as if ready for a WI meeting or rubber of bridge at any moment. But all was less serene than it seemed. Just as so many times before, within seconds she had loaded the conversation. Caittie knew that Mum would now pursue the usual routine until she had gotten the answers she wanted. Caittie had planned to tell her mother about the tiff with Keith, but her plans about the box had to be kept secret. Her father's note had bound her to that.

Of course, it was always going to be contentious, given that her mother wanted not to investigate the box but instead to destroy it. She had always maintained that she wanted no further harm brought on the family by whatever it was her husband had brought upon himself. However, Caittie had refused, because to destroy the contents of the box would have felt like destroying her lost father. As she headed to get her bags from the car, she froze. Keith. He must have phoned Mum and warned her that things were worse than ever. Caittie longed to be honest with her mother, but it was more than likely that whatever she told her would be instantly relayed back to Keith. All she had mentioned herself was that she was staying the day and probably staying over, as usual, which was true. Only this time Caittie was planning to leave her car here and head off to London without Keith's knowledge or approval.

In the end she turned back to the house without retrieving her bags. It was a case of either devising some plausible explanation or simply cutting and running. In fact, the thought of driving to London and abandoning her car while she started her investigations filled her with a kind of excitement. It soon dawned on her, though, that after twenty-four hours or so, Keith and her mother would probably have the police looking for her; the thought fuelled her determination.

'Go through, dear, it's almost ready. I'll bring it through.'

Caittie went through to the sitting room

'Mum, honestly there's nothing to worry about. All that's happened – well, I suppose you've guessed that I've had another row with Keith?'

'Yes?' – a long slow inquiry that seemed to be the start of a sentence that never came.

Caittie sighed. 'Well, things haven't been right for some time. It is hard to put my finger on why, but I need some time away.'

'Away where?'

'Anywhere. Just to sort out a few things.'

Caittie tried to sound confident, painfully aware that she was failing – and also that her mother's dream (the ideal white wedding, grandchildren) was failing too.

'Oh dear! Would you like here to stay for a few days, then?'

'No. To be honest, he wouldn't leave either of us alone if I did, so it would be pointless. You know he calls you.' Into the uncomfortable silence she plunged on, 'I thought I'd pop over to Limoges to see Wendy.'

'Wendy! Does Keith know?'

'No, and I'd rather he didn't.'

Her mother shook her head. 'You expect him to hound your footsteps?'

It did sound absurd, even melodramatic, but that was actually what Cattie feared. She answered, as casually as she could manage, 'No, no. He's just very tenacious. I don't want to make a bad decision for the wrong reasons, simply because he's pushing me.' Caittie hoped her mother would play along agreeably, but Mum, typically, was thinking in moral terms.

'I can't lie for you, or for anyone, Caittie. If Keith asks what's going on you may depend upon it that I'll tell him the truth. And so ought you. At any rate, shouldn't you talk to him first?'

Such lovely manners, Caittie thought, with resignation.

'I have, many times. Why do you think we have so many arguments? He can't – or won't – accept or even *allow* anything outside his particular view. Instead he turns to silly mind games, and –' Caittie stopped herself on the verge of mentioning almost hating him, just in time. Should that get back to him, it would only increase his panic and inflame his determination to find her.

'And what?' Mum asked, suspiciously.

'And that will suffocate me. I need room to breathe. I need room to find the strength to take the good bits of Keith and deal with the bad bits in such a way they don't – don't suffocate me any longer.'

Mum switched her attack to a different flank.

'I thought you were over this – this Wendy thing.' As much as her mother had loved Wendy, once Cattie had confessed the reason for their separation, she had never spoken of her without revulsion.

Caittie said calmly: 'There *is* no "Wendy thing". Wendy is married and living in France. But we're still friends.' (Which was stretching the truth, she admitted inwardly.)

'Why don't you choose another old friend?'

'Perhaps I haven't got an open-ended invitation from all my other friends! Why can't I go where I want to? Listen, I've got to figure some things out! If I can't find a way of making my relationships work I'll never get married and never have children!'

Caittie hoped that using children as blackmail would prove irresistible. How often in the old days her mother had mentioned it, fantasising about the days when she and Wendy would both bring her their children! But Mum remained stubborn. 'I still don't see how seeing Wendy will help, so particularly.'

'Wendy understands men on a deeper level than anybody else – and she's found out how to use her strength from when we parted.

Perhaps she can show me.' Caittie had never shared the secrets about Wendy's cynical view on men and sex, so she hoped that this sounded profound.

'I still don't see how I can help you without lying.'

'Simple. I leave my car here in your garage. I phone Keith at home while he's at work and leave a message on the answerphone. I tell him I'm staying over with you and won't be back tonight. Tomorrow I phone him from France. So if he calls tomorrow you can tell him the truth.'

'I was actually taking you to the theatre tonight with some friends of mine. We'd already booked, but I specially got you another ticket to collect at the door.' The pause was almost theatrical. 'I suppose I could do what you ask. But surely there's an easier way?'

'Also, you don't phone Keith today for any reason.'

Her mother looked hurt, as if unjustly accused. 'As long as you call me from France.'

'Of course.' Caittie tried to sound dutiful, though secretly chafing. 'But I need a couple of other favours, just small ones. I'd like to borrow the rucksack from the loft. It's just easier, I mean, it's loads easier than a suitcase on trains, especially when transferring. Also, would you mind giving me a lift to the station?'

Her mother was curious about Caittie's job applications but as soon as she could, Caittie successfully steered the conversation towards her mother's friends. All she had to do was to mention another name for her mother to hold forth (in remorseless detail) on what each was – or had recently been – suffering or enduring. It was an hour before her mother suggested she get lunch, while Caittie climbed in the loft for the rucksack. As Caittie was transferring her things, she couldn't help reflecting dryly how she had come home considering telling her mother the truth, in hopes that she might even impart some crucial insights from the past. How could she have forgotten Mum's loyalty to Keith, and to the possibility of Caittie's bearing him children! She could only console herself by recollecting that she'd given nothing away, and that she might possibly be able to abstract some information on the phone from London.

The longer they sat over dessert, the more clearly Caittie seemed to understand her Mum's train of thought. Starting with looks of puzzlement and culminating with a nod of conclusion, her mother then smiled with the smug confidence of having finished the *Telegraph* crossword. Caittie recognised this look from the many confrontations they had endured in her teenage years. She knew her mother had a killer question, or objection, or had discovered a hole in her story.

'What's up, Mum?' Caittie had no choice other than to ask directly. She had to show some degree of her newfound strength. If she was following in the footsteps of her father, she couldn't leave her mother with the impression she still needed Keith's protection.

'What do you mean?'

'You look like a question waiting to burst.'

Her mother paused and then submitted. 'Well, dear, this idea about seeing Wendy, it doesn't make sense to me. Surely if you're off to France you'd have left the car at home and taken a plane, especially as you live next door to Heathrow?'

Good point, Caittie thought, but not checkmate.

'I want the car here when I come back. Also, it costs a bomb to park at the airport.' This part was true, but she disliked negative spin when she had tried so hard to make it positive earlier. 'Besides, Wendy suggested the train, because the nearest airport's a hundred miles away. The railway stops just half a mile from her village so it's just – well, easier.'

Caittie stopped, feeling that she was trying too hard.

'I see.' Mum sounded less than convinced, but the car was duly housed inside her garage, and they said their goodbyes at the station. It was a three-hour journey to London, as she had to change at Leamington Spa for Paddington, but Caittie still felt a rush of relief as she left the house. Keith still knew nothing, and soon she would be in London.

5

Name, rank and serial number

Pierre opened his mouth and then closed it again. Andrew resisted the urge to speak himself, instinctively guessing that a slip of the tongue could unwittingly destabilize the entire process. But then, perhaps that was what he wanted? What was it about Pierre – that texture of quietness – that made him doubt that he'd been kidnapped? When would he start playing nasty, and demanding information (and what information, exactly, was he after)? And – sharpest of all – was Pierre merely trained to sound like a psychiatrist, or was he, Andrew, actually being detained in some asylum or other? Andrew had never felt so unsure of his ground before. In the end, he elected to keep his responses vague but relevant. He seemed to remember having read something to that effect about hostages in Iraq.

He said guardedly: 'So what's the timescale?'

'You are neither the first nor the last for me to interview, so we'll take any time that might be needed.' Andrew waited for Pierre to add something to his statement – just the smallest morsel of explanation would have tempered his fears – but none was forthcoming.

'Listen, I want to get this over and done with. I own nothing of serious monetary value – except the house, of course – and I can't understand what anyone would want from me. So unless you can give me a damn good reason, I'd be obliged to be allowed to get home to my family.'

'Then cooperate. You must understand there is no "getting it over with" here. You will be finished only once you've reached the necessary level with your answers. Don't ask me what level, I can see the question on your face. Just believe that I need real answers to confirm our thoughts on certain questions before you can be released. Then and only then can we talk about such things as "home".'

'"Real answers" and "certain levels" to me are just ways of saying you're after some sort of confession.'

'If that's how you want to see it. But please remember that there's no point in telling me what you might presume I wish to hear.'

Andrew repled, nettled, 'It doesn't sound like a normal interrogation. Are all your interviews like this?'

'What is "normal"? I need some information and you don't want to stay here, so surely it can only be a matter of time until we find a solution.'

'Right, so you mean I can't go home today?'

'My dear Andrew, I enjoy the sharpness of your mind, but truly I cannot give you any indication. Your time here will be as long as it needs to be. Now, perhaps you could stop trying to piece together some kind of picture.'

Andrew could see he would need to employ more subtlety if he was to get anywhere. He sighed and said, 'So what do you want to know?'

'Good! I want to know what you think is the worst thing you have done.'

'The worst – what? Look, just tell me what am I supposed to have done! Aren't you legally meant to actually *accuse* me of something?'

Pierre shook his head. 'There's no such obligation.'

'At least tell me who I'm dealing with, a politician, a policeman or a shrink!'

'If only it was that simple! Much as I'd like to help you, I honestly have no intention of giving you an answer.'

'"Honestly!" That's a pretty odd word to use, since you won't even tell me what's happening.'

'But it is also the correct word, for surely only your own ego or pride will prevent your being open with me. Of course, it would be easier to lie or trick you into confessing something, but that is not an option.' Pierre's hands pressed heavily onto the table, as if part of him was finding the strain on his patience too much to bear.

'Because you have orders?'

'Because it is not an option.'

'That's just it! If my detainment was above board, shouldn't you be charging me with something – murder, insanity, whatever it is?'

'Next you'll be asking for your right to remain silent,' observed Pierre, amused.

Andrew didn't smile. 'You pretend to want my cooperation, but unless you reciprocate in some way with a little assistance it's hopeless. Try rephrasing the question.'

31

'I can only assist when you start working with the process instead of fighting it and me. So the question remains: what's the worst thing you have done? How could that need rephrasing?"

'It's not easy.'

'No?'

'Perhaps I've got too many "worst things" to choose from.' With no accusation and a disturbingly open agenda, deflection seemed the easy way to buy time to think.

'Try free association. Try the first one that comes into your head.' Pierre was smiling again. 'Let's start from there.'

More pseudo-psychology, thought Andrew acutely, though he'd never actually been in therapy. In fact, for the last few minutes he'd been scouring his memory for anything he could possibly be accused of. Yet the first thing he recalled surprised him, as it was a childhood secret he'd never confided to anyone before. 'OK, how about stealing a few pennies from my grandmother?'

'That's very interesting.' Pierre did not react with any surprise, but an invitation with his hands to continue.

'Interesting?' he repeated, in disbelief.

'In that this is the first thing you think of. Tell me about it.'

'There's nothing to tell. It was only a few coins from the small change pot, not much money, but the trouble was, I never got the chance to say sorry.' How odd, thought Andrew – sharing his feelings, even with his wife, was unusual for him. Perhaps this Pierre was gifted after all.

'Do you think she knew?'

'I don't know,' Andrew admitted, 'but my not saying sorry still hurts me, so perhaps she did, and it hurt her.' His eyes fell with the admission. Fact was, he'd only ever considered his own pain. Now his guilt and discomfort seem insignificant against the hurt of others. His clever distraction had turned into an own goal.

'Why did you take it?'

'Because of my friends.' Which was why, he now realised, he'd never told anyone before.

'I don't understand.'

'Well, peer pressure, if you like. All the parents seem to have the same sort of arrangement for their change, and all my friends were swiping from theirs, and I was made to feel that I was either "one of the gang" or – or an outsider. I hated myself for doing it and I suppose that's why it has stuck in my mind.' Half justification, half admission of his failure, he thought, hoping that the subject would change.

'You knew it was wrong?'

'Of course.'

'But you still did it?'

'I just admitted it! But surely a few pounds doesn't mean that I deserve to be incarcerated?' Each admission seemed to be banging the emotional nail deeper into his skull.

'Then why introduce the subject?'

Andrew said hotly, 'You said the first thing I could think of!'

Pierre leaned back with a sigh. 'Let's try again. What is the worst thing you have done?'

'Listen, as you obviously already know whatever it is I'm supposed to have done, why not just *tell me* and give me a chance to prove my innocence?'

'Why don't we assume that, had I wanted to share this information, I would have done that in the first place? We will get to it one way or another, but it must come from your words, your thoughts.'

'Sorry, but that makes no sense. Since when does the prisoner create his own charge sheet? Surely there must be some allegation I should be responding to, supplying my alibi, discovering some mistaken identity, that kind of thing?'

'Is the word "worst" not specific enough?'

Questions without answers. Andrew had heard that this was common in psychotherapy, but it still made him fume. How dare they hold him against his will, anyway? And why in some hospital setting with walls that moved at will? As if he could understand what was going through his mind, Pierre stirred and rose. 'Perhaps I will let you think for a few moments in peace. I have other things to do, so I'll return once you have had a better chance to focus. Possibly my presence is making you rush your thinking and not helping you be honest.'

'With you?' he flung the words at him.

'No. With yourself.'

Pierre stopped just before the door. 'I'll return shortly.' *A threat or a comfort?*

The door opened at a gesture, he turned and left.

6

London

The train carried Caittie like a steel wave intent upon beaching her upon London's rocky shore. She felt precarious, weaving from crest to crest of nervousness, excitement and doubt. Sweat beaded on the surface of her cheeks: fear, mixed with a strange sense of thrill. It felt refreshing to be dealing with the baggage of her life, removing the weariness from having carried it for so long.

Stepping down from the train at Paddington, she stood for a few seconds, bracing herself. The journey had been quiet, but now it felt as if people were somehow looking at her differently. As if the excitement inside was unwittingly showing on her face, or – the next moment, she realised why odd and even resentful glances were coming her way. Everyone else seemed to be marching purposefully, a river of driven humanity, while she was dawdling at a pace inconvenient to everybody else.

Moving faster, she recognised that she needed to make a decision. Her heart wanted to find somewhere she could sit and think as a base to work from, while her head forcefully urged that she go straight to the deposit box. The problem was that if she booked a hotel room and then found her instructions didn't require she stay there, it would be a waste of time and money. However, the box could easily contain too much information to absorb swiftly. She could only anticipate needing to take some of it away at least and study it.

Luckily, mid-afternoon was generally the perfect time to book a room in London, after earlier incumbents had checked out. Even if the rooms were still being cleaned, it would be reassuring to have a hotel room to go to upon her return. It was the height of the summer tourist season, although recent IRA shootings had certainly deterred any number of Americans from coming. The question was, which hotel? Too plush a place and she might appear memorable, with her casual clothes and rucksack, yet too small an establishment couldn't possibly provide the safety of a constant mill of people. She looked up and down, mentally crossing off the ones where there seemed to be no noticeable clientele or a constant rush of visitors. Slightly down the road she could see a nice-looking hotel set inconspicuously in the shadowed terraces of several buildings: the Ascot Hyde Park.

Walking into the reception, she worried that it seemed rather more posh than she had anticipated. A smartly-uniformed male receptionist immediately started shuffling papers upon sighting her, as if hoping to convey an aura of importance. When, just as randomly, he stopped, it was simply as if she had passed the test of waiting long enough. She asked for a room, any type or size. The jeans and rucksack that had seemed perfect on the train seemed to somewhat shake his confidence, but she smiled reassuringly.

'How many nights, Miss?'

'Just the one.'

'A balcony with a view?'

'Oh no, I'm not bothered. Just a quiet room.'

'And do you intend to pay by credit card?'

She smiled again, though she perfectly understood the implication: 'No, I'd prefer to pay cash – and immediately, if that's convenient for you.'

'But the minibar, the room service – '

'I don't expect to use either.'

The actual sight of her cash seemed to relieve the hotel receptionist immeasurably. After a further attempt to talk her into a balcony room, he beckoned to a porter who had been lurking out of sight to deal with the rucksack and show her upstairs.

Her room was generic London, well-appointed but also very well used. Caittie's window overlooked a back alley far shabbier than the frontage had been, being the usual cluttered chaos of every London back street. She dumped her rucksack on one bed and lay down on the other, almost pinching herself with excitement at having accomplished even this first basic step. The events of the weekend and today flashed past as she recalled how her mother had attempted to entrap her – she would need to plan more thoroughly from now on, though aware that no amount of planning could cover every contingency. In the end, she permitted herself only ten quiet minutes. It was hovering over the edge of her consciousness, almost beckoning to her. The box.

She decided to leave her rucksack unpacked so as to be ready to move on at a moment's notice. Slipping through reception with an artificial smile for the young man at the desk, it felt safer to hang on to her key, which seemed to impart an illogical sense of control. She joined the Paddington taxi queue, as with just a few people waiting, it seemed a quicker option than wandering the streets attempting to flag one down. Soon she was telling the cabbie, 'Twenty Regent Street, please.'

'A shop?'

'The bank.'

'Gotcha.'

She was enjoying the unusually light traffic when the unwelcome recollection of Keith obtruded. How *could* she have forgotten to call? Not that she wanted to speak to Keith – the exact opposite, in fact – but she had promised her mother that she'd be in touch. Also, if by any chance he doubted that she was still at Mum's, he'd be on the phone pronto, just to check. Luckily, the taxi driver had taken back roads across to Marble Arch and fifty yards ahead she spotted a phone box. She tapped on the partition screen. (*'Sorry, but could you please pull up at the phone box briefly? I need to make one fast call.'*) The taxi pulled in with that typically slick movement while Caittie grabbed some change from her bag and left Keith a short, sweet message, mentioning the lasagne in the freezer. Only later did she stop to think it might have sounded a bit *too* sweet, even artificial. However, by then it was too late to do anything about it. Soon the driver swung out on to Regent Street and, after a few minor traffic hiccups, pulled in just before Piccadilly Circus. She slipped a note to cover her fare (plus a generous tip) into the tray. Before her lay the discreet black anonymity of London Safe Deposit Company.

Urgent as she had felt before, once the taxi had swung back out into the traffic, Caittie seemed stuck to the pavement, overwhelmed by the noise and brusqueness of Regent Street… or perhaps there was more to it that that. After all, until she'd accessed her father's box, she could always have changed her mind. But once Pandora's Box was opened – actually opened – she subconsciously knew that there could be no shutting it, no forgetting its contents, no easy return to normality. Perhaps nothing – once she returned to Regent Street – would feel the same again.

Suddenly, as if prodded, she stepped into the path of a gaggle of teenage shoppers. Temporarily unnerved, she stepped backwards only to be almost flattened by a heavyset black executive. Turning and weaving through the pedestrians, she pushed open the front door as if it represented her only hope. Inside it was cool and dark and Caittie's breathing slowed at last.

As with so many places in London, the address on a prestigious road gave no hint as to what lay within. The further she ventured, the more she was convinced that little or nothing had changed, from when she had returned the box last via the same solicitor who had delivered it on her birthday. The silent corridors remained, its polished surfaces smelling of a discreet hidden opulence, along with the occasional but silent, grey-suited men and women intent upon their own concerns.

Arriving at the reception area she showed the unsmiling man behind the counter her safety box key, which she had always kept hidden in a reinforced leather pouch disguised as a key fob. Even when she lent Keith her car, she would always separate the two sets, with the excuse of preferring to keep her house or work keys with her.

'You do know this box is password access only?' The young man behind the counter had finished inspecting her and was prepared to make her feel inferior. Despite his (perhaps forty) years, behind his computer, he portrayed the self-importance of a rather bored youth, and the keenness to use his new toy was obvious.

'Of course, but isn't that a strange question to someone who must expect to be asked for a password?'

He cocked an eye in her direction, and said flatly, 'Yeah, well, maybe, but we've recorded no fewer than six failed attempts to access this particular box in the last seven years.'

Caittie said steadily: 'Well, this isn't one of them,' thinking nervously that danger had moved from the realms of fiction into reality in just a few seconds. Six attempts! Who had made them? Had she ever been in the habit of doubting her father's warnings she could no longer doubt them now: *'You will be followed.'*

She forced herself to ask, 'Do you know who they were?' A chill shivered down her shoulders. In a room surrounded by walls, she could not help feeling as if someone was looking over her shoulder.

'They were all you! Or at least, they claimed to be,' the man said, more seriously, as if sensing her reaction might be genuine.

'But they couldn't prove that, surely!'

'They had passports with your name on them, but, believe me, I've seen a few of those fakies. Having said that, they had everything except the password.' The man paused and looked back at his desk, as if to suggest that he had a job to be getting on with. 'Look, if you sit down I'll call you when the room is free. Then if you can pass the manager's security I'll take you to the room personally. Can't say fairer than that, can I?'

Waiting, Caittie found herself recalling the actions of the solicitor on her birthday, which she had at the time dismissed as hopelessly overdramatic. How he had set himself up with a metal bin, files of papers in front of him. Burning everything, but only once, he'd most politely insisted, Caittie had read them thoroughly. Now she recalled how easy the information was to remember and how simple it had seemed to brush it aside. She also recalled the panic on the solicitors face when she'd acknowledged that she'd had no plans to deal with the box for the foreseeable future. How he'd wanted her to go with him that day and put it in the safety deposit, but her refusal to interrupt her birthday made him break out in a deeply unattractive sweat. And how, to oblige him, she had reluctantly agreed to accompany him the next day, to go through all the laborious arrangements for the safety box and her trust fund, and then her surprise – even displeasure – when he left her ('so sorry, a previous, ah, appointment') the minute she had entered the security door to the vaults. It was clearly some game he was unwilling to play, as well as a reality check that Caittie would prefer not to have faced.

The door to her side suddenly opened and a short, powerfully-built man strode past her toward the exit. Caittie paused, uncertain, until the receptionist asked, 'Would you care to follow Mr. Matthews?'

For whatever reason, standing up and taking her first step felt more significant than any other preparation to date – Caittie's heart hammered inside her like a small imprisoned animal. Inside the room, she seated herself at the far side of an intimidating walnut desk. The heavy-set man took the seat opposite and opened an entry ledger, saying briskly, 'Now, may I see the key again, and your passport, if you please?" Without a word, Caittie proffered the key, which he turned over twice, frowning, as he scribbled on his ledger. Her passport was flicked through, and, after checking different pages and scribbling down what appeared to be numbers, he asked her for the word that had absorbed her thinking for the past few days.

One word, without which all her efforts must come to nothing. One word, after which he didn't raise his eyes away from the direction of his ledger. One word, after which he fell challengingly silent.

'Password?'

'Bikini,' she whispered.

'Sorry, again?'

'Bikini,' she returned, with more confidence.

This word had vivid memories for Caittie and she had very few doubts, despite the thudding timpani in her chest, that her father had chosen it. The reason was amusing – embarrassing, almost – and buried in her past. She had been only five or six when she had overheard fragments of conversation between her father and some of his work colleagues. She had been playing on her own, not even half-listening, as children so often do, when something sounded wrong. Dad had said something that it seemed important to clarify (it's so crucial for children to know that their parents are normal and that any doubt can be clarified).

In Caittie's case, she had to ask, *'But Daddy, why are you going diving in a bikini? Mummy wears the bikini, not you!'* She still blushed at the recollection of her father and the other men convulsed with indulgent and patronising laughter, as she stood before them in purest bewilderment. It took some time for her father to recover sufficiently to explain that they were talking of a new discovery, an ancient road at the bottom of the sea. How they were planning to go as soon as possible to investigate and how her father would have all the best scuba-diving gear, featuring a proper wetsuit (and assuredly no bikini). Yet still she doubted, at least until she learned that the area where they were planning to dive was just off the island of Bimini. It was the mishearing of consonants that only a child could combine in order to irresistibly leap to the wrong conclusion.

Meanwhile, the man had picked up the phone, muttered out the numbers from her key and the word "bikini", then waited for someone else to respond. He seemed to offer only a series of grunts, all the time looking down at his desk until he put down the receiver while she almost stopped breathing.

'The manager will be along shortly. Will ten minutes be enough, do you suppose?'

'I'm not sure. Could I have a bit longer?'

'Well, there's no one waiting, not so far as I know anyway. Look, there are lights on that wall and you can carry on while the green light shows. If it turns red you have two minutes to pack up before the manager'll be round to bring you back. If you finish early, just press the little button below the lights.' He returned her passport and key. 'Also, sorry but I just need to search you and check your bag before he comes.' Caittie stood up while he just patted her pockets then glanced into her bag.

'What are you looking for?' she asked, emboldened by her success.

'Don't worry, just for cameras or the odd hammer and chisel. Don't want people taking pictures of our security or breaking into other boxes, do we? Not *you*, of course. Safe as houses.'

The other security door then buzzed as the lock opened and the manager impatiently beckoned for her to follow him. Silently, she followed a short way to a safe deposit room with boxes, each with two keyholes, on every wall and a long table down the middle. He worked his way along the numbers until he came to Caittie's box number. He turned his own key in and then curtly motioned for Caittie to do the same. She did and the lock clicked.

The manager was all business.

'Right, now once you've finished with your business, put what you want to keep back inside and lock the box with your key. I'll lock the other side personally. Meanwhile, please pay attention to the lights, especially, of course, if they turn red. If you need assistance, contact me at once. I won't be far away.'

She couldn't remember when he left. Later, all she remembered was the moment when she turned and looked at the safety deposit door. Just as all those years ago, the box loomed towards her: black, rectangular, ominous. Taking a deep breath, she took it out and placed it on the table.

Opening the lid, there was the letter and the parcel, with, still wrapped around it, the Roxy Music poster her dad had used on her birthday presents the year before he disappeared. She picked up the letter first, which had a bold number two scribbled on the front of it. Turning it over, she noticed that it was sealed with the same strange tape as before, obliging her to tear it open sideways in order to read it.

Thank you, Caittie, for standing there, and for not giving up on me.

What started out as harmless fun when we were at university became a lucrative enterprise, before gradually turning into this nightmare. As you might by now have suspected, previous diving trips are what funded everything (we have organised channels in place in order to offload our treasure trove). The proceeds are what created your trust fund and what enabled Michael and Frank to fund their own disappearances.

Michael. George. Frank – and me. GAMF, as I mentioned before. George, as you probably know, has as far as I know never been found – whether he escaped, took on another identity or died is unknown to us. Therefore, what I've done is to make plans with Michael and Frank for when I return, or if you follow after me, but first you need to know why I didn't return – or why I SUSPECT I didn't return, at least.

I had arranged to join Dr Zink on the next exploration of Bimini Road. I had been lucky enough to attend the first attempt in 1974, because GAMF had done a lot of scuba diving around there and we retained quite a few local contacts. As the most experienced diver I'd also taught diving to Michael and Frank (George was just not the athletic type!) This next trip with Dr Zink we're taking a team of psychics with us. I can imagine you raising your eyebrows, Caittie, but at least one of them is a specialist in a field that I need for a particular purpose. I admit that it's a long shot but we don't have many other options at the moment. In short, it's the protection of the secret that drives me, and only by seizing every chance might the threat be removed. If there is the slightest chance I can do this, I have to take it – for the sake of others, not only for myself.

I can say no more here, for you must protect yourself. All the details of what we were investigating have been hidden. To find them you will need to find Michael. Don't open the packet with this letter – not yet, at least – as the purpose of what it contains will become much clearer later. All the time it stays wrapped they will think it's the final piece of the jigsaw – yet trust me – it's of no use to you or to anyone until you've recovered the rest.

The man at the desk will have checked your bag on the way in and he will check it on the way out. As we put this plan together, we assumed that the man at the desk may be bribed to give an account of your visit. So from here just take this letter with you and burn it the first chance you get.

Caittie, I've written all this on the assumption that you would want to try and finish what I started. This is because you're the only person I trust who would have the ability and motive to even try. All I can assume is that the inquiring mind of the girl I left at thirteen has matured into the promise of a brilliant and determined woman. Yet if, here and now, or at any point in the future, you feel it's too dangerous, PLEASE stop and go no further. Don't put my past before your future!

It's important to make your decision before you recover the rest of the information, as then you'll be in real danger. If at any point the integrity of this information has been breached, Michael will know and will attempt to make a connection to Frank. I'm telling you this because when you do contact Michael – assuming you do – he will detain you and question you until he is sure you are the genuine Caittie.

So, how do you contact Michael? As I mentioned before, withdraw plenty of cash before flying to Elounda, Crete. Once settled there, you'll need to place an advert in a seafront taverna called Artemis, around Schisma harbour. The advert should be a simple want-ad for a boat, skipper and scuba gear; to train and assist for four weeks in local waters on a diving project, English speaker preferred. (This is all relevant to the sunken city of Olous, just off Elounda, the significance of which will become clear when you meet Michael. It is also very much on the theme of our work, on its more innocent side.) Michael will leave a message with the bar owner, so ensure you visit each day, for whatever reason. You may get other people applying to your advert but you'll know Michael because he will refer to you as – forgive me – Miss Muffet. He will also urgently need to check whether or not you are being followed so don't worry if it takes a while for him to make contact. I'm hoping that no one intercepts you until Michael can make your identity safe, but – if you are intercepted – you'll still by this point know nothing compromising, either to you or to others.

When completely alone with Michael, you need to recite the nursery rhyme about little Miss Muffet. His answer will, I hope, trigger a response in you. Should it not, he'll give you a second chance, with another word. This isn't just his obstinacy, there's a need to be sure. Believe me; his life might depend upon his recognition of your true identity.

I only hope I've written all this clearly enough. Just remember I always loved you regardless of my apparent obsession and my numerous absences. All I can hope is that you have come to share my own ethos in that some beliefs and truths matter more than risk. If upon reading the hidden information or at any point thereafter you decide not to proceed further, please give the information to Michael. He'll need this to contact Frank as the details were placed in a chain for reasons of protection. The idea was that once I returned then I would be able to let them know what I had found. And yet you're only reading this because I never returned.

You'll never know how much I've missed you.
   Dad.'

Caittie had been so absorbed in reading the letter, going over the important bits several times for fear of forgetting something, that she had forgotten the light. Glancing up, she noticed that the light was already red, without her having noticed it switch to amber, although she could hear no noise, only the whizzing motor of an unblinking camera in the corner above the entrance. Nonetheless, she felt the need to get the box back in the safe deposit before the manager returned, instinctively feeling that the less people saw what she did the better. Holding the letter in one hand, she picked up the lid in the other and pretended to replace the paper in the box as the lid went on while actually sliding it to the side with her thumb. With her own back to the camera, she slid the letter inside her shirt while slipping the box back in its compartment. She was just locking her side when the door opened and the manager came in.

'All done?' He didn't wait for Caittie's response. Moving to the box and locking it swiftly, he was obviously a person wanting to get on. He walked straight to the door and held it open for Caittie to walk through and then locked it behind her.

'This way,' he told her, and she moved behind him, following the faint clipping footsteps down the corridor. Her father had warned her that they would check her bag again, so without thinking she put it on the table. Her mind was so full of what she had read that it seemed like a long time before the security man returned.

'Right you are, can I check your bag again?' The guard didn't hesitate, but rifled through only very casually. Glancing around, Caittie spotted the reason – there was a camera directly over the table. All the guard was doing was moving things around for the camera's benefit. He then came round the table towards her, causing her heart to move unsteadily, but he only patted her pockets, said, 'Thanks, miss,' and opened the door for her. She glanced at her watch, no wonder he was eager to be finished. It was a few minutes to five – going home time.

She nodded her thanks and walked as unhurriedly as she could contrive through reception and out towards Regent Street.

7

Inflections

As Andrew watched Pierre's shadow flicker down the hallway, he found himself desperately hoping that he wouldn't be plunged back into darkness. Transfixed with the image of the liquid door, he allowed some moments to pass in trepidation, until the illuminated stillness of his room felt trustworthy enough to allow his body to relax.

Emptying his mind of everything peripheral, he tried to focus on the reality of what was happening. It was, first of all, clearly essential to find some way past the futility of Pierre's questions and the illogical nature of his detention. The key had to be the "worst thing he had done", only once he'd realised what that was could he make sense of his arrest. And yet whenever he tried to recall anything direful in his past, his memory pulled a blank, and whenever he almost forced his mind to focus, it just seemed to jump from one nonsensical event to another (the coins taken from his grandmother, for God's sake). Apart from the recollection of his signing the official secrets act, nothing fitted with the nature of his detention – and, even then, he could see no relevance, as he hadn't broken it.

Trying a different approach, he lay back on the bed and closed his eyes. Perhaps he needed to *see* his thoughts rather than only think them, after all. Pulling down the projector screen lids in front of his eyes, he started to replay his version of his life. Perhaps this chronological sequence of the bad or worst things, along with the best, might trigger something? Not that he anticipated finding anything bad enough to warrant his current treatment, but something must have brought about this misunderstanding. He truthfully didn't know whether he liked Pierre or detested him, but he was clearly not a person to be messed around.

His mind drifted to the gang fighting of his early childhood and the petty crimes and pranks boys got up to. The teenage years of avoiding violence, just to find how remorselessly violence would catch up with him. Event after event rolled before him, with no escape even from the most excruciating emotional episodes – missed chances, putting the move on a girl more in hope than in expectation, rejection and embarrassments. And more – raw nerves, raw feelings, still darker episodes; he felt himself obliged to prise open the most heavily cobwebbed boxes of recollection. But even in his most despairing moments, he could find nothing worthy of the word crime, or vengeance, or even simply worth this much trouble.

Forwards and backwards his mind trawled over the early immature relationships, his education and then his work and training in those formative years. Drinking too much and driving too fast, yes he admitted it, but he had been fortuitous enough not to be left with any scars other than a few evenings he could not remember. Then business and local politics, overlapping with marriage and children. Reaching the end in what seemed a rush, he started again, this time trying even harder to find the smallest event that could have possessed the seed of such disturbing consequences. Surely somewhere – his chess club, his flirtation with the Communist wing at university, his short-lived passion for the bass trombone – some such circumstance had to hold a key as to why had had been mistakenly linked and held for questioning.

Whether it was around the third or fourth frustrated re-running of his life when his attempts passed from the conscious to the unconscious, it was hard to point to the moment, just as it's hard to point to the moment when mist deepens into fog. Yet the longer he drifted, the more chaotic any sequence or direction became. The jumble of thoughts soon lost all direction, giving way to the surreal world of dreams. His mind wrestled like a python, wanting to get back to the task but fascinated by the images now playing. It was as if someone had taken a series of pictures from several events and randomly mixed them in a slide projector stuck on rapid repeat. He couldn't recognise any of the places or people, the scenes moved in sequential stages, with its own illogical logic. He was irresistibly drawn to understand what they were trying to say. His mind lost the struggle of focus, it was now chasing visions, still trying to put any pieces together, the segments dropping away into shadow, unreached and unreachable, lost.

He was left with a surreal close-up of a shepherd in a woollen cloak, standing by the gate, beckoning and calling to his flock, trying to beg, deceive or entice the panicky sheep into the safety of the pen.

Andrew's mind wanted to move on from this irrelevance, but, as if the projector's controls had broken, he could not stop. The shepherd's stupidity annoyed him, as his efforts more often than not just befuddled the sheep, though some were steered in by some instinct, or even simple exhaustion.

As the vision widened further, it became clear that there were hundreds of sheep in the field nervy, scattered, darting around in small groups. Just as he began to be intrigued at such random behaviour, the film lens widened and he could see various different dogs taunting, worrying and chasing the flock. Some of the dogs resembled sheepdogs, though even these paid scant attention to the shepherd's terse rebukes. Others were clearly wild, revelling in the chaos they were causing. There were pockets of sheep seemingly unaware of the havoc, but this tended not to last long. Panning down the field towards a river, some were enjoying the thickest, plushest grass. For some reason, these sheep's attitude irritated the dogs into madness, yet even when some of the rabid dogs ripped through the flocks, nipping and attacking – even killing, it seemed – some sheep seemed oblivious of the risk.

The longer Andrew watched, the more frustrating it felt that he could neither make sense of these images nor rid himself of them. Suddenly his eyes blurred as if a force in his back propelled him face to face with the shepherd. He told him, 'What use is your shouting? Why don't you have sheepdogs to round them up?'

The shepherd looked nettled. 'I have the authority of my master and the safety of the pen, surely that's all I need! After all, this is the only completely safe place and the ones already here show this is the best place to be!'

'Has it not occurred to you they are too busy running for their lives to take much notice of you? And you didn't answer the question, do you not have any sheepdogs?'

'My master trained some for me.' Following the direction of his arm, Andrew's eyes were drawn to a group of dogs sitting waiting patiently in an adjacent field. 'My instructions are clear enough and I am repeating what my master told me to do!'

'Do you not think that using your dogs might be better than letting the sheep suffer?'

'Their suffering cannot be my fault!'

'But why do you think your master gave you trained sheepdogs if they were not for you to use?'

'I don't know. The problem is if I let them into the field I will not know which dog is which.'

'Don't you think it's worth a try? Or will you wait until your master sees your failure and clears the wild dogs for you?'

The shepherd turned his back and continued shouting at the sheep. Sickened and denied, Andrew now found himself standing in front of the shepherd and his pen, but no longer as a bystander. The wild dogs rounded towards him – they were lean and ugly, with matted fur, and the whites of their eyes were yellowed. In a moment, there were several wild dogs in front of him and, even with the prospect of being overwhelmed, he found that he couldn't move, something held him there, protecting the remaining sheep. The dogs – they looked like wolves by then, unless it was only imagination – stepped back, disconcerted, almost shocked. As Andrew turned back towards the shepherd in modest triumph, he became slightly disorientated. To see the shepherd's face, he now had to look upwards, for now he was eye to eye with the wolves.

As if the fight had begun, his vision was masked and his body felt tense and desperate. Blindly he tried to thrash himself free, before finally breaking the aching wrenching from long yellow teeth as the dream evaporated. His eyes flickered as he sat up in a start. Sitting opposite at the desk was Pierre, watching him.

8

Leaving London

As Caittie moved towards the hustle of Regent Street, she felt so dazed
that each step seemed no more than a single pulse of thought. Yet at
the same time, some niggling worry recalled how essential it was to
ensure she wasn't being followed. In one sense, it felt paranoiac
preparing for danger in the absence of any indication of its presence,
but her father's warnings had left her with little choice, especially
when she recalled, with a lurch of the heart, that what precautions he
had taken had not been good enough. The feeling she had endured
when standing on the train platform had only been amplified by his
letter – one of those rare occasions in life when a single phrase appears
to change everything. She looked around Regent Street as if the entire
world was new.

Ideally she needed a travel agent, but Regent Street was not
designed for travel firms, and, after walking up and down a short way,
she decided she was wasting valuable time. Doubling back towards a
small coffee shop near Piccadilly Circus, she managed to buy a couple
of large soft rolls surrounding limp tomato and cheese, which she put
in her bag, along with a package of biscuits. The shop assistant looked
at her rather strangely when she asked for the change entirely in coins.

Upon leaving the coffee shop she attempted to hail a taxi, but it
was rush hour and the endless stream of taxis, some with lights
switched off but several with lights defiantly on, swept past her as if
she was invisible. Taut with nerves, she suddenly noticed a dark saloon
car parked on the opposite side of the road. An executive sports car
was never unusual on a busy London Street, but still it commanded
her attention. Surely, she had seen this car before. Her mind relived
the moment when her taxi had pulled away after her arrival. As the
back of the taxi disappeared it had unveiled exactly the same car just
behind, AEG 22H. It seemed strange that police hadn't moved them
on, strange because of the awkward situation where they had parked
and doubly strange in that a policeman was still within sight, but

casually walking away. Still scanning the road for a taxi, she tried to make her glances casual towards the black car, but could make out nothing through its darkened windows. Just as the eyes of a painting sometimes follow the viewer, it seemed to her that this dark beast of a car was looking at her... or was she going mad? It had to be some incipient paranoia. Meanwhile, to her relief, a cabbie had wheeled up beside her.

'Paddington station, please, and without going along Regent Street!' Caittie wasn't going to take any chances. Her father had said think clever and she wanted to prove to herself that she could.

'OK, love, no problem!' The taxi driver was an older man, with an East London accent, which seemed subtly reassuring.

He pulled out, as taxi drivers do, with minimal indication and a clear presumption of other vehicles' giving way. In Piccadilly Circus, they shot round the first left. Caittie waited until they were some way up the road before allowing herself to check behind. The image of the black car combined with her father's warnings was growing in her mind to the point of neurosis. And yet, sure enough, there it was, the shape of its wing edging out from the traffic, its elegant dark lines with blackened windows, only two cars behind. Although there were probably hundreds of similar cars in London, this one seemed to be driving with a purpose, a purpose linked to her taxi as it mirrored each twitch or adjustment in direction. She tried not to make it obvious that she was looking – had she turned around fully, they would almost certainly have spotted her. As soon as they saw her looking, they might switch the tail and she might not know who was following her until it was too late. Of course, she reminded herself, it was perfectly possible that some executive in the car was also headed to Paddington, she mustn't over-react until she was sure.

What was totally unacceptable was the prospect of failure just seconds after she had started. How her family would love that – it would be so Caittie! *Think clever; think clever.* If she was really being shadowed, she needed to incorporate some form of evasive action into her plan – plus, she needed to make sure she wasn't being followed, while all her old insecurities warned her not to take risks she lacked enough experience to cope with. But she needed to know!

Delving into her shoulder bag, she located her 'emergency pack' and removed a small compact. After this, she used the mirror periodically to check the car was still there and – sure enough – each turn was precisely replicated by the menacing black vision behind her. Also, was it her imagination, or was the taxi driver becoming aware of it? She caught him checking his own mirror repeatedly. For a dizzying moment, she was tempted to confide in him, but London taxis aren't constructed for James Bond-style manoeuvres, and surely the executive car could keep up regardless. Besides, if they were the kind of people her father had warned her about, it wouldn't take them long to discover where the taxi dropped her off. A better idea was to draw them into a place where she could slip away, something she could only manage while appearing unsuspicious.

The black car was hovering about fifty yards behind as they approached Paddington Station. As before, she slipped some money onto the taxi driver's tray and told him to keep the change. While the taxi was still in motion, she shot out and ran into the entrance toward the main concourse. Pausing just for a second inside the main area, she glanced down the rows of shops and spotted a simple fashion boutique. In a matter of seconds she had picked out two identical cotton summer jackets in different colours and a patterned headscarf. By the counter was a rack of sunglasses, including a pair of big round reactor ones. On paying, she slipped on one jacket and tied the scarf around her head. The bandana style was strangely comforting – as if she was preparing for a role in some action movie – but it created a contrast in appearance that was a subtle disguise. She checked herself in the tiny mirror from the sunglasses stand as she put them on. In normal light the glasses looked perfect, as they were tinted enough to diffuse the shape of the face but not conspicuous by being dark enough to appear to hide behind. Putting her shoulder bag into the carrier with the jacket, she wandered back into the concourse. She had memorised the travel agents' number and had hoped to visit personally, but now felt she couldn't risk it.

As she looked round, she found a row of phone kiosks and without hesitation went straight into the first empty one. The resolute stride to the kiosk was all she could do to lose her feeling of being exposed on the concourse. Not knowing who of the many people milling around may be looking for her, it seemed foolish to stand in the open attracting attention, as static people always do in a busy place.

She had asked for change at the coffee shop so she could make some phone calls – she needed coins sooner than she had guessed, but only ten minutes later she had what she needed – flight times and availability for Crete.

Turning back to the concourse, she instantly noticed, in the midst of the hustle of people rushing about their business, four men in earnest consultation. The older two wore dark suits – pinstriped versions of the black car – and the others jeans and scruffy leather jackets. She hoped that their discussion had nothing to do with her, but as moments passed they appeared more and more menacing. *Or was she imagining it?* Nerves turned to eels inside her stomach as she realised that she ought to leave, rather than to excite suspicion by sticking around the phone booth too long. As she braced herself to emerge casually from her booth, she noticed the two bikers jogging off in opposite directions, while one of the two dark-suited men was clearly using one of the new – and still fairly rare – mobile phones. Still stranger was the fact that his mobile was small and sleek, in no way resembling a brick. Caittie had seen people using mobiles before and they had appeared far too cumbersome to be practical. Yet from somewhere came the recollection of seeing something on the news about the development of batteries small enough to be incorporated into smaller handsets. It seemed a logical inference that only the very rich could afford one already – apart from those spies with access to such things before the public. She hadn't even seen them in the shops yet.

Her original notion had been to obtain some kind of disguise and then to pass the men as discreetly as she could. Now, however, she felt less sure – could there be others on the lookout? The girl at the travel agents had long since hung up, but Caittie kept the phone to her ear, pretending to talk, buying time to think. She suspected that it would be only a matter of minutes before they scoured the place and tracked her down if she stayed put. It would also seem equally odd if she remained on a call for very long, for any searching and seeing her there several times over, would inevitably have their attention drawn to her. She checked the position of the two men, but a railway worker on an industrial-style electric buggy was blocking her view. Pulling a chain of tall cages, he was heading towards a service area. On impulse, she quickly moved to the side of the tallest one, adjusting her pace to his mobile six-foot wall, hoping that she wasn't too visible between the gaps as it snaked between passengers. In a matter of moments, the buzz of people and trains retreated as she went past the restricted area signs and down the service corridor.

Once she was out of sight of the main platform, she dropped back behind the last cage as the corridor passed through rubber doors into an enclosed non-public area. Looking behind momentarily to check there was no one following, she found herself tripping into the back of the train as the driver brought it to a standstill. However, the clang of her body against the metal of the trailer just added to the sequence of clangs as each part of the train came to a cranking halt. As much as she was tempted to cry out, some reflex response took over, stopping her cry and freezing her beside the last carriage. She could hear the driver fiddling with the cart and its coupling before he finally turned, whistling, and entered a site office. On her right was a large steel roller shutter for lorry access, plus a sign that she could just make out as a fire exit. The longer she stood there the more exposed she felt, as she would be instantly seen the minute anybody came from either direction. Swinging her bags and attempting to look casual, she moved out of sight with ever-quickening steps. When she got to the buggy, she just had to go full speed across the opening toward the fire exit. Out the corner of her eye she could see the worker in the office on the phone. As she passed him, he called out urgently, 'Miss! Hey, Miss, stop! You're not allowed in here!'

'Sorry, can't stop!' Caittie briefly turned her head to see the man leaning out of the window of the office, phone still in hand. In the next few steps she had reached the door and hit the emergency bar hard. The pain of impact shot up her arms but the door yielded into a fenced yard in bright daylight. Several vans and trucks were there, but nothing was blocking her path to the open gates. She ran to the gateway and looked up and down what was obviously a rear access – but, more importantly, a public road.

It was a long way up the side of the station to a main street and she could see the traffic roaring past the junction. Perhaps one of the bikers had been put there to watch for her… or perhaps someone was just behind. Along the road in the other direction was a police vehicle compound with a reception office. A man in a typical police uniform with starched epaulettes stood behind the reception, writing something down in a thick-nibbed pen.

'Can I help you?' The policeman asked, still carrying on writing.

'Um yes, I know this sounds silly but my boyfriend's car has gone missing and he has asked me to check if it has been brought in.'

The man sighed in irritation. 'Listen, he needs to report it stolen if it has gone missing! Plus, if it was brought in here that would be cause he'd abandoned it, hadn't he, or parked it in a dangerous position! Either way it's only because he left it somewhere silly.' The man seemed most at ease talking to others as if they were stupid.

'Yes, of course, that's what I told him myself. Only he insisted I called in.' Caittie leaned forward to whisper. 'Someone also told him it was shifted away on the back of a council lorry.' She took off her glasses and smiled, remembering Wendy's advice about how good-looking women prepared to flirt a little generally get what they want from officialdom. The officer looked at her for a few seconds, and then smiled grudgingly back. 'Oh, well. Just this once, mind, I'll check for you.' His attitude was that of a man going to trouble above and beyond the call of duty.

She gave him Keith's registration number and he went to his computer. Meanwhile Caittie strolled back to glance along the road to the railway service yard. She could see one of the men in dark suits standing at the emergency exit door. As she stood there one of the bikers came running up to him. After a brief exchange they both entered together – she could breathe again.

'Sorry, Miss, we got no record of this vehicle being picked up – and if we had, your boyfriend would be the first to know. You tell him from me that we don't pick 'em up by mistake, right?'

All Caittie could think about was that the men had gone inside and she needed to get moving. She said, 'Thank you so much! He'd have been so annoyed if I hadn't checked for him!'

'Well, we can't have that now, can we? That'd be a domestic!' The policeman chortled at his own joke as she slipped out the door. There was no one about as she moved along the road and round the corner into Wharf Street. Walking as quickly as she could without running, the heat building under her new jacket, she suddenly remembered that it might only be a matter of time before they knew she was attired in red. The vision of the mandatory terrible photo, flashed in every corner of the station, unnerved her. Taking the jacket off and folding it as she went along, she swapped her jackets over without a missed step. She then re-tied the scarf around her neck before making up her mind to get off the street, as she was feeling exposed in these back roads. Luckily the exit she had taken from the station had bought her out on the general direction of her hotel, but she needed get there without being seen.

Just ahead was a sign for St Mary's Hospital and Imperial College. She used the first hospital entrance she could find. Taking the general direction towards the main street on the other side of the block, she mapped her turns in her head to keep on course. In the maze of corridors it felt safer to walk more slowly, as she still didn't want to attract attention, though she had visions of men and dark cars prowling round the streets in search of her. The hospital by contrast seemed a haven of safety. Although she had changed her jacket, so much of what she was wearing was still the same that she feared any professional would soon pick her out. The beige jacket should be fairly safe for now, as even if they had full details from the shop, it was a far less obtrusive colour. From the station to the duty policeman people would only recall her as a girl in a bright red jacket, though it was possible too that a description would include the lurid shopping bag and scarf, which made them seem a liability. Just before her she spotted a full rubbish bin, a new carrier bag to one side. She looked in the carrier bag to find day-old sandwich packaging, which she emptied into the bin. Taking her shoulder bag out of the shopping bag she transferred her belongings into the carrier.

Round the next corner, she found herself in the waiting areas, to one side a block of empty chairs. Two women were talking, facing the other way. Caittie's eyes were attracted to a large floppy straw hat on the corner chair nearest to her. Picking up the hat she slipped it into the carrier bag, placing the shopping bag on the same chair with the red jacket and receipt inside, all in one swift fluid movement. She nervously sped off before anyone noticed what she had done, allowing herself a little smile once out of sight, smug in anticipating that few women would complain if they lost a used floppy straw hat and in return gained a brand new jacket, including receipt.

As she approached the main reception the streams of people going in and out grew thicker. Taking the scarf off, which was making her neck too hot, she slipped it in her bag and donned the hat instead. The smell and noise of London traffic was striking compared to the disinfected tranquillity of the hospital. She could see her hotel from the road and felt very tempted to go straight toward it, but in the interests of double-checking decided to walk away from the hotel and cross further down, adjusting to the overall automaton pace of busy city-dwellers.

At the next road intersection was a pedestrian crossing near where she had spotted a side road at the end of the block of hotels. Venturing down the side road, she noticed what looked like the start of the service alley she had seen from her room. It seemed so easy, striding across the main road, down the side alley, a quick look round and darting out of sight, yet it felt such a relief not to feel the need to keep checking behind her! Her care was soon rewarded with the sign for Hyde Park Hotel Goods Entrance Only. She could smell the kitchens – stroganoff – at an open door. An emergency exit, her entrance caught two cleaners unawares, sharing a smoke and a gossip out of sight of their managers. They stood up straight to make room for her to pass.

'Good evening.' Caittie's confident demeanour attempted to suggest that she could claim some rights of entry – all the more since she knew she didn't – or not here, at least. The cleaners said nothing, though one managed a nervous grimace in return. Without stopping Caittie took the back stairs to her floor. A cleaner's trolley was parked by an open door along the corridor, but as she could hear no cleaning it seemed logical to infer that it belonged to the women she had passed. She unlocked her door, entered, and pushed it shut with a sigh of relief. The last few hours had tested and tormented her – it was a comfort to be able to let down her guard, at least temporarily, and yet, the more she thought about it, the more the adventurous part of the business also excited her. Never had she felt so alive as when she had been tested, but even more striking was her new faith in her ability to act spontaneously.

The truth was that, since her father's disappearance, her life had been shackled by her mother's protectiveness, which had encouraged her to do everything possible to ensure that Caittie's thirst for adventure was thwarted. Then of course there was Keith – his control mechanisms for putting her down, his ability to suck all confidence out of her, until her presumption of her own inadequacy had almost become a habit. Yet here she was, an adventure veteran of a mere couple of hours, completely addicted! Had she suffered any doubts about risks while reading the letter in the vault, she had to confess to herself that danger felt more of an attraction than a deterrent.

Locking the door behind her, Caittie checked round the room, though everything seemed exactly as she had left it. She knew she still needed to keep moving, keep thinking and keep prepared. Whoever was after her was unlikely to give up easily and would try and track her down. She went methodically through all her movements, checking for any weak spots. If they contacted Keith or her mum, they would follow a trail that would have her *en route* to Wendy's, but with luck, Keith wouldn't know even this much until tomorrow morning. All anyone could be certain of is that she disappeared at Paddington. Even if they guessed she hadn't taken a train, it was surely impossible to check each hotel in the area until morning. She must have a little time and space before she had to be back on her guard.

About the idea of moving on, she felt torn. How long could it be before they checked the registers on every hotel working from Paddington outwards? Yet if she tried to move to another hotel now, she might only be advertising her desperation. Who knew how many bikers might be looking for her? What if her slipping off the radar had activated the panic button until the full resources of these people were made available? It was even possible that spending a night on the streets would be better than risking another hotel. This might be the last chance she had to make herself comfortable, and the clothes she was wearing had all been compromised.

She was accustomed to taking archaeological trips – sometimes at very short notice – but staying out of everyone's way for twelve hours or more was a new experience. Although she hoped that she had managed so far, she would need to be even more prepared next time, as they would not be likely to underestimate her again. Stripping for a shower, she saw the letter she had tucked in her clothes at the vault dropping to the floor. Her father's instruction had been explicit: destroy as soon as possible. She read it once more and then considered the best way to get rid of it. She was contemplating tearing it to pieces and flushing it down the toilet when she spied the metallic dark green rubbish bin. She grabbed the complimentary matches from the ashtray and torched the paper, the flames dying down within seconds.

After her shower, she felt hungry, so she opened the food she had bought at the coffee shop. Suddenly something made her freeze. It was not that anything in the bag should not be there, but something, something, didn't feel right. There was a needling warning there, that something was wrong. Looking blankly into the bag for several seconds, she tried to work out what it was that worried her. In the end she sat on the bed, forcing herself to down the rather stale rolls, though at any other time she would have thrown them away and gone hungry. At each laboured chew she worked logically through her steps to find out what was spooking her. The missing link eventually struck her hand as she brushed the crumbs across her bed.

The room key. It had been in the bag all afternoon, at the vault, at the fashion boutique – the security camera must have photographed it when her bag was searched. The large key fob had the room number one side – which was probably not of importance – but the hotel's name and insignia on the other was. How much and of what side did they see? At best they may have seen only a number and take hours to track down all the hotels. At worst they would have enough information to be only minutes behind her.

Caittie felt that she needed to move fast, but it dawned upon her she might be overreacting. What she needed to do was to not just evade her pursuers, but to use cunning to confuse them. She dialled reception and asked for a taxi at eight o'clock to Waterloo (since she was supposed to be *en route* to Wendy's, she might as well leave them this distraction for whenever they tracked the hotel down – assuming that they did, of course). There was, however, something rather strange: the receptionist only said yes after attempting to say something else, stopping abruptly and then instantly agreeing.

Putting together her intuitions of unease, Caittie decided that she needed to leave the room. Swiftly she gathered up her rucksack and shoulder bag, yet, upon automatically picking up her room key, she just as quickly tossed it back again, as if it was compromised. Opening her door, she swiftly glanced along the corridor. She had a superstitious desire to gain a view of the main road and sauntered down the hall in case any of the rooms up the hallway might command a front aspect. The cleaner's trolley had long since moved down the corridor, and glistening on its corner handle was a set of room keys. On impulse, she grabbed the keys from the trolley and rushed back along the corridor to a room she had observed being cleaned earlier.

It seemed like ages, fingers fumbling through the keys, for her to try to make sense of them, but finally the door yielded to a room sterile and unoccupied. Propping the door open with the luggage stand, which was in a recess nearby, she returned the keys under the reassuring buzz of the vacuum cleaner next door. Running swiftly back up the corridor, she went back in the room and shut the door gently behind her. At the window she could see the top of a bus going by. Almost squeamishly, she slowly inched herself forward to check out the pavement below. Just as she was looking up and down the road, a dark car similar to that that had tracked her to Paddington curled into view. Stopping as abruptly as possible without screeching the tyres, three men jumped out, two in biker gear, and moved elastically towards her hotel. The part of Caittie that still doubted – that such things happened in Britain, that evil existed, that her father had exaggerated – felt a clammy hand of doubt put upon it.

Her rucksack still on her back, she slipped into the wardrobe and squatted on the floor, closing the doors behind her. For about five minutes all was still, then she heard heavy footsteps and commotion, voices shouting up and down the corridor, including the outraged tones of someone – presumably the hotel manager – which went on for a couple of minutes, making her heart race faster with each passing second. Biting her lips, she could feel the salt of sweat and shook her head in self-disgust, recalling how her father had told her not to make a call from anywhere unless you're about to leave. Her new sense of independence had overruled her father's advice. Just as she thought things had died down, she could suddenly hear voices again – much closer – and they sounded instantly louder as the door opened.

To Caittie it seemed as if her heartbeat alone was loud enough to be heard, but the aggrieved tones of the manager were powerful too, especially after he walked in. 'See? These are the only empty rooms we have, this one and this. All empty, all clean and locked!' He was addressing an audience owning what sounded like several pairs of heavy boots. Caittie clamped both her hands over her mouth, as if not trusting herself not to give something away. From the hallway she picked up occasional words from someone talking with a deeper voice, rather further away. *'Burned... Yeah... In a bin.'* After a few seconds, she realised he was talking into a phone. She imagined the man from the station platform, using his new toy. Then she heard, more clearly: *'The back fire escapes... Yeah, next door, no, no, yet another hotel... Right. Got it.'*

Then the door closed on her and all she could make out was the high bleating tones of the manager. 'Sir, you are mistaken. No, indeed, you are not searching the other rooms, not without a warrant.' A few muffled noises followed and then footsteps retreated. Caittie was exhausted. Too frightened to move, she just sat listening intently. Still, the noises went on.

9

Deductions

Andrew sat still, half looking towards the table, his head still reeling from the dream. He felt it better to wait for Pierre to make the first move – better for him and possibly even better for Pierre, while he tried to regain his composure. He felt horribly strange – a state of mind he had successfully avoided for decades. The dream, so disturbing, still rioted through his brain. But it was not the shepherd causing the turmoil, it was one image from the cascade that preceded it. A flash of a fragment that once released was now expanding and pushing its way to the front.

It was a daunting thing to have to face, awakened after all this time to what had happened in the pit. Climbing down the cliff face to the slurry and walking out on its thin crust was fine, when the end result was to show his friends how brave he could be – that merely separated those with bravado from the pretenders. It was only when, trying to emerge, he had climbed about halfway up that the ground gave way, sending him plunging down the steep slope toward the sludge. That moment a nightmare was born, strong enough to dismantle a whole lifetime of dreams. Each night thereafter he relived it all: the scrambling desperate grasping at the stones and weeds in a wild effort to slow his descent, the growing avalanche of debris as each section of rock gave way beneath him, the baked-on crust braking his fall, only to find that his feet had cracked through in spite of all his efforts. The treacly slurry started to suck at him, until the frenzied punching of fists found something firm enough to hold his weight.

It took a few seconds; it lasted nearly a lifetime. The horror he faced was not merely the thought of that day, nor the weeks of nightmares that followed, but the fact it was with him again. How quickly and successfully he had blocked this cycle of torment by night and reflection by day, so that it stopped any section of the dream from being part of his conscious life and thus making it intolerable! Since that time whenever he awoke, any dream would instantly evaporate beyond any recall or recognition. Yet now a dream was still playing in his mind, every image, every sequence, forcing the unavoidable question of having to live once again with the consequences of his dreams.

'You look worried, Andrew.' The silence had grown until it became the elephant in the room.

'Oh well, I'm not really quite awake yet.' This was almost wishful thinking, that he could go back to sleep, leaving the dream behind, awakening as he had always used to, clear-headed, himself, whether he had been kidnapped or woken in his bed at home. But Pierre's voice was grave.

'I hope you've done some serious thinking and have some sort of answer for me?'

The questions were a welcome distraction, but frustrating in that they were preventing any hope of being allowed to sleep. Andrew had to let time pass before he attempted to answer. He knew he had little to give, but needed to make sure Pierre could see it was a considered response. 'I have certainly done a lot of thinking and have turned over every stone to try and find something that you would consider the worst.'

'And so, you've found – what?'

'Lots of things, but after our last debate I frankly doubt whether any are important enough.'

Patiently, 'I didn't say the most important. I said the worst thing!'

Andrew had to stop and pause. They were back to the same impossible question and he had to find some way round it. 'Let me put it this way. I've been in a fair few fights. I'm guessing that I hurt somebody I shouldn't have?'

'You make it sound like a bit of a hobby. Did you go around beating people up for fun?'

'Not at all! I was maybe dragged in occasionally when I probably should have known better, but I certainly got beaten up at least as much as my opponents. Learning to deal with people bent on violence – or just with the bullies existing in all walks of life – well, it means you have to get your hands dirty. I never considered violence as fun and if I've ever hurt anybody I never meant to. In fact, once I even let myself get beaten up just so my mates could get away from a mob.'

Pierre raised his hand. 'Please. Do you really think I'm here to listen to endless justifications for your every juvenile misdemeanour?'

'How should I know? But, if not, it must be connected to some person or business where I've hurt someone – hurt someone badly. I mean, *something* must have happened in order for me to warrant this treatment.'

Pierre said quietly: 'I can tell you this much, that whatever you have done revolves around pain – but then, there are so many ways of hurting people, aren't there?'

Mortified, Andrew asked, 'Is this some kind of revenge, then?'

'Do you really think I would go to such lengths in order to seek revenge, when pain, punishment or other retribution would be so much simpler?'

'There are no lengths some people might go to if they are mad!' In the face of denial, provocation seemed the best way to force some guidance.

'My friend, I might just be mad by the time we finish! But back to the question. You know the answer, perhaps you are the mad one – if you don't tell me.'

Andrew held the words on his lips a few seconds trying to at least make his response seem considered. He knew his ideas for stalling would run out and he needed a subject that would give him time to think by being relevant enough. The pressure was building and he was dreading the next few moments.

'All right. This is where I am. This cell – if it is a cell – is certainly not under police jurisdiction, as there is no tape recorder or second officer. But then again, it is a bit more than what you might expect from some nuthouse for nutcases.'

'Go on.'

Andrew paused again. 'You know I signed the official secrets act, but apart from a curiosity about the three-minute warning systems when still an apprentice, I can't see how I could be involved in anything so sinister. Yet I sense that this place, my detention here and your obscure questioning has to be connected to some mix-up to do with espionage.'

'I can tell you that it's official, but then that depends whose office you think I operate under. Then again it is also a secret, but that depends on who's supposed to know and who is not.'

Great, thought Andrew, but at least not a complete denial.

'So can I take it from that answer I am on the right track?'

'No, you can assume I have given you a couple of clues. That's all.'

'You see, my assumption was that I've done something wrong toward my government. But now you leave me with the feeling that I know something that another government needs to know. However, the truth is that I've never been anywhere or done anything to make any other government want to treat me like this and certainly have no such secrets to give you. I don't know who you really are or where you come from, but you cannot ask a man to admit to treason without giving good reason first. All you leave me with is a paradox that I cannot answer, for nothing is right.'

'Finally we are on the right track!'

Andrew braced himself. 'So you are from a government or anti-government organisation?'

'No, I fear not.'

'But you are still asking me to commit treason of some kind, whatever you want the information for?'

'Not at all.'

'Then how am I on the right track?'

'As I said at the start, the difficulty would be the honesty. That's why you cannot see how close you are to the answer.'

'But all you leave me with is the paradox of this situation and the vagueness of your question. I'm no nearer to knowing why I am here or what it is you think I might have to give you! Can't you *help* me with honesty, if I am so useless at it?'

'At this rate I might have to!' Pierre's hands moved the folder slightly on the desk as he considered. 'In your own words just now, you confessed that there is no real answer to a paradox because it contradicts itself. But you gave me a kind of an answer. Perhaps the answer to my question also contradicts itself. So, Andrew – what is the worst thing you have done?'

'You mean, if I want to get out of here alive?' he said sardonically.

Very quietly, 'I can say nothing about *that*, at this point.'

For the first time since Pierre's appearance, he felt a spasm of pure fear. He had been lulled into trust by his interlocutor's urbane style, but these people, whoever they were, weren't just playing mental games. He thought of his family, his house, even – absurdly, at such a moment – his vegetable patch. And then he thought, more grimly, *I'm not going to let them take everything away from me.*

10

Leaving London 2

The longer Caittie squatted, her back pressed against the back of the wardrobe, the safer she felt, and the longer the quietness continued the more she relaxed. Even the musty smell seemed less oppressive, connected as it was with the wooden cloak of safety. But nothing could prevent the unanswerable questions running through her mind: would the men come back with a police search warrant, set up a watch around the place, or leave for Waterloo? They needed access to the police for a search warrant and she had watched enough TV detective series to suppose they needed a valid reason to get one, not to mention police support. After all, what reason could they give? Unless her father had stolen something – something she couldn't believe – she hadn't committed any crime!

It had also seemed from their actions that the bikers merely pretended to police-style authority, their every move suggested they wanted to cover their tracks at all costs. After all, when the manager had challenged them about searching the rooms without a warrant, they had quickly retreated. Of course, there could be reasons for this: they might be secret service, they might not want to waste time, and perhaps they felt confident of locating her elsewhere. However, it seemed obvious that the less time she stayed in the area, the better.

The longer she thought about it, the more she realised that she was only undiscovered because every problem had been countered by a plan (or, at least, spontaneous action) that had saved her. She was at least better than any of her mistakes or she would have been caught by now. This moment of self-assurance welled into a powerfully warming feeling, to think that with no experience, she had so far eluded a team of what seemed to be well-equipped professionals.

Doubly determined not to give in, she attempted to analyse what her father's enemies might or must be thinking. Without a search warrant, they would probably scour the hotels in the block until some other trail distracted them, especially as they seemed agreed that she'd left by the fire escape. Yet she also thought they might very well leave behind someone to keep watch. With twelve hours – at least – to pass before she could attempt to fly to Crete, her heart clamoured with impatience and pent-up nerves.

Once the men had frustrated themselves by searching along the hotels, they might conceivably contact Keith, by this time putting his dinner in the microwave. (He didn't think of himself as chauvinistic, but still, he expected a woman to present him with his dinner. It was almost deliberate denial of what to do, as a child pretends not to know what's required when asked to do something.) All Keith would say, if asked about her whereabouts, was that Caittie was at her mother's: then they would have to wait until her mother returned to find out that he was wrong.

Yet whether they caught up with her mother later tonight or first thing in the morning, everything should still point towards Caittie's decoy of getting a train to France and Wendy. She had visions of bikers trailing through Waterloo – even down to the port at Dover – trying to head her off. At the same time, she still didn't know how many people were looking for her, and how many places they could cover – she was still playing blind man's buff without a script.

Yet unless they actually tracked down Wendy (how? Her movements were always uncertain) they might not imagine that Caittie was planning to leave for a third country by air, yet these men seemed to be well-connected if not actual law-enforcement operatives. The policeman ignoring the black car across the road from the vault and the worker reporting her at Paddington station (assuming that this latter event had occurred, of course) stood testimony to that.

All things considered, it seemed sensible to lie low for a few more hours, by which time she might reasonably hope that the search had switched over to Waterloo. Certainly staying put was far preferable to spending any longer than necessary on the streets. Strangely enough, after worrying for some time what might become of her beyond her present fugitive lifestyle, Caittie found herself praying. She had never been to church much, apart from the odd school event, since her mother stopped making her go to Sunday school, yet at this moment she longed not to feel so alone. It felt as if she longed to make contact with one old friend.

The faint light visible through the crack in the wardrobe door clicked off as night fell. Street sounds changed from the constant drone of daytime to the intense and often intrusive bursts of noise that early evening brings. The day's events seemed progressively less fearful. In fact, the more Caittie considered, the more it seemed to her that the men chasing her hadn't been outwitted so much as befuddled. Why else had they not opened the wardrobe? Why else had they been just too late to track her through the service area at Paddington? She couldn't even consider herself lucky – it was more than that – it was as if she had a guardian angel inspiring and protecting her.

This suggested a new strength that had either been awarded to her, or which had, though dormant, been there all along. She couldn't resist the hope that perhaps it was her father looking over and protecting her. That perhaps they were doing this venture together and together they could do anything. This whole thought gave her a warm glow inside. Closing her eyes and leaning her head, the exertions of the day caught up with her. Her eyes flickered and blinked twice, first swiftly, then slowly. The third time they didn't open again.

As the anxieties of the day filled her resting consciousness, it also flooded her unconscious dreams, where the thoughts and activities of the day replayed again and again. Restless because she had not intended to sleep, it was only when she reached the point in her dream when all she could envisage were the men in dark suits roughing up her mother that her restlessness fought her into consciousness. Her head shot forward as she woke in a start, thinking about her mother – even Keith. In all her planning, all her objectives, she hadn't considered the consequences for those left behind. Just as her father before her, had she become an equally selfish seeker of their shared objective? All she knew was that somehow she would have to find a way to check Mum was OK before she left.

Her head was so busy with her thoughts that it took several seconds before she realised there was some sound in the room. Perhaps it hadn't registered at first because it was a vaguely familiar sound: a gentle, rhythmic, consistent snoring, hardly noticeable from inside a wardrobe. Her body stiff from being squashed up in such a small space with a rucksack, she tried to peep through the crack in the wardrobe door. Not being able to see much, she pushed the door to open it a fraction. A faint light streaking across the room from the window dappled the darkness with dimly-lit patches, already suggesting the early hours of a summer dawn. Her eyes adjusting, she could make out some large black object in front of the wardrobe: presumably, the snorer's suitcase. How stupid she felt, the rooms being cleaned yesterday evening, naturally they must have expected night arrivals. Whoever heard of hotel cleaners otherwise bustling about their cleaning in the afternoon? Her only consolation was that only an innocent and innocuous hotel guest would be snoring in bed instead of looking for her.

Yet she couldn't avoid self-condemnation for allowing her guard to drop once the immediate danger had passed. Yesterday she'd had no choice other than to leave a trail, as they had followed her so closely, but from now she needed to up her game – and she also needed to get out before there was any chance of the person in the bed waking. Pushing gently while steadying herself with her hands, she gradually eased the door open a few inches. As the door opened she glimpsed the snorer. The sight of a heavily overweight man snoring in bed wasn't an attractive one, but the pinstriped suit laid out over the chair proved creepily reassuring. Keeping hold of the doors in order to stop them from rattling she pushed them open a little further and swung her legs out. How stiff she felt!

Pausing just to check she had everything with her, she slung her shoulder bag to balance the rucksack on her back and leave both hands free. In slow motion – keep snoring, please keep snoring – she reached the door and eased the handle sideways. Opening it was not a problem, but she recalled from yesterday that the heavy doors made an unavoidable *clunk* when shut. Moving into the hallway, she pulled the room door to as slowly as possible, easing the lock so any noise would be minimised. Almost simultaneously with the snap of the catch, she sprinted off as if from a starting pistol, darting down the corridor and well out of sight, starting to breathe again some moments later.

To avoid the night porter she had decided to use the emergency exit that she had taken advantage of before. As she pushed the door open she still had a bizarre apprehension that one of the men would be waiting and watching; but she had to take the chance. Running into the yard she felt rather than saw a security light blaze onto her back, which despite proving that there was no sign of anybody else, still made her feel uncomfortably exposed. As soon as she was out of sight of the hotel she slowed down to a brisk walking pace. It was as fast as she dared go, as she was determined not to give any casual observer reason for recalling her. There were few people around – security types, catering staff – but soon she gathered her composure enough to slow a little more so as to look as inconspicuous as possible from the perspective of anyone on their early morning business.

With each corner and each bend in the road, she hesitated in nervous anticipation, giving a casual glance to ensure no one was following. Every time her anxiety evaporated further. Zig-zagging through back roads had two advantages: it avoided long straight sections and it made it less likely that anyone would see her. The peculiarly random blocks of London made it tricky to keep her bearings, but the just-rising sun was one constant to rely on. In no time she came out onto a main road and swiftly moved across into another block of roads on the other side, slowing as the weight of the rucksack was making her puff just a little from the pace. Ahead was another road already busy with steady early morning traffic – it led her out somewhere she recognised, not far from Hyde Park.

Surely there would be taxis here. There were not many vehicles around yet, but a reasonable number of these were taxis. The first few went by without stopping – perhaps her backpack was a deterrent? – yet they seemed to operate within obstinate rules of their own. As yet another without a light on seemed to be sailing past, she kept her eyes open for another cab, but it suddenly pulled over sharply twenty yards further up the road. Joggling with her rucksack, she ran to one side and pulled open the door.

The cabbie was late fifties, critical, fatherly.

'Where do you want to go?'

'London Bridge.'

The cabbie frowned. 'I ain't working yet, but I'll take you to Charing Cross and you can swipe a train. Seeing as its so early, like, and you're only young.'

'You mean that you don't think I ought to be here on my own?'

He explained he was not on duty, but would give her a lift to Charing Cross from where she could connect by tube or train. He was what you could only describe as a cockney gentleman, who did not think it was right for a girl to be wandering through the streets at that time of the morning. Asking him if there was anywhere to get a coffee and some breakfast near the station, he explained that's where he was heading, and as he couldn't charge her, with a teasing wink he suggested she could buy him a 'nice bacon butty and a cup of real tea' instead. His fond description of the Cabbies' Shelter only added to the temptation of what he described as the best food in London.

She agreed, and then hardly listened as he spent the rest of the journey telling her the hundred-year-old history of the charity set up to provide cabbies with food, and how it had dated from the days when they weren't allowed to leave their cabs, when they were horse-drawn. Caittie, meanwhile, was reflecting on these latest events. How she had wanted London Bridge to throw the scent towards the Kent coast line, but Charing Cross would do. Better still, she was in a taxi that was neither charging nor officially on duty, which meant he wouldn't radio or need to tell anyone of where he had picked her up. It had seemed just conceivable that the men chasing might have the ability to monitor radio frequencies. She recalled the man snoring in the hotel room and it dawned on her that, as bad as it seemed at the time, he had unwittingly shielded her through the night. How different her luck would have been had he chosen to hang up his clothes late at night, instead of going straight to bed!

Quiet roads meant that it wasn't long before they rounded the corner into Embankment Place and she spotted the railway bridge going into the station. The Cabbies' Shelter was a large over-decorated painted garden shed, just as described, though the cabbie, old-fashioned soul that he was, paid for the food before she could intervene. He seemed happy to enjoy the conversation of an attractive young woman, along with the raillery of his friends. They leaned against his cab, Caittie doing her best to stop the rich butter running down her chin, as he asked where she was off to.

'I'm going to France to see an old college friend.'

She felt that she had no choice but to maintain this fiction, but his questions possessed no underlying threat. It felt pleasant and safe being in this secret world of London, one which people didn't generally see. They chatted long enough for Caittie to find out where the nearest phone boxes were on the way to the station and for him to wink at his cabbie mates as they walked by. When she was finished she kissed him on the cheek, thanked him profusely and walked away, amused to think how he would be ribbed by his mates about the mystery girl he had hosted. Up the road and round the corner was a whole bank of phone boxes and luckily she still had plenty of change from yesterday. It wasn't long before the phone was ringing on the other end.

'Hello.' It took a long moment, as if her mother had just awoken.

'Hi Mum, it's Caittie!' Caittie was hoping that by now her mother was being watched and was almost certain she actually heard a second click, just after her mother answered the phone. It was always there on detective programmes and she hoped it actually occurred when phones were tapped.

There was a short pause before, 'Caittie, dear, do you know what time it is?'

'Sure, but I said I would phone to keep you in touch.' Caittie waited for her mother to respond, but no response was forthcoming. 'Also, I thought you ought to know that I stopped off in London and picked up the box Dad left me.'

The low wail cut through her last words. 'Not again! You can't! You mustn't! Haven't we all suffered enough?'

Caittie forced her voice to sound calm. 'It's OK, there was nothing very interesting in it – just some advice I didn't quite understand.' Caittie hated lying to her mother, but as far as she was concerned she was talking to whoever else was listening.

'Right, well, please just bring it home! Remember, your father said it could be dangerous, and surely you don't want to risk that?' Her mother's voice had lost all restraint.

'Believe me, Mum, it's nothing to worry about.'

'Have you told Keith where you're going yet?' Her mother knew that this was a sore point and it showed in her tone.

'I was hoping you'd let him know for me. Also, warn him not to expect a call for a couple of days. You know how disorganised Wendy is.' Caittie knew her mother's use of voice for effect, so she reciprocated by using her most youthful tone, normally effective when asking her mother for a favour.

'You're not leaving much option!' Her mother was now voicing disappointment in a way only mothers can. 'So. Where are you now?'

This was the question Caittie had been hoping for – she needed to be sure she left a decoy trail. 'I'm at Charing Cross, just waiting for a train to Dover.' With this she had defeated her worst fears from her dream – there would be no conceivable need to harm her mother if it was clear that she knew no more than anyone else. Her mother sighed heavily down the phone.

'I do wish you'd just come home and forget all this, dear.'

'There's nothing to worry about. I'll phone when I can.' Caittie recalled her father's words: phone only when you are about to leave and since she had just divulged where she was, she should be leaving directly. 'Got to go mum, sorry. Take care, love you!'

'You take care, dear.'

Caittie put the phone down and jogged past the station and down the Strand. She had done all she could to lay a false trail and could only hope that it would buy her enough time. It wasn't long before she was passing Nelson's column. There was much more traffic now, but still she felt safe, like any other early morning person busy about their business. It was simple enough to hail a cab and to ask for Heathrow, but she knew if her decoy had failed they would surely be watching the airports. The only trouble was that it was difficult to get to Crete in one flight unless it was a charter. The travel agent, during her brief time on the phone, had seemed unsure whether there were any spare spaces, although she suspected that there would be, since the schools were yet to break up for the summer. Caittie, however, had still decided that the scheduled options sounded better and, if her timing was right, fairly opportune.

As the cab worked its way laboriously up to the A4 and onto the M4, queues of early morning commuters were forming on the roads trying to get into London. The driver having dropped her off, it didn't take long for her to find the British Airways desk and buy a seat on the first available plane to Athens, it seemed conceivable that her father's enemies might eventually find her details on some computer flight record, so it was best if they did not have it too easy. In addition, Athens would be a good place to change.

'Boarding in two and a quarter hours,' said the man, and Caittie waited impatiently for her tickets to be issued, as she didn't want to wait in the airport and she still had things to do. Joining the queue for a taxi this time was no trouble, and she was soon en route to Uxbridge town centre, as she needed to reach her bank for more money. Yesterday's excursions and today's flight was eating up money fast and she might needed a lot more if this was the scale of things to come.

Arriving in Uxbridge a while before the banks opened at half-nine, she took the opportunity to pop into a supermarket. She had done a few foreign digs on her archaeological expeditions and worried as to what familiar branded comforts were to be found in Crete. She located her favourite sunscreen and moisturiser, though in truth she was merely browsing in order to pass the time and to avoid standing awkwardly outside the bank's door.

By the time she had finished shopping, the bank was open, and there were about a dozen people queuing inside. Standing in line, she passed the time checking, even practicing, every possible angle or glance that someone might use watching her. The queue moved in short bursts, giving her the chance to make out a cheque for cash using the barrier posts to lean on.

However, once she proffered it to the cashier, the bank teller looked at it and passed it back, 'Could you sign the back of the cheque for me, please? And do you have a form of identity on you?'

Caittie tried to look calm as she signed, offering her passport as form of identity. Then came the questions she didn't want, firstly 'Has this been phoned through?' and then the 'Wouldn't you prefer a banker's draft?' All she could answer was no and no, but this didn't appear to satisfy the teller. Instead she looked in her drawer, closed it, apologised – in some confusion – and said that she wouldn't be long. In less than a few minutes she returned, accompanied by an overweight man, already sweating in a suit.

It was a relief to see him squinting apologetically behind his glasses, as he was so much what you expect from a middle-management bank official. It was a short negotiation as he tried to offer travellers cheques and rather less cash; as they would need to get that much out the safe. After explaining to him she was going to stay with a friend for three months and backpack thereafter, she opted to keep the cash at ten thousand, with three thousand in traveller's cheques on top. Then a face she recognised appeared and the two men exchanged a few hushed words.

The newcomer was an assistant manager, someone who had previously advised Caittie about some investment bonds: while the two men were in conversation, she caught his eye and smiled. He smiled back, still talking to the other man, and finally things began to happen. In no time they had started to count the cash in the drawer while waiting for the rest to arrive – later, someone else brought in the travellers cheques. The activity soon made the minutes pass more quickly, while the bank tellers neatly parcelled the money into several different envelopes.

With the money in her bag, she was soon onto the street – she'd been inside too long by her liking. She needed to keep moving, but she still needed to kill some time, as she hoped to arrive at Heathrow with the minimal wait before departure. Still worse would be to go to Heathrow with someone on her tail. Walking up the high street she entered the shopping centre, moving in casual shopper's style, but occasionally doubling back in order to take better note of any person she passed. She was fairly sure she'd spotted no one suspicious, and with a relatively light heart took a seat in a coffee shop commanding a view of both the bank and the entrance to the shopping centre.

Half an hour or so later, with a muddy excuse for coffee already inside her, she sat behind a second cup. She had no intention of drinking it as her thirst could stand no more than one: it was merely to justify her remaining at the table. She considered changing clothes, since she had by now been to several places in the same outfit. It had been her main weapon yesterday to cause confusion and it might make her feel more comfortable today. Ferreting through the rucksack, she found a change of top – a good compromise and easy to manage in the ladies'.

The weight of the rucksack reminded her back of the pointlessness of carrying it around more than necessary, especially as it was after all at far greater risk of being recognised as a feature. And yet just sitting around watching the multitudes of people busily going about their business soon made her fidgety. It seemed ridiculous doing nothing when she had so much to do, but the alternative was to return to Heathrow sooner than she would like. Leaving her second coffee, she made her way to the taxi rank just along from the supermarket. In the back of the taxi she took out the beige jacket she had bought at Paddington. As soon as she got out of the taxi, she put the rucksack on a baggage trolley and carefully folded the jacket over it to obscure its colour.

Along the main concourse, the throngs of people moving in all directions was matched by the masses queuing or sitting, passing time. Too many strangers, resulting in an abundance of caught half-glances impossible for any amateur fugitive to make sense of. Even the man at passport control seemed to take too long looking at her passport for Caittie's comfort, and for a second she thought that it might be queried. It was a relief when he gave her passport back and waved her on.

Walking into the departure area she found that she still had nearly an hour to kill – a difficult balance of time in view of thousands of strange faces. She read her book for a few minutes, but then felt the swarms of people walking by just too much. After all, any one of them could be looking out for her and sitting there on view seemed to be merely tempting fate. She needed to remain out of sight as discreetly as possible. Since her pursuers had all been male – thus far, at least – it seemed sensible to spend a fair bit of time in the ladies' toilet, surfacing occasionally to see if her flight had been called for boarding. Nearer boarding time it felt more natural to wander around those shops round the outside perimeter, spending as much time as possible in the quieter ones as if she was working the crowd and using them as cover.

It was a relief to board, surrounded by Greek families and placid business travellers – even the in-flight meal, stodgy as it was, seemed surprisingly welcome. Relaxing, trying to make her seat comfy, she couldn't help but reflect over the last couple of days – only this time, less with a sense of failure, than a sense of anticlimax.

Had her decoy been so good so as to give her a clear run to Crete? Or might 'they' simply be awaiting her in Athens? In either case, she seemed to be missing the excitement of yesterday – not only missing it, but even contemplating how exciting it might be if she could almost court danger only to elude it – a strange thought to have, especially since she suspected that her inexperience would probably lead to mistakes enough no matter how hard she tried. All of this made her wonder whether her mother had been right to fear that she had inherited her father's 'risk addict' gene.

If she drifted too deeply into these contemplations, she had at least the convenience of being periodically interrupted by the couple inside of her aisle seat. They not only went to the toilet or asked the attendants more questions than anyone else, they also did it (very annoyingly) five minutes apart rather than simultaneously. After a couple of hours it became very frustrating, especially as they took no heed of Caittie's annoyance, or the irritation of the other passengers.

She forgave them, partly because they were obviously nervous travellers, but, more importantly, because they gave her an insight as to what to do in Athens. She had considered various options when she arrived – perhaps take an immediate connection flight or possibly to lie low for a couple of days and then to charter a boat. But after the couple spent about an hour discussing how to get to the ferry port and how most of the boats leave in the early evening, this seemed a much less obvious way to reach Crete, and, although certainly a bit slower, had the advantage of avoiding much hanging around. Her resolution made, Caittie slept the last hour before landing.

11

The cost of nothing

Pierre failed to answer directly, seemingly content to leave Andrew to his own conclusion and seeming sure he was close to saying what he had wanted all along.

As Andrew recalled his answer there was only one word that had not been repeated or explored – nothing. How ridiculous! How could 'nothing' be the worst thing he had done?! Still harder to recognise was any way that 'nothing' could have lead to his detention as some sort of criminal.

Andrew sat angrily staring at the floor, richly inlaid and rather fine, considering. All his deliberations had been bent upon what he might have done, rather than what he might not have done. His frustration now was that this insight (or was it even an insight?) made the whole scenario still more confusing.

This 'crime' of doing nothing, to his mind at least, included such examples as people failing to maintain safety equipment on trains or planes, yet at no time had he ever accepted such a responsibility. Instead, his every effort had been focused on finding that answer, proving his innocence, solving that mistaken identity and achieving release. Now it felt as if all his notes had been chalked on a slate, which had been mysteriously wiped clean. He felt lost, stranded by his own assumptions. The short time he had anticipated this process to take seemingly stretched out endlessly before him.

'I just can't see it, I've never been in charge of anything where negligence may have caused a crime!' Andrew had to fill the silence to prevent his mind crumbling further.

'Can't see or refuse to see?'

'How can I possibly know?'

Pierre shook his head. 'I never said that such honesty would come easily.'

'What do I have to do to convince you that it is the truth? Surely your folder details enough about me to know I'm not lying. Then again you could just open it up and accuse me of something – anything! Anything to put this confusion straight!'

'Andrew, I have no doubt that you fully believe you're telling me the truth, but this is with the honesty of today. The question you have to address is different. How honest were you in the past?'

'You seem determined to talk in riddles,' said Andrew, in disgust.

'On the contrary, I have already spelled out for you that *nothing* is the key. This ideally needed to come from your deliberations, as only by your own personal exploration can you completely understand what – and besides, easy as it might be for me to accuse you, you can't know the consequences of all that you might ask.'

Andrew drummed his fingers.

'Surely being locked up in a cell for something that I know nothing about still leaves only two options – either guilt or innocence. Personally, I'd rather just get to the point, however that fits in with your plans.'

'Isn't it a universal principle of justice that admission and regret are the best ways to obtain leniency? By telling you all that you ask – assuming that I could do this thing – I'd remove any chance of your really understanding what you've done.'

'But I've confessed already! I've done nothing. Nothing, nothing, nothing! Whatever crime that is, I admit it and I regret it. So, when can I go?'

'Never if this is your attitude!' said so sharply it stunned them both. Then, with a deep breath, 'Let's compromise. I will guide you towards the answer if you promise to cooperate. Which means no flippant responses.'

'One-way traffic again. But hey, you make the rules. I have no problem with cooperation if we can sort this out quickly. Anyway, who wouldn't be flippant when they are being teased over some mistake of identity?'

'And if there is no such mistake?'

'Listen, I'm trying to be helpful here.'

'Andrew, as I said before, you're trying to be honest in the way you see things now, which can be very different from the honesty of the past. Just as the victor of any war gets to write the history, so we as people continually try to remain victorious within ourselves by justifying our actions. Ego, pride or convenience can all neatly adjust the facts so that our very sanity is protected. It's rare to see any person hold on to any degree of reality or compassion, in such emotional or extreme events, beyond any reasonable time. Selective memory soon ensures all such recollections are less painful.'

Andrew, dangerously, 'So you're saying I've selectively forgotten something?'

'Less forgotten than – reassigned… you remember it, but as a positive decision to do nothing, whereas in fact it was a negative decision whose consequences you've conveniently glossed over.'

'But surely that's what everybody does, to some degree. If I've conveniently glossed over something – in common with everyone else in the world – I still can't understand how I uniquely deserve punishment.'

'Oh, don't worry about punishment – when your honest self comes face to face with what you failed to do, you'll gladly accept punishment. For instance, if you saw a gun lying around in a room full of children would you just leave it there?'

'Of course not!'

'You'd remove the gun because you can see the danger and the risk of what might happen?'

'I would. So would anybody.'

'Then instead let's consider what happens when the danger is far less obvious. Imagine that the gun was lying just out of reach of a man you cared for, no children for miles around.'

'What does the man want with the gun?'

'I don't know. Do you?'

'Right, well, if this man's committed a crime I couldn't help him conceal it, but I *could* help him own up to it.'

'Even if it's inconvenient?'

'If it's really urgent, of course you'd drop everything.' The more positive spin Andrew found for his answers, the more comfortable he felt.

'Yet who judges what's urgent is the question.'

'Each judges their own – isn't that how friendships are built and destroyed? These questions are quite pleasant, but where is this heading?'

Pierre smiled. 'Tell me about Philip, then.'

'Philip who?'

'Philip George.'

'Philip… '

'The Philip who came to see you just after you moved house.'

For the first time in hours, Andrew stared in disbelief. 'How the hell could you know about *that*?'

12

Athens – Elounda

It was just before the plane started its descent into Athens when Caittie made her decision. She had already established that her flight was due to land at seven-fifteen local time and that the majority of island-bound ferries sailed after half-eight. Yet she had felt so unnerved about leaving Heathrow safely, and so relaxed in transit, that it was a reality check to recall what the time difference would make to this ferry option. Also, relaxing as the ferry sounded, the meagre hour or so allowed for her to get through the airport and to the docks made her think twice.

She again considered taking a train to somewhere obscure and then perhaps crossing a border in order to charter a boat, yet – faced with this swift, neat alternative – every other option seemed altogether too laborious. In addition, sticking to internal Greek transport would probably entail much slacker passport and ticket controls. Of course, it would also mean a slower journey, but if she could only make this first connection she should be able to keep at least one step ahead of any pursuers. She hoped to get some money changed and then to access the docks as quickly as possible by taxi. (If this failed, with luck the ferry should still be an option.)

Yet she still felt convinced of the need to move swiftly. Whatever she did, the only other person concerned was her father's friend Michael – with luck, still waiting, despite the past seven years. Yet at the same time, she longed to learn to control her emotions, and to only rush when under direct threat (as in London.) Her father's enemies would probably pick up her trail sometime, but all she could do was to attempt to reach Michael safely. Whichever way she looked at it, it was important to keep moving, and a planned dash for the ferry would enable her to do so.

As the plane reeled to a stop and the seatbelt light went out, Caittie was one of the first on her feet. It dawned on her, as she waited to disembark, how handy it might have been to have risked a last-minute arrival at the airport and bluffed her rucksack on as hand luggage. However, without such foresight or experience she just had to hope it was a good day for baggage handlers and that the evening was the part of the day most likely to ensure swift service.

As the door opened and the stewardess beckoned the passengers forward, the leaning sun and blue sky felt crisp against Caittie's eyes, while the air warmed her entire body as she left the plane. It was a very different kind of warmth in the southern parts of Europe: hairdryer dry, lacking the sauna-like, soporific quality of the English summer. It was the same dryness that on various work trips to such climates inevitably made her realise how dusty the earth can become. Yet the atmosphere felt cleaner than British airports, the people more relaxed, compared to the sticky, impersonally busy mess of Heathrow. Standing by the side of the luggage conveyor, with hundreds of others, the desire to keep moving became almost a thirst. With little else to do beyond fretting at the delay, she started praying that her bag would be out soon. Sure enough, it was only a matter of minutes before her ancient rucksack slid out amongst the holiday suitcases.

Perhaps it was luck, perhaps it was prayer or perhaps the last bags on are always the first to come off, but all the same Caittie found herself dashing towards the passport and customs area with still – theoretically, at least – enough time to make the ferry. Her passport got the usual cursory grimace that subliminally suggested, why bother when they are white and English? It was only when walking through the customs, with its series of obligatory aimlessly wandering officials, when it suddenly dawned on Caittie that she was carrying far too much cash in her shoulder bag. If she was stopped and searched, how on earth could she explain it? All she could hope for was to successfully impersonate a busy tourist in the usual rush to get the holiday started. As it happened, she had worried for nothing. The customs officers didn't even bother to disrupt their conversation as she passed by, hesitating just for a second before being pushed on by the flood of passengers coming along behind.

Moving into the main lounge, she scanned the concourse for a Bureau de change or for some form of bank. Only one money-changing kiosk remained open, with a series of rates on display. Since she couldn't be bothered to compare rates of exchange, she recovered one of the envelopes the Uxbridge bank had divided for her and passed it over the counter, while the man looked at her carefully and checked the notes, muttering laboriously in Greek. Caittie flicked open her passport and said, '*Ne*' – 'yes' being one of the few Greek words she could remember. She couldn't recall the Greek word for hurry, so she pointed towards the exit and moved from foot to foot as if she desperate to get going. The man nodded absently, still counting, humming to himself, as if ending a lucrative day. Time was the only thing that could complicate her plans and the taxi rank sign ahead of her represented another milestone to safety.

Standing impatiently in the taxi queue, Caittie couldn't help notice the arguing drivers, as – or so it appeared – one might have jumped their turn. Such overt opportunism always shocked her, compared to the patient queuing in England, at no matter what the cost. However, it only took a few minutes before she was first herself. It was a relief to be just seconds away from the exposed grill penning in the queue and the hundreds of eyes potentially watching her. She had already convinced herself that one man, clearly taking a break with a cigarette, his eyes glued to her top, was identical to one of the customs officers. Yet there was no time to worry, as her taxi was pulling in. She lent forward to negotiate with the driver.

'You speak English?'

'Yes, so.'

'The Piraeus harbour, ferry for Crete. As quickly as you can!' The man nodded without concern and it was difficult to know whether he really understood her urgency. Peeling off five thousand drachmas she continued. '*Kontino.*' It was the Greek word for short and the nearest she could remember to get her message across. She caught the driver's calculating eyes in his mirror as he headed off, as if to check out what sort of tourist he had in the back seat. Then he almost imperceptibly nodded and without a word shot away through the cars that were shunting and waiting for spaces, horns blazing away, as he forced his way into the traffic. Meanwhile, just behind, Caittie adjusted her position so as to glance both forwards and backwards, which was becoming a habit.

As they pulled away from the airport onto the main road, she spotted the man who had been waiting near the taxi rank turning and sprinting back inside the building. It might have been coincidence, but he had – in the flicker of a moment – turned from an innocent bystander into something altogether more sinister. Her father had warned her that the danger would come from those in authority. Or was it merely her own overactive imagination? – she couldn't be sure. Anyway 'they' – whoever they were – couldn't know where her taxi was going, while her driver appeared to be relishing his instructions for dispatch. There was none of the usual slogging through traffic lights; instead they were zig-zagging through back roads at speed. Every few seconds Caittie checked behind, though she felt confident that it would have been impossible for anyone to follow them unnoticed at such a pace.

She still had the wad of money, at a quick count just over five hundred thousand, which was a little short compared to the exchange rate advertised. No wonder the man had started humming as he served her, taking advantage of her hurry in order to give himself an end-of-day bonus! Being cheated would have normally annoyed her, but now it seemed an irrelevance. She thought she could smell the sea. Peeling off another couple of thousands, she held the driver's bonus in her hand as they screeched to a halt in the car park outside the ferry terminal. It was five to eight and the ticket office was doing a marvellous interpretation of a shop about to close.

But she wasn't too late – just. As she handed her driver the money he pointed to the door and said 'So! Hurry.' A quick exchange of where she wanted to go and she had secured a ferry ticket to Heraklion. A few minutes later she was on deck and watching the sailors' departure routine. A series of service connections and gangplanks were taken away, but she wandered across the deck watching the dockside for anyone or anything that might be perceived as even vaguely suspicious. The boat was reasonably crowded, though – to her relief, it was almost entirely peopled by tourists of various nationalities. As soon as the boat left the quay, she felt freed and took a celebratory stroll round in order to get her bearings.

A passing steward gave her the itinerary: the boat would take all night to sail the distance, arriving about five or six the next morning. Her economy ticket had secured her passage on board, but unless she had pre-booked there was no chance of getting a cabin. As she strolled round it was clear many people were settling down for the night, greatly reducing the number of people on deck. She had really done almost nothing all day, but somehow she still felt tired. The sea air blew fresh on her face as the temperature dropped and they had left the heat and dust of Athens behind.

In the ladies', it seemed a good idea to take the opportunity of changing into warmer clothes before facing the night's sharper breezes. Checking the mirror, Caittie was shocked to realise just how dry and neglected her skin looked. Her task gave her little sense of having excess time to kill and so, not knowing when she would get another chance to spend some time on herself, it felt good to steal a little. She set up camp at one end of the basins, until brushing her hair, cleaning her face and applying moisturising creams made her feel herself again. Too busy, too nervous or just too frightened of late, it had been a routine completely neglected, despite representing essential parts of what recharged her batteries and allowed her to face the world. She had spent the last two days thinking logically and clinically and – stimulating as it had been – life felt a barren place without the other parts of a girl's life. She had often wondered how men ever managed to remain sane in their macho world, with so many thinking it was somehow unmanly to take a little care, preferring the hard-worn look.

While sorting through her clothes, Caittie took the opportunity to divide her money. Putting most of her sterling and half of her traveller's cheques at the bottom of her rucksack, she put some drachma in her jeans, splitting the rest between the cotton jacket, her bag and the little wallet next to her skin. Once washed, she decided to venture back on deck, as she needed to find a quiet sheltered place to spend the night – there wouldn't be much time to rest in the morning if they docked as early as predicted.

She made a brief excursion into the lounge area, which dismayed her, as it consisted of a few groups of teens getting ever drunker and louder, while the remainder looked uncomfortable, as if attempting (without conviction) to sleep through the noise. Settling for some warm food, a steaming cup of coffee and a bottle of water for when she awoke, Caittie ventured back on deck. Finding the end of a quiet bench sheltered from the breeze – the other section was occupied by an older Greek couple – she settled down to eat. The second sip of coffee only served to confirm the first's utter lack of flavour – by contrast, the food went down quickly, too quickly – perhaps nerves increased her appetite. Afterwards, using her jacket as a pillow, her shoulder bag as a cushion and her rucksack as a leg rest, she improvised an easy chair and sat back enjoying the needled stars in the clear night sky.

Caittie tried to recall something Wendy had told her when she had moved out. She couldn't recall the words – or not exactly – but she knew it was something to do with true friends being like stars – no matter where they are or whether they were visible, they are still shining somewhere. This recollection was part of an attempt to make sense of this experience, despite its dangers and discomforts, simply because she had so few friends like Wendy (Caittie *made* friends quite easily, but Keith had always managed to destroy or manipulate away any chance of her building close friendships). He seemed to need her to be dependent upon him alone.

Caittie had to wonder whether her current peacefulness was due to the freedom to be herself: new life, new choices and the potential of new unfettered acquaintances. Surely it was freeing enough not having to take any heed of what Keith might think or say! Then she felt a surge of guilt at having only left him dinner for Monday, he'd be furious at not being catered for tonight. Besides which, she hadn't phoned – indeed, she couldn't, there was far too much at stake. The call to her mother and her 'Wendy decoy' had seemed to work, as far as she could know, but any call she might make at this point could lead her father's enemies straight to her. Besides, her fragile strength, though it seemed to grow each day inside her, could still crumble in conversation with Keith. There would probably come a time when this wouldn't matter, but she couldn't risk it yet.

Caittie was just starting to put on her jacket when, out the corner of her eyes she registered something vaguely worrying. Along the side of the boat twenty or thirty yards away was a young man slipping towards the bench, can of beer in one hand, cigarette in the other, his movements loose and easy, as if dancing to some music in his head. She sat impassively as he processed slowly towards her, his head lent forwards, mumbling occasional words to his imaginary song. He stopped at the end of the bench, leant his head back and puffed on his cigarette, looking at her through a grey puff of smoke with drunken eyes.

'Hello, sweetheart! Why doncha join the party!' He had obviously not shaved for a couple of days, though it resembled the patchy fluff of alopecia more than 'designer stubble'.

She ignored him. In her experience, conversation with drunks just prolonged the irritation.

'How about it, have a few drinks, liven the place up a bit?' He was still bobbing around as if he was trying to disguise the swell of the boat and his inability to keep his balance.

She was just about to say something when she noticed another two lads running up noiselessly behind him. Taking one leg each, they yanked down his trouser, his pants half following. He barely flinched or even looked round at his friends who were scurrying away at speed giggling pathetically. Rather than show any embarrassment, he stood blankly for a few seconds trying to pull his trousers back up before he realised that for this to succeed he needed to undo them first.

'Sorry, but I don't do babysitting!' Caittie jumped in while he was still trying to adjust himself.

'Hey, look, don't take any notice of them. My mates are arseholes if you 'scuse my French – they won't bother nobody!' His enunciation, attempting to compensate for his condition, only produced the odd piece of unnoticed spittle. 'Come on, love, what d'you say?' He started to edge closer.

Caittie instantly gathered up her bags. Yet before she could even move, she heard a tirade of abuse coming from her other side. In a couple of seconds the Greek woman had got to her feet and was pointing and poking her finger in the face of the young man, firing Greek words at him with such venom that he backed off, hands before his face. 'OK, OK, sorry I spoke! Keep your hair on!' He edged swiftly backwards, eventually managing an awkward turn and mooching away.

'Are you all right, lady?' The old woman asked Caittie.

'Fine, thank you! I'm very – very grateful.' Caittie was stunned and sat with her mouth open slightly trying to find words to say. 'What did you say to him?' The old woman had returned to her seat, before saying, with some satisfaction, 'I said he looked like a cross between a goat and a monkey's bottom!'

Her husband added, 'I'm sorry, but our own daughter was attacked a few years ago.'

'Don't be sorry! I'm very grateful to you.' It didn't seem enough, but Caittie had to respond to his apology – though assisting someone seemed an odd thing to apologise for. She settled back, much comforted. The old Greek couple, despite appearing like something off of a film set, were sensitive, intelligent and caring people. Their warmth extended to someone they didn't know, because they felt an empathy with her, an empathy that removed any doubt of intervening or the danger to themselves. She tried to guess their age and thought it was probable their daughter could easily be the same age as she was.

The safety she now felt in their proximity allowed her to nod off for brief bursts of sleep, but she found the slightest noise and lack of a real pillow meant that she woke often, half-remembering rather short and stormy dreams that only increased her sense of worry. She fretted that she hadn't told her mother the complete truth. She recalled that she hadn't contacted Keith properly. She wondered whether she had been grateful enough to the old Greek couple. Guilt seemed to stalk her dreams without reason.

The engines of the boat changed from a constant drone to a throttling noise, which forced Caittie to completely awaken. The Greek couple immediately began to busy themselves assembling their belongings as if they were expecting to move at any moment. Moving into the gangway and looking ahead, Caittie could see lights clearly shining on the hand-drawn silhouette of land in the distance. The sun had not risen, although a faint glow was visible on the horizon, as it was just about to soar upwards from the eerie half-light. Looking for the water in her bag, she found some biscuits she had bought in the coffee shop on Monday. They were a bit broken up, but it counted as a breakfast of sorts. She sat picking at the biscuit crumbs, wondering what to do next. Her thoughts drifted back to the man at the airport – he might have simply been curious, but what if he had prompted an entire team of people now tracking her movements?

Looking back, she had at first been forced to rush to evade the men, then – having lost them – rushed to leave the country. Now there was no need to rush, especially if, by doing so, she might run straight into her pursuers. The ferry seemed to be a good idea, as being harder to trace, but the nine hours' journey time could certainly have enabled anyone to fly ahead and be waiting for her. The best way she could avoid this, she thought, was to wait on board upon arrival and check out the quayside. Once the stampede of the passengers had gone, then anyone waiting would probably stand out and she could decide what to do. Chances were it wouldn't be necessary, but to hold back would give her options, whereas to rush straight out might give her none.

'You all right now?'

Caittie hadn't noticed the older Greek couple preparing to depart, but the old lady stopped and bent forward, clearly worried by Caittie's expression, her ornate crucifix dark gold against her black top.

Caittie almost jumped. 'Oh! Yes, yes of course.'

'Someone here to meet you?' The old lady persisted.

Caittie paused again, taken aback by the warmth and friendliness, but more with the comfort of suddenly feeling less alone. Then she admitted, 'No, I'm travelling alone.'

'Where you go?'

'Elounda.'

'Elounda is good. You come with us to Neapolis. Short bus ride to Elounda!' The lady tugged at Caittie's arm to get her to stand and as if to suggest they wanted to hurry.

'Great, thank you!' Throwing everything together, she grabbed her bags and followed the couple into the main area and down the central stairwell. They emerged into a large flat area full of cars and vans. Weaving their way through they came to a small beaten-up half-van, half-car seemingly welded together. It had two seats in the front and a rusted metal box in the back. The man got into the driver's seat and the lady held one of the back doors proudly open.

'Come!' she urged.

'Thanks so much.' Caittie had thought of them as old because they were both small and weather-beaten, it now dawned on her that they were just middle-aged but wrinkled like prunes in the sun. The back of the vehicle also suggested that they ran some kind of farm or smallholding. The straw was no problem, but she tried to find an area without too much what looked like animal droppings, by brushing the rest aside with her foot. Tucking herself in behind the driver's seat, she used her rucksack as a backrest.

'You speak good English,' she ventured.

'Please. Our son has taverna in Neapolis. We give best vegetables for him. You come to taverna?'

'I'd love to, once I finish my business!' Business sounded the wrong word for someone in casual clothes and a rucksack, and the woman looked puzzled, so she added. 'I have to meet a colleague. I'm an archaeologist.' This lady had been so kind and genuine that she quickly added a reasonable truth to the statement.

Once they were moving she could not see anything worth noting, and it seemed desirable to remain hidden. All the time she couldn't see anyone, no one could spot her, which felt illogically comforting as if the anxiety of being discovered couldn't start until she could see it coming. The odd half-glimpse of a dock worker or security guard, between the processions of traffic, was all she could make out from her pit in the back. As they came bumping out over the causeway of the boat, the light had shone in through the back windows that were frosted with mud, and the sun had risen dazzlingly while they had been below decks.

It wasn't long before they were on the main road. Caittie was relieved that the man drove cautiously, as the noise in the back was already deafening. The sterile concrete of the dockside buildings flashing past the back window gave way to a new kind of dust, different to Athens: redder, less industrial. Often, the shadowing outline of various vehicles came zooming up to the back windows and then at the last minute pulled out to overtake. She relaxed back to reflect how lucky she had been to choose to sit next to this couple. It hadn't seemed relevant at the time, but she now connected the golden crucifix round the woman's neck with her prayers the other day. She had remembered those prayers last night on the boat, not that the prayers were bad, but she had asked for help and given nothing to God, other than indifference, of late. It seemed a bit shallow to promise to herself, she would be more faithful, if she survived this quest. She resolved to try and pray each day, whether she desperately needed help or not.

It took almost an hour before they halted, the woman offering her help to emerge and the man turning for a gap-toothed smile – Caittie felt embarrassed when he refused money for petrol. Instead the woman pointed to the over-painted café of her son's up the road, while saying proudly, 'This belongs to Nectarius. You bring friends also.' It was obvious that she wanted nothing for herself, merely success for her son. Caittie thought how different this felt to her own experience, with one parent wrapping her defensively in cotton wool, as something fragile, while the other had simply disappeared, loving adventure more than her. At that moment, all Caittie wanted was a parent that loved her the way this woman loved her son. Impulsively, she put her arms round the woman and hugged her.

The husband said something in Greek, pointing across the road to the bus stop. Caittie waved goodbye as she crossed the road – and they'd been right, it was just minutes, before the bus turned up. Then a few minutes more she was looking out the bus window at the beautiful views as it carefully wound its way down the hills to Elounda.

13

Philip

It was a name from Andrew's past. One word, and an instant summary conjured up a picture of childhood, full of baggage. A bloody nose on his first day at school, an influence he thought he had moved away from at the age of ten. A face that surely stood watching as he struggled to cling to life in the pit that day. A photo, neatly filed, dealt with, taking the positives into a new life, with any fear quashed by the anticipation of leaving the negatives behind. Perhaps most of all, a wound reopened.

'For someone uninterested in my petty juvenile crimes, you ask the strangest questions!' It was avoidance, even denial, but he couldn't stop himself.

Pierre said calmly, 'Just tell me what happened that day he came to see you.'

'There's nothing to say. He came to see me and went away again!'

'Surely after those intervening years it must have taken some effort, and a journey, to track you down? Didn't you wonder why he came?'

'Not at all. He told me himself, just as soon as I asked about the others from the gang. It was pathetic to hear how the bully was now being bullied, claiming to be the victim of some kind of injustice. So, frankly, no matter why he had come to see me I felt that I couldn't take any chances.'

'Hadn't he taken a chance coming to see you?'

Andrew ignored this.

'The only thing that seemed to have changed in those years was that he hadn't grown as big or as strong as the people he bullied. Once deposed, he didn't fancy being the victim. There's no bigger threat to a leader than an ex-leader, and to combat this constant threat it would be essential to make an example of him by keeping him beaten. Basically he was just looking for a nice way out. And also, I wasn't the only one. I knew there would be a queue seeking retribution.'

'So, your own revenge was to send him away?'

'I didn't send him away as such.'

'What did you do then, invite him for tea and arrange to meet him next week?'

'Of course not!'

'Isn't that what old friends do? He was beaten, after all. What could be the harm?'

'I had new friends, by then, kind people – the sort of people he used to prey on. While to me he still seemed like the injured animal. How could I trust him?'

'But you'd changed and your new friends had accepted you, right? Didn't you think they might have given Philip the benefit of the doubt?'

'That wasn't a risk I wanted to take.'

Pierre stirred in his chair, but refused to lift his eyes.

'So, your friend turns up desperate, lonely and – we assume – seeking some change in his life. You must have done what he himself hoped to do and instead of offering anything, you decide to not risk your own comfort. Is that right?'

Heat flooded Andrew's face. He said, impulsively, 'Listen, I know what you're getting at! But where you're wrong is that it was a matter of trust. The truth was, I'd started over and learned to use my strengths to protect my weaker friends. He needed to find his own new place, his own friendships, without the baggage of the past. Then he might stand a chance.'

'This is mere self-justification.'

'Self-determination, more like.'

'So what am I getting at?'

'How can I know? You only want me to have done nothing!'

'Or perhaps to let you hear yourself glossing over your past.'

Andrew frowned. 'It was a decision I had to make, unexpectedly, on the spot. I still regret any hurt it may have caused.'

'And by hurt you mean –'

'And certainly no part of my decision was concerned with revenge. You may still see "doing nothing" as a bad option, but to me there was little choice.'

'Or perhaps you had a choice, but you panicked?'

'I was a teenager, for God's sake! That's what teenagers do, they make mistakes and they learn from them. Is that a crime?' The wound was now bleeding inside Andrew's head. 'What has this got to do with anything anyway?'

'Perhaps it's just different ways of looking at things.'

'Meaning?'

'For instance, we could talk about Kevin.'

14

Elounda

When the bus pulled into Elounda town centre, known as Schisma, it was just before eight. Caittie's anxiety seemed curiously at odds with the drowsy tranquillity outside, where there seemed hardly any sign of life. The sea, which had seemed so distant from the hills above, was now so close that she could smell it. The bell tower, long visible, was now a stone's throw away and a glimpse of the harbour between the buildings reassured her that it was indeed Schisma.

For the rest, it was a place eager to embrace the tourist, but without losing the character of an old town. On the way in they had several times passed large hotels being built, along with long stretches of land that seemed almost uninhabited. A few people were strolling in and out of the small supermarket, for it remained the time of day when the locals at least had the sense to keep out of the later heat. Caittie had the impression that there was no point in even trying to sort out accommodation or anything else until the town had awoken again, in a tourist sense. In the meantime, it seemed sensible to scout out the tavernas near the harbour with regard to placing her ad.

A little farther down she spotted a hub of restaurants and bars around the small square harbour, as if a corner of the square had cut a right angle into the coastline. Further along she could see the beach down the shoreline, past the harbour, where other possible tavernas were visible, though she guessed that the harbour might be more logical with regard to the boats required by her advert. How strange it was, to think that Michael lived here! Assuming, of course, that he still did. She noticed that the road dividing the buildings from the water seemed to be the place where locals gathered, with the remnants of cigarettes in several places near the harbour edge.

Returning to the supermarket, she bought a pad of plain paper, a large felt-tipped pen and a fresh bottle of water. The girl at the till seemed tired and over-heated, taking her time before starting to ring up the few items on the counter. Caittie noticed some local tourist maps tucked in a rack on the end and quickly slipped one onto the counter (much to the girl's disgust, as she had just pressed the 'total' button). Moving back down to the harbour, Caittie perched on a conveniently abandoned piece of concrete near the boats and tried to work out what her father had said in the letter. Her aim was to get the essence of the message so imbued with the atmosphere of the place that it would pass unnoticed by anyone other than the mysterious Michael. After a couple of abortive attempts she decided on short and simple, with the key words in bold:

Wanted, Boat, Skipper, Scuba gear, for 4 weeks diving project, some experience but also some guidance and training needed.

She would need to ensure it was placed as near the road as possible. It was an odd advert in such a place, but she guessed perhaps that was the point, in order to limit unwanted if innocent responses, which she might have to talk her way out of accepting. Caittie was careful not to overstate her own diving ability, which was OK, but not advanced (though she recalled with amusement how Mum had gone berserk upon learning that she had signed up to learn scuba diving one holiday). Those years after her father had disappeared had been so painful! But since it was just instruction in the hotel swimming pool, Mum had been persuadable. It had been far easier to follow that up while on holiday with Keith, by booking a day's diving at the same time as he attempted water skiing. Considering her final draft one last time, Caittie eventually added instructions to any respondent to leave a message with bar owner. That might weed out a few well-intentioned boat-owners, as well as shielding her (wherever she was staying) from the overly keen.

After a time, she began to feel twitchy with frustration at having to wait before movement and life in the town would awaken. So often, back in England, she had been the one impeding busy people, but now she was the busy person in the midst of a sunbathed tranquility! She breathed deeply and slowly, while trying to relax and take in her surroundings. But her mind stubbornly refused to appreciate much beyond the probable futility of placing an advert in a restaurant window swamped by canopies, tables and chairs. And, beyond that, who was to know whether Michael would be willing to meet her – or even, to put the worst possible case – if Michael was still alive?

Once she'd reached this point, Caittie pulled back from the brink of panic. Her father obviously had his reasons and she would have to stick to his instructions if she was to have any chance of doing what she was meant to do. She would learn soon enough about Michael. Leaning back she caught sight of the church tower, prominent and admirable on the apex of the square harbour – a fantastic place to overlook the entire area, as her eyes caught and admired the hills in the distance. All around the town they rose, hot, dry, and already almost wavy in the heat of the morning sun.

As she looked along the stretch towards the beach, her attention was arrested by Kalypso Hotel. It wasn't so much that it had the advantage of height, instead it was the apartment balconies, and the small black sign hanging from one of the top railings saying 'apartment to let' in two languages. It seemed to be almost beckoning to her. She sat there staring for a second before grabbing her rucksack and heading straight for the entrance of the hotel.

Breakfast and her advert would have to wait, she had a gut feeling that she needed to make that room hers. Inside there was a nice young waiter called Stafis, perturbed by her inquiry, who started to protest that he was not allowed to let the rooms and that she would have to wait for his boss' arrival. However, he confirmed that the room was still available and had been cancelled on a two month let for July and August, so there was still plenty of time left.

'So there wouldn't be any harm in my taking it?' she said, flicking back her hair, which looked fairer than usual, as if the sun had already tinted it. It didn't take much more, just a coaxing tone, slightly puppy eyes and every other ruse she could summon that might possibly weaken a young man's doubts. Counting out the cash for two full weeks at the maximum rent clinched the deal. She probably didn't need to tip Stafis or to promise to move on immediately if his boss had let the room in his absence, the key to independence was already in her hand.

Moments later, Caittie was standing in the room and thanking Stafis with genuine feeling before he left her to let her settle in. Methodically, she sorted her out her rucksack so as to rinse through a few garments at a time, while still keeping as packed as possible. It had been the first chance she had had for relaxation over the last few days and didn't know when the next might come. She must have stood on the balcony for half an hour, admiring her luck at the view over the harbour, tavernas and the horizon of Spinalonga, before contentment gave way to hunger. She had promised Stafis to breakfast in the hotel, so she would be there when his boss arrived in case there were any problems. The boss' pat on Stafis' shocked back was all she needed to see to know that she was safe. This place felt comfortable, compared to the ever-increasing tourist blocks sprouting all around the area. Its style and size must once been modern and prominent, but now seemed delightfully rustic, homely even, and certainly ideally placed (she would have suffered a modest degree of squalor for this view from the balcony).

Caittie ordered a deliberately large breakfast with plenty of coffee, another luxury she had missed (she wasn't naturally a big breakfast eater, but the plan was to skip lunch). In terms of the advert, it would probably be a gamble getting the timing right, as with the Kalypso, the actual owner probably wasn't always around, even over mealtimes. Still, even if she had to return later, it would only be in the response to a good prospect and with perhaps a name of the person she needed to see. Stafis came to clear her table the moment she had finished; impulsively, she arrested his attention.

'I need a favour.'

'Anything!' said the boy gallantly.

'It's just this. If anyone comes here looking for me or asks about a British girl with a description like mine, I need you to say that I'm not here. That you've never seen me.' She seized his hand imploringly and he froze, shocked.

'You are in trouble? Police?'

'No, no, nothing like that! It's my – ex. He's quite rich and very angry I left, and his friends are bastards!' The rich part was a bit of a lie, but at least the boyfriend and bastards ticked two out of three. Her main hope was that it sounded convincing, and there she seemed in luck.

'Trust me, no problem!' He winked and carried on clearing her place.

Strangely enough, Caittie didn't feel nervous any longer, but she had to assume those chasing her would have the resources to catch her up eventually. When the manager had counted her rent in cash, he had also put it into his pocket – she hoped this meant he might have declared the previous cancellation deposit for the room and wouldn't record her stay officially. If Stafis played his part he too might throw any enquiry off its tracks.

Back in her room, she sat on her balcony watching the tourists and locals gradually gathering by the sides of the harbour until it was positively busy. Changing her top to a grungy T-shirt and scraping her hair back casually, she completed the look with no make-up, so as to seem like someone more likely to consider serious diving. She had long realised her face could easily look normal when scrubbed, but as soon as she dropped her dark blonde hair and put on make-up, the beauty of her pointed chin and lovely cheekbones altered remarkably. Sporty transformation completed, she had another stroll round the harbour before deciding where to start.

In the first few tavernas, it was hard to get anybody to understand what she wanted. She did not want to offer much money or raise suspicion, so she didn't push. The result varied between brisk refusals to vague offers of assistance from possibly non-existent cousins. It even crossed her mind that she should return in the evening with a short skirt on, making it easier to get some owner to put up her ad without caring if she was really serious. She had been trying the smaller places in the hope they might prove more receptive, but eventually slumped into a chair in the biggest and showiest place in the coast. Camelot's had a prominent frontage with a permanent awning, which made the windows hard to see. However, it was still nice to sit in the shade, and the chairs were marvellous. A man in a dark crisp shirt came over to her table. He appeared a bit more than a waiter, but as they were quite busy it seemed to be all hands on deck.

'Madame looks hot, would she like a pleasant drink?' He was tall, with a confident twinkle and rather affected, gigolo-style, good looks.

'Could I have a coffee and a glass of iced water?' She couldn't make up her mind whether to cool down or just top up on caffeine.

'Of course! But perhaps Madame would like something else to make her smile?' His voice was full of innuendo.

'Yes, actually!' Her voice dropped to a soft whisper. 'Could you put this sign up for me in your window?' His face seemed concerned when he first read the note. Then he gave a rather knowing laugh. 'Have you asked anyone else this?'

'Just a few!' She tried not to show her frustration at his amusement, as it was the first time she had received any reaction than indifference.

'Allow me to tell you why, young lady. The man who does most of the scuba round here, his brother owns the restaurant at the end and his cousin owns that one two doors down.' He lent forward now to whisper. 'He is not the sort of man most people would wish to upset.'

Caittie tried to speak but the man raised his hand to stop her.

'Frankly, I do not like this man. The others may not want to help you because they are frightened to ask permission of him, but I will accept simply to annoy him!' He stood back reading the message again. 'You say here, leave message with the owner, but how are we then contact you?'

'Don't worry, I'll be here every day!' Caittie had to focus on making her response sound unworried as to why others would be frightened or why this owner relished the chance to annoy. It didn't seem ideal, but at least it no longer felt impossible. She was in no position to refuse, so as not to waste whatever space she had succeeding in putting between herself and her pursuers. It would be all too easy to now sit back in this seeming tranquility, drifting along pleasurably enough, only to be awoken to danger when it was far too late. As for Michael, it was essential she found him, because her father promised her that Michael could help. By the time Caittie was ready to leave the bar, the man who had put the sign up was serving another table so she merely waved as she left.

The mini-supermarket next door was geared up for seafront tourists so she wandered in for a few supplies (if she had to spend time keeping watch, then a few home comforts wouldn't go amiss). Yesterday's English broadsheet, a trashy novel, some snacks and her own small supply of gin and tonic comprised the rest of her basics. She had forgotten to pack a beach towel but spotted some by a variety of parasols and beach toys. It was easy spending the rest of the afternoon and early evening lying on her balcony, occasionally checking over the top of the book towards the harbour – nothing seemed strange, but then, how would she recognise 'strange?'. Yet it still seemed necessary to watch, as if to get a feeling of what 'ordinary' meant. As the afternoon passed, the boats slowly returned, filling the half-empty harbour of the morning until they packed the area, mooring anywhere they could manage. The contrast was striking between those still used as fishing boats and those significant few that had obviously been converted to cash in on tourist trips.

With so many venues advertised merely as holiday destinations, it was pleasing to find a place that embraced commerce and tourism side by side. On her balcony, she could take in the panoramic view of the horizon of the Kolokitha peninsula, with Spinalonga at its tip, which made Elounda feel as if it was perched at the end of a lake. The tourist leaflet she had picked up explained how different occupiers had ruled Crete and how Spinalonga itself had once served as a leper colony. It made for interesting reading, as she had to consider what she might tell any real diving companies responding to her ad.

As darkness fell, she changed into warmer clothes and resumed her watch. The busy road was often jammed as taxis dropped off tourists intent on soaking up the views of the picturesque harbour, along with rather too much alcohol. Preferring to keep a low profile, Caittie waited until the restaurant had thinned out before going downstairs for dinner. Everybody wanted to sit outside, so it was easy to get a table inside, at the back. A girl on her own could attract trouble and attention, as she had found on the ferry from Athens, but here Stafis, who gave her a knowing look, was attentive in looking after her. He bought her a small carafe of wine she had not ordered, and – responding to her puzzled look – explained that it was his personal gift for the bonus his boss had also given him for her rent.

It was easy to sit there drinking, almost celebrating how far she had come on this journey, but by the end of the carafe Caittie was more exhausted than elated. She had not drunk more than a glass of wine for a long time and was glad to see her bed after the bad night's sleep she had suffered on the boat.

Sleep she did and it was only as the traffic noise increased with the heat of late morning that she woke, her mouth dry and her head fuzzy from heavy sleep. It took her fifteen minutes and a whole bottle of water before she even felt like getting washed and dressed. She castigated herself for drinking too much, as she needed to stay alert, but her body had absorbed the alcohol as if to ensure she caught up with her rest. It didn't matter hugely, but she had slept longer than she'd expected and was now anxious to get out and see if her bait had lured any 'bites'. All the things – including prayer – she had planned for the morning were curtailed, as well as a brief spell on the balcony. To her eyes, everything looked normal across the road, so, wanting to get moving, she went down to the Kalypso bar for a coffee. After assuring Stafis that she didn't need breakfast, she sat and sipped coffee as he prepared the other tables. It wouldn't be long before she could go and ask if there were any messages across the road, but it also dawned on Caittie it might not be very strategic to be seen walking straight across from one place to the other.

Taking her bearings from the day before, she walked left out the hotel and down past the beach area, away from the harbour. Half looking for a better place for her advert, half admonishing herself for having little faith so soon in her choice, she obliged herself to wander almost to the outskirts of the town, determined to keep any premature prospect of failure not only underfoot, but also under control. When she reckoned she had gone far enough, she doubled back, but stayed on the main road around the back of the hotel. As she came near the town centre, it was a simple matter of following the road past the far side of the church, round the back of the row of buildings with the Camelot in the middle and then returning to the harbour from the other end. This progression felt right as it gave her a chance to walk past the Camelot and into the supermarket from the other side. This gave a full view of anything potentially suspicious at a glance, but was probably also what any tourist might do. Buying an English paper and more bottled water was as good as wearing a badge that said 'tourist'. Yet, back in the Camelot, seated as near to her advert as felt reasonable, it was difficult for her to relax, as her slight hangover, mixed with the growing heat, left an inherent tension along her entire body.

Caittie took her time with lunch, pretending to search through her paper. Her body instinctively craved salad and fresh food, which she had missed in the last few days. Two courses spaced as long she dared seemed to justify her extended stay. Strictly water with lunch and two strong coffees after, yet there was still no sign of the man who had accepted her advert. After getting the waiter's attention, she described him only to learn that the man's name was Nikos and that he was the son of the owner. When she explained why she wanted his name, she was at once relieved and disappointed to find he had left a message to say there were no messages for her yet. An afternoon on the balcony, a late dinner with two glasses of wine and the day seemed to have repeated itself.

The next day she rose much earlier. Stafis had given her lots of ideas for long walks, and, after deciding that the mornings were cooler she ventured past the beach and down the coast towards the saltpans, which led to a nice circle at the end with open views full of light and seagulls. And yet, lovely as the scene was, Caittie was aware that this was her second day in town and she couldn't avoid wondering whether anyone was tracking her. How could she notice anyone in particular? It was an impossible task in the busy place full of strangers. Anyone could be watching her – barring the men she'd seen in London – and she'd be none the wiser. However, here in the open and doubling back on the path meant it would be difficult for anyone to approach her undetected.

Again, coming back into town she followed the main road round past the back of the church, down the back of the Camelot and came in from the other end via the supermarket. Today Nikos was serving, complete with his natural flirty charm, but today it did not seem so arrogant. He asked about her diving and she had to evade the question, while managing to assure him it was essential to find the right person, someone used to more than the occasional day trip. Nikos had a friend who knew somebody into diving and said he 'would put the word around'. His meaning tone prevented her from objecting, as it would look odd if she put him off. All such risks would have to be taken, if there was any chance of finding Michael some seven years past her twenty-first birthday.

On Friday, Saturday and Sunday, the same pattern repeated itself with a different walk each day, though the others were in striking contrast to the flatness of the saltpans, as they seemed to lead to different hills that encircled Elounda. Each day, Caittie made sure she doubled back over her tracks at some point so as to get full view of anyone attempting to follow. Often she rested before descent, sitting on some throne-like rock while surveying the kingdom below. On Friday, taken with the beauty of the hills, she recalled that she had been skimping on her promises to pray, which invigorated and revitalised her walks still more. Although she was conscious too as each day passed her prayers seemed to get more desperate, spurred by the feeling that the time was running out before she might be caught, and mixed with the sense of impatience and longing for something to happen.

Monday was Stafis' day off, which was a little annoying, because the other waiter's English was very poor and Caittie was considering visiting Spinalonga, the island that beckoned to her from her balcony. Instead, she found herself wondering around town, feeling a bit purposeless. She took the path up the hill to the cemetery she had passed the other day. Today the cemetery made her feel unsettled rather than giving her the calm she normally felt from such places. To Caittie, the graves no longer seemed peaceful and historic – today she could only see them as plenty of hiding places, stone blocks built over dead bodies in order to conceal live ones from view. Picking up her normal route through the town, she moved round the back to take her usual seat in the Camelot. She glanced over and did a double take – had her sign really been taken down? Nikos was serving, rushed – she tried to catch his eye. She was sure he had seen her but he didn't approach. Another waiter took her order, but only looked blank when she mentioned her ad. Finally Nikos arrived, with a puzzled look she had never seen before.

'What, have you been frightened off like all the others?' Her voice was mocking, but also nervous.

'Not so. You have a message!' He handed over a sealed envelope. 'The scuba man I told you of, he is an angel – this man that sends this message is the frightening one. You want my advice, you go home before you get involved with this man.'

With a long, serious look, he left her. Caittie tried to take it all in, but it had made little sense – the Nikos of last week seemed so different from the Nikos of today. Meanwhile, her fingers were fumbling with the paper.

'Miss Muffet, your instructor has seen your message and has had it removed. Do not put it back up, either here or anywhere else. Arrive at this taverna again tomorrow morning before ten and choose a table at the road's edge. At ten o'clock precisely a white van will pull up. When the side door opens, get straight in. I'm sure you have questions, but there will be plenty of time for those later.'

The note was unsigned. She sat there for a moment thinking, her heart bounding. If the writer wasn't Michael then how would he have known about 'Miss Muffet'? Even if her enemies had gleaned this information somehow, surely they wouldn't bother making such public arrangements. As for Nikos' all too obvious doubts, well, she had to take the chance that he was wrong. Having come this far, how could she *not* take a chance? Besides which, it was taking a chance simply being here, assuming the men were searching for her, because she had probably already stayed longer than she should have, in the same place. When Nikos approached to clear her place, she looked up with a reassuring smile. 'It's OK, good news. This man can help.'

'Not this man.'

Caittie tried to sound reassuring. 'Why do you not like this man? Do you know him?'

Nikos shrugged. 'I don't, but he doesn't look like a diver, or talk like a diver. He has strange eyes. Perhaps my friend's friend can find someone to help you dive.'

'I don't see how you can –'

He leaned forward. 'I tell you, this man is not good. Is danger!'

With this, he left again, taking her plates with him. Caittie's lack of response now seemed to make her the escaped leper who had swum from Spinalonga of old. It was now a choice of staying in a dangerous place or taking her chance – with regard to which her mind had long since been made up. Going back to her hotel had real purpose and definition now. She laundered most of the clothes she had worn over the last few days and packed her rucksack with everything she could. A spare T-shirt in her shoulder bag and rebalancing the money just in case anything got stolen made her feel better prepared.

Her father had assured her that Michael would make her safe, but all the same she felt constrained to be sure she left little trail or clues behind. Time after time that afternoon, and into the evening, Caittie felt compelled to slip onto the balcony and check the streets, but there was nothing to lend credence to Nikos' comments so she had dinner as normal, responding with nothing beyond small talk to those diners who said hello to her. After dinner, she sat on her balcony watching the comings and goings at the Camelot while finishing her tiny bottle of gin with tonic. In the morning she decided it would be best to say nothing, slip out with her bags and send the key back by post if needed. Then, if the meeting with Michael led to nothing, she could always come back. Much worse was the recollection that, should it prove to be her father's enemies pretending to be Michael, her accommodation and keys would be needed no longer.

Caittie endured another restless night's sleep. She did sleep, but the more she slept the less easily she could get back to sleep as her thoughts spurred her to wakefulness. By seven, she was on the balcony eating the rest of her snacks and drinking her water. It was a breakfast of sorts, as much as clearing the room, but she would rather do this than face breakfast downstairs and tempt any questions. The minutes seemed to drag on for hours, until, as if from nowhere, the time was twenty to ten. She couldn't wait any longer. Downstairs, Stafis was out serving a group of tourists their breakfast. Pausing at the counter, she crept out through the staff door while no one was around. She could hear noises in the storeroom, but the kitchen was empty and she was soon out on the street by the church.

She felt that she just wanted to keep moving, as waiting would soon feel unbearable. Wandering from shop to shop, counting the minutes, she casually progressed round the block. It was five to ten when she finally chose a chair along the Camelot's frontage. No one rushed to serve her, as she sat with her rucksack on her back as if she was just resting.

Each second seemed to tick by unendurably slowly and yet it was probably a couple of minutes past ten when the sound of a car engine started to overpower all other noises, scattering sea gulls back over the water. A blue car, followed by a white van, with its engine equally screaming and then a black car, all screeched to a halt right in front of her. The side door of the van flew open and a man bent forward, beckoning, and saying something in Greek, which she assumed meant 'Come, quick!' There was no time to think and both cars were revving as Caittie leapt forward and stumbled into the van, falling upon her knees with the weight of her rucksack on her back. She was trying to pull herself up using the back of the front seats, as all three vehicles shot off at full throttle, sending her lurching backwards against the man behind. There was a cacophony of horns from the traffic ahead as the white van seemed to plunge through. The Greek behind her was struggling to keep his balance on his knees, as he pulled off her rucksack. If it were not for the extreme g-force, she would have thought she was watching an action movie, but this one she was involved in.

Suddenly the man pulled a sack-like thing over her head. She started to struggle, whereupon the driver called back in very English tones, 'Don't worry! You're just not allowed to see out the back window! Just relax!' Struggle seemed futile in the circumstances and she sat breathing the Hessian sackcloth – she could still feel the vehicle rise and fall as it hit bumps and corners at speed. Just when she decided that the vehicle was going at normal speed, a hand suddenly covered her face. As soon as she felt the vapours in her nose, the fuzz of unconsciousness smote her hard and suddenly.

15

Kevin

'Kevin?' Andrew paused, looking for an answer, but all he got was a knowing smile. 'OK, well, I accept that I didn't do quite enough that night, but you can hardly say I did *nothing*.'

This was live guilt, constant guilt, and no matter how much he had changed since it had first seemed raw. The death of a friend! What greater price could there be to pay? If only, back then, drink-driving had been the scourge it is today, rather than the frowned-upon – if still socially acceptable – habit of the time. Although, on Kevin's twenty-first birthday, the car wasn't left behind, or even driven directly home, but instead was made part of a bet.

The question, then – how hard do you hit a friend when they won't listen to reason? How tough do you have to get, in order to reach hold of the keys before the struggle turns nasty? Remembering, after all, that Kevin had more than once driven neatly after drinking before, making it all too easy to kid himself he was only slightly the worse for wear, and that there was nothing really to worry about.

And yet, no punch – and no reaction – would have seemed too extreme the next day, compared to the iron railings that killed Kevin that night. A wet road, a sudden loss of control, his upside-down soft-scooped ice-cream-coloured car. So many of them who could have done something – it was cruelty masquerading as hindsight.

'I'm glad to see that your mind has focused straight to the point. Do you notice how both these circumstances come down to the same basic decision?'

'A decision, yes, but hardly the same,' said Andrew, frowning. The truth was that this still hurt, that the decades that had passed had never eased the feeling of that horrible night.

'But you were the one who said such decisions are about relative judgments. So do you admit that you did nothing?'

'No, I don't, not at all. We *did* do something, we tried – and not only me! Instead each of us looked at each other, as if to say, "What more can we do without losing a friend?" It was a step none of us took, simply because we wanted to keep being friends.'

'I'm sorry, but in fact what you're saying is that you weighed the risks, the certainties and uncertainties, adjusting your actions to a nicety until you decided to do exactly nothing, nothing at all.'

Andrew's colour rose. 'But this is a part of being human! Every day, our decisions go wrong. It's so easy to criticise after the event! All one can ever do is to accept what happened, and to try to do better. After all, I did change – both these and other events had an effect on me!'

'You say you changed, but did you really?'

'Listen, after Kevin's death, I changed without a doubt. Every ambition, every value, altered beyond all recognition.'

Pierre said rather coolly, 'Your thoughts may have reflected some degree of new thinking, but I would suggest your interactions with people in general were still engrained in the habits of the past.'

'Sure, it took me some time to grow up, but what sort of crime is emotional immaturity?'

'To me it seems more as if you were trying to take the blame for what happened to Kevin.'

'Well, if I did, at least that means we agree on something!'

'Not at all, Andrew, because there *is* no blame for what happened to Kevin.'

'But you just said – ' Andrew halted, uncertain, knowing that it was still wrong – all wrong – the wrong way round altogether. 'And now you've contradicted yourself!'

Pierre shook his head, 'No, not at all. Instead, I've simply made you look at the process of your own decision-making. The crucial question is: can you see the difference between when there's a limited risk, when you decide to do nothing, and when there is a certain danger, when you still choose to do nothing?'

Andrew's temper flared. 'Of course, but taking action's not always the best thing!'

Silkily Pierre replied, 'Yet knowing something needs to be done, shouldn't you choose the best option?'

'I'd like to think I always try to…'

'To do what, exactly? In short, despite all that happened, despite these very changes you've supposedly made in terms of your life, how could you still decide to do nothing, when it really mattered?'

'I don't know what you are talking about!' It was pure denial, while in desperation he tried a different tack. 'How you can guess what was in my mind at any given time, is beyond me.'

'Is it? But weren't you the one who took every opportunity to boast about your confirmation class in 1984?'

It was a scramble, a jump in subject he wasn't expecting, and suddenly his mind was racing to make the connection. He said, suddenly, 'You *are* a strange bloke!' The words slipped out without his approval. It was an acknowledgment that Andrew's manly island mentality had been well and truly breached, something half-acknowledged by Pierre's thin smile. Andrew's half-formed theory about aliens returned, but hopelessly, as if already aware that there was no choice left beyond being stripped (emotionally, at least) quite naked. As for the rest, he knew the year, the boast and where it happened – the confirmation class he'd attended during the preparation for his marriage. Religion had been omnipresent throughout all his life, even if at times actual attendance was neglected, so it had seemed natural to accept the offer, prior to his vows, in order to collect the full badge.

'So, Andrew, you were a boaster. Well, boast to me now. Tell me the question and give me your answers.'

He knew the question referred to, but realising its relevance and under the whip of Pierre's taunting, he couldn't just say it all in one go.

'It was just the simple question about what it meant to be a Christian.'

'And your response?'

Strangely enough, the evening returned to him vividly: the vicar's bowed head and pale, still face, listening to the answers from the room full of people. Time after time, each person starting with 'do not' this and 'try to be' that, upon which the vicar would gently answer 'True, true, my son, but not enough.'

Andrew himself had said nothing. He believed that he knew the answers, but he yearned for someone else to step up and give it. Only when the room fell quiet and the suggestions stopped could he not resist speaking up. And afterwards, the man's direct, friendly gaze, the overt admiration of an attractive woman in a navy blue blouse.

Pierre needled him. 'And what about you, Andrew? Come, come! You can remember when it suits you!'

'I said it was not enough as a Christian to do no wrong, but also –
but also to do good whenever you can.'

'You see? That was, let me see, as early as 1984, wasn't it? So how
was it that you still failed to follow your own advice?'

Feeling humiliated, taut, Andrew longed to stop the game, he
didn't want to play anymore. 'If you say so!'

'I do say so. And so, in 1984, you still did nothing.'

'Right.' How many old wounds would have to be spurred into
recollection before Pierre would get to the point?

'You know what I mean now, don't you Andrew?'

He did, but he didn't, simply because it was too much like the
most diabolical variety of nightmare. 'I might, but why don't you help
me out?'

'Ok. Tell me about your work on Russia in 1984 and why at the
end of the day you did nothing,' Pierre's voice rose with the vigour of
accusation.

16

Interrogatory

Caittie's eyes finally opened, her lids scraping over the clammy surface. Feebly, she tried to locate some clarity in the room. Her brain still felt numb and she could still feel the effect of the vapour in her nostrils, from what must have been chloroform or something similar.

All she could discern, from the shafts of hazy light squeezed through a few cracks, was waves of floating dust in a place so unkempt that, if not exactly a barn, it was certainly derelict. Sensation returned, in her first seconds of consciousness with the realisation that her arms were aching profusely. Also, as if her legs weren't entirely under her command, it took several attempts to get the soles of her feet solidly on the floor and her body closer to a standing position. The floor felt very dusty; she could feel grains of dry dirt grinding against her bare feet.

As Caittie's eyes adjusted, she could see why her position felt so strange. The stiffness in her wrists was accounted for in that each wrist had a shiny leather strap around it linked to the beams above (the chain dispelling any notion that her circumstances were improvised, as the fastenings were purpose-made). Her fingers were also thickly taped, so she couldn't grip anything. Still worse, she had, while still unconscious, been stripped naked except for underwear (having gone from fully clothed to near-naked in her unconscious state made her feel intensely violated). Her ankles were also bound, a short chain connecting them together.

Caittie briefly pondered the prospect that she had somehow been tricked and even caught by her pursuers, but the likely consequences were far too frightening to contemplate. Besides, her captors *had* to know the codeword, so they must have either captured the codeword (from someone) or be connected, in some way, to Michael. Unless Michael had somehow deceived them, there was probably still some information they lacked, but in either case, her fate was now out of her hands.

She guessed it was mid-afternoon, as the heat penetrated even the darkness of the barn. Each time she tried to move, she felt raw leather scour her wrists and ankles. The lack of air and the stillness made her start to sweat, as if her mind and body were in shock, or perhaps reacting to the fuzzy after-affects of the chloroform. Futile as it was, she kept tweaking the bonds at her wrists and ankles, though it was unsettling to realise that this was because she subtly enjoyed the pressure of the straps on these places, an enjoyment rising from deep inside. As irresistible as the temptation to keep testing her restraints was to the secret person on the inside, her outer self flushed with at least as much embarrassment as heat.

She had twice allowed Keith to tie her up, at his request, when he had wanted to introduce some 'fun and games' to their sex life, but it had never worked for her. All that had happened was a sense of feeling silly, while she had privately taken the view that the only pleasure arising from it was Keith's, in binding her. This felt very different (perhaps because it was real). Her mind continually seemed to drift towards a fantasy of 'Michael' (still handsome, with his strong brows and mobile mouth, even if he was about the same age as her father). A stranger, someone keeping her for his own pleasure – and at the same time a man so intimately in touch with her innermost desires that he would not only punish but adore her – so much so that, should he remove her chains she would choose to put them back herself. She was secretly shocked to discover that these thoughts had an evolving life of their own.

She knew that most men were nothing like this, instead they took what they wanted and therefore were scarcely to be trusted with such submission. Yet, at the edge of her thoughts, she suspected it was only pleasurable because she assumed that her current position had something to do with her father. For the same reason she was almost willing Michael to be here – she couldn't face the idea that her trip had been wasted and that even her nervous anticipation was purely because her new-found lust for danger had crossed into physical – even sexual – pleasure. In the end, she found that she had to block out the thought, as it challenged everything she had lived by until this last week.

Instead she forced herself to think logically, to 'think clever.' Focus, plan, prepare: words she repeated in her head, trying to work out how careful she would have to be until she was sure of what was coming next, blocking any more transient illusions.

Suddenly a shiver of light flashed across her, but too fast for her to register anything beyond a larger space than she had expected. The force of the light slicing through the darkness made everything afterwards almost black by force of contrast. Then, Caittie stiffened, hearing, closer than she expected, the sound of footsteps, a car's revving engine – then more footsteps, closer. Turning her head as far as she could, she could just about determine a rustic door faintly illuminated by light seeping round its edges. The grinding noise of shoes into dusty gravel grew louder as purposeful steps neared the door. The timber door rattled momentarily and then stuttered open, scraping along the ground as if unaccustomed to being used, filling the space with almost unbearable, Mediterranean sunlight.

The brightness hurt Caittie's eyes so much that she winced and blinked in her attempts to focus. A young, tautly-built man stood in the doorway, briefly drinking in her body, as a child would thirst for something denied him. Then, face averted, he spoke swiftly in Greek to someone behind him.

The only word she picked out was "Zoniana", a place once recommended by Stafis as one of the options for walking in the mountains (that is, if she hired a car and wanted some serious exercise). It was only when the young man at the door finished talking, did his eyes stop occasionally flashing towards her and he then stood in silence.

Realising he was either unable or unwilling to communicate with her directly, she followed his gaze across the room. There was the dim outline of a tall dark man rising from his seat in the corner. As he moved towards the guard at the door, she could see he was middle-aged but fit, tanned but somehow not of Mediterranean complexion, dressed in a sharp black shirt and trousers and, bizarrely in that half-light, wearing sunglasses. She thought, with a bounding heart – Michael. He must have been there since the first flash of light! Just as she realised this he walked across to the younger man, saying something in Greek. It was obviously some kind of instruction the young man was loath to accept as the older man flicked his fingers in dismissal.

The guard took the signal with a sudden sense of embarrassment, closing the door behind him. The tall dark man waited for a few seconds before reopening the door a foot or so to let in enough light to expose the room. In the distance, Caittie could hear the car pulling away – the wheels spinning in the dust created a gentle cloud that wafted in through the gap and into the beams of sunlight.

Walking slowly around her a couple of times, as if he had all the time in the world, Michael's every step crunched as his feet contacted the grit of the floor. All the time, she was aware of his eyes looking up and down her body. Even when he was behind her, she could still feel his gaze burning onto her skin. It remained hot, even stuffy, yet his silence was chilling. Finally, she said, as lightly as she dared, 'Look, you can untie me now. I presume you're Michael?'

Either you're Michael, she added silently to herself, or I could just be about to be raped. His silence, and his pacing together steadily evaporated her original optimism. She added, 'If you are not Michael, I happen to know he'll be angry when he finds out how you're treating me!' Still the man didn't respond, and she was debating whether it might be a good idea to add, 'Let me go and I'll try to forget it ever happened' when he finally responded, 'Little lady, you presume too much!'

His voice was calm and deep, English over the barest hint of Greek. He *must* be Michael! Except that, under these circumstances, she still couldn't bring herself to believe it.

'Who are you?'

He paused before her and it seemed to her that he frowned beneath the sunglasses. 'It is not a question of who I am, but of how you are going to convince me about who *you* are, and what you might be doing here.'

Caittie felt a rush of temper. 'I don't know! You brought me here, you tell me!' But before she could say any more he raised his hand to stop her.

'The trouble is, you understand that you are not the first to come here and claim to be Caitlin. You would think by now they would have given up such bald attempts to take us in. I think they have disposed of her and send these silly bitches here to make a fool out of me!' His voice deepened into anger by the end of this comment, but Caittie felt a surge of hope. If it was only a matter of proving her identity, she must have nothing to fear, though she couldn't keep her voice entirely steady. 'No, it's me: it is, really! I *am* Caitlin, from London, it's just taken me seven years to get here!'

A moment or so passed after she had spoken. He crossed behind her, his head meditatively bowed. Then, without warning, she heard a whoosh behind her, just before the rush of pain down her back. A slur of pain from some kind of whip. Caittie gasped in shock and felt tears fill her eyes instantly. The man came back in front of her, so close that she could smell strong dark coffee on his breath.

'Public knowledge. Tell me something new.' He walked round again.

She thought frantically, trying to picture something the real Michael might relate to. 'You – that is, Michael – used to come to my house with George and Frank to see my father – ' The same level pain electrically skidded into her back.

At first she didn't think it hurt quite as much second time, but with the impact over the top of the first one it stung with greater intensity as the seconds passed.

He returned to face her, 'All this I have heard before, four times, five times.' This time she could see from the cruel line of his lips that he was enjoying himself – and that he suspected he had more enjoyment to come. It didn't take much imagination to work out that this was someone who had done this before. She remembered her father's words '*Michael was set up on murder and sex charges, he's perhaps a little strange, but not that strange.*' It fitted, if – indeed – this was Michael before her. But he had moved behind her again.

'GAMF met at my house!' She needed time to think, but fear of pain drowned out thought. It took a couple of seconds, but when it came it stung worse than before. Sharper, thinner and more intense, even the sound through the air was different. She was now praying to help with the intensity of the pain, as a narrow trickle of salty blood wavered down her back. And yet, as if the physical and the mental were now perversely separated, she was still thinking as logically as she could, realising that, if she went quiet, he could conclude the worst and inflict more damage on her. She needed to engage him, to provoke his curiosity, to find out what had never been told before.

Slowly he crossed before her again, removing his sunglasses, almost insulting her. She was suddenly confident he *was* Michael, despite all the years that had passed – she recognised the hooded eyes and heavy eyebrows, the sardonic line of mouth, even the same basic hairstyle, groomed but not too groomed, though his hair now glittered with glints of silver. The bizarre part was the triumph in his fine eyes, as if he was feeding off and even absorbing every tear on her face. It was almost – almost – as if it was some form of exaltation – what he had done to her body, or at least the response he had elicited from it.

Yet, strange as all this was, the strangest thing was that she could find no rage against him. The more clearly she recognised him as Father's friend, the mercurial Michael, the more secure she felt in the final outcome. As they stood in silence, she even found inside the courage to try to accept the needling pain in her back, as an inevitable part of the process of finding Michael. Still stranger was her lack of anger, for, after all, one endures pain for the people one loves – not on behalf of a stranger. But she had made him wait and now her pain had half-seduced him, though, at the same time, the sane part of Caittie resisted the sickness behind such thoughts.

She knew, all the same, that she had put her idealized partner on so high a pedestal that it was hugely unlikely that anyone could ever match up to it, as she could only envisage any such man going about his selfish pursuits, just like her father. Still, she longed for the man who would protect her, and how passionately she would absorb any pain in return! As if conscious of her thoughts, Michael, if he *was* indeed Michael, moved closer, sardonic, 'And what are you thinking now, my little friend? And are you thinking clever, because now is the time when you really need to?'

Impulsively, she responded, 'Father told me to "think clever" in his letter, but then, anyone might have said the same.' The familiar words – thinking clever – felt welcoming and inspiring on her lips.

'Now, now you are *thinking*!' He moved, close enough to so that his warm breath felt almost arousing. Slowly, he dragged his nails down her back over the thin, vibrant whip marks along her back. It felt like barbed wire being dragged across her skin as it penetrated the inflamed area.

He breathed, 'Does this help you think, then, you little cheat? Because you're running out of time!'

'My father trusted you!' As she said the words she looked up and saw his mocking eyes close, dizzyingly close. It was as if he had planned to kiss her, but instead chose to suck the impending scream out her mouth.

'And to *think* that I played in the room while you talked!' she spat out, though part of her half-longed for the rough command of his lips on hers. He remained frozen for several seconds. Then his face changed, his hands returned to his pockets, and he deliberately stepped back.

'You must realise that I need more than that?' He said, though his voice showed that she had awakened some dormant recollection of the truth. Then he said, quite slowly, 'Do you know why you played your childish games in the same room as we met?'

It was window of opportunity and she needed her full focus to seize it, a focus all the harder to grasp in that her fantasies had concocted a powerful mixture of feelings. She determined to wash everything extraneous from her mind while trying to deal with his question, a scrambled visa back to her childhood.

But this time, at least, he waited for her answer, and the tension in his shoulders suggested that he knew how crucial it might be. In the end, she whispered, 'I think I remember... my mother didn't care for what she regarded as Father's games. Therefore, your meetings were deliberately planned for when she was out, meaning that babysitting me was part of the price that Father paid for your friendship. I think – no, I'm sure – that was why I had to play in the same room.'

He said, 'So we must now talk some more, but I must warn you now about the poem.'

She said eagerly, 'Would you like me to repeat it? I just assumed that all the impersonators had –' however, he cut across her, sharply. 'On the contrary! It is entirely up to you to decide when to tell me the poem. All you have done so far is subconsciously determined how much time I will give you once you start to recite. The more truth you have admitted – the more truth I sense in you – the more time you get. So remember to ask for this only when you are completely ready.'

'Because?'

'Because everything changes if you cannot answer.'

His words were laced with a new and raw sincerity.

She shook back her hair, saying, 'I choose the poem.' There was no time to waste, she had to trust in herself, as only (the new) Caittie could.

'Are you sure? And aren't you first meant to tell me why you're called Caittie, as all the others have?'

'No. That would be pointless. My father called me Caitlin so he could call me Caittie, so everyone would spell it wrong and it would make me different from all the other Kates and Katies. That's been with me all my life, surely there's no more public knowledge than that!' She couldn't hide the resentment in her voice.

'So, you can also be clever. Tell me the line of the poem.'

'Haven't you heard it enough?'

'All of it please. I need you to say it!'

'I remember wild flowers, cornflowers. They spoke to me.' He raised his hand to stop her. 'Well, you would not want me to say the obvious rhyme like all the others, let's assume we both know it.'

She had shaken him, that much was obvious. He glared at her, and swung his shoulders towards the door.

'All right, I admit it. You are perhaps a better liar than the rest. But now, Dartmoor!' He uttered the word and stepped backwards, relaxing as if he was expecting to wait a little while, as if he had been this far before.

Her mind raced: she suspected he was beginning to believe her, but what could Dartmoor – or even Miss Muffet – to do with her father? She forced herself to run any connections with Dartmoor methodically through her memory. It was a process of elimination that drifted seconds into minutes.

Then she suddenly visualised the place on the edge of Dartmoor where, to her recollection, her father had managed to come on holiday with them a couple of times (the first time seemed vague as she was so small, but the second time was surely when she was twelve). Recalling the last, she could remember an unusually serious row between her parents. Then the next day she had gone out with Father all day, while Mum had chosen to attend some workshop or other. She remembered the guide's annoyance when her father explained that they were heading off separately. And then they'd stopped for a picnic when they got to some Iron Age ruins.

It was that day she had her father all to herself. The first such day she could remember, perhaps the only day she had been allowed time to fall in love with her father. For so long he was never there, or never entirely there, for her. That day, she'd spent the afternoon wrapped in his sweatshirt while he made do with some plastic raincoat. That day she had spent wrapped in his smell, his warmth, as if she had finally been fed, after so long a time of starvation. She recalled walking until her legs ached. This entire new world he gave her, just to find by the next year it had all been taken away. She said, suddenly certain, 'The Manor Hotel.'

Without a word, the man started furiously tugging at the chains above her head. The links spun round, jarring through the eyelets, as if her sudden exhaustion was pulling her down. After releasing her numbed arms, he undid the bonds securing her feet. Caittie could only imagine that his anxiety was due to the impostors that preceded her being half-dead by this point and allowed to drop to the floor. Then, placing one arm round her waist to support her, he eased the final chain through and discarded it. Flinging a towel over her, in one effortless movement he picked her up and carried her to the straw. There he hugged her fervently to him – forgetting her flayed back – saying, 'Caittie, forgive me. I am – I was – your father's friend.' The fire in her back warred with the ache in her arms for her attention, but still she felt comforted. Pain alternated with confusion, but if this man *was* Michael, she needed him, as her father had promised that he would make her safe.

The longer they lay there, the more she realised, almost disappointed, that Michael's embrace was sorrowful in more than one sense: parental, protective. This thought was warming to her, but the remaining straps still on her wrists still felt sore. She raised her hands towards him – he removed the tape delicately, almost reverently, from her fingers. He had also lifted part of the towel off her back and began applying a cold sponge to her pain. The anguish of the first contact subsided into more soothing dabs, as the medication took the heat out of her skin.

Confusingly, he was the sadist who had himself caused – even enjoyed, or so it had seemed – her injuries, but the thoughts and confusions of why she couldn't hate him all returned to her, with powerful force. He had loved her father. He had punished her for only as long as he had believed her to be her own impersonator. While his sorrow, his regret, had moved her, how loyal he must have felt to her father, to have induced him to wait all these unwavering years, when she could – perhaps should – have come to him. No wonder he was overcome with relief or sorrow! Even the thought of what he might have done to the impostors she now felt as her guilt, for it had been her delay and confusions that had created circumstances allowing it to happen.

Michael had stood as the guardian to her inheritance without even knowing her. Yet now, in their first real meeting, in the strangest of circumstances, he had to come to terms with the fact they were in this together. How they could work together – this man who had beaten her – was still to be determined. All she could do was to wait and hope that he retained command of her father's instructions and of his own men's trust. Much as she longed to get on with the agenda in her head, she had been subjugated and humiliated and was therefore in need of reassurance. Yet despite the throbbing pain, the longer she lay down, the stronger seemed her sense of calmness and peace. It was a sensation difficult to comprehend, as it seemed related to a freedom of thought to which she was unaccustomed.

Still stranger was the feeling of nervy relief when she heard a car pull up outside, tyres skidding in the dust, a welcome distraction. A few seconds later, the door swung open and the man who had left stepped into the doorway again, and did a double take at her lying in Michael's arms. Caittie had to avert her eyes from his gaze as he waited for Michael's instruction. Though Michael had covered her after washing her back, she still felt very vulnerable.

They spoke in Greek, Michael ordering – or so it seemed – and the man listening – he shot one look at Caittie, though whether of awe or disdain she couldn't determine. Then, with no response beyond a nod, he shot out the door. Michael meanwhile returned, guiding Caittie to her feet. As soon as the young man returned with her clothes, he took them, and placed them down beside her, touching her as if he needed assurance of her reality, saying, 'Get dressed. I'll be back in five minutes.'

It was a painful process simply to get dressed, when it involved stretching or – worse – touching her back. The pain had eased with Michael's ministrations, but the swelling ridges in her flesh left her in no doubt of the level of pain she had still to endure. Jeans and shoes were easy, but the T-shirt was agony. Holding it above her head she hoped it would slide down on its own, but her skin was now sticky with medication and it bunched on her shoulders. Soft cotton as it was, it took some moments before she could ease it down and get used to its contact with the skin of her back.

17

From Russia with love

Andrew sat motionless, feeling as if the word Russia was scorched mockingly on his forehead. How could he have been so foolish as to not realise that this was what Pierre had wanted to know all along? Now that the answer was before him, the line of questioning could seem no longer vague but ridiculously obvious, and the failings in his memory unavoidable. Simply because he had glossed over this memory, it had been repainted and justified a dozen times to keep his sanity. Yet having been inspired to forecast the collapse of Russia and the carnage that would follow, at least he had tried, so how could it be the "worst thing" he had done?

'Come on, Andrew, I'm doing all the work here.' Pierre pushed for his response. A wince of a smile was forced upon Andrew's face, but no words came. The question was not only what to say but, with this new direction, what would be the consequence? He felt hot with indignation at the notion that it might be considered the worst thing he had yet done, especially as he had done all that anyone could have managed. However this alien – for he was half-tempted by the 'alien' theory again – clearly had some powers that he was loathe to test out. There was no doubt he would have to give up something, if he was to ever get out of this bizarre place alive. Finally, as the seconds passing became increasingly uncomfortable, he choked out a response. What he needed utmost now was to avoid digging a hole deep with his fears.

'That's a big subject, Pierre. What exactly do you want to know?'

'Well, I don't need the annual grain harvest. Just tell me how you knew the USSR, as it was then of course, would collapse?'

Strange, Andrew thought for someone to ask *how he knew* and not *what he knew*. They obviously thought he had obtained some secrets, when doing his research. He had never been a spy, but now he felt the accusation suggested that he had been. Well in that case, then why not play the part?

'How are you so sure the grain harvest was unconnected?'

For once, wry humour almost seemed to annoy the older man. 'Andrew, we can do it the easy way or the hard way, the choice is yours.' (How dare he repeat, yet again, those precise threats that Andrew had so often used upon his own children!) Sure he knew it was time to give a little, but this interrogation was all about control. There could be little enough to do with queen or country here, as the Russia issue had simply become too vague and remote in history. He knew the routine: tell them enough to keep them interested and hold onto the essential – the value of his life. Whether in the playground, daydreams or spy movies, he had rehearsed this part before.

'Well, there's no easy way, because, even if I wanted to, I couldn't remember all the data. Grain harvest, currency, industrial output and even their ability to tap the natural resources created something of incalculable complexity –'

'More games! How did you come to your conclusion when others did not?'

'So you *are* really Russian then?'

'Answer the question!'

Serbian or Bosnian even, with that line of jaw, he thought, saying, 'That would be a lot easier if I had good reason to tell you. But since I still have no idea for what crime I'm supposed to pay, let alone its price, why should I hang myself? At least that way I retain some measure of integrity!'

'I could give you half a million reasons to tell me! Shall I name them all?'

An approximation in terms of casualties, of course, but it confirmed everything he feared and certainly that there was no doubt what this was about. He could still so clearly recall the fighting, hatred and mass genocide of the Balkans. Headlining the news, whole villages destroyed, bodies stacked and rotting, all that he had predicted at the end of his Ph.D. thesis coming to pass. Yet why would anyone seek revenge on him for not doing enough? Surely it was more reasonable the blame should lie with the governments of that time. But blame is what these Balkan people were good at, hooking into past hatreds! And if Pierre – or Piotr, even – was now, however urbanely, projecting this guilt onto him, he needed to combat it – and fast.

'If it's revenge you are after, I'm not so sure that the governments of the time missed much.'

'Don't try to deceive me, Andrew, you know full well that the governments of that time did not agree with you! And you had a letter from Margaret Thatcher saying just that, didn't you?'

Shaken, Andrew almost whipped out another, 'How the hell did you know that?' – but instead held his tongue, bemused. 'They' seemed to know every detail about him, but still wanted more. A letter that only a handful of people even knew existed! How could anyone obtain such things?

He said, 'She didn't actually say there was any disagreement, nuclear weapons were all she focused on. Besides I'd say they – the Foreign Office, MI5, you know, the national specialists – knew more than I did of the facts, but just found a different, less pessimistic, way of interpreting them.'

'How could they have more facts than you and then still do nothing about it?' Pierre snapped.

'I don't know! All I know is that I had no secrets. The governments of the time had the secrets, plus the intelligence factotums to sift truth from the fiction.'

'You suppose that they had all the information and did absolutely nothing?'

Andrew said dryly, 'Oh no, quite the reverse – they were doing something all right. Cruise missiles, supporting the US' Star Wars programmes – and all because they were driving the USSR into economic collapse. You don't have to be Einstein to realise that any war with the USSR, let alone a nuclear war, would cost billions of dollars, and tens of millions of lives. Genocide on the collapse of Communist block would be mere collateral damage in comparison.'

'But you not only knew the collapse would lead to untold loss of life, you had a solution, only to give up at the first hurdle. Why?' Pierre leant on the word 'why' as on the thrust of a knife.

'Don't you think it frustrated me just as much? I was furious! But at least I'd impressed Roy – Roy, my MP – enough to get the document read by the Prime Minister. Besides, where else could I go where I wouldn't just be seen as yet another lunatic making silly predictions? Let alone how futile my attempts would look once I realised what the governments were up to – thereby making my plans the last thing they would pay heed to. With so much history between them, and victory sensed just around the corner, how would I convince them the better way was compromise and respect?' Andrew had to ask himself how many ways you needed to pull out the way of the blame, as if wrestling the bone from the dog's mouth.

Pierre leaned forward. 'But you are the one who talks of integrity! Isn't it better to try and fail no matter what people might think of you, than to calculate its futility and give up? In short, surely such a cause deserves better?' His eyes flashed, causing Andrew to mentally downgrade his probable age by several years.

'Look, if I thought it would have done any good I would have – just as, if I could go back and have my time again, I would! It was a prediction, untested, and in my naivety I did not have the confidence to believe that the worst – even if predicted by myself – might really come true. I died a death inside with every victim that could have been saved and now you want to finish the job. Don't you think I've suffered too, living with this?' It left his mouth as heartfelt honesty, but rang in his ears as a plea for mercy.

'At last we can agree on something, Andrew, but as I said we shall have to agree the price you pay. After all, you just told me you would want to try and make amends if you could.'

Andrew thought dizzily, *what does he want? My knowledge, my life?*

'But I don't see how! I have no power or influence and I still seem to have not told you what you wanted to know.'

Pierre sighed. 'Don't make me have to squeeze every last bit of information out of you. Sure, you have admitted – finally – the basics, but you skipped the most important bit. In your own words, the facts were incalculable, so how did you calculate them? How could you, on your own, predict the unpredictable?'

Yet again Andrew felt a step behind, he had to stall for time to think.

'How do I know I can trust your intentions?'

'You can't,' said the older man calmly. 'It is only your assumption what my intentions might be. So come, explain to me how you did your calculations?'

'It was just assumption and the laws of approximation!'

Very quietly, 'I believe it was more.'

Andrew snapped, 'I need to know that anything I say will not be misused and, unless you can convince me otherwise, I must limit what I say.'

'I understand the sentiment, but you will have to trust me.'

'If you understand the sentiment then you knew all along I could never go public with my predictions, because to do so would require proof and publication of the calculations! So why taunt me?'

'I'm not taunting you. We have – though I realise you doubt it – the same aims. Why don't you give me an outline of your theory? Then perhaps we can exchange some information and – I would hope – some trust.'

Andrew breathed deeply. Trust! After being abducted, harangued, lectured and insulted – that was a good one. But had he any choice?

18

Allomorphic

It was a good five minutes before Michael returned, during which time Caittie swiftly washed and dressed, every minute feeling more and more alone. Wet from the tepid water – which further teased her wounds – she shivered too from a growing sense of shock. As she moved about, she happened to pass through one of the shafts of sunlight crisscrossing the barn. Its warmth cut through her like a therapeutic laser that made her yearn to move her whole body into the direct sunlight, as if it would absolve her and convince her mind to calmness.

She longed to see Michael again, and yet when he appeared blackly in the doorway, he grimly beckoned her to follow, with neither words nor any apparent sympathy. It seemed strange to feel chilled in the heat of the day, but once into the sun the shock, pummelled by the warmth, left her body, as if she was secure in the covers of her own bed or held in protective arms. Yet Michael himself, as if embarrassed by what he had done, simply strode away as if trying not to look at her. Following him, her eyes stunned by the day's brightness, she felt pained by the sense that he was deserting her, in an almost brutal style, without heed to her feelings. And yet, she had to accept that whatever connection lay between them was deeply abnormal and they had only known each other for a matter of hours.

She dealt with disappointment by gathering herself up and thrusting all such thoughts aside, as if placing it in a 'pending' tray in her mind, as with so much of her life it enabled her to carrying on functioning, always promising to deal with it later. It just seemed a retrograde step to return anything, after emptying so much of her lifetime 'pending' tray in the last few days. But there was no choice, her father's instructions had its own agenda and she had to keep up.

Going down a pitted farm track, away from the flat dusty yard area in front of the barn, she spotted a large farmhouse about a hundred yards ahead. There was a rocky path up the side of a mountain, from which she could see fields of watermelon, lemon trees and olive groves below. The air was still very warm, but with each yard in the open stretch between the buildings, the shock of heat through her body was now giving way to the breeze cooling her skin, making the fine hairs on her arms rise gratefully. By the time Michael reached the house, Caittie had almost caught him up.

Two growling mongrels emerged out of a kennel to the side, but with a word from Michael they returned to their quarters. The pair walked into a kitchen in which six local-looking men slouched, playing cards. All of them somehow had managed to obtain badly fitting smart clothes as if trying to emulate Michael's tailored attire. But they still looked a class apart. Upon sighting Michael, almost all of the men scrambled their cards and left the room. The last one hung back and took some tomatoes, olives, stuffed vine leaves and drinks and swiftly transferred them to the table, waiting for an approving flick of the hand from Michael before disappearing..

Michael ordered, 'Please, eat and drink! There are some things we need to discuss now. Then I need to do things and, I presume, you can make yourself more comfortable.' Michael's tone was more of a relaxed growl, as if he was concentrating on not showing some turmoil underneath. His rearranging of the plates in front of them, so they could share the food, was slow and meticulous to show no matter what conflict, calmness was still in control.

'Do I eat first or would you prefer me to talk with my mouth full?' she joked, rather breathlessly. Perhaps it was her state of embarrassment and stress, as such times with Keith, she had become used to responding with either wit or sarcasm or both, when facing such contradictions.

Michael smiled, as if he enjoyed such spark, even when combined with rudeness. 'You do the eating while I'll tell you what you need to know right now.' His voice had immediately softened into warm growl, like a pacing tiger that had just been fed and now wanted to be playful.

The stuffed vine leaves, olives and bread were welcome, but she seized the water first. As she started to eat, he startled her with, 'I am sorry to tell you, but you were being followed!'

Caittie swivelled to face him, but he said, 'Believe me, we knew. We were watching you for two days before contacting you. The men on your trail were Greek secret service and you, of course, wouldn't have noticed them. We only did naturally, because we get to know who is or is not meant to be around.'

Finding her voice, she said, 'And the others – the ones pretending to be me. Were they followed too?'

'Absolutely. The Greek police look for us all the time and do not find us. This is why we had to remove you in so dramatic a way. It's also why you couldn't be allowed to see where we went, until we knew it was you. Each time we have a so-called Caittie, we check with friends in UK to see where you are. This time you not there. Another time you not there, but we found out just in time, as they tried to take us in while you were on holiday with your boyfriend.'

The way he said the word, almost in disgust, made her think, he knows everything about me, even about Keith. With the same wry distaste, he added, 'This man, do you love him?' He looked at her quizzically.

Caittie's hand paused, halfway to her glass of water. She had perhaps expected some questions associated with Keith, but not this one. It was a question she had answered herself, but still had not met the promise to her mother, in that she would tell Keith. He waited impassively until she shook her head, then he said, reassured, 'Good. You must not trust him or tell him anything. We think he may be giving them information or worse. To continue, once you disappeared from England, they knew where you were heading, so they only had to wait. We hoped that they might think we had given up, as we found out about the last impostor beforehand and that occasion we did not answer their advert. It had also been almost a year since their last attempt. Anyway, somehow they only tracked your movements to Athens. We have some informants in the Greek police and apparently you caused some confusion when you lost them on the ferry. How did you give them the slip?'

'I got a lift from an old couple in the back of their van. They dropped me at Neapolis, where their son has a restaurant, near the bus stop to Elounda. I didn't tell them anything, but I did promise to try and eat there at some point.'

Michael smiled. 'Don't worry about your promise. I'll send some men to reward them in a better way on your behalf. Also, the secret service in the meantime may have lost you, but they will now question everybody from that boat, until they find out about your plans. They would have worked out by now you had to be in one of the vehicles.'

He walked over to the door the men had left by and harshly shouted a couple of names. In seconds, two men came bounding into the room, from what by Caittie's second look at their appearance must be a thug centre just down the corridor. Michael gave them some instructions, but she again could not make out anything beyond 'Neopolis'. If these were the ones sent to the elderly Greek couple, she could only hope that their arrival wouldn't alarm them. The men shot past her and out the back door.

Michael slowly selected some olives, while in the distance she could hear a car grinding away. 'Now, Caittie, I need to do some work and get things organised. I'll show you to your room, where you may have a few hours' rest. I will call you later when I return, when we will have dinner. Any questions you have we will cover then, if that's alright.'

Disappointment hit her again. She had so hoped to know more! About what he knew, about what her father had promised her. In addition, Caittie wanted to keep her mind occupied, so as not to dwell on what had just happened. She had to accept, reluctantly, that this was Michael's agenda and she had to let him get on with it, if she had a hope of resolving the awkwardness between them. So she submitted to being guided along the corridor and up a set of stone stairs. En route she could hear a television, along with male voices. "Her" room was small with plain wooden furniture, but clean, with a small shower cubicle and basin. Unlike the wide-open view from the pathway, as she walked across the room to the window it looked on to the scrub of the hillside. Apart from wasting hours trying to spot lizards on the red-crusted rocks, this offered her very little by way of diversion. Perhaps Michael was subliminally encouraging her to nap.

He moved back toward the door. 'The guards downstairs won't disturb you unless there is a problem. I hope you can rest.' Was it her imagination, or was there some latent tenderness in his tone? Raising her hand in response, she caught him give one intent look at her. Then he was gone.

Upon checking her bags, she noticed that her things had been removed and put back, because the order had altered, but everything seemed to be there, including the money. She decided to take a shower, assuming her back could stand it, and wash her hair (afterwards, she tried to dab her back with cream, but decided against it). Face down on the bed, the dampness of her back and hair made the most of a cooling breeze from the window. In the silence of her room, she registered again the abundance of cicadas, whose activity seemed to intensify as dusk fell and evening set in. She normally hated sleeping on her front, but in minutes she fell asleep, exhausted.

The knock on the door startled her. The sun had slipped with milky-pink speed over the hills and, still half-naked, she scrambled for the bedside light. With the fall in temperature, her back felt almost chilled, so slipping on her top was much easier.

'It's OK – it is me, Michael. Dinner is in ten minutes downstairs. We have lots to discuss as things are moving fast.' Then she heard him walking away.

She sat up amid mounting nervousness. The ten-minute warning was thoughtful, as she had time to get out her moisturiser and brush her hair, acts that felt healing when she knew it was about to round another corner ahead. From Keith to her father's box; from London to Crete; from Elounda to finally locating Michael – each had been a corner turned just to find another path ahead, with tonight there would be yet another step into the unknown. In ten minutes, they could finish what was left undone. In ten minutes, the sick excitement in her pit of her stomach would be answered. She was desperate to know what things 'moving fast' entailed. Down the stairs, she followed the exuberant noise and herby smells emanating from the kitchen.

Pushing the door open, she was confronted by a room bewilderingly full of people. The large kitchen table, at which they had sat before, now had a smaller one tucked on the other end of it. Eight men, along with Michael, were already seated, and there were several empty places. An old woman dressed all in black – very Greek – guided Caittie reverently to a spare seat reserved next to Michael, who acknowledged her with a glance.

Another man then entered, carrying a couple of jugs and placing them at either end of the table. As soon as Caittie had been poured a drink of wine from the jug, Michael beckoned to the old lady behind him. Smoothly she began to ferry bowls of food onto the table, with each being offered to Caittie first. She was careful to take only a little from each, partly thinking of all the men to follow, and partly too nervous to feel hungry. She took a sip of her wine, which kicked with an astringent intensity that she was unused to. She tried not to let her surprise show on her face, and quickly took another bite of the lamb, which made the second sip of wine taste marginally smoother.

Michael's voice, so near her ear that her heart raced, said, 'Little lady, you live a charmed life! Not only have we not been traced here, but I have already arranged for you to leave this country and return to England.'

Return to England! What was the point of that? Caittie felt crestfallen, but he continued, 'Believe me; once you're at the airport you'll be completely safe, and even better still, it is for tomorrow morning. Normally I would change your identity and give you a false passport, but the Greek Secret people would be checking the flight bookings. Then again, I might give you more than one identity, but that could prove a problem if you were searched. So instead tomorrow you'll leave on a charter flight booked months ago, which no one should suspect.' Michael was looking complacent, as men tend to when secretly begging for someone to ask them to explain more, just because they have held back a vital part of the information.

'How can I do that? Don't we have to get the flight changed?' Caittie played along. She needed to move past the remaining awkwardness between them, for one thing – and, for another, he was the only man she had ever first encountered at the point of a whip.

'Not at all! That's the last thing we should do. Instead, we're going to change *you*! Tomorrow, you will become Sharon Wilkinson, with a passport to match.' Somehow Michael managed to eat so swiftly that he hardly had to pause. 'She is, in fact, the girlfriend of one of my uncle's employees, who came here on holiday for a month and is due to fly home tomorrow. She wants to remain in Greece, to be with him in Athens – in short, to stay longer. To be honest he is not very bothered, but she has no money and is desperate to stay. So instead of paying for false passports, we will switch passports with her. I have taken the liberty of negotiating some money for her expenses. If she is to pretend to be you, she will need English currency and traveller's cheques. This I could get, but it will look better if it is yours. They may trace the money from your bank knowing you are here. No, don't interrupt yet. We will fly her from here to Athens on a local scheduled flight under your name, so when they pick up the flight register, they will be watching her in Athens. It is unlikely that they will have a good photo, so her description has to be near to yours and then the local agents tracking her will be none the wiser. This will be valuable time for you as they should be instead watching this Sharon in Athens.'

Caittie had quickly finished eating the first round of food and the old lady brought more, but she needed to ask questions. 'It's very likely that her passport picture will look nothing like me. Won't we get found out if it's checked?'

'In the morning, we have a passport man coming here and at the same time Sharon will arrive. They're coming in on the morning ferry. Then we decide to either switch the photos or adjust both of you to look more like each other. Don't worry, we have done this before – we'll make sure it is a good job.' Michael made it sound routine even by the tone of his voice.

'How much?' asked Caittie, for something to say.

His smile teased her. 'How much is your life worth? Two thousand for the girl – by the way, make sure it's mostly traveller's cheques. The passport man will need about five hundred Sterling or the same in Drachma.' Michael's tone indicated that he thought it was a good deal.

'I'd hope I was worth a lot more than that,' she returned, but then, seriously, 'But listen, doesn't it mean we're setting this innocent girl up? Would they actually go as far as harming her?'

'No, no, no – not harm. Worst-case scenario, she's imprisoned until she confesses she's not you,' he said impatiently. Caittie couldn't be sure without knowing him better, but she sensed that his answer was intended to placate her rather than engage the truth. It was obvious, simply from his treatment of her, that he could easily distance himself from an unknown girl's welfare, especially for his own cause. The question was whether she had any choice, other than to do the same and risk more than just her own safety.

After a moment she said, 'Only if you promise me you look out for her.' The moment after she said it, she felt almost embarrassed, considering that he retained such loyalty to her father. Her father must have deserved such loyalty and that both their actions – however apparently selfish – must have at heart a greater purpose. After all her father had put forward his own life and had it taken away.

'Believe me, this girl will be with my uncle's top man, who will guard her like a daughter. Michael placed his hand on his heart, suddenly all Greek, the Englishman inside entirely swamped.

'I'll accept your word if you tell me what this is all about.' It was the question that had been burning in Caittie since she arrived.

'Are you sure that you want to know?'

'The fact that I'm here should answer that!'

'Tell me what you know,' he said, with resignation.

'I know very little – I know about university and GAMF and your first explorative journeys as a group. Start with your side. I know you left the UK under strange circumstances.'

'Alright, you win.' His voice softened so that his men who were busy chatting could not hear easily and he then started in clearer, properly accented English, each word low and sharp. 'I hope you understand that I have to talk English in the Greek manner because of my position here. It is important that I seem Greek and not so obviously the Michael who was brought up in England.' He leant back more and continued in his more usual relaxed tone. 'It is not only the Italians that have a Mafia, Caittie. There are many different branches of the Mafia in Italy, hence the problems when they moved to the USA.

'In short, we are just a Greek version of the same style of organisation. My uncle is the head of the family. My father turned his back on the family when he married my mother. That's why they moved to England, as there could be no peace for them in Greece. What Father did was an insult to my grandfather, as my mother's family was not acceptable to him. Equally, my father was not welcomed into my mother's family either. That's why I was brought up in England. I only met my uncle when my father brought me to Greece for my grandfather's funeral. He had a quiet word with me, just to say that if ever I needed anything I was to call him – job, favour or money. He made it clear I was still family and had special privileges.

'When I first met your father at university I had forgotten about all this. I read psychology and was doing a research paper on self-induced belief.'

'Meaning?'

Michael considered. 'In layman's terms, when someone wants to believe in UFOs or similar, why it is that they so often see what they want to see? What makes them imagine such things? That is why I joined the UFO society and your father's group sounded intriguing, especially as he then taught me to scuba dive. You may think – as I thought at first – that there was no connection, but your father always believed that if any evidence of such strange things were likely to be found, it was in water where the mysteries would stay undiscovered by the authorities. It was not long before I was sold on the whole idea and became involved in some of the planned projects. So I soon found it useful to phone my uncle and ask for some supplies – a large ocean-going fishing-type boat, scuba gear, all of these things – but most importantly a trusted local skipper who was used to evading the authorities. The rest of what we did I think is best read by you from your father's documents – when you find them. If you are caught then the less you know the better.

'My study of psychology brought me into contact with the power of mind control. I had had some strange thoughts as a teenage boy, which I only later discovered were connected to my unusual early upbringing in Greece. They coalesced in my desires – in my desires –'

She was aware that she was flushing, as he continued, 'to control women, by whips and other punishment. The strange thing is that when I looked, I found a small number of women that also enjoyed such treatment as much as I enjoyed giving it.' He stopped and looked closely at her. 'You looked shocked?'

'I'm puzzled. Are you saying that women enjoy what I went through earlier?' Caittie could not concede more. The scabs forming down her back still hurt and as much as the odd aspect might have seemed exciting – if not pleasurable, exactly – she still couldn't consider it acceptable behaviour.

'"Enjoy" is perhaps the wrong word. It is just a very small minority of women, often those who have suffered rare events or a series of things, which then triggers a need within them. A need which gives satisfaction from punishment, a need that derives pleasure from pain.' His voice had lowered and mellowed, it was his favourite subject, which oozed from his lips.

'So they're slightly mad, then?' She could not help herself, but tease a question in the hope he would make sense of what she had felt.

'"Damaged" is more the word. What I do is to give sensation of pain without violence. It is an art form to inflict it with as little damage as possible – besides, the damage is already inside them. It is their damage that gives them the need to receive as much as my damage does to give. Without each other, we would adopt perhaps some self-destructive lifestyle, so as to give or get the pain we need. All people have these feelings to a degree, but most have only a little that is easily contained. I talk of those were it has been engrained into them. But you distract me from the issue.' He stopped and sipped his drink, and Caittie could see the same look in his eyes as he had when he was enjoying causing her pain. He sat and composed himself to pull away from those thoughts.

'Is it normal?'

He looked at her intently. 'There is a wide range of normality. Many normal people have secret desires to try such things. They play with people's minds because they are bored with their sex lives and do not realise the damage they can do.' He gave Caittie a knowing look. It was if he knew she had enjoyed certain aspects of the straps – even as if he was waiting for her confession that she had experimented with Keith. 'Yet still you distract me and if you do so much more, I might keep you here when you have important work to do.' He paused with a teasing look. 'In fact, we both have to do an important job, as wherever your father's instructions send you I am designed to follow. But to return to what you need to know. What you need to know is that just after university I met a girl in a club designed for people like her and me. I won't mention her name, but we were together for many years. To cut a long story short, when George went missing and the problems with the GAMF Society got out of hand, I arrived home to find her hanging from an eyelet on the wall, strangled. It was clear that I had been set up for her murder – there was no sign of a break-in and all my special implements were laid out – deliberately, but strangely. I didn't even wait to change. I phoned my uncle and he got me out of the country.

'I had sold my soul to my uncle so as to get supplies for GAMF and now I was asking for more! I had the choice of spending most of my life in prison or coming here and running his operation in Crete – an organisation designed to protect itself from the reach of the law. So for fifteen years I have been waiting here, the last seven waiting only for you. You have certainly taken your time!'

Caittie couldn't bear to go into all her fears, her subjection to Keith, even her remaining loyalty to her mother. Instead, she said, 'Sorry, I was a little confused for a while. But what I still don't understand is this – why you are still waiting? Surely, with all your connections, you could have found a way to change identity and disappear for good?'

He said quietly, 'Caittie, you were just a little girl when your father left you and never came back. Had you known him better then you would understand. I would willingly have laid down my life for him, for his integrity, and long ago I made him a promise to help you.'

'He asked you to promise?' she said, almost wistfully.

'Absolutely. As for why I kept my promise, well, very few people have that special quality that makes people want to follow them. Your father not only had this, but he always used it with the interest of the greater good, whereas people like my uncle use it for the advantage of a selected few. Anyway, I had no choice than to live by looking over my shoulder at every turn, no matter what option I took. That is, until you came. We can together release us both from this nightmare.' He sat back and started talking in Greek to a couple of his men.

The old lady had busied herself in clearing the plates and bowls from the table. It seemed like a break in what had been a busy constant flow of activity. To Caittie, his use of the word "nightmare" grated against her high-minded justifications for trying to complete her father's work. Stuck here all this time, though, Michael may well have grown impatient and wanted it over, but to her this was still fresh and exciting, and she longed to be able to think about what he had said about her father. Caittie got up, rather shy suddenly. 'I think I'll go to bed now.'

Michael was perturbed. 'Wait, wait, I am not done! First, you must be careful whom you contact from now on. Not just who, but when and why. No phoning this "Keith" (still with the same disdain), any of your friends or even your mother unless it is planned or agreed!' He held her wrist to stop her walking away. 'Have you made promises to contact people?'

'Only my mother, and – and Keith can – I don't care about breaking a promise to him.'

A curt nod, with just a suspicion of approval. 'I also need you to do something for me tonight, as there won't be much time in the morning. I want you to write a letter to your mother, telling her how you got from where you are supposed to be and giving a persuasive reason to be in Athens. Make it sound as if you will stay there for some time. This will give cover to Sharon and to those that want to spy on you. If you feel that you must, enclose a letter to any other friends that fit in with this. When you are gone, I will arrange postage from Athens to England. But these letters must be in your own handwriting, your own style – ha! Still better, can you write a second letter to your mother dated in a week's time, making up some stories of what you have done?' He let go of her wrist and clicked his fingers at one of his men standing by the side.

'But if this Sharon is being watched, she could give the lie to everything I write, couldn't she?' While she was asking the question he instructed one of the men to fetch something he was pointing to, which the man duly did.

Putting a tourist guide of Athens in her hands, he placed it with a controlled gentleness that felt odd in its assurance and familiarity. 'Do you think me so simple? From here you can pick two places to visit, see or eat at, each day – the choice is yours. Whatever you choose I'll make sure Sharon does them on those days. She'll be spending your money, so get your money's worth!'

Caittie could not help but smile. The difficult bit now would be finding the words for her mother. The old Cretan lady suddenly leant awkwardly past to pick up a bowl, as if deliberately jolting her into action.

'Brilliant, can I have some stationery as I am travelling light?" As she finished the words the same man that had got the guide was already bringing envelopes, writing pad and pens. She thought, *of course. They already knew everything that was in her bag.*

She had a last word from Michael, in his 'Greek tone'. 'We need to be up early in the morning, little lady, for when the ferry comes in. We will knock on your door for breakfast, so don't spend too long on the letters tonight. Anyway, the more you write the greater chance of making a mistake!' Michael now gave her a quizzical look, as if he knew shorter would in fact be easier. 'And I hope your father was right and you know where he is directing you with his clues?'

Caittie gathered all the things together from the table and made her way to her room. It felt strange writing to her mother, seeking to make some sense of her aborted trip to France and her telling her of the definite decision to end it with Keith. In the end, she pretended that Wendy had given her a lead on digs going on in Crete and outside Athens, meeting a nice man there who simply made the farce of going on with Keith impossible. It was difficult to suggest she had a boyfriend without mentioning his name, simply because Michael had not told her who Sharon's boyfriend was, and she longed to get her notes finished as soon as possible. It was only while writing it she realised that this restriction was in fact a blessing. Left to her own devices, she would have tried endless self-justification of her actions and thereby be tempted to overstate them (she knew from experience that such things are often blind to the writer, but instantly ring to a discerning reader as false).

135

The second letter was all about her fictitious digs and its on-off pattern, which gave her time to do some touristy things (this was, as Caittie knew, not how it usually worked, but it just had to be this time). It was even harder choosing some enjoyable things for Sharon to do, as she had hardly got used to spending her own money, let alone spending it on behalf of a person she'd never met. Momentarily she contemplated what this girl might prefer, but then again tomorrow she would be Sharon, so this other girl would have to enjoy whatever Caittie would want to do.

Keith's letter was also much easier than she thought, because here she was on truthful ground. Out was any notion of lengthy explanations, which might result in endless self-justification – or even a correspondence, which she desperately longed to avoid. She wrote that the experiences of the last week or so had told her there was more to life in Athens than what he had to offer (in fact, he did not offer life, he starved her of it, she decided not to say). She had finally realised what was missing in their partnership. "Acceptance" seemed a silly word, but she would be happy living any life with someone that wanted her for who she was. Actions, patience, devotion and many things we look for in a partner meant nothing to her without this acceptance (she secretly believed that even the pain Michael had inflicted upon her earlier would be easier to tolerate, if it was with a man in mutual love, adoration and acceptance, rather than the negativity Keith had forced upon her for years). She left out much that she shrank from mentioning, and concluded with "good wishes".

The letters finished and sealed, she reflected on Michael's words, but she knew where she was heading. Her father may have given her the keys to a personal box, but she would deal with the detail later, as it seemed impossible to open another emotional box right now. She put out her light and tried for the first time to sleep on her back. It was an uncomfortable, drifting and rather disturbed sleep, but the dull pain was strangely comforting. Part of why it had taken so long to break with Keith was because she could still not easily bring herself to hurt anyone. But now having duly signed off on him, she subconsciously – if perversely – felt the need to punish herself for having done it. Only after such punishment and hopefully by tomorrow would she feel truly free to move on.

19

$$E = MC^2$$

'As you've probably guessed,' said Pierre calmly, 'I'm talking about emotional energy here.'

In one short phrase, Pierre had not only called Andrew's bluff but also dispelled a fear of incipient madness. Assuming that one's thoughts are uniquely odd, in a world where sanity is by majority, it is tempting to seek protection in silence. And whereas a woman might well tend towards some resolution, a man will more often prefer the sullenness of denial, despite all the evidence that many men feel the same, and that he is part of an archipelago of men who might feel similarly.

All his life, Andrew had seemed to see things differently to those around him, as if he was looking at a layer of life invisible to the vast majority. So often his optimism at finding some expert or scholar who shared a piece of this thinking was squashed by the seemingly natural obsessive behaviour they then apply to just one element of a subject. In short, he had long since decided that information had become a battle of strength over truth.

Not by choice, but by admission his island seemed invisible to others. Here, now, he faced a man that knew the phrase – "emotional energy" – and perhaps even how Andrew had theorised it. He wanted to hate Pierre for keeping him against his will, but he also longed to know how he knew so much about all these things, how deeply he seemed to think and to feel. But then he was perhaps making over-eager assumptions! The question was, how much did Pierre know? Andrew had shredded so much of his work when the Balkan conflict started and thousands started to die, as if taking out his frustration on his own ignored material. Yet at the end of the day, he was still left with the constant torture of justifying his every action one minute and believing that he deserved to suffer for his failings the next.

'Andrew?' Pierre prompted, bringing Andrew back in time. 'Emotional energy. Does that ring a bell?'

Andrew looked at him, straight into those strange hazel eyes. Deep within, he knew Pierre was right when he had not done enough, even if at the time, he thought it was his best effort. Even the haunting dream of earlier was still subliminally disturbing his thoughts, as it flashed images of the shepherd trying to do the right thing and failing miserably in his task. What a delight it would be to confess his failings and let someone else take on the burden of being critically judicious! But how could he share, how could he embrace it, if he still had no information behind the purpose or consequences of his detention?

He said, 'As I understand it, it's a simple enough concept, that emotional energy is a form of energy like any other and obeys similar rules.'

'Very good. Yet if it's that simple, why isn't it universally acclaimed?'

'But it is! People just don't realise or associate the different forms together into one entity. A therapist might call it positive stroking or a padre might call it forgiveness, but the many forms are still all out there.'

Pierre stroked his chin.

'So how did you, Andrew, take all these things that everyone else could see, but make them into a form of energy force you could predict with?'

Andrew flashed back, 'Haven't you ever considered what creates big historical events? How you can trace back from the genocide of whole nations and end up looking at the abuse of a small boy? Just like a snowball released at the top of the mountain, it only becomes an avalanche because nothing stops its path. Even worse is the fact that conditions meant that it was able to gather power as it went along. All this you have to understand and calculate.' Andrew slipped a disguised oxymoron on the end, for to understand was to know how impossible to calculate it really was.

Pierre was unimpressed. 'No, I can't accept that! No man could calculate the myriad of emotions, events, fate, coincidence and any other variable, for any mass of people. History is littered with leaders and governments who have tried and failed. There is more to it than simply calculating.'

'But that's what mankind has learned to do, to work out the mathematics of chaos theory and the cosmos. Why not this? What makes you so sure?'

'Andrew, you're very intelligent, but no mathematical genius. There has to be something extra, some formula that allows you to calculate in simple terms!'

'Is that what this is all about, your wanting the formula? Right, well, you're out of luck there. I destroyed them!'

'Want *the* formula! Destroyed *them*! You trip over your own words now trying to evade my questions. I know there is more than one formula and to answer your question, no, I do not need them!'

Andrew snapped hotly, 'What else would you want? What use is any other information without them, and apart from that, I'd guess I'm here because the only copy is inside my head?'

Pierre shook his head. 'The outline will be enough.'

Nothing made sense to Andrew. Each bout of questions just seemed to lead round another corner. Was this some kind of reverse psychology – having some empathy with his position, getting him to talk and then egging him just that bit further?

'I still don't see what use any general outline will be if you do not have the formula – the formulas – needed to take it further!'

'You're assuming that I want to abuse the information. Give me an outline of how you started your work and I will tell you why this is all I need to know!'

At long last, the promise of something tangible and immediate. Perhaps it was the sacrificial chess piece laid as a trap, but it had the appearance of a lit path to the door.

'Ok, I'll play.' Andrew paused, waiting for a reaction, which didn't come. 'It was as I said before, following through major events. Dictators, assassinations, terrorists, Communism and all manner of extremes always came back to a primary emotional cause and only ever succeeded – or even happened – because of a series of emotional energy-forming events. The more you understand how that works, the easier things are to predict. Understand a little more and I believed – I believe – that you can start to prevent the worst of these. I worked out a politics versus progress chart and it was clear that changes in political systems were inevitably accompanied by some degree of emotional turmoil. From that I began listing different emotional energies.'

'Such as?'

'Hatred, conflict, desperation, love – there are just so many. Each category has a subtle mix of several influences. Eventually, I started to list them in order of strength and whether they were positive or negative. The problem was working out which ones interact with each other and how. After that is the complexity of how they neutralise or amplify each other. Individuals already do this unwittingly when they pick on someone's weakness, but the trick is to convert this information into the effect it has on the masses.'

'Is this not back to the untold calculations?'

'Not at all! If I drop a beach ball and a cannon ball into a pond, although the beach ball is larger, its wave is swamped by that produced by the cannon ball. You calculate the effect of these waves upon each other and more importantly how a series of events ends up producing such a wave. It is not a question of calculating everything, but understanding where and how the larger events happen.'

'Understanding these larger events or calculating them?'

'Oh, both! Everyone tries to understand them, but unless you have a method for calculating them, I guarantee that people will miss key ingredients. Without all the ingredients you cannot accurately apply the approximations that make the calculations ultimately possible.'

Pierre toyed with his papers. 'I may be beginning to get the picture, but could you perhaps give me a clear example of what you found using this method that other people missed?'

One example. Well, what harm could it do? Suddenly Andrew said, 'The Balkans works as an example. With all its history of war and hatred, it seemed frozen in a state where communism ruled and religion was suppressed. The deprivations of the region and anger at the system found an outlet in transference to the hatreds of old. But such a system doesn't freeze these emotions, it contains them allowing them to amplify with no positive counterbalance to these negative influences. Remove the containment of Communism and you have genocide.'

'Perhaps an oversimplification?'

Andrew flushed. 'An oversimplification because you asked for one example and I didn't want to detract from the point.'

'Don't get me wrong, I find you cogent. But what do you think were the main differences between your calculation and the many governments that should have been aware of these issues?'

'There are very subtle differences between energy capable of growing into a national or international problem and one that dissipates into something less serious, as it duly does in most places and times. I would say they all understand how to take action to get a result, but they have little idea how to calculate the accumulated effect of their actions. International politics seem set on throwing enough negatives into the mix until both sides have no choice other than compromise.'

'I see.'

'And that's all you want?'

'I never said that. The truth is that I have from the outset wanted your words, because I need awareness in your mind of these past years.'

'What for?'

'Because I want you to do a similar task for me. Because I have a job for you to do.'

'You're wasting your time,' said Andrew flatly. 'I don't do jobs. I don't betray my country.'

'I think you mean the country that you've already betrayed.'

20

Sharon – and England

A rumbling clout rattled the door, waking Caittie with a start – a man's voice, speaking Greek, disappearing down the hallway, banging on other doors, leaving a trail like a passing storm. She sat there realising that it had been some time since she slept without a swirl of troubles and dreams: clear liquid sleep like fresh water. Once her back had released her she had dreamed nothing, and still felt slightly soporific. Her state was not helped by the darkness outside, without a glimmer of dawn on the horizon. Thinking back to last week's morning ferry, she thought it must be before half-five, though the knock suggested some haste in getting ready.

It was difficult choosing clothes that would suit both Crete and England, but once she'd changed and repacked, Caittie set aside the traveller's cheques and money Michael had asked for. By the time she got downstairs, she faced an identical scene to the night before, the only difference being the type of food on the table.

'Good morning, Sharon. Today I will call you only Sharon, as you need to become accustomed to it. Please sit and eat!' Michael leant forward and pulled out away from the table the same chair she had sat at last night.

Once she had mouthed the words good morning, as if her voice had not awoken, she stood holding the back of the chair for a moment. Taking in the activity and scene of the room, her attention was drawn to one of Michael's men picking up an egg out of a basket from the centre of the table. As he banged it on to the surface her instinct told her that there would be mess, but instead he rolled it forward then backward and then began to peel it. The pastries, bread and cheese just seemed to be the natural choice to these Greek men sitting here, such combinations were never seen in tourist hotels. The bread and cheese particularly made her feel like she was joining a picnic.

The old lady appeared with fresh pastries, which explained the smell of baking permeating the room. They were clearly homemade and by the number to feed, she must have been up incredibly early to get them ready for the crack of dawn. Caittie felt obliged to take a pastry so as not to offend the woman. Only once she had taken her first bite, with an appreciative nod, did the old lady seem satisfied. The pastries were delicious, but rather rich for Caittie's normal breakfast, and she felt thankful for the sight of coffee.

'I hope you slept well and are feeling more comfortable?' Michael having finished eating, had waited for Caittie to finish her pastry and subsequently decline an egg before asking his question. He had been obviously waiting to ask for some time and his eyes averted to her back as he said the word "comfortable".

'Yes, I slept very well.' Understanding what his eyes were asking, along with his words, she answered both questions.

'I'm glad. I hope that you are less angry with me?' Michael's face and words tried to show respect in almost a sense of gratitude.

'It was my own fault for waiting so long and leaving the door open to impostors. But I expect you enjoyed the wait?' Her words were short, but her face showed she had understood more than she was saying. Any discussion would only open wounds for him, especially as she half-suspected his sadism had been steeled by the death of his girlfriend.

All such thoughts were disturbed by the sound of a car pulling up outside. It had now started to get light, as if their hillside position allowed them to see the sun breaching the horizon before the rest of the island, but unless they were very close to the ferry terminal, it seemed a bit early for Sharon to arrive. Michael stood and went to the door, escorting in a woman and a man, both Greek. He chatted to them both for a couple of minutes, occasionally looking at his watch and occasionally turning in Caittie's direction. Despite his apparently urging them to join breakfast, the pair persisted in standing, looking as uncomfortable as if they were waiting for the dentist. The man was older than Michael, sweating in a jacket that looked the same age as the furrows in his brow. The woman, who was perhaps thirty, wore too much make up and fake-tan and had elected to dye her hair an extraordinarily unlikely reddish hue. She had sat down and was leaning back with her legs crossed, trying to look relaxed, but the constant picking at her nails argued otherwise. There were no introductions – everybody seemed in waiting mode.

Michael obviously hated this hiatus and left the room, returning about a few minutes later awkwardly carrying a ladies' shoulder bag. 'Well, my little Sharon, the new Caittie will be here shortly so we might as well get you started. I hope you have not packed your things?' He could see by Caittie's face that she had.

'Sorry, it's become a habit – anyway, keeping it packed is less complicated!' Caittie could not even consider whether his voice was teasing through the wryness of his tone.

'Good practice normally, I agree, but today we're changing you into Sharon, so we need to leave as much of Caittie behind as we dare.' He put the empty shoulder bag in front of her. 'I need your passport, driver's licence and any other things that have your real name on it; your own shoulder bag will be used by the new Caittie. Plus you'll need to take all your clothes out of your rucksack and lay them out on the bed.'

Caittie hid her embarrassment with a laugh: 'I didn't realise I'd have to go through kit inspection to get out of here.' As flippant as she sounded, Caittie wanted some more information on what Michael was doing. As with Keith, flippancy and sarcasm had become a habitual way of posing a question.

'We need the rucksack for the new Caittie. She must be seen with it as it will be part of your description. We also need you to pick out a few pieces you have worn either in London or here in Greece, as they too might be recognised. This will give the new Caittie that genuine touch. If we are lucky, they will stick with the long-distance use of agent's reports and not ask for detailed photographs. As long as we keep ticking their boxes, they might buy it. Remember that they could well be suspicious after you disappear briefly and then suddenly book yourself on a flight. They might assume many things during this gap, so we need them to think they've just got lucky.'

'Don't worry. I can do that.'

'So far you have been very good, especially for someone who knows little about this kind of life, but now we need to get professional. Remember that the new Caittie will be with one of my uncle's men and we will leave a few clues to make them think she is waiting and arranging to meet me. They shouldn't disturb her all the time they think they can use her to get to me.' Michael pushed the shoulder bag with his hand, as if to suggest she get on with it.

'I thought you were going to come with me?'

Michael smiled into her eyes. 'I'll be close at hand and meet you once we know where we are going. But, well, there are – reasons – why I can't risk going back to England. That reminds me – we need to sort out our communication system.' He reached into his pocket and pulled out a piece of paper. 'This phone number is in London. When you have recovered your father's information, immediately phone this number. All you need do is say "I have new lucky numbers" and then give the name of the city or airport you are going to. This along with the flight number you will have to encode, but say nothing other than this opening phrase and the series of numbers. You will encode the name place and date by numbering from the pangram – the quick brown fox jumps over the lazy dog. The first letter is one and the last thirty-five. Try to use different numbers where the letter appears more than once.'

Caittie nodded. 'Then what?'

'My contacts in London will get this information to me and I'll meet you there at the airport you have given. I'll need two full days from the call to my arrival. Now, go and get your stuff ready – it won't be long before the others arrive and we still have lots to do.' Michael went back to the other end of the room.

Picking up the bag and going back to her room, she first emptied her rucksack. It was the spare money at the bottom she wanted to transfer to her new shoulder bag while all this sorting out was going on. Once she had packed her new shoulder bag, she put it to one side and placed her personal papers along with the promised pay-off money by its side. Sorting through her clothes seemed both crucial and trivial. She really adored some of the pieces and tucked them at the bottom, hoping she could avoid parting with them. Eventually she selected a few sets of things she had worn and could bear to let go, including the beige jacket and the scarf, which had probably figured in any description. She was shutting her case when she heard Michael call up that the others had arrived. Carrying all the shoulder bags, papers and money in her arms, she went back into the kitchen.

Michael was standing behind his usual chair, talking to the orange-headed lady next to a tallish girl with her back to Caittie. Caittie looked dubiously at the girl's short skirt and cheap shoes and wondered what she was letting herself in for. Her hair was definitely mousey as opposed to Caittie's dark blonde and the Greek woman was inspecting it with her fingers while still talking to Michael.

'Good!' Michael, seeing Caittie, pulled her towards the group, swinging the other girl round. 'Sharon, meet Caittie and, Caittie, meet Sharon.' The two girls stood and inspected each other over the top of Michael's pointing fingers, whilst the orange lady looked on.

Sharon's appearance struck Caittie as an average but not overtly attractive girl, who was over-compensating with her tarty clothes so as to increase male interest. She was a few inches taller than Caittie and her mousy hair was full of unnatural loose curls, which must have taken ages to do each day. This was complemented by her exaggerated make-up, as although she was only probably a couple of years younger than Caittie it looked as if she had not progressed from her teenage worries into adult assurance.

'Nice to meet you, Sharon.' Sharon put her hand out to shake with Caittie, pleased with herself as she looked across to the other new man in the room, as if she wanted praise for remembering her lines.

'Likewise!' Caittie couldn't quite hide the dread in her voice as she contemplated what was about to happen. Although Sharon was everything she couldn't bear to be, she could see Michael's plan better now as the reality was falling into place. All she could do was accept that by adopting the opposite persona, it would be a deflecting and natural disguise, as she would be just another amidst the multitude similar looking holiday makers (Sharon's signature hairstyle, in fact, was a real advantage in that respect).

Michael quickly moved forward, took Caittie's papers and put another set back in her hand. Counting out some of the money, he tucked it into his shirt pocket and passed the rest to the new man – Greek, thin, rather sulky-looking – who was accompanying Sharon. He then handed Caittie's passport to Sharon.

'Have a quick look. Anything that you think is strange or can't be carried off safely – now's the time to say so.' Michael stood over them, anxious to get moving. He had for some time been dashing round the room in nervous energy while everyone else seemed to be in slow motion. Even now, he couldn't help fidgeting as he stood.

Both girls flicked through the passports – as far as either could see, it was a done deal. Michael's undisguised impatience made both of them feel this brief flick through was one of courtesy. In terms of the photographs they were of similar height, a couple of years and a few pounds in weight apart. Caittie could see from Sharon's photo that the lightly curled hair was actually the calming of positive ringlets in her passport. She hated perms and was secretly shaking her head in disbelief at why anyone would want one. Sharon, on the other hand, seemed to be looking rather pleased.

'Now, don't get hung up on the photos, as we are going to make some adjustments.' Michael took the passports back and handed them to the older man with his briefcase in hand, who immediately moved off into the hallway. 'We're going to change the photos but first adjusting hair colour and style so that the description is true to the original.' The fake-tanned woman was now tugging on Caittie's arm and Michael, seeing Caittie's reluctance, put a steely hand behind both and pushed them towards the door.

As she left she heard Sharon say, 'Hold on, you said I would be called Katie and in the passport it says Caitlin. What sort of weirdo name is that?'

Caittie reappeared, to say, 'It's the sort of name that says you have a father that gives you an awkward name, to call you a common name, just to confuse everyone. He said it gave a different individuality and classlessness, which is something *you* might understand.' Caittie had completely confused Sharon, but before she could work through it, Michael pushed Caittie from the room. She had enough time to see him frown darkly at her, though with a glint of humour.

Everything was at high speed now, as if infected by Michael's own pace. Her hair was prepared and darkened slightly with what Caittie could only hope was a temporary colour dye. The woman, who had no English, had a whole selection in her box and made a good job of adjusting the colour and curl. Much to Caittie's relief the curls were more relaxed like Sharon's hair now, with none of her tight passport-type ringlets. It felt more awkward being made-up, as Caittie couldn't recall anyone having made her up since the days of *As You Like It* at school. Yet in a strange way it made the whole process suddenly seem easier, as if she was now an actress getting into character.

At length, she was ushered into another room where the old man had his briefcase and tools spread over a wooden table. Standing her in front of the propped up sheet of plastic, he took several photos of her, each time minutely adjusting the light. Once done, Michael collected her and took her back to her room, where Sharon was trying on and checking through her clothes ('hate that colour. Hate that style'). Caittie gritted her teeth and refused to respond.

Alongside Caittie's clothes was a wheeled suitcase containing what was obviously Sharon's dubious wardrobe. There was now no time to worry about whether she wanted to be like Sharon, there was no choice – it was part of the plan to finish her father's work. Her previous hatred of his selfishness now seemed more like self-pity, as she could see further and further into his world. She had never trusted him unconditionally, thereby condemning the start of her life to failure. Now there could be no vanity and no obstacles – just challenges.

As the two girls tried to take on board the objective of picking out some symbolic outfits from each other, they naturally gravitated towards the few styles that they had in common. Michael's impatience reached in towards the end to force the exchange of reluctant items. The longer Caittie chatted to Sharon, the more she could recognise the kind of behaviour that Wendy used to use with men (the difference was that Wendy exploited her sexuality out of cruelty, whereas Sharon's motives were closer to vanity and hope). Michael had left the room as soon as it was time for the girls to get changed and repack their new bags. As each piece of clothing added to both their new looks, they looked at each other with unacknowledged unease as it became spookily close to looking in a warped mirror.

'We'd better go back down now!' This from Caittie, too brightly – now fully packed, she was eager to get moving. Sharon, however, was slouching against the wall at the top of the bed.

'You can, I can't. The guy Michael said I was to stay here and not come down. Something about staying here until you're safely off. Bloody overkill if you ask me.'

'Don't worry, Michael knows what he's doing!' Caittie went over, bent forward, and gave her an impulsive hug. 'Thank you!' She did feel grateful, as well as regretful for not liking her. She couldn't help pausing at the door as she left, thinking – does this girl really know what she might have let herself in for?

'No probs,' said Sharon, and watched her go.

The first thing Michael did when she entered the room was to proffer her the faked passport photo. She had expected to be impressed, but in spite of this, when she met his gaze she couldn't disguise her admiration. It was as authentic-looking a traditionally bad passport photo as she could imagine. The plastic behind her and the bleak lighting gave her that police mug shot look, with dark and shiny patches all in the wrong places, managing to suggest both Sharon and Caittie at the same time.

Whilst flicking through the rest of the passport, she was startled to notice that Michael's men were taking longer and more appreciative looks at her than they had done before. Inside, she had to shake her head in disbelief. Her hair done, make-up plastered all over and clothes adjusted to show lots of flesh instantly made men's behaviour primeval (the skirt, instead of being fashionably just above the knee, had been taken up to show half the thigh – it was tight on Caittie so on Sharon's few extra pounds, it would have been very tight indeed.) She was relieved when Michael, always conscious of her mood, clapped his hands in anger and gave the men various orders to get going. There were still nagging doubts in her head, but she knew she was safe in his hands.

Once they were alone, he said, 'Your flight leaves in a few hours, but we need to get you to the airport the long way and do a changeover of vehicles so there can be absolutely no connection with you to this place or my men – or to me. I'll travel with you halfway. You'll finish the journey in a taxi.'

'Can I take the tickets?'

'Of course, and the suitcase labels.' A vehicle outside tooted its horn, which in turn spurred Michael into still faster mode.

'Out you go. I'll be with you in a moment.'

Caittie towed Sharon's suitcase into the heat where a small van and driver were waiting. She had some reservations about managing Sharon's skimpy clothes in a van, but Michael soon caught up and led the way to a padded bench seat, though she shuffled in Sharon's skirt like a crouched penguin. The inside of the van was very clean with low lighting. It was obviously designed to look inconspicuous and business-orientated on the outside while actually discreetly transporting people. No sooner had Caittie tried to sit down did they both have to adjust their seat at the swift surge of the van pulling away.

'So my little Sharon, you have some questions for me?' Michael seemed quite relaxed at last.

'I don't want to seem ungrateful or untrusting by keeping on questioning you.' But, she thought, I do want reassurance that you have all things covered.

'You're certainly your father's daughter.'

'To me, there are a few things that still need explaining.'

Michael looked at her with a little twisted smile. 'There are always gaps in any plan, and even alternatives, in case various things happen. The thing to remember is that the more fragile the plan, the faster you have to move. The more cover you have, the longer it will take for it to be broken down. Some things I've had to leave telling you until the last minute because it's perhaps better for my men not to overhear. Not that I don't trust them, but if any were caught then they must not have a complete picture.'

After this, he told her a good deal. All the details emerged of how Sharon had come to Greece with a girlfriend, who had returned early when they started to run out of money and was annoyed at being left alone with Sharon being so boyfriend-obsessed. Meaning Caittie should have a clear run with little complications if they ticked the right boxes ('remember,' he said, with a sudden grin, 'You don't have to be Sharon for all time, if that's any comfort!'). She took in what Michael was saying clearly, committing it strictly to memory like a school lesson, but there were so many unresolved thoughts going round her head! So much had happened in just over a day that it felt as if her life had changed forever.

Yet the journey felt too quick, as if the time had just evaporated. The van slid to a sudden halt, the back door opened and the driver beckoned her out into an underground car park of some shopping or office complex. Caittie looked at Michael for that split second, but there was no voice to express the fog of a doubt she could not see through. Michael could or would not answer her puzzled look, but he shocked her by crushing her lips to his warmly, before looking away.

'Soon!' Michael grabbed her wrist momentarily as if he had found one word that meant they wouldn't have to face any others. Then he nodded bleakly to the driver, and the moment was over. He was gone.

Minutes later, Caittie was inside the taxi they had rendezvoused with. As it came out into the sunlight, the driver appeared to be about to join the end of a queue of taxis. A crackled message on his radio and he instantly pulled out into the traffic, leaving Caittie breathless.

She was now to all appearances a tourist again, with the carrier bags and baggage credentials suggesting Sharon. Yet she couldn't feel calm until she was sure she could *be* Sharon. From the way she stood, to the way she talked, she would have to effortlessly blend in and avoid any undue attention. She spent the journey practicing each detail in her head.

When the taxi pulled into the airport, she paid the driver – she probably didn't need to, but it looked realistic (the driver didn't refuse). Even her pacing at the airport did not look out of place. Caittie had long since noticed that holidaymakers always seem divided by those impatient to get home and those so shattered or so relaxed that they could scarcely move. It was hard to get used to the different stares the men were now giving her, as they automatically eyed up any attractive girl sporting a short skirt, but in the same way that made her feel awkwardly exposed as such gear also labelled her as not Caittie and therefore more comfortingly invisible. She practised the prickly smile Wendy was so expert at, so useful at deterring men from being over-friendly.

The visualisation of being Sharon, now put into action, even seemed a strange relief from the frustrations of check-in and boarding. Once seated, it was a relief to know that another corner had now been turned and the troubles of Crete were almost behind her, the mission at least partly accomplished. Settling into her seat, she drew out the pale pink chick-lit novel she had bought at the airport as being suitably Sharonesque. Not that she wanted to read it, it just acted as a busy sign and gave her time to think without people being tempted to make polite conversation.

As the plane gained height, her head cleared. She now found herself aware of a different kind of thinking, as if her brain had subtly rewired itself. In such a brief time, she not only felt as if she had lived more than years of her previous existence, but she also seemed to see people in a new way. The old Caittie had rarely considered people in any depth – she had tended to take their actions at face value without further thought. It was almost as if she had distanced herself from her own life, in self-protection. Now she had had no choice other than to look at others, even those she had never met, with a view to trying to predict their actions.

This more psychologically-based process had shown her things she had never looked for before. For example, she had realised that her instinctive initial dislike of Sharon was born out of her old self. Too quickly trying to judge her by her own standards, frighteningly like her mother, avoiding the need to look at her own actions. She had in reality nothing but gratefulness for Sharon, as she was taking a risk, even if not bright enough to realise its value. Her old self had utilised her intelligence in every transaction, save that of her relationship with other people. It was as if she blocked out connection with most of those around her so as not to get close enough to be hurt. Few had made it past her first defence and those who had were still left frustrated by her inner shell.

Possibly these problems stemmed from her relationship with her father and how she dealt with his disappearance, but it had surely been engrained by her mother's actions in wanting to over-protect her.

The man across the aisle cleared his throat, as if working himself up to a conversation. Before he could find any excuse, the stewardess approached with the food trolley acting as a lucky distraction. Caittie was surprised to realise that, despite her dread of the four-hour flight seeming endless, she had managed to pass a large part of it effortlessly.

Food dealt with and rubbish handed in, she examined herself to see whether the problems with Keith were largely down to early sense of loss, whether that was what hadn't been right. He too was blocking emotion, or truth, or both, and – despite all she knew of him – she couldn't see why. After just a couple of encounters with Michael – for that was all it had been – she still felt closer to him than she could now ever conceive to Keith (was it imagination, or had his kiss something certain and possessive about it?).

Perhaps it was because he was the same age as her father and a substitute she desired, but it opened a connection and cemented a strange trust. Thinking back to the whipping, she tried to work out what those feelings were that had confused her. She definitely liked the restraints, both physically and mentally – she could finally sense why Keith had proposed them – but their symbolic presence in giving control of her life over to someone else was something Caittie resisted to her bones.

She was confident that pain wasn't intrinsically anything to fear, for if she was ever going to experience the real joys of life, then she would have to risk pain. But she couldn't help smiling when she recalled his silent admonition when she had been sardonic to Sharon's complaint about 'Caitlin'. This man had in less than twenty-four hours shown so many times he understood her completely, body and mind, and the experience – a first for Caittie – was a heady one. It was this level of integrity she had lacked in her life and a taste of Michael's lips, assertive yet tender, had made her cease to despair of someone she could trust.

For her, an ideal partner had to be a man that could command her respect while letting their thoughts somehow run *through* each other, someone she could follow wherever he climbed in life, knowing he would always ensure she ascended with him. And, although physical attraction might have triggered these realisations, it was at the psychological level where yielding was ultimately required. After this, however it ended, there could be no more reverting into the shell of her previous surface life, with its sugar-coating of deluded intelligence.

An electronic ping drew her attention to the overhead seat-belt signs. She had heard the captain announce their approach to Gatwick, but it had only just now registered. How fast the flight had gone! Putting her book away, she now wanted distraction and remembered that she hadn't prayed this morning. She had managed to pray previously at the apartment, but somehow in all the excitement it had slipped. The next part of her father's adventure would bring new troubles, as well as old ones. She closed her eyes and prayed not only for herself, but for Sharon, her mum and – even – for Keith. As for Michael, she could only pray that her father's instructions and trail would be a righteous one and not a selfish waste of time. She finished with a prayer of longing for the strength to see and accomplish whatever task lay ahead of her.

The plane landed and with the usual delays and endless walkways, until Caittie was finally waiting in the scrum of baggage collection. Sharon's suitcase had been round at least once, before she remembered it was now her case and not her beloved rucksack she was looking for. A customs officer smiled appraisingly as she passed, as Michael had supposed, no one was bothered about holiday flights. While queuing, she had reminded herself of the instructions Michael had given her in the back of the van. And she couldn't help wondering. *Is he thinking of me?*

21

You turn if you want to

Pierre waited to let the peak of tension pass. Then he said, 'Yet why should this have to come down to honesty or betrayal? There are greater loyalties than to whatever piece of land you are born in. You presume that I want to you to betray one country in favour of another, which is not the case. Forget countries or any such tribal grouping – this involves the whole of humanity! Don't you agree that it's about time you *truly* tried to do enough? The difference this time is that I will give you the understanding to take it that bit further.'

Andrew said, 'It sounds as if you've been reading too many cheesy spy novels. The classic turn of the traitor is taking some naïve eager young mind and convincing them to do some mission for the greater good. Anyway, you haven't answered my questions about what this is really about.'

'What if I can't give you an answer, as to nationality?'

'Then tell me why you called yourself Pierre, when you don't sound a bit French.' It had been brewing inside Andrew for some time, this warm but bland creature, speaking in universal English without hint of origin.

'Call me Peter, if you prefer, as all I did was use one of many translations of my name.'

'Peter,' Andrew tried it out on his tongue. It didn't seem to suit the older man any better than Pierre had. 'OK, Peter, I'm still waiting for some explanation of what you want me to do and who I'd be working for. If you want me to consider the offer, that is.'

'I don't want to get to a point where you agree to the task out of some fear or dread. I need you to agree to the task from your heart, because only then do you possibly stand a chance of succeeding. Look, let's exchange promises, Andrew. I give you the principles of a higher moral ground behind the task. If I can convince you on all counts, then all you have to do is agree to the task in principle.'

'I'll give it a go.'

Peter glanced sharply at him. 'Remember, once you agree there'll be no going back.'

Andrew thought about reminding him that there was nothing Peter could do once he was back home and free to change his mind, but decided there was no point in slamming the door in his own face. He nodded.

Peter lent forward earnestly. 'I want to give you information that will eventually change the way the world sees itself. Your job will be to take this information and bring it to the public realm. To affect that you will have to make some changes.'

A madman, or an alien, thought Andrew, with an unexpected sense of deflation. When, just for a moment, he had almost imagined.

'All due respect, but I have no public authority. If you want me to stand on street corners shouting, well, frankly there are just too many roads.'

'It would be your task to set it to public record – in a modern way so that it cannot be rescinded.'

'Do you mean you want me to *write* about it?' Andrew could not hide an element of disbelief in his voice.

'You will have to find a way of making it work – the most important thing is empowering someone that understands and can defend what I am to tell them. There are many vested interests against the truth – those who lied and those who gain by its perpetuation.'

'Is it dangerous?'

'Upsetting people always has its risks, but the task has a prerequisite to be as non-confrontational as possible. When you push past the vested interests that are set against peace, as those that blocked you before, they will just get a bit rougher. Name one country that does not have a connection with the cycle of lending money, buying weapons and control through indebtedness! Whether as a perpetrator, victim, player, or resistance, you either join the game or risk being swallowed up or victimised.'

'Agreed! But what can I do?'

'Only someone that understands the effects of emotional energy and its consequences can implement a controlled procedure for changing opinion. Eventually, this will create a wave of public opinion that slowly builds into an unstoppable force.'

'Why should your government pick me?'

'You still assume I work for some government, Andrew. I work to re-educate governments! And no, I do not expect all this to happen from your work! Others will follow your footsteps.'

'Hold on! There are more considerations than just my decision. Do I get some protection?'

'When you light a fire, you shield the first flame until the fire is started. You will be the first flame.'

Mad, madder, maddest, thought Andrew, and yet he speaks so well – so movingly!

'So you want me to take on some public opinion mission, exposing some truth, taking some small risks and all towards peace?' Andrew's hand rose quickly to stop Peter from interrupting. 'Why would such a worthy-sounding cause need to employ such covert tactics? Whether it's the defence mechanism of a small country or the destabilisation tool of a competitor, there's always an element of revenge in conflict. The trouble is that it's not the language or impression I am getting from you. My instinct tells me that there is another twist to this.'

'Andrew, I told you at the beginning you'd agree with the punishment set before you – and you'll also have an unquestionable accord with who I work for. And there will be no betrayal of country allegiances.'

'What happens if I don't agree?' he asked warily.

'What reasons have you not to agree?"

Andrew secretly thought, 'And what choice do I have?' As if his mind could sense a crack of light, a door of hope, a situation now ajar. He nodded.

'Good, Andrew!' Peter leant forward again. 'Now, I'm afraid that I have some shocking news for you that will be difficult to explain and even harder to accept.'

'As long as my family's OK – they are OK, aren't they?'

'They are fine, Andrew. It is you who is technically dead.'

22

Dartmoor

It was early Wednesday evening by the time Caittie got to St Albans and set about finding Sharon's rented flat. The directions she had been given were clear: to walk from the station, up Victoria Street, past the police station and onto the town centre at the top of the hill. The signposts to the cathedral were also obvious enough. However, her first instructed stop (the estate agents' office) wasn't where her directions indicated. It took some minutes of searching before piecing together Sharon's disjointed instructions. A tour of the town was the last thing she wanted in cheap high heels that did not fit too well, towing a surprisingly heavy alien suitcase.

The ordinary, almost shabby buildings of the outskirts were in stark contrast to the abundance of quaint old buildings in the very centre, but served as a natural indicator that she had probably walked too far in the wrong direction. The Peahen pub was a great landmark, but she only found it once she had almost given up and ventured towards the cathedral. The problem seemed to be that Sharon had somehow confused the directions from the station with the instructions for dropping off the letters. It was annoying, but perhaps only to be expected.

The main thing was that the letters she had been given would shortly be posted through the estate agent and bank post boxes. If her cover was going to hold, and Sharon was not to be reported missing, then Sharon's notice to quit her flat and cancel her standing order for the rent were essential. It had seemed odd when Michael had told her not to take a taxi, but instead to be seen walking down St Albans high street. But Michael was right – doing this she felt like Sharon, taking an expensive taxi would feel like Caittie. This wasn't about taxi drivers, loose tongues or even breaking her trail, but about attempting to be Sharon until she was clear.

Nearing the flat, she came through a huge arched gatehouse with an array of old buildings behind it. Standing in a pretty gardened triangle in front of a sign displaying "St Albans School", she wanted to stay and absorb the atmosphere in what instantly struck her as something that seemed like a 1950s film set. Although the school was closed, all she could imagine were teachers in gowns and the boys in some old-fashioned uniform that, in the wrong part of town, would get them beaten up at the bus stop. Instead, Caittie forced herself to continue down the hill. The more modern houses, many converted into flats, set along the fringes of the town, were sidled in between older ones.

She thankfully identified the building, for as far as Caittie was concerned, heels were for posing in and not for any prolonged walking. It took a couple of seconds to take in how small the rooms were, especially as her shoes didn't travel far after being kicked off, while the only place to put her case was on the table (it was described as a studio flat, but only if you were a painter not requiring a large canvas, she thought). Not that it mattered – she had a bed for the night, a bathroom and a telephone, though its size did explain how Sharon could afford to live in such a nice part of the town.

She opened the fridge without much hope. Sharon had been away for a month or more which meant that it was unlikely to expect anything edible (in fact, there was only a wizened apple). At least from her unexpected tour she had a good appreciation of what food the town centre had to offer, but it would mean walking back up the hill. But first, and most crucially, she had to find the information on where her twelve-year-old self had first bonded with her own father. With the help of directory enquiries, she finally had the phone number.

The receptionist at the Manor Hotel near Okehampton was very helpful. Despite her initial statement that they were fully booked and certainly had no single rooms left ('we only have two singles at the best of times') she kept looking. With a steer from a colleague and some heavy rustling of paper, she unearthed a double-room cancellation for the weekend ('someone taken ill in a large party booking, so two weren't expected, if she cared to pay for the double…'). If they could re-let the room, it would save them the fee. Paying the deposit with Sharon's credit card was the scariest part, as Caittie did not know how creditworthy she was, by this time, though it worked. The receptionist couldn't be clear on transport arrangements, as Sharon's inability to drive complicated things, but she recommended a taxi from the train station. With the room secured for a long weekend from Friday to Monday, Caittie thought it was best to sort out all the details at leisure.

Michael had urged her to only stay in Sharon's flat for one night, as part of the plan was for Sharon to phone her mum the next day, with a simple message that she was going back to Greece and had quit her job. The letters Caittie had delivered gave notice on her flat and Sharon would ask her mother to clear it of her possessions over the weeks of the notice period. This ensured a plausible-enough set of events and items that should mean no one would be looking for Sharon.

By this time, it was getting late and she was hungry. Having located a pair of jeans and some trainers from her case, she made a quick trip back to the town centre. She couldn't face any of the variety of greasy burgers on offer from the high street so she settled for a Chinese takeaway and a bottle of wine. It seemed appropriate under the circumstances, as she was required to play loud music to make sure the neighbours registered that 'Sharon' was home, however briefly (there was luckily no chance of a neighbour dropping in, according to Sharon).

Back in the flat she started to make a list of what she needed, but apart from an ordinance survey map and some decent walking boots, everything else seemed secondary. The hotel would require some dressing for dinner and a fresh outfit to complement the crushed and creased clothes would not go amiss. Looking at her options, she decided so she would travel to Okehampton tomorrow. It might prove less than ideal for clothes shopping, but, being close to the moor, the map and boots should be easy enough.

All she would have to do is find a hotel for the first night and do her shopping in town, reaching the Manor Hotel in the afternoon. This would give her the whole of Saturday and Sunday for search.

As for the search, well, it had been fifteen years ago – she could only hope and pray that she would remember the place. She'd have to buy some tools and rather than carry them, it would be easier to get them in Okehampton as well. Her programme clearly set in her mind, she relaxed with the TV news. The appointment of George Carey as the new archbishop and the renewed trouble in the Balkans both troubled her. Her recent upsurge of belief made her feel she should have some opinion about the archbishop's appointment, whereas she had none. As for the Balkans, to Caittie it was almost incredible that people living alongside each other for so long could still hate each other so much. Still worse was the thought that this new person she was becoming, with a new awareness of people, was someone who had escaped from her inner shell to now find the news actually interesting. It was something she had seen her mother and older people do, but she had deemed it to be a middle-aged thing for which she was still unprepared.

The next morning, she left the flat as instructed. The takeaway cartons on the worktop and meticulously unmade bed were all telltale signs of a short stay. Sharon's gifts, her duty-free, along with instructions on how to clear the flat plus Sharon's note apprising her mother of what clothes to bring as extra luggage to Greece in a month's time, were all designed to leave even the closest person no doubt or reason to worry above the information they had been given.

Which, Caittie thought, wouldn't stop Sharon's mother probably worrying about what sort of Greek man was taking advantage of a daughter. It was Michael's plan that Sharon would then be living a double life posing as both herself and Caittie, as all trails for both would lead to the same person. Michael anticipated that this would give them at least a clear week.

Having to trek into London and take a tube to Waterloo, she only had time to grab a processed sandwich, before the four-hour train journey to Okehampton. All this travelling was giving her too much time to think and had started to become tiring, as if this new person she was becoming was growing day after day and had the pains to prove it. Even just sitting on a train and looking at people, she noticed things she had never taken time to notice before. There was the dignified man with the MCC tie and the weary-looking eyes, the family of too-many children in hand-me-downs. Caittie felt a strange kinship – her people. Her country. She tried not to think of Michael.

Arriving in Okehampton at its very provincial English station, she stepped into an even more provincial town. It was certainly a place where you would start to feel out of place dragging your suitcase along further than a short distance, but luckily a B&B was all she needed. Looking for the quickest relief from this feeling, Caittie spied just along the station road, an older renovated house set back discreetly from the road, with a sign showing Bed & Breakfast and a still better sign beneath it: "vacancy".

A quick knock at the door secured her a very hot and bothered landlady. After listening to her explanation that she was fully booked for six weeks as the schools had just broken up, she confessed that she did have one room free for one night as long as she didn't mind not having sausage in the morning. Settling into her room, it seemed hard to believe that just yesterday she had been still in Greece with Michael.

Still, at least there was one single advantage. In this town, no one would care if she looked like Sharon or Caittie. She could take pleasure in sorting out some of her own clothes and dress down for comfort. Her hair scrapped back into a ponytail, undermining the effect of the "Sharon" curls, she felt relieved to be more herself. It wasn't hard to find a pub with families enjoying early evening food in the garden. A quiet corner seat inside, an abandoned newspaper and a large salad meal ordered along with a pint of shandy ensured little attention. The usual looks a girl or woman gets on her own didn't worry her, as it was mostly family men looking but not daring to talk to her. She almost spoke to a sensible pair of older women in tweed, but decided against it, wanting to keep her ghost-like drifting existence unnoticed.

The next morning she set off with a list of essentials which she methodically gathered up in a series of shops through the steadily rising summer heat. Just as she'd thought, the OL28 Ordnance Survey map and boots were easy to find. Locating a DIY shop took some time, but she managed to find a hardware shop and settled for a basic large pointed trowel, a crowbar, hammer and a hand-held digger. Juggling her parcels reminded her to seek out a cheap rucksack and extra carriers to stop the tools chinking as she walked (later she had the leisure to be amused at the shop assistant's puzzlement, as Caittie wrapped the tools as delicately as if they were made of glass).

The only thing now on her list was some evening wear for the Manor Hotel. It was hard to find good fashion without the slightly Margaret Thatcher-style out-of-date shoulder pads, which left little choice other than a simple summer dress (Caittie had long since recognised how just a few hours on the train equated to around a year in fashion). After a sandwich lunch, Caittie settled her bill with the owner of the B&B and phoned for a taxi. It seemed to take ages to arrive, but she was in no rush – the weather was fine and she could either wait here or at the Manor Hotel.

Her heart fluttered unreasonably as she turned in the hotel's gate. Here, after all, she and her father had come, all those years ago, on that memorable walking holiday, yet all she could remember was a lovely old Georgian house with a few facilities and a bit of an extension. As the driver pulled into to a jumble of car parks, she was hard put to recognise the old original building. Walking down a driveway between the buildings, she noticed an impressively extended dining room while out the back were buildings like miniature aircraft hangers promising extensive indoor sport facilities.

Caittie didn't know whether to be more shocked or pleased. Since it was still before three and her room wasn't quite ready, she chose to wait in reception, courteously declining all the receptionist's suggestions to check out the activity board and book something. It seemed to be the "expected" thing to do, but Caittie longed to get on with things and everything around her seemed to be occurring in slow motion. Opening her Ordnance Survey map, she eagerly looked around the local area, hoping to spot where her father had taken her all those years ago. As she had feared, though, her clearest recollections surrounded being with a father, she hardly had visions of the scenery itself.

She could just recall passing the main road junction and stopping in a pub car park. There were several Stone Age and Neolithic sites marked on the general locality, so it was likely she would have to walk them all until she recognised the one at which they had enjoyed the picnic. As it turned out, the man sitting next to her was friendly enough to ask what she was looking for ('I know the area like the back of me hand'). Moving her finger along the 386 to Tavistock, she stopped at a mid-point PH sign and said she needed to get there the next day.

'Well then, tonight is your lucky night. I'm Toby and I own the minibus parked outside, see? I shuttle guests to their golf, don't I, so I can shuttle you tomorrow while I'm at it.'

As she glowingly thanked him, it occurred to Caittie that the way things were falling into place made her feel strongly that it was all "meant to be". Fate had applied the brakes on her rush and anxiety and she could let go of worrying until tomorrow. Here at the hotel, under Sharon's alias, she felt for the first time in ages confident enough to leave her bag unpacked. It seemed a delicious thought to have nothing ahead of her for several hours other than (at some point) dressing for dinner.

Descending to the dinner hall in her new dress, she felt confident and unfazed, as the staff tried to work out where she should be sitting. The evening meal had changed from the more personal service she recalled from her childhood to a large schematic plan with allocated tables. She found herself sitting on the end of the table of fourteen orienteers, the same fourteen presumably who had had two of their party drop out the day before. Blending in was actually a relief – Caittie had to stop them trying to separate a table for her, as it was more comfortable to sit in a group rather than conspicuously all on her own.

In Greece, no one really passed judgement when she sat by herself. Here in England, she knew that eyes would be looking and people would not only judge, but wonder about why a young woman should eat at a restaurant on her own. She had little in common with the group to which she was included, but the dinner was good, especially the salad – so refreshing in this hot weather.

Not wanting to go straight back to her room after dinner, Caittie took a casual walk round the hotel, at the end of which she bought some bottled water and a selection of snacks from the bar. Her intention was to stay out all day without stopping for lunch.

The next morning, she awoke nervously early and without appetite. It was an effort to ensure that she consumed more than she normally would of fresh fruit, porridge and toast. Changed and with the digging gear safely stowed in her rucksack, she waited outside by the minibus stop with the golfers, taking no chances. Toby waved her on blithely with a group of other people, some carrying golf bags bulky enough to make her rucksack seem almost invisible.

'Golfers first,' the driver said to her, 'and you second, love, if you don't mind. Tournament today.'

'Not a problem,' said Caittie hastily. She was hoping to recognise the route and visions she had in her head about that day long ago, vague as they were. Although she had picked a pub along the right stretch of road, was it the right pub? What do girls of twelve remember about pubs? She could be walking and searching needlessly and wasting valuable time!

After the golfers had gotten off, the driver carried on straight, until, turning off the main road, he weaved expertly through narrow country lanes. Eventually, they emerged into the tiny village of

Bridestowe and from there back out onto a main road on which he promptly pulled into the Fox and Hounds pub car park.

'Here you are, then,' said Toby. The pub was on the correct side of the road but Caittie still felt disorientated by the journey and direction of approach. That flash of an image stored in the memory was instantly tainted with doubt when it had not appeared in the same expected pattern.

Any reservations about it being the right pub were too late, as his hurry meant that Caittie had no choice than to take it from here, right or wrong.

The pub was deserted so early in the morning, and, once her rucksack was settled comfortably on her back, she headed towards the back of the car park following the public footpath signs. The order and sequence of events when she walked with her father that day fifteen years ago were still confused, but she felt fairly sure that they went to the Widgery Cross before ending the day at (what was then) the new Meldon reservoir. All she could do was to plan a similar route, zig-zagging across as many as she could of the places marked "settlement" on her map and hoping something would strike her as familiar.

It was relatively easy from her own studies to eliminate the best-known settlements, such as Grimespond, along with others of the wrong age or type that her memory said it should be. The sun was hot, and climbing the first ascent to Bray Tor, she felt sure that the day would be long and tiring. She kept going over the visions of the picnic that day and was with each reflection more confident that the answer was nestled in some valley or other. First came this trek to get her bearings, and then, with the compass, she could plot the best way to weave through the ups and downs of the rugged landscape. She had decided to ignore the warnings signs on her map for the military firing range, as the risk of the range seemed far less than her taking too long. Time would not allow her any such courtesies as to find out whether or not it was safe, though it usually was.

Once standing at the summit, it occurred to her that Widgery Cross was a strange place for a monument to Queen Victoria's Jubilee, but at least it was a memorable one. Setting off on the mining tracks around Great Nodden seemed the quickest way to make ground, but even the tiniest section of the map seemed to take ages.

Whenever the tracks stopped, it was slow going. While her feet got wet and chilled in the boggy areas, her head felt constantly hotter, regardless of how much water she drank. It was always a relief when the tracks reappeared – some old railway routes with the odd sleeper still left intact and other strange, granite tramway-like constructions. It was mid-afternoon and still nothing had resembled the image tumbling in her head. By the time she could see Stourton Tor, Yes Tor and the Meldon viaduct in the distance, she started to question her approach in her mind.

Perhaps she should have done some library research and not just relied upon her memory? Perhaps she could eliminate the possibilities down to a couple of sites if she went back and did this? She instinctively felt that she'd gone too far and with many doubts she started to zig-zag back, crossing over her previous tracks to spot-check as much fresh ground as possible. She felt sure that even her father would not have dragged a young girl so far.

Caittie couldn't say what exactly suddenly snapped in her brain – a smell, a curve of land – but suddenly the scenery seemed to strike a chord at the back of her mind. The map said there should be a settlement to her right, but she couldn't see anything. Off the track was a large, flat, boggy piece of ground that seemed to hold a ridiculous amount of water, considering the long dry spell. The map showed a settlement on the edge of it, but the ground sloped away and had remained out of sight as she had skirted the small rise on the other side. The more she stood there and looked at the view, the more hopeful she suddenly felt.

Even being as careful as possible, a small slip managed to fill her boot with water. In just a few minutes, her right foot squelching, she reached the other side and looked down into a trapped valley out of view of the easier pathways. There was a stream running through one side of the valley and a series of low stone circles and walls, and with a surge of sudden hope she knew she had been here before. All her walking and searching throughout the better part of the day had been a waste of time, just because she had decided to take the easy route around Great Nodden. If only she had started the other way round!

Making her way down the bank, she didn't care too much how she crossed the stream as her feet, already wet and soggy, were becoming sore. The question now was where had "Miss Muffet" – her youthful self – actually sat?

There was undoubtedly a whole series of flat stones her father could have used as seats and a table for their picnic. With tools in hand, she decided it would be quicker to flip over the most likely in turn, rather than to waste more time in possibly useless meditation. It went against all her training and instincts at such an historic site, but her need was stronger than her reservations.

She bent down and started to hammer the crowbar under the first stone. Suddenly she was aware of a rumbling noise that went from distant roar to ear-piercing suffusion, making her whole body rigid with fear. By the time she realised what was going on, she was in time to spot the rear of an RAF jet, just visible for a second before it disappeared over the next tor.

Looking towards the horizon, her eyes drifted to the hills at the back of the valley. Emerging on the ridge she could see twenty or thirty people, the bulk of the group walking and half a dozen at the rear standing and pointing. Not pointing directly at Caittie, but still, their gestures seemed agitated, even from a distance. The fact they were on the trickier but more scenic paths made her instantly assume that they were ramblers. Such people were bound to take a very dim view of what she was doing with her hammer and crowbar. She had little choice other than to grab her tools, pick up her rucksack and head swiftly towards Meldon, in the opposite direction to theirs.

Her plans to walk back to the pub and then to take the bus were now aborted – instead there was no option than the long walk along the reservoir paths and then finding her way back to the hotel. The main thing was to keep moving, there would be little chance of them catching her up from that distance and no questions to answer. So near as she'd been to her father's papers, her heart urged her to sneak back and to wait till they had gone, but the light was almost gone and her head forced her toward safety.

It was getting late by the time Caittie had tripped through the old ice works on Stourton Tor and found the Saxon Kings Way path, which circumnavigated Meldon reservoir leading past Place farm. She hoped she wouldn't be too late for dinner at the hotel, though part of her only longed for rest and sleep. Having walked so long, she felt unusually hungry and chose her normal portion from the self-service items rather than to wait and order from the menu. Trying to decide how much to take suddenly flicked a switch, turning the problems of today into plans for tomorrow. Going back round, she took a few selected items and a handful of napkins. Almost on her own at the table, it was easy to tuck one of the Cornish pasties and an improvised sandwich into her bag.

The trouble was that, despite the remoteness of the moor, she had been working in the late afternoon, when any hiker could see her from miles away. The simple answer to this problem was for her to miss breakfast and go at first light. A hard march the way she had come and she could almost certainly be there before anybody else would dream of wandering the moors. She knew her tiredness yesterday was likely to have been dehydration, as she had run out of water too early in the heat, so as before she went to the bar and got more snacks, plus double her water rations. Once she got back to her room, she set her alarm-clock for half-four – she would risk the first part in the half-light of dawn.

When the alarm went off, she dressed as fast as possible and headed off. Moving softly through the dimly-lit corridors and the hotel yard, she tried to ensure avoidance of any suspicion and with luck wouldn't be seen – or even heard – at all. It was much easier once she had left the grounds, walked down the main road and picked up the deserted lanes past the farm towards Meldon, though it was a couple of hours forcing her legs to keep to a pace they would rather not have kept to.

At seven-thirty she felt confident enough to stop for her reserved breakfast, whilst she strolled and pondered the stones around her. On a second look it was clearer, cooler, with the heat of the sun not yet started.

An hour or so later, she had lifted several stones with no luck. She was trying to focus on the most likely ones to lift, but, as time went on and more stones had been moved to no avail, she realised the choice lay beyond anything that she might have visualised that day with her father. Looking back, there were two stones she doubted that she had the tools to lift. Again, she forced herself to "think clever" as her father could have only picked stones that people couldn't easily – or accidentally – move.

It *had* to be one of these stones, but the question was how to lift them? She knew how to do it from her archaeology work, but it was the materials she needed. Yesterday's trek along the track to Meldon came back to her. There up in that bog were odd bits of metal, probably discarded from mining or railway works. Ten minutes later she had located a couple of loose ones. Starting from the crowbar and using sharper rocks as fulcrums, she managed to lift the first stone, propping and leveraging with ever-larger rocks and bars under the edge each time.

As soon as there was a sensible gap she threw herself on to the earth in order to peer under it. There before her, thrillingly, was a large leather pouch, covered in mud. Pulling it out and brushing it down, she looked at it. The prospect of opening it in the open air suddenly made her feel very exposed, as if now finally in possession she needed to protect it. Yet surely to leave without being one hundred percent sure of what was inside had to be an act of utter stupidity.

She glanced inside to see a letter in her father's handwriting with the words 'Dearest Caittie' on the side. Snapping it back shut, she put it in her rucksack, feeling that with her hands so muddy it seemed almost sacrilege to spoil the papers' preserved status. Then her professional archeologist instinct took over – she returned the stones and tidied generally so there was almost no sign of her having been there.

Walking back, her legs, which had earlier felt so laboured, seemed charged with a fresh sense of purpose. It took probably the same amount of time to walk back, but her mind was so curious about what lay in the envelope that the time seemed to pass in a flash. Back in her room she carefully wiped and cleaned the pouch and her hands, trusting that the abundance of muddy tissue would flush down the toilet without blocking it. Opening the yellowing security pouch, only the first page was readable as its inner wrapper was a heat-sealed polythene bag. From this, a folder of loose papers fell to the bed in her father's neat script:

Dearest Caittie.

I prayed that you would find this safely and that your journey has not been a hard one. I hope that you have found Michael well and he has made plans for your safety. I also hope that you understand my reasons for involving you, in that you were the only one I could completely trust.

The fact I'm not here means that someone is onto us – someone who obtained private information passed between my friends somehow. We knew we were being watched, but things started happening strangely after the Cuban dive. Because I didn't know who to trust, I had started a policy of exclusion. By taking one person out of the communication loop, wherever I could, I was trying to see a pattern. The fact that you're reading this means that I'm likely to have been killed, so trust nobody. Michael knew the least, which is why I trusted him to help at this stage, especially as his skills and contacts would be invaluable to you.

As I described before, GAMF was heavily into diving for treasure, as it to a great extent funded our archeologically based non-profit expeditions. We were therefore interested in discovering all we could about the two Spanish gold fleets caught by hurricanes in 1715 and 1733. Much of the treasure was never recovered, because so many ships were damaged and scattered in the storms. This little enterprise proved to be profitable as well as interesting, as Michael's contacts and George's research gave us an edge that our rivals lacked.

Frank was helpful too, in many ways, though he was always desperate to prove himself. He was ten years younger than his brother and loved to practice spying on him. We tended to take all this with a pinch of salt until one day he let it slip that his brother was a top CIA operative. Frank was mortified and admitted he'd never told us this before, in case he compromised his brother's safety.

At any rate, what Frank described (and latterly showed us in his boyhood diary) were notes of a conversation his brother had had on the phone, which Frank had spied on. His brother was reporting in on a radio ham that picked up Russian submarine B130's distress call, when it ran into an uncharted shipwreck in shallow water, just inside Cuban territorial waters. This was Oct. 25th, 1962, and the radio ham had recorded this message without knowing what the message was, but Frank's brother secured the tape and had it translated.

The sub apparently had sustained only minor damage and was ordered to proceed to the edge of the quarantine area imposed by the USA before surfacing. The commander Shumkov was annoyed, but had no choice other than to patch up the minor repairs and checks necessary. Only on the surface with no pressure could he effect the repair, but his masters in the Kremlin wanted to make sure that if any accident happened, it would sink in deep water and stop the USA conducting easy military salvage.

George ascertained that the coordinates of the shipwreck ruled out missing wrecks from the modern era, so it became very interesting to us. The only trouble was its position in Cuban waters – even ten years later, these waters were heavily patrolled. Eventually Michael came up with a contact that would take us in under cover of darkness. This contact was a contraband runner and not only did it cost us a lot to hire him, but we had to front a lot of bribes as well. The bribes made sure that the patrols that day reported a floating container in that area (this was a common problem with the ever-growing number of container ships and their tendency to lose the occasional container overboard. Other ships steered clear of the reported area, in order to avoid hitting them). Anyway, we went in and found the wreck precisely on the coordinates where the Russian sub had recorded them. In the dark it took a little while to cover the search area, but we had a few hours of diving time left once we located it.

It was a completely untouched Spanish galleon and just like picking candy. We knew from our research where the best stuff was generally kept on board and soon removed enough debris to expose some of its treasures. We tried to keep it professional by crating things up so as to keep pieces together and get as much information for provenance as we could (most ships, especially the Spanish ones, collected gold and precious objects from a wide variety of sources). To cut a long story short, when we got back and went through it all, one piece just didn't fit. We had the remnants of a French casket and some coins; and the sort of ornamental box that a ship's captain would give pride of place in his cabin. It was elaborately worked in silver, with an inscribed lock plate. It stood apart because although we found it roughly in the captain's cabin area, it didn't fit comfortably with the other finds.

Frank took a small piece of wood remnant and had it carbon-tested, as this new technology fascinated him. Meanwhile George, back on shore, was convinced that he had seen the inscription before. When a couple of weeks later Frank called a meeting in London, we thought it was about how the proceeds would be split from this latest find. There he presented us with the results of the carbon dating. The casket by this method was made in about 1780. The ship, however, dated from around 1700-1710 and everything else we had taken for sampling proved of that similar age. Everything suggested that this ship was probably from the 1715 or 1733 fleets. But how could a casket made fifty or sixty years later be buried amongst this shipwreck? How could this ship have sunk carrying a casket fifty years before it was made?

Ironically, GAMF had started by investigating just such oddities and turning them into treasure trove, but in this case we were confronted with the strangest mystery of all. At first we asked questions and help from various academics, but the more we asked, the stranger things got. Not only did everything seem to lead to a dead end, but also we were certainly being warned off. The break-ins at home you may remember, as everybody on the team suffered similarly, until eventually Michael's then-girlfriend was killed in what was surely a set-up.

I have always suspected that Frank's CIA-based brother might be monitoring our activities, but again it all seemed more than that. It became international wherever we went. All this dragged on over a couple of years during which George became more and more distant. Only recently did I discover why, *when he phoned me (I've not been able to contact him since). As I mentioned, he had recognised the inscription and had spent all his holidays and any spare time over those two years researching it. Unfortunately what he found solved the first puzzle only to give him an even bigger one. So much so that I had little choice than to make this last trip and – with luck – emerge with some proof of what George and I suspect.*

But first, George told me how he had seen the inscription in a report when he was researching the missing ships of the 1715 and 1733 fleets. It was memorable because it was a French phrase inscribed in a Spanish record, yet since part of the record was missing and since it didn't seem to lead anywhere, he ignored it. At that point of his research when he first saw the noted inscription, we were consumed by the need to find projects with clear financial opportunities. However, after returning to his notes and spending two summers in Spanish monasteries, George assembled the story. The ship we found off Cuba had been left behind from the 1715 fleet, because of rudder difficulties, when it had been forced to stop mid-Atlantic for temporary repairs. The rest of the story he pieced together from various reports from survivors, including one from a Spanish Monk who had later been rescued.

On the monk's report of the outward journey, the ship had been moved to sheltered waters near Bermuda for repair, with the intention of catching up with the fleet later. This was a dangerous area for a Spanish ship, so once ready they left under the cover of bad weather. Sailing into the area of what we know as the Bermuda triangle, the next day they came across a small French frigate. The weather was poor, but not bad enough to warrant the damage the frigate seemed to be suffering from. In addition, its crew appeared slothful and confused and did not run. This French ship was fast and well made with excellent guns and could have taken flight or fought harder, but the superior size and proximity of the Spanish ship easily overpowered them. Even though a large part of the crew and its contents were captured, by the time the fighting had finished, the ship was so damaged that it was useless as a prize and was left to sink (the Spanish captain made notes because he had never seen a French ship of this style before).

Shortly after the loss of their ship, according to the monk, still stranger things happened and he was called to the captain. They had interrogated the French crew and they were talking so strangely that the captain thought they were mad – or even possessed by demons. As the only priest on board, the monk's advice was sought. This monk's transcribed notes, that George had uncovered in the monastery that served as his final resting place, gave these interviews, in detail. The French sailors, with rare unanimity and emphasis, were united in maintaining that France was now a republic and all aristocrats had been guillotined. They even declared that all of Europe would soon become a republic under Napoleon's rule.

Since to the monk (as to the Spanish captain and crew) it was fifty or sixty years before any of these events, they had never heard of Napoleon. The Frenchmen's testimony was therefore dismissed as evil madness and of no worth. The records were then misplaced in the archives of the inquisition, who interrogated the monk upon his return.

As for the captain, crew and Spanish monk, there was less dispute as to what kind of madness beset these French sailors than as to whether it might prove contagious, especially to an illiterate and superstitious Spanish crew.

According to the monk's papers, the captain determined to kill all the Frenchmen. Such instances of un-Christian carnage were still largely viewed as the fortunes of war and the Spanish inquisition had taught people to distance themselves from any kind of lunacy, or risk punishment still far worse themselves. The monk, however, was moved by the young Frenchmen, and talked the captain out of killing them, instead suggesting that they be marooned on an uninhabited island with a couple of guards (this is where the French captain's inlaid casket sailed off with the Spanish captain, along with its inscription "to help a stranger is to help Jesus").

Leaving them marooned with a small guard would not only save his own crew's souls from devilry, but also leave a chance of the prisoners being picked up by a prison ship once the Spanish ship returned. Not only was the monk's plea successful, it was successful enough for the captain to leave him there with the French to save their souls. The monk was not to know that the Spanish ship would be lost off Cuba in another storm when the repairs to its damaged rudder failed to hold.

As the time on the island passed, the Spanish guards became more and more disturbed by what they heard, despite the monk's assurances. As the French were verging on the psychotic with the confusion they were in, the monk tried to calm them and by giving counsel the best he could in French. The more he talked to them the more he was convinced of their genuine belief they lived a hundred years ahead. Months passed and it was not long until some of the Frenchmen lost any care for their lives and freed themselves to rush the guards. Carnage ensued as the two guards killed five prisoners before they were themselves overwhelmed. The French buried the dead in a mass grave. The monk was spared because he had helped them, but before anything could be constructed that was remotely seaworthy, another Spanish ship landed on the island.

Naturally, the rest of the French were then executed at sea. The strange thing is that the monk recorded the French as appearing almost glad, as if hoping for relief from their madness. All this transpired from an account that the monk wrote upon his return to Spain (as it turned out, he was very lucky, even at this late stage of the inquisition, not to be tortured to death for refusing to repent it as lies. He was declared mad, but never wavered from his account of the Frenchmen. He lived out his life in a monastery of his order).

Caittie, this was where George was astonishing: because of the confusion over the names of different places, as each country seemed to have a different name for these islands. It was George who figured out where they were dropped off – the very island where I'm headed now, once this letter is placed for safekeeping. The drop-off point the monk describes was the last island on the end of the cays at the south tip of Bimini, and the reason why I'm going – of course! – is to locate the grave of the guards and French sailors – the grave that marks the only place on earth where men of the same age, dying at the same time, are as much as one hundred years apart in time and birth.

Their bones may hold the explanation of this secret, a secret that a handful of people and several governments hope to keep at any cost. If I can locate the grave and bring back some samples of bone for carbon dating, it should be possible to verify the monk's story. Although the grave is said to be fifty yards inland, due west of the highest point, I still back my chances of finding it. He describes a large round stone with a cross etched into it, but nearly three hundred years may have changed things. This is why I must risk the journey, as one of our team for this trip is a psychic who specialises in finding such burial places.

My dear Caittie, this opportunity is too great to miss, the mystery is too enticing to leave and I'm running out of people I can trust!

For you to follow my path, you'll need Frank, who can be contacted in Miami. To contact Frank you need to find the Brickwell Harbour Condo in Miami and post a message in box 161. You just need to say 'GAMF reunion', naming a place and time to meet. He uses this box for other things so hence the hint to whom the message is from. If he doesn't respond, then repeat the process the following week (of course if he never responds, then I'm afraid he too is dead).

I have to go; I hope you understand. I hope you know I love you and trust whatever you decide to do with this information.

I must ask you one last favour. Can you tell your mother I always loved her? Tell her I loved her despite her attempts to stop me or emotionally blackmail me, simply because in many ways she was right. My secrets caused distrust and rows between us but, had I told her what it was I am about to do, then she may have loved me enough to let me go, but then I would have to leave knowing that she held information that people were prepared to kill for. If you can, Caittie, help her understand.

With love always, Dad.'

Caittie flicked back through the pages of the scribbled notes, reading bits over and over again. Some pages had faint fingerprints on them, suggesting that, although he had taken care, he couldn't have had much time for their preparation. She suspected that he wouldn't have written anything down until the last minute, in case it was lost (or worse, found). The sheer amount of information was hard to take in. It wasn't so much the detail of the story, but its very essence, as being something she had never imagined.

In a sense, all her father had offered her was a small box and a story that confused both time and characters. The problem was that even once found, she might not have an answer so much as a key to an even greater mystery. Butterflies filled her stomach as the hopes of changing life direction were now likely to be more life consuming. Small wonder he had never dared to confide in her mother!

She now felt trapped in a hotel room, on the edge of Dartmoor on a Sunday afternoon, with little hope of getting to London or anywhere until tomorrow, since a train journey now could only get her there uselessly late in the day. She noticed the muddy marks her clothes and shoes had left on the carpet, but, compared to everything whirling around her head, it didn't seem worth worrying about. Looking at her watch, she realised there was just time to grab some kind of meal. It was almost a reflex to stock up on food while she considered what to do from here and plan accordingly. Tracksuited types and rushed families grabbed their meals around her while Caittie felt terribly separate, and unutterably alone.

'Excuse me,' said a young blonde man, 'Are you all right? You look as if you've gone one round too many with your trainer!'

He was attractive and clearly up for a mini-flirtation, but Caittie only flashed a smile back. 'No, just a little absent-minded!'

'They're showing some Woody Allen films later on,' he said, 'maybe see you there?'

'Maybe,' said Caittie, but she knew she would have neither time nor energy. She could only think about her letter.

23

Terminal decisions

'I'm *what?*' said Andrew weakly.

'I realise that it's a shock,' said Peter.

'What do you mean – technically dead? You're mad!'

'If I could explain –'

'Sorry, but since I'm sitting here talking I have to assume that I'm not 100% dead...'

'Andrew, my friend, be still for a moment. Let's just say that your life on earth is in flux. You could remain dead, adopt a new identity or – as I hope – rejoin your family.'

Andrew struggled with this. There was no choice – his decision had been made, so why did Peter see this as an answer to the question of being – or not being – technically dead? His mind couldn't help but to slip into spy mode, trying to make sense of things. It was possible (wasn't it?) that he had been abducted under cover of some faked death, ensuring that people stopped looking for him. Of course, being supposedly dead might be useful if he was meant to work 'off-radar', but what on earth must his family be thinking – or grieving? He couldn't even imagine it.

The hoped-for option had to be a return home, however complicated that might make things. But he couldn't help saying accusingly, 'You said that once I'd agreed in principle you'd tell me what this is all about! From what you just said it sounds more like, had I not agreed, you'd have bumped me off!'

'No, I needed your agreement so the decision was one made freely – not one emerging out of fear or dread, which it might have been if you knew the consequences.'

'So tell me straight, who do you work for? Russia? Serbia? Somewhere in the Middle East?'

Peter replied, 'I told you before I do not work for any country or nationality!'

'Then why would you want to destabilise any other country?'

'It is more about a – a correction, however unsettling that may be.'

'OK, then as I can't see any terrorism angle, I guess we are talking lunatic fringe group.'

Peter smiled thinly. 'I can't imagine you being likely to help any such group, unless you were forced to.'

'Isn't *this* force – this detention?'

'Circumstances, Andrew, which are necessary!'

'I deny it. This is extreme, what you've done to me is extreme, and I can only assume you have an extreme end-use for me!'

'Even extreme becomes mainstream occasionally,' objected Pierre mildly, but Andrew had lost interest.

'So who do you work for, Pierre? Straight answer!'

Pierre stood up. He was taller than Andrew had realised, much taller, and broader in the shoulders than he had seemed sitting down. Perhaps he was Andrew's age after all, or even younger.

'I work for God.'

Nearly every thought and conjecture in Andrew's head was felled by that single word. A Christian himself, he scrambled to recall fragments of knowledge relating to religious sects or fanatics, but he couldn't begin to relate any of this, either to the person in front of him or to their discussions. His head began to swim, which might be why the new and glowing Pierre appeared to be flickering around the edges.

'You mean – THE God?'

'Of course.' Peter's voice had an unnerving surety.

'Not some Middle East fanatics or something worse who think they are acting for God?'

'No.'

Andrew struggled. 'But it doesn't make *sense*! God – if anybody – has the power to do any of this without my help and certainly doesn't need to go to these crazy lengths to get me to agree. In short, what good am *I* to *God*?'

'There's a difference between a decision made by choice and a decision made through fear.'

'Beautifully put,' said Andrew sardonically,' but how can I be sure this isn't all part of some extreme fanaticism? Disinformation is something I've seen all too often – strife dressed up as innocence, with only the intention making the difference.'

'So you're worrying about being part of some fanatical plot, which will brutally enforce, torture or murder in the name of religion?'

'Yes. Spot on.'

'But you know better than that! You know that the extremists you're alluding to use just a sliver of God's word mixed up with endless distortions of their own, just to excuse their thirst for punishments! God wants people to be free to choose, not forced to choose. Your task will be to give people more freedom to choose.'

Andrew remained unimpressed. 'Sorry, but I still can't see how you expect me to take on fanatics and authorities single-handed. How can anyone do that?'

'Do you think God would ask you to "take on" those who work by force and fear? What could be the point of simply replacing one fanatic with another?'

No longer was it a matter trying to work it out, it needed to be given proof. But all he got was the conflict of his thoughts with Peter's words, and the strange throbbing sensation at the back of his head.

It's an aneurysm, he thought, it's a brain tumour.

God's out to get me after all.

24

Michael

The Manor Hotel on Sunday was as frustrating as an English Sunday afternoon could be. Caittie so longed to get on, yet she was stuck in the middle of nowhere with nobody answering phones. Normally she regarded Sunday, by its nature, as being a delightful part of the week, when people stopped rushing around on their daily tasks and did something different. Here – despite being surrounded by people very obviously enjoying their breaks – she felt Sundays to be a useless institution, providing an invisible but immovable obstacle towards the completion of her plans.

Reluctantly, having put down the phone on her tenth attempt to find out about flights to Florida, she had to come to terms with the fact that this was her rush and no one else's (indeed, it wasn't even the right season to travel to Florida).

As the initial surge of desperation that her father's information had given her subsided, so too did her urgency to share it with Michael. She had precise instructions to complete with regard to meeting Michael and all she could hope for today was that the fragments might come together tomorrow. The task her father had set her had proved almost too easy, in that it would have been more comfortable to have spent another day searching and less fretting in the limbo of waiting. A heavy expectation and responsibility weighed her down, clenching her stomach painfully. Until things started to happen again, calmness would be a struggle.

Suddenly she straightened up, remembering that in her rush that morning she hadn't prayed. She had promised to pray, but each time events turned, her determination had been forgotten. She took a deep breath, as if to oxygenate a prayer into her brain. Praying was what she thought she was doing, but it was a sense of control that came over her body. Part affirmation, part sorrow, but either way this was God's day and she had not given him anything… remorse fed upon loneliness.

Wandering through the lounges looking for a quiet place, Caittie found herself in an odd little square room just off the lounge, surrounded by activity boards, where a dozen or so people seemed constantly on the move.

The busyness spun her back into the main hallway, where the faint chlorine smell from the swimming pool distracted her from her surroundings. Slowly the words on the small notice board started to register, with its list of names and times for treatments and massages. A dense scrawl of names and crossing outs on the booking sheets, most fully booked that day, a few slots open throughout the rest of the week.

Before she had motivated herself to turn and walk away, a pretty but over-dressed woman addressed her, while crossing out her own name on the booking form.

'Hey, are you free now? I'm supposed to have my facial and massage in five minutes, but my kid really wants me to watch his tennis.'

Caittie was taken aback. All this time she had almost deliberately avoided conversation, and people had only really talked to her on an official basis, except for the young man at dinner. Yet, it was a simple enough idea – a facial, a massage and time to kill. It seemed an unavoidable combination, but she still said, rather doubtfully, 'Are you sure it's OK for me to go instead of you?'

'Definitely. She's expecting somebody! Just scribble your name above mine and wait down that corridor, second door on the right.' Without further explanation, the woman dashed through the hotel, probably late for her son's tennis.

As Caittie was scribbling her name on the sheet, it dawned on her that she had never actually agreed. But she was holding the baton and she supposed she had to run with it. A few minutes later, a pristine beautician emerged from the room and called the other woman's name into the corridor.

A short explanation later, Caittie was leaning back while having delicious things done to her face. She started to pass into a drowsy trance as her mind relaxed and she found herself in her own type of conversation with God. As with most conversations with God, it was curiously one-sided – rhetorical questions that mysteriously cleared into answers. She wondered what Sharon would have thought of the massage (having scribbled Sharon's name on the booking sheet) and decided that Sharon would have undoubtedly loved it. Tomorrow she would have to throw herself back into "being" Sharon again. She could put the massage down, therefore, as essential preparation.

The beautician's touch was professional and, although Caittie was no expert on such matters, it dawned on her that sometimes the smallest things could make a difference. It reminded her of when sometimes she would exchange a foot rub with Wendy when either of them had endured a really bad day – it was distinctively the touch of a caring friend, whereas for some time all she had felt at Keith's hands was an inconvenienced "business as usual" sensation. Michael's touch, despite the strangeness of the circumstances, had appealed powerfully – probably because it was full of emotion. Caittie felt as if something had been pressing down and smothering her, almost as if she was only now regaining full feeling. As the beautician tidied her up, Caittie thought, *like so many troubled children, I was almost starved of emotion, which makes people desperate to avoid the madness of no emotion at all.*

Once she had paid, she seemed to float in a glow as she made her way back to her room. Life – and crucially, any adversity – seemed far less troublesome or difficult to cope with. She bathed and got ready for dinner, taking time out to stop and think, plan and pray. She had to keep faith with her father and Michael, but above all, with God. The complexities of what to do next no longer seemed some kind of panic, but rather a sequence of events where she had clear objectives to make and optional routes to follow.

Her faith felt drawn from what she had felt growing inside her throughout the past weeks and – especially – her recognition of those doors that opened in front of her whenever things seemed impossible. Now she felt different, as if she had been given a new life, above mere existence. She now she felt that she could be satisfied with anything in life as long as she lived it with integrity, whereas before she always felt inadequate against peer, partner or maternal pressures.

Making her way to dinner, Caittie felt alive and glowing. She hadn't been sitting down long when the same families from Friday arrived at the table. This time the children rushed to the seats, vying for best position. One of the mothers started to sort them out, while reserving herself the seat next to Caittie. The men seemed to be together on the other end and the children were now split up between the mothers. Caittie turned and smiled a friendly greeting.

'How are you? We didn't see you here yesterday. I'm Kathy, by the way.' The woman's voice was slightly nervous, but friendly.

'Yes, I was pretty late yesterday. I'm Caittie.' Instantly a slight flush hit her cheeks as she realised her real name had slipped out.

'Have you been to any of the badminton nights?'

Then followed a series of polite questions, typical questions that were warmly predictable: are you here on your own, what have you been doing today and have you been here before. This made it easy for Caittie to describe her facial and tell her about how much the hotel had changed over fifteen years. When the questions got more personal, she managed to steer back into the safe topic of all the children. Caittie sensed a touch of guilt in Kathy's attempt at friendliness, probably from having left her abandoned on Friday – Kathy seemed the sort of person that would care if she offended anyone.

As the evening wore on, Caittie couldn't help observing the interactions between them all. The atmosphere had definitely changed since Friday. The need for friendly reassurance on that first evening had excluded Caittie, but now (only a few days later, but having been in each other's pockets) Kathy was not alone in seeking some distance. In this microcosm, one could sense how holidays put friendships to the test and distance took away the overheating that was evident today and – if left to the extreme – could even end them.

The next morning Caittie was up, dressed, breakfasted and packed early. She had decided to keep hold of her father's notes. Despite the risk, they were precious to her and until she could decide what else to do with them, she would hold them. Checked out and taxiing into Okehampton, she tried the local travel agent. Last-minute holidays to Miami were hard to come by, and the girl was obviously unused to such requests. It might be easier in London, where she had the choice of plenty of shops, and specialist ones at that. The longer she stayed here, the less time she would have in the afternoon to sort something out.

On the long train journey Caittie contemplated what to do. She needed to give Michael two days' notice of her destination, but first she needed to get rid of her bags as it would look odd (not to mention feeling cumbersome) dragging them round London travel agents. Arriving at Waterloo and exiting the station, Caittie kept up a steady pace that made the wheels of the suitcase squeak reluctant behind her. After buying a London paper from a kiosk, she asked the seller for directions to the nearest hotels. Ten minutes later she was in the reception of the Mad Hatter Hotel, purely because she found the name irresistible. With a room booked for two nights (paid in cash), the receptionist was delighted to loan her their telephone directory.

Travel agents. Caittie needed to find the right package holiday, book it and pay for it as quickly as possible, so although phoning might be quicker, she would still have to show up in order to complete the full details and to pay. From the directory, she picked out some pages with a good cluster of agents in close proximity, so she could visit as many as she had to as quickly as necessary (her back-up plan was to just book a flight, but Michael had advised that package flights draw a lot less interest and if anyone was still seeking to intercept her, then any girl about her age or appearance might be checked). Ripping the pages out, folding them and putting them unobtrusively in her bag, she handed back the slightly lighter directory to the receptionist and set off to the tube station.

The first couple of travel agents didn't seem to have anything available immediately – or else lacked enough gumption to find out. What she did discover was that this time of year was early in the storm season and too hot generally for holidaying. Parts of Florida apparently shut down their hotels during this heat and humidity. Although a few holiday companies were now using this situation to offer Britons sun-scorched holidays, the strength of the pound had caused them to be pretty fully booked already.

The next agents sold more specialised holidays and with more persistence and a few phone calls, she had some options to consider. The sales rep was keen to get a whole package together and when Caittie suggested leaving out anything she didn't need from the list, she was soon pressured into changing her mind. The rep assured her that unless she had a complete holiday package or business trip in place, American immigration would cause her difficulties. This was the last thing Caittie wanted, so she stuck out the process of booking a full ten-day, three-centre trip. Over an hour later, she had a flight booked for Miami late on Wednesday. According to the holiday plan, it was to be a few days at Miami, followed by stops and tours of the Everglades. Not that she had any intention of going to the Everglades, but she would land with a pre-arranged hotel and it would be a good back-up and cover should anything go wrong.

After her previous experience of hanging around and trying to sort things out at the airport, it was relief to have all the paperwork delivered by courier Wednesday morning. While the holiday sales rep was sorting the money and doing the paperwork, Caittie had started to make notes on some borrowed notepaper, as she needed to encode the information and phone it through to Michael's contact as soon as she could. The timing was tight and wouldn't give her the full forty-eight hours if she waited until she got back to the hotel. Even worse was using the hotel phone. Scribbling furiously while the agent made the endless phone calls and her attempts to line up the holes punched down the side of the continuous paper feeding into the printer meant that she had enough time to encode the place, date, times and flight number. Then she needed to double-check it and be sure Michael would know everything, as they had no real back-up plan.

In the travel agent's, she realised things were coming into place, yet her stomach started rumbling embarrassingly as she had forgotten to eat again. Paperwork finished and with receipts in hand, she looked down the busy street. Surrounded as she was by office blocks, it wasn't hard to find a wine bar. They had improved after the stock market crash, not quite so obnoxiously full of yuppies and usually boasting a payphone for calling taxis. Still better was the time, at the end of the working day, with shops just closing and post-work office drinks not having started yet. The first one she found was quiet enough to make her dare to call the number Michael had given her. The gruff voice on the end said simply, 'Hello', and then 'Wait' in response to her 'I have new lucky numbers' opening, followed by an even gruffer 'Proceed' and 'Thank you' once she finished. She wondered who the contact was and how long and patiently he had been waiting for her. Once putting down the phone, flooded with relief, she remembered that, should Michael miss her for any reason, she could use this same number to encode a new message with alternative meeting place and time, even if she did have to make an international call.

Her call made, Caittie felt an unusual sense of achievement, although she knew from experience how quickly it could unravel if she took anything for granted. As Michael had told her, the more gaps in the plan, the faster you have to move, but at this point she had little choice other than to wait. The question was whether to wait doing something useful, assuming her cover was secure, or to continue to be evasive.

Back at the hotel, she decided to reread the information her father had given her over the two letters. The trouble as she saw it was simple – the biggest questions remained unanswered in her father's notes. Yet still more critical were the technical issues – if this time-shift was true, how had it happened? And why would anybody go to so much trouble to hide it? If it represented a natural occurrence then surely the authorities could have nothing to hide? If it was unnatural – if it even sprang from something literally alien, or supernatural... the deeper she went, the crazier the questions seemed. But it gave Caittie comfort to think that her father must have also run through such thoughts in his head, even if he never found enough time to put it into words. Having a whole day to herself tomorrow, she decided – despite any danger – she had to risk going to the British Library. It was something she had not done for years, but a greater research project she could not imagine. Even with her mind set for tomorrow, she had a restless sleep with so many unanswered bits of information floating round her head.

The next morning, she breakfasted early and was at the library by the nine-thirty opening time. Dr David Zink's books on the Bimini Road were disappointing in that they had nothing conclusive to say. Compared to how she had been taught herself, there seemed less system and more speculation to his investigations. Yet she had to agree, in the absence of proof, that there was little choice in some of his conclusions. She could easily imagine her father being unable to resist helping out on such expeditions. Although GAMF itself was taking a different route, it would seem logical that they might keep tabs on Dr Zink's trips in case they could sense an opportunity. The most worrying parts of the material she read were government-sponsored experts claiming that such a strange formation of stones were part of a natural formation. Of course, places like the Giants' Causeway initially seemed inexplicable, but in modern times the natural and unnatural were easily separated. From what she could read of the mineral findings they were unnatural, so why would a government expert say the opposite? She could certainly now understand her father risking his life on these expeditions, if he thought the truth was being hidden.

Flicking through other material linked to the Bimini Road she found the name Edgar Cayce kept cropping up. A psychic, he predicted in 1930 that Atlantis would be found in this Bimini area in 1968 or '69. From her notes, Caittie recalled that Dr Mason Valentine had announced this discovery in 1968. Cayce in his day had become a weird, almost religious, cult-like figure, having clearly impressed many learned people of his time. Some remained still desperate to prove his seeings true, but there was not enough in the Bimini Road that fitted with Atlantis.

After a sandwich in the library restaurant, Caittie continued her reading agenda for the day, including reports on the Bermuda triangle, the endless lists of missing vessels and strange occurrences. Harder to find and understand were the relevant reports from centuries past, as they couldn't separate the natural from the strange or the realistic from the superstitious.

Like any area of the world plagued by sudden storms, an element of superstition was not unexpected. Yet there was a degree of intensity and strangeness in the pattern in Bermuda that she could not see anywhere else. It wasn't just the sheer number of reports, the number of storms and their ferocity – by the end of the day, Caittie could see how easy it was to be dragged into the fantasies that so many people grasped at, using such things as UFOs to explain the inexplicable, but to her – a trained scientist – any calculation was strictly analytical. She was determined to keep an open mind until more information presented itself. Looking at her watch, she felt exhausted – it was four-thirty. She dreaded returning to the hotel, as it would make the evening interminably long.

Changing tables, she seized an abandoned newspaper out of an almost involuntary compulsion to stay in touch with the real world. However, instead of flicking through a few news pages and then jumping straight to the books, theatre and fashion, she found herself snatching at headlines and skimming. Well towards the end of the more obscure news items, she gasped. The watcher in her half-grasped that the people in close proximity to her looked over in annoyance – yet she had every excuse, as it was her name, her description, her job and most importantly her life in the column. She had been reportedly thrown from a balcony, with her boyfriend shooting himself afterwards. The police were not looking for anyone else in connection with her own murder.

Caittie's head spun sickly. Sharon was dead – instead of her. What *could* have gone so horribly wrong? Michael had promised that Sharon would be OK and now Sharon was dead. Poor silly Sharon! Yet her shock and guilt soon gave way to worry. Soon, somebody would spot the identity switch. All she could hope for was that although they might work out quickly that Sharon wasn't Caittie, that it might still take them time to identify Sharon as Sharon.

It was as if a time bomb had started to tick inside her chest. Sick inside, Caittie gathered her belongings up.

'Are you all right?' asked an older woman.

Caittie longed to confide in her – in anyone – but she couldn't allow herself. She said, 'Thanks, I'll be OK,' and in a numb blur headed back through the city to her hotel, though she couldn't help but weep when she was out of view and thus out of reach of sympathy. Yet at the same time she knew that sympathy – even from a stranger – could dissolve all the strength she had built up inside to complete this investigation. If she let this huge weight of remorse overcome her, she would be back to the same little girl that her mother and Keith had so effortlessly manipulated. All she could do was to hold back and to count the lives of her father, Michael's girlfriend and now Sharon as being wasted unless she stayed strong and completed her task. Only in finding the truth could all their sacrifices be remotely justified.

As much as she knew she would be hurting, the question was how to make sure her mother found out from Caittie what was going on rather than from anyone else – and in an untraceable way. She stopped by two phone boxes before finding one that worked.

The phone rang several times until it was answered, then just as she was about to blurt out her speech, it started her mother's recorded message ('so sorry, not around just now. Please leave a message after the beep'). Desperate and relieved at the same time, all Caittie could do was jumble out an abbreviated assortment of phrases. 'Mum, *so* sorry, but believe me, it wasn't me in Athens – I'm going to find what happened to Dad. I'll explain later, but I'm *still alive*! Love you, Caittie.' The more she thought about it afterwards the more it seemed the coward's way out, as it was too easy. It was a failure not being able to fulfil her promise of talking directly to her mother, but it was all she could do for now. More importantly it was short enough not to be traced, but without being rude.

The rest of the evening she felt too knotted up to eat, though she also didn't want to walk, where her red puffy eyes would draw attention. Instead she focused on the next day, finding solace in going through her clothes. Sorting out those unworn, those rinsed out but just dry, and those slightly worn that would do another turn. They had all been squashed into a rucksack or kept in a suitcase for so long that Caittie found it daily more difficult to assemble an outfit that didn't look shabby. Using the hotel trouser press and iron, she methodically checked, freshened and pressed every item she had. Even small marks were selectively sponged and then dried with the hairdryer. By the end of the evening, she was physically and mentally exhausted and went to sleep without resolving or even entirely facing the question of what her mother must be feeling right now.

The next morning she longed to be dressed and breakfasted early, but equally didn't want to be hanging around an unopened travel agency. Making tea, she consciously slowed herself down by thinking about the day ahead and how the disastrous news of yesterday might affect her plans. As much as she feared the little girl within her, she found herself kneeling and praying by the side of the bed. Such a humble and positive position for prayer she had not conceded to since she was around ten, but she was subconsciously seeking find that same simple style of prayer that as a little girl had brought her comfort. She needed to offer herself without question or doubt and just ask for the forgiveness, which was essential to enable her to carry on, carrying the heavy weight of guilt about Sharon. She kept reminding herself that she had seen the danger and had asked the right questions and only under Michael's reassurance conceded it was safe to proceed. The trouble remained that now, in full knowledge that the worst had occurred, she couldn't separate whether she had done it consciously for the right reasons or unconsciously deluded herself.

Once Caittie had taken the time to dress and do her hair as Sharon, it was a matter of keeping on the move again. Yet, despite this, all she could focus on was getting some answers from Michael about what had happened to Sharon. However, if she made it safely to Miami, at least he should be there. The thought of seeing him provoked a pounding heart, but she was also aware that she wanted explanations – that she was in fact quite angry at him at the moment.

At the travel agent's she had to wait for the tickets to arrive by courier, but at least that meant she didn't have to wait long at the airport. It seemed to take ages on the tube to get to Heathrow, especially dressed as Sharon with those long, male glances that Sharon's attire attracted. It seemed cheap and cruel to still use Sharon's image and passport as her own, but she had no choice.

Once at Heathrow, Caittie felt blissfully lost in the crowds of families jetting off on summer holiday season. Each queue kept her moving and hidden – only at each passport check did she feel really tense. The shock of the previous day had left a guilt inside that gave her a false sense of bravado, half wanting to be caught and punished, yet everything went smoothly as she slipped through with the package holiday procession. Once through passport control, she found herself in the bar trying to calm her nerves.

The nearer the plane came to takeoff, the more relaxed Caittie became, her attitude almost comically at odds with the behaviour of those around her. She was soon relaxed enough to doze most of the long flight – her brain was still trying to recover from a night of restless guilt and the shock of what had happened to Sharon.

25

Simply Impossible

All Andrew could do was to shake his head in disbelief. Yet another hope of a simple answer dashed before it had a chance! Even if this man wasn't part of some extremist group, how could he ever prove that he was truly from God?

This was beyond proof – and into the realms of pure belief. On the other hand, did it matter if Andrew only agreed to act on a good cause? If there was even the slimmest chance that he could get back home, he longed to take it. Yet how absurd was the question of how a dead man could convey such a message in the face of near-certain hostility? If the most prominent peace campaigners and scientists struggled to gain acceptance, what chance could *he* have? And also, what chance would there be of the greater public accepting anything without solid proof?

In the end, he told Peter, 'Look, no disrespect, but unless you're an expert in today's world, you don't have a chance of gaining attention, let alone acceptance. I agreed to help and I still don't mind trying, but what's the point unless I have enough credentials to succeed?'

'Emotional energy is what I need. There's no new science to divulge, only a new interpretation of what mankind has deduced so far. For many reasons, most people – given the absence of a more complete knowledge – simply fill in the gaps, using their best guesses. All you have to do is to convey the realignment of this reasoning. For example, just look at any genuine understanding of history and you'll see it dissected into convenient blocks or periods, whereas in fact it's a constant stream with each period affecting the next, or (in human terms) an interaction and flow of emotional energy. The trouble has been that the false assumptions of the past are often held onto in the absence of any alternative, just because they seem to fit. So don't worry about credentials, you just need to be able to defend the reasoning. Moreover, it is not about delivering anything as *fact* –

instead, it's about giving a new reason to enable choice. This will let people again be free to choose a path closer to God and truth.'

Andrew objected, 'But people are already free to choose! They're freer now than they've ever been!'

'How can people be free to choose when they are blinded by science and false assumptions? Mankind has adopted the philosophy that it either has or else will soon have all the answers, making God superfluous. They even believe that they're in control of their own destiny! Some accept God's laws, while others abuse the same laws to achieve social control. Many still respond to religion out of deprivation or in hopes of better things to come, on the strength of God's promises. Yet for most, religion has become marginalized.'

'I still don't see how a few bits of information would free people as you describe, enabling them to choose! If it could, well, to be honest, then I'd just head off and, well, do it.'

Even if only to get out of here, Andrew added to himself.

Peter half-laughed. 'Think of it as a jigsaw. All the pieces are there, but without the cover they'll mostly be put together wrongly. Introduce the picture and then one can search the pieces, choosing which ought to go where. Your job is to paint that picture – clearly, simply and plain for all to see. Then it will be up to individuals to see what it means to them.'

'I don't mean to be difficult, but frankly, what kind of people would set a task like that, only to contradict its supposedly noble aims by kidnapping and even coercing someone into helping them? Twice now I've asked why you keep me here under these circumstances and you've just avoided the question!'

Peter retorted, exasperated, 'But I *have* told you everything, you just choose to hear it differently! This is a common problem for people, as they consistently elevate the importance of their position. Look how throughout so much of history mankind was determined to believe that everything revolved around the earth, as if to exaggerate its importance… no, don't interrupt! Andrew, many years ago you worked out where you are, though for different reasons. Put everything I have told you together and create a new picture. One that agrees with your boyhood theory! Remember that deduction you made that you felt too frightened to share?'

It was more in anguish than anger, but Andrew knew he had to find or force the answer in some way, even if it meant playing along. The worrying thing was that, having accessed some seemingly impossible stuff from inside his own head, this man (or was he a man? The alien theory felt better and better) had every sort of information on him. The maze of questions spun round in his mind: 'Emotional energy', 'technically dead'...

'Oh my God,' the words slipped out, as if too powerful to keep inside. The boyhood theory sparked by the words that Jesus descended into hell and, on the third day, had risen again. How back then his juvenile mind had played 'scissors, paper, stone' with the reasoning and logic behind Jesus' descent, and then all such interactions between good and evil.

'You always knew,' said the man before him (if he was a man). 'Part of you always knew you would be called, and would then have to answer.'

And this was the strangest thing: one part of Andrew had always known.

26

Welcome to Miami

As the plane bumpily landed, Caittie's head felt fuzzy, still half-asleep and throbbing with the surging sound of the engines (why did the reverse thrust sound angrier than the take-off, she'd often wondered).

All the prospects of what might happen upon landing (having encircled her several times, both awake and dreaming) were now pushed aside. There was little she could do now if her assailants had tracked her down and were waiting for her, beyond praying and hoping. Part of Caittie still hoped that the notoriously laidback attitude of the Greek police and the lack of time for any enemy to track the connection should be security enough for now. Her emotions were instead consumed with the call to her mother, which now felt inadequate, clumsy, and incomplete.

Yet, even though she now knew she had no choice other than to make the call, the possibility that it might still have provided a clue to her father's killers added insecurity and nerves to her list of current failings.

As she walked off the plane and queued at immigration control, she got a sense that if internal European holiday control was perhaps over-relaxed, then the USA was by comparison perhaps over-intense. People ahead of her were being questioned in turn, some for ten minutes, others for much longer, while papers were being checked as fastidiously as if the authorities were paranoid about anyone's spending a second longer in America more than they were allowed to.

It was almost a relief when it was her turn. The polite black man said, 'And why are you here, Miss?'

'A holiday.'

'A vacation,' the man corrected her.

'Yes, it's – it's all in the papers, the Everglades, especially.'

'And all on your own?'

She smiled faintly. 'That doesn't bother me.'

It seemed to satisfy the official, who went on to make sure that her itinerary was as clear in her mind as in the documentation. It was indeed all in her papers, but really in order to make sure she was genuinely here on holiday and knew where she was going. Meanwhile, in the queue to her left there was a sudden commotion, with a garishly-shirted man now surrounded by unsmiling security.

He shouted, 'It's a dark-blue pen! It's practically black! Is this some kind of joke? What price American tolerance?'

'But only black is acceptable,' objected the official, over the heads of the massively overweight security men, all with guns strapped to their flanks.

'And that's in the Constitution?' whipped back the objector.

The man's protests continued as he was escorted down the corridor. The last Caittie heard was a grovelling apology at the prospect of being arrested for his sarcasm. For her, life was less problematic. It was merely a matter of being Sharon, where simple questions demanded straightforward answers. Despite this, the man behind the desk seemed unnervingly distracted by something on his screen. Just when she thought he was about to become rather more intense, with a click of a button he handed her papers back to her and told her to move on: she was clear.

Sailing through customs, Caittie started wondering what to do next, her heart pounding unnaturally at the prospect of possibly seeing Michael at any moment.

Her holiday supposedly boasted a shuttle bus towards the first hotel, from which the tour would start. However, it seemed simpler to search for Michael first, and get a taxi to the hotel later if all else failed. Caittie strolled up and down the rows of people inside and then the rows of cars and taxis at the pick-up point without luck. Twice she imagined she had spotted him: once a dark man lithe as a whip but rather too young, another time someone of the right age and cast of countenance but far too heavy-set.

In the end, she decided to find a seat just inside at the airport and wait a couple of hours, periodically patrolling for any signs. After all, she had given Michael less than the 48-hour notice he had asked for and it was more than possible his connection flight was unavoidably later than hers. Perhaps if no one had showed up in an hour or so she could investigate flight connections from Greece.

Sitting on the end of a row of seats, she took several minutes making herself comfortable, pulling her bags close to her as if preparing to camp out, while ensuring that all of her gear was out of the way of the constant stampede of people near the entrance.

Her heart bounded as she suddenly imagined that she'd heard his voice. Although it wasn't quite his – instead there was some twenty-something of Mediterranean countenance holding her gaze for a moment before saying quietly, 'Don't worry, Michael sent me.'

The relief freed her throat. She hadn't realised how taut she had been.

'Michael sent you? Is he all right?'

'Absolutely. He knows about the trouble with Caittie's identity in Athens and he warns you to be careful. He'll explain everything when it is safe.'

Caittie picked up her gear, which the young man helped her with.

He said, 'Now, when I've finished going through your instructions, just name the hotel where you stayed on Dartmoor and leave. Please don't turn or acknowledge this conversation in any way. From here you are to get a taxi to Dadeland Shopping Mall on North Kendall Drive. Repeat, please.'

Caittie did.

'Good. Please ask to be dropped at the western end. Walk straight through the mall towards J C Penny's. Go straight through and out the other side. No matter what, just keep walking – don't look worried, don't look round. Please repeat these instructions.'

Caittie repeated them – again she was word-perfect. The man said, 'Excellent. Now, as you enter the car park, keep walking straight towards the orbital road. A car will stop alongside you. It will have something you immediately recognise on its back seat. Throw your case in, get in and lie down across the back seat. Please don't sit up until instructed to do so. Is that clear?'

'Yes,' said Caittie. She had been stunned at first, but with each second her mind gradually caught up with the words and the situation.

'And have you a word for me?' asked the man, softly.

'The Manor,' she whispered, 'The Manor Hotel.'

'Good luck,' he breathed, and she started to gather her things. Smoothly, without hesitation or rush, her bags in hand, she made her way to the exit.

The taxi driver insisted upon putting her bags in the boot – not her personal preference, but Caittie decided not to draw attention to herself by insisting otherwise. She was still disappointed not to have seen Michael, but she didn't doubt that he was behind everything she was doing. Miami was humid and seemed disconcertingly, achingly bright, its wide roads covered with cars. Twenty minutes later, after deflecting the usual taxi-driver questions with vague answers, she arrived at the western end of Dadeland Mall.

It seemed such a huge site that Caittie felt a bit odd as she started out on her instructed trek, lugging her case behind her. Loaded down with shopping bags would have felt fine, but a suitcase seemed rather out of place. As she dragged the wheels along, they seemed to make more noise than ever, as if they too were secretly protesting. Slowly she walked straight down the centre, wondering whether someone might be watching her every move. It was some comfort, though, to realise that all she could do was keep her head down and follow the instructions.

After crossing what felt like acres of shopping area, she entered and weaved her way through J C Penny's. Finally, just when the exit door in front of her began to feel like an anticlimax, an ear-piercing crack whipped behind her, freezing her instinctive flinch into shock. It could only be a gunshot and the sound lasted an endless second, during which she almost longed for a bullet to hit. Then, as Michael had once instructed her, she landed on the floor, twisting her left wrist with the impact. The stunned silence of what seemed like a lifetime was instantly followed by multiple screams behind her.

Resisting her immediate impulse to flee, Caittie took cover under a rack of discount clothing. The noises behind continued so surreal, with the echo of shots giving way to shouting, and she decided to take her chance on heading for the exit. Within moments, she heard police sirens blaring, and sweating, she half-walked, half-trotted down the slope outside the mall. Halfway between the mall and the road, a car sped, only to stop abruptly beside her. On the back seat was a plain black leather strap that her back remembered instantaneously. It had to be Michael, she thought, as the driver's arm was furiously waving for her to jump in.

Opening the back door, she dived in. Before she could turn to shut the door, the driver had hit the accelerator. She had glimpse of a crowd of onlookers – white, dark, pale. She said sharply, 'What the hell is going on?' Her fear and helplessness demanded the question, though she had already relaxed, recognising Michael's taut, toned back.

'Shut up and keep your head down,' he told her, as it was clear that his driving absorbed most of his attention. Even if Caittie had dared to insist upon an answer, the force of directional changes at speed shifted her around as the car braked and cornered. With each passing minute, Michael's eyes constantly checked his mirror, as the intensity of his driving slowly subsided.

Finally he said, 'Right, you can sit up now!'

Caittie slowly pushed herself upright and for the first time got more than a vague glimpse of their direction. Expecting Michael to have set up somewhere cosy and safe in order to exchange information, it was confusing to see that they were now in what she could only imagine was downtown Miami. Both houses and people were in stark contrast to the forced cleanliness of the airport and the ostentatiously affluent mall. Had she not been with Michael, she would have felt worried. Even as it was, she asked, 'Where are we?'

'Don't worry, we're not stopping,' Michael sounded almost amused.

Within just a few blocks and a couple of corners, they turned onto a main route out of town.

'When are you going to tell me what's going on?' Caittie made sure that her impatience showed.

'Soon, very soon. In just a few minutes, we'll grab something to eat and have a chance to talk.' As he talked, he pointed up the road – just ahead were flashing blue neon lights urging the passer-by to stop: 'Hot food, great diner.'

Pulling in, Michael drove through the car park and round the back (she had forgotten how muscular his shoulders were). Still without speaking, he jumped out of the car, opened the trunk and reappeared with a screwdriver and a new set of number plates. As swiftly as if he had done it a dozen times before, he moved round the car and in a couple of minutes changed them, urging, 'Come on, chuck your things in the boot!'

A moment later, in a quiet corner, Caittie could see him better. Was it stress or were his eyes more shadowed, his lips tauter than she remembered? Pity seized her, but she was still angry.

'What happened to Sharon, then?' she demanded, as softly as she could. 'You promised me!' Caittie went to continue but Michael put his hand up to stop her.

'Please. Keep your voice down and I'll explain. You were only let into the country because it's likely that they suspected the switch and were hoping to follow you. In other words, the Americans had two choices: either to detain you, in which case we wouldn't now be talking, or to suspect that they needed you for something – meaning that they needed to follow you.'

'But those gunshots – were they meant for me?' Caittie's voice betrayed her worry that events were outside her own planning and thinking. She had only ever really considered being politely arrested in a true British style and shootouts were as beyond her imagining as any other abrupt awakening of fear.

'Of course not! When they let you through, you were undoubtedly picked up by the secret service. I sent you to the mall because several drug-related gun battles have occurred there in recent years, making it a target for undercover police and security. When one of my men fired his gun in the air it was to cause a diversion. In short, we stopped them from taking you out, especially if that was their instruction, to avoid the risk of losing you again!'

'I don't understand,' said Caittie flatly. 'Why would the Americans be against me?'

Michael held up his hands. 'OK. Fine. I'll tell you. The reason we're in this situation now is Keith!'

'What the hell could Keith possibly have to do with this?' Caittie's voice rose as she couldn't control her fear.

'Your boyfriend –'

'He's *not* – I mean, I dropped him!'

'Caittie, I know this will shock you, but we're pretty sure that Keith killed Sharon.' Michael put his hand on Caittie's arm as her eyes blanked out whitely. 'Once we did a couple of trips with Sharon dressed as you to kick up a false trail, he suddenly turned up. Even stranger is that we're 99% sure Keith was seen entering the flat just before she was killed.'

Caittie found her voice. 'But why would Keith harm me? Or someone he thought was me?'

Michael's arms held her so hard that it hurt, though she could only imagine it was meant in support. He said, 'We can only assume he was supposed to be on a surprise visit. The only trouble was that at the door, he could tell Sharon wasn't you and that he had been fooled by our tricks. All we can assume is that, in this confusion, he had no other choice than to kill Sharon, followed by her boyfriend. Although he probably tried to get as much out of Sharon as he could first.'

Caittie cried out in panic, 'But Keith couldn't kill anybody!' Caittie either couldn't or wouldn't take in what she was hearing. But Michael was still surer.

'Listen, your precious Keith knew the address of my uncle's man – an address possible for none to know or to trace unless they had some connection with the secret service. And then – and then – your Keith was seen afterwards talking with some authority to the Greek secret service agents who we believe to have been duped.'

Caittie interrupted, 'Are you telling me that Keith is a spy?'

'Figure it out yourself! Killing Sharon also forced the official identification issue, which will soon expose the switch and enable them to access an international arrest warrant on an official and public basis. All I can hope is that the information you have from your father will let us move quickly before events overtake us!'

But Caittie was in no mood to agree. Instead, she said, deliberately slowly, in an attempt to calm them both, 'So, however you look at it, I killed Sharon?'

'Of course not!'

'Excuse me. We set her up and I practically led Keith to her!'

For a moment Michael seemed to tower above her – no longer sexy, or benign – or indeed anything except furious.

'Look, they've already killed my Katya, your father, almost certainly George and probably anyone else that gets in their way! We can either let them have the information, in which case they will doubtless kill us for daring to know it, or make sure there's no secret to keep anymore. Giving up would only be an option because it's easier than fighting!'

Caittie sat silently for a few seconds, until Michael started to drum his fingers on the table. Finally she said, 'OK, we carry on, but only on condition that we don't risk anyone else besides ourselves.'

'That may be difficult depending on what information you have, but I can at least assure you that I will only involve those not already committed by informed consent only. I'll tell them enough to be able to understand the risk.'

She said, impulsively, 'Then the first person we need is Frank.

George told my father, just before he disappeared, about the casket found on the Spanish galleon. The one that didn't carbon date correctly. George had tracked down the words on the casket to a text he had seen before and it led to a manuscript from the Spanish Inquisition. A monk's report of a French ship captured and sunk. This monk was marooned with the prisoners and it turns out these Frenchmen showed up in the 1715 storm, but sailing under Napoleon. They had been time shifted nearly one hundred years and the report tells how they died, with the bones of the guards and some prisoners buried together. What my father was doing was going with somebody called Zink –'

'Ah,' breathed Michael, 'And his psychic!'

'Well, he has *ties* to psychics, I think. I believe that's why he called him, in order to locate the mass grave. Dad called it a "forensic utopia of bones" that might prove to be the final piece of the puzzle with regard to some kind of time-shifting in the Bermuda Triangle.'

'Which is where Bimini comes in!'

'Exactly. He was heading towards Bimini when he disappeared. I also suspect that there might be more to it than this, but my father never left any hints as such?' Caittie inflected this into a question, hoping that Michael's memory might be able to add some additional information.

He frowned thoughtfully. 'I don't know whether I actually have any hints, but I do have a couple of worries. Firstly, do you have a precise location on Bimini itself? It's a larger and busier place than you might imagine and would take a lifetime to search. And secondly, if you *do* have a location, why need we involve Frank?'

Caittie could hear the pent-up resentment in his voice. Her power now resided in the secret location, she had worked that out already. It was why she hadn't just told Michael before – and why she wouldn't tell Frank. Each would learn the story only a piece at a time and only when she felt sure it was right.

Michael had a good point though – why tell Frank? Plus, how would she feel if the adventure put Frank's life in danger too? But in the end she couldn't find a strong enough reason to disagree with her father. This had all started with GAMF, so perhaps they should finish it together – even if her father had to be represented by herself.

She said, 'Dad instructed me to get Frank involved – that's why. Also, we have fifty miles of ocean to cross from here and he believed that it would be far better than walking into any obvious trap at Bimini airport.'

'Oh well,' said Michael, 'If your father wanted it that way, then I guess we should go along with it. Let's hope poor Frank finally won his skipper's licence!'

'What kind of licence?'

Michael said sardonically, 'Frank was training to be able to take us out as our very own ocean-going skipper. It would be nice – though surprising – if Frank had ever completed something successfully! So! Tell me, how do we find him?'

'We need to leave a message at Brickwell Harbour Condo, post box 161. In the note we have to specify a place to meet him the next day – and, if that fails, we need to repeat the process the following week.'

Michael said flatly, 'Frankly Caittie, I don't think we *have* a week. We need to move fast and then either use what we have or reach safety until we can! Look, why don't we make a deal? We leave Frank a message and if he doesn't get back to us then allow me to locate a skipper who can take us instead. Then, once we return, we message Frank again and tell him what we found. Remember, he may not even be alive.'

Caittie knew that they needed to keep moving. It felt faintly disloyal to her father's instructions, but his intention had to be more important than the words themselves.

'I suppose you're right, under the circumstances. After all, it can't be long before they trace Sharon here.'

'Exactly. Now I need to make some calls. I left some men keeping watch on our trail. If they say it's clear, we need to make plans.' A couple of minutes later he was back, half-smiling. 'Still mayhem at the shopping mall, but it seems that they have no idea where we went. So I'm going to book us into the motel here for tonight, if that's all right with you.'

Caittie nodded, and he continued, 'I've also decided on a place to meet Frank, should he pick up the message – a bar called Cap's Place Restaurant up at Lighthouse Point. It's on a spit of land with a single access causeway which will let us easily control the situation.'

Caittie had found herself thinking while he'd been gone. Finally she said reluctantly, 'I recall something Dad said about Frank. I know he wanted me to contact him, but it also seemed clear that he doubted

Frank somehow – or at least, as if he thought Frank might be holding something back.'

'I never liked him, as you might guess. He's not a man of honour. In fact, I think we should ignore him – it would be a lot easier.' Michael's relief was as if a hostess had admitted there was something wrong with her food and he could at last confess to the bad taste in his mouth.

But Caittie still shook her head. 'No, I feel that we should honour my father's wishes. If we post the message tomorrow morning, with a meeting time in the afternoon, we could allow a choice of being there the same time the next day. Of course, it'd be safer to keep moving, rather than hanging around, so if he picks up the message immediately we could gain a day. But can you really get everything ready as soon as tomorrow?'

'Sure – the men will act as an early warning if they spot anyone suspicious coming near the place.'

'Thank you,' she said impulsively, and he responded warmly, 'I like this plan, you have your father's brains!'

'I have my own brains – my father wasn't around long enough to leave me much!' Caittie gave Michael a glance that suggested that such subjects of comparison were taboo. 'And another thing, I'd like to have some kind of watch kept on the postbox. I don't know what Frank looks like, but you should, even if it has been a long time!'

As always, Michael's attention to detail was reflexive.

'Yes – why not? I'll organise a change of vehicle for tomorrow, we don't want to be using the same car even if I've already changed the plates.'

Back in the motel, Michael had left instructions that if she wanted to change and freshen up she was afterwards to remain dressed. He had only booked the one room as it aroused less suspicion if anyone at the motel thought he was someone with a prostitute and – still dressed as Sharon – Caittie could pass for one. However, his reassurance that he would sleep in the chair for a few hours seemed genuine if also unnerving, but then, he could always – if so disposed – have taken advantage of her in Crete. As for staying dressed, this was just a precaution in case they needed to move quickly.

Michael's men had spotted a couple of dozen secret service

personnel at the mall, enough to allow them to extensively trawl local hotels in hopes of picking up their trail. After a couple of hours Michael returned in a different car, wearing an easy smile that jerked Caittie's heartbeat (was she really spending the night with him – at least in the same room – and yet not *with* him?).

Everything was ready for tomorrow, but first they had to wait out the night. Trying as she might to sleep, she couldn't help noticing that he was calmly reading a book as if it was just another day in the undercover life he had long since grown accustomed to. All those years holed up in strong houses and covert travel had made this near-normality for him. Yet to Caittie, the strong muscles of his shoulders were at once a comfort and a provocation, the taut lines of his thighs spurring an uprush of desire.

She fell asleep eventually, only to be awoken by Michael's hand softly stroking her side, just where her back morphed into her breast. Caittie held her breath, conflicted with nerves and feeling. His hand moved more surely, locating the nucleus of her breast, then the core of her sensuality. His lips, warm and urgent, sought hers – was this a final admission of her inadequacy? Yet she couldn't help responding. He had found her, after all, and he owned her – he owned her more than any other person could ever hope to do. They finished up convulsing in unison, her above him, him inside her, and they both knew – however resistant she still felt in some ways – that for her nothing would ever be the same again.

The next morning she awoke to find Michael already gone, though he had left a note: 'Come to the next-door diner when you're ready, M.' Because they wouldn't be coming back to the same place again, he reckoned that it was safe enough to breakfast next door. She met his eyes with embarrassment until she saw that his were smiling.

As soon as they were seated and placed their order, he produced a notepad and began to write to Frank.

GAMF reunion. Cap's Place Island Restaurant, Lighthouse Point. 4pm today if possible, or we hope to see you at the same time tomorrow. If you're away we'll catch up soon.'

The envelope simply marked *Frank* felt warm in her hands as they drove across Miami. Eventually they made their way along the waterfront and past the many new high-rise condo blocks, until they found Brickwell Harbour condo. As soon as Caittie entered the lobby, she put the envelope through the postbox. Back in the car, Michael weaved across the car park, stopping when they had a clean line of sight towards the lobby door. From under his seat he extracted a set of binoculars and propped them on the seat between.

Caittie said uneasily, 'Do you want me to use these?'

'Not necessarily, but I need your clever young eyes. Keep a lookout for anything and anyone looking stressed or out of place,' and he gripped her hand, momentarily, just powerfully enough to leave the mark of his fingers on it.

They sat with the radio on, in a state of equal tension, but by three o'clock Michael seemed relieved and pleased that no one had appeared out of the ordinary – certainly there had been no sign of Frank. It therefore seemed reasonable to accept his suggestion to leave a little early, so as to get to the restaurant ahead of time. This would enable them to get a bite to eat, as they hadn't lunched (though Caittie, at least, hadn't even noticed).

Surprisingly, the journey took almost no time. Once they reached Interstate 95, the miles slipped past, and ten minutes after leaving the off-ramp they were in the restaurant car park. Caittie's first impression was that it seemed an odd place, boasting storm damage both old and new. It was hard to avoid the impression that there had been a management decision to do only minimal repairs, in case another storm would be along soon.

By the time four o'clock came, they had been seated and served a drink and snack. By 4:15 they were discussing what to do when Michael halted mid-sentence. A heavy fellow with still-ruddy hair, appearing nearer sixty than fifty, had come up towards their table, extending a hand.

'Howya doing Mike, old man?'

'So you're still alive then?' Michael's hand met Frank's.

'I think you could safely call me a survivor,' said Frank. 'So, what sort of reunion is this? – You never said to bring wives, partners or floozies!'

Michael said coldly, 'This is Caitlin, involuntarily co-opted, by her father, as the fifth member of GAMF.'

Frank whistled. 'Not the famous Caittie! Won't she find it hard to talk about old times? Besides, I thought we'd agreed to drop any further GAMF activities?'

Michael said evenly, 'No, though I do recall that you were in favour of it. What actually happened after we split up was that George uncovered an ancient document on the French Captain's box. He knew where it came from and how it got there. Caittie's father died looking for the answer. I don't know about you, but if this answer might give us our lives back, then why shouldn't we give it a go?' Michael's hand was raised in order to stop Caittie interrupting.

'I told you before to leave this alone, didn't I?' snapped Frank.

Caittie cut in, 'Look, we're going ahead, either with you or without you.'

Frank looked surprised.

'What do you mean?'

'I mean this, it was my father's wish to keep you involved – but we need to move fast!'

Frank said mildly, 'But hey, what's all the rush? It's been fifteen years already, right?'

Michael's hands gripped his seat so hard that his knuckles whitened. 'Listen, this time we've got the location to find the *proof.* A proof that will rank us amongst the most famous discoverers of all time!'

Caittie was distressed, but Frank's expression quelled any protest. Michael knew Frank of old, she quickly saw he was attacking him at his weakest point.

Frank said, slowly, 'You mean, there's something genuinely new here? Wow, great! Why don't you give me the location so we can all figure out what we're in for?'

'Have you passed your skipper's exams yet?' asked Michael shortly.

'Years ago!'

'And can you get hold of a boat that could take us to Bimini? If not, I'm sure I could do it.'

'Listen, mate, I own one forty-foot ocean-going beauty! It's got –'

'When can we take it across?' Caittie beat Michael to the question.

Frank, beaming at her, was in his element. 'Best time to sail is in the evening, overnight. It's a good fifty to Bimini and can take roughly eight hours – depending on the weather, of course. But, before we get too excited, perhaps you might give me a clue about what we'll be doing once we get there?'

Ignoring Michael's entreating brown eyes, Caittie said, 'We'll be digging for graves, so we need to plan for a few days, at least.'

'Graves?'

'If you remember, my father got hold of a box capable of being carbon-dated far out of line of any probability. The graves we're looking for might just explain the carbon-dating problem.'

Conscious of an involuntary movement from Michael, Caittie finished, rather lamely, 'Which is, well, where you come in.'

Frank objected, 'Sorry, but I still don't quite understand –' causing Caittie to rush in with, 'Look, can we sail tonight or not? If so, I will tell you more once we are on the boat – enough to convince you before we get too far.'

'Tonight?'

'She doesn't mean…' Michael broke in, but Frank interrupted, 'OK, tonight, then – have it your own way – but only on the condition that you tell me the rest as soon as we leave harbour.'

'Frank, she can't even tell *me* until we get there. If she says we have enough information to find it, then I have to say, I trust her.'

'And so do I, of course!' Frank agreed, adding, 'I'll get the boat fuelled and ready, though we don't have a whole lot of time if you really want to leave tonight. If you two can swipe some food supplies and digging tools, we can meet at the Brickwell Harbour condo.'

'I know it well,' said Michael drily.

'Good. Just across from the marina, wait out at the end of the jetty. Maybe seven-thirty?'

Michael looked at Caittie, but she said firmly, 'Seven-thirty.'

Once Frank had left, first shaking their hands in a much friendlier way than previously, Michael and Caittie had plenty of time to drive back. At one point Michael stopped and made a couple of calls while Caittie rushed into shops buying supplies. He kept continually checking his watch, as if the calls might be timed (probably speaking to his men). Well before the named time, they arrived in the car park that Frank had specified.

'Ready?' he asked, after drumming his fingers irritably for several minutes.

'When you are.'

'Good. Then let's get the supplies out of the boot and wait at the end of the jetty.'

As Caittie helped him, she caught a dizzying sense of his closeness, reminding her of the previous night. And yet at the same time she thought, bleakly, *But that's all over, in the past. And, whatever happens on Bimini happens for good.*

27

Hell hath no theory never scorned

Hell.

But how could that be? It was fine to theorise and contemplate, but every inch of Andrew passionately longed to reject his own conclusions. Sitting on the edge of his bed, breathing almost theatrically slowly, he felt so *real* – even though (still more powerfully) came the feeling that such considerations were never intended for the here and now. Surely sanity itself demanded that such theories be kept distant?

Even as a boy, Andrew had always felt that the announcement of Jesus' post-death descent into hell perilously conflicted with everything he'd been otherwise led to believe. For example, how could the seeming collusion between God and the devil at the beginning – and also the end – of the Bible be reconciled with the Bible's every other portrayal of Satan? Psychology, realism, rationalism and every other tool Andrew found to hand served only to reinforce this conclusion. It came down to weighing such contradictions against each other, and his irresistible conclusion was that the image of Satan was largely man-made.

The reason was, when he had to accept the presumption that there was only one all-powerful God, then its corollary seemed equally insistent: Satan could only exist if God *allowed him to*. And surely such an allowance could only be collusion by some other name. Only then did Andrew notice, with sinking heart, that there were no contradictions, just the same paradoxes he had long since discovered in most spiritual matters, where something appeared to be both true and untrue at the same time. In short, it wasn't about which interpretation was right or wrong, but instead about how mankind had wilfully elected to misinterpret God's agenda at different points of its history. Which seemed – very annoyingly – exactly the conclusion that Peter/Pierre had given him before.

'You seem shocked. Do you need a few minutes to consider?' Peter waited, but his voice couldn't quite lose its edgy eagerness that suggested that they needed to carry on.

Andrew said testily, 'I don't know what you want me to say! One side of me says you must be pulling my leg, but the other side has to concede you know more about me than seems humanly possible. Or – in other words – you are who you say you are.'

'When you were anticipating something so very different! However, you agreed to the task and therefore you have a job to do, a job which might even be considered *earthly*.'

But Andrew remained troubled.

'But why didn't you just say you were – *the* – Peter, Jesus' rock, right at the beginning? If you'd done that, you should have known enough to assume I'd comply with anything you asked!'

Peter said, as patiently as he could manage, 'You had to accept the task *without* knowing, for this is not only about doing right, but about doing right for the right reasons. In other words, anyone acting by God's instruction could be acting out of *fear* of God rather than for the *love* of God!'

'But in the past –'

'Exactly! Different things might have been necessary in the past, due to the fear and superstition of those times, but all this has changed. If a criminal is prevented from committing a murder out of fear of punishment, then he may well lead a better life, but might still remain full of murderous desires. Being good – or godly – is all about losing even such intent towards evil and thus gaining integrity of the soul.'

'Of course I accept what you say, but it still makes no sense, in that God doesn't *need* to empower any messenger!'

Peter said irritably, 'Haven't you heard that there will be no more prophets? In the past, any man doing God's work would have needed miracles to prove his saintliness. A prophet then would either be working with the blessing of a sovereign or be seen as a serious threat to one! Travel, communication, the written word, the printed word and every other thing that has flowed from these have all grown, one upon the other, to be a greater power than any single sovereign or government. There's no longer any need for a prophet to prove anything – instead, it's for mankind to hear the truth and discern it amongst the clamour of falseness!'

'I think you're still slightly missing the point, which is – how do we convince people of God's existence without God?'

Peter said tolerantly, 'Oh, I think most people by now know that God exists – or could exist. The problem is what will require them to put in some effort into sorting out the truth from all the falsehoods surrounding them. For atheists, agnostics and all those that hold fast to a superficial belief (or disbelief), there comes at some point a problem that every rationalist explanation in the world cannot solve. They can peevishly claim that God failed to make things clear enough for them, but in truth, God has done more than mankind could ever have hoped for. Therefore, should any of these aggrieved sorts complain, 'It's not my fault, because God didn't prove Himself!' then they could be said to have sealed their own fate. As for you, as much as you try and question the intentions behind what is being asked of you, it will still all come down to the simple question, did you do enough with the information you had to enable others to see the truth?'

Andrew said honestly, 'Perhaps that's why I keep trying to say that this all seems a bit impossible.'

'Is that your answer?'

'Of course not!'

'And your answer is?'

It was the moment of his life, but he scarcely knew that. He drew a deep breath and said, 'Yes, of course – with reservations, mind.'

After all, if you have a mountain to climb, the sooner you get going, the sooner you'll get to the summit.

28

A long beach trip

Michael gestured towards the water. They had been standing at the ocean's edge for some time and – beautiful as the setting was – Caittie had felt nothing more than both awkward and exposed. Yet (what a relief!) coming towards them was a largish yacht with its searchlight flashing in their direction, crossing the fading light.

'That's got to be Frank!' said Michael, with a frown.

'How do you know?'

'He was always like a kid showing off new toys, especially to a friend who had never seen them before. Luckily we're not trying to draw attention to ourselves!'

A few minutes later, the middle-aged man had pulled in and jovially beckoned them on board. Although Frank was keeping the boat as tight to the jetty as he could by using the engines, it still sounded as if he was deliberately revving them. Michael, holding onto a side-rope until they were both embarked, couldn't disguise his irritation. When Frank pulled away with an over-zealous burst of the engines, it almost made Caittie lose her balance. Frank's immediate glance said it all, while Caittie could only imagine what Michael was thinking. As for her, she was deciding that Frank looked like good 'cover'. With his Hawaiian shirt and loose beige shorts over his taut legs, he looked absolutely nothing like a person on a covert mission.

'Weren't we were going to talk first?' Caittie had now reached Frank at the steering wheel.

'Hey, I thought you guys were in a hurry!' said Frank, with a grin. 'Look at it this way – if you tell me something I don't like, we can always turn back.'

As Caittie told Frank most of what she knew about the monk and the events, he stroked his chin thoughtfully. As the techno part of GAMF, Frank was the perfect person to run some of her ideas across. At the same time, she managed to avoid his subtle questions with regards to the location the monk had described for the graves.

Frank seemed neither surprised nor unsurprised by what she told him, as his eyes stayed focused on the sea. All she could assume was that her story was enough, as he held the same course. Caittie had anticipated rather more questions, but in the awkward silence that followed, it seemed more logical to locate Michael who still hadn't joined them. The light was fading when she went below deck to where Michael was sitting, frowning, at some papers. She busied herself putting the supplies in the proper cupboards or in the fridge. Just as she finished, the boat suddenly lurched far more than the waves had caused before. Caittie's heart leaped into her throat – surely this was some change of mind – or at least, direction? She still had a compass in her bag from Dartmoor and sure enough they were now heading farther south than required.

'Michael.'

'Yes?'

'Have a look at this.'

His eyes met hers. In another moment she was scrambling up on deck in his wake.

'What's going on?' challenged Michael, but Caittie doubted that Frank could hear him over the engine.

'Why have we changed direction?' Caittie shouted, more forcefully.

Frank glanced at her, but said nothing.

'If you're going to back out at least tell me why!'

'Keep your hair on, we have to go round the waterspouts!' Frank pointed over to the side.

Caittie turned and went to the rail at the side of the deck as if she couldn't believe what she was seeing. 'My God, what's that?' All she could see in the dim light was some kind of monster sucking up the water with a straw. A tornado-like column of water, some way off, stretched from the ocean right up to the clouds. The menacing twilight of the very low sun, combining with the darkness of the clouds, completed the sense of the surreal.

'The weather forecast was a bit tricky, but you have to put up with that at this time of year. The only course of action is to turn at right angles away from them in case they are travelling at speed. We will get back on course as soon as we can pass this one!' Frank sounded very casual.

'Aren't they dangerous?' Caittie had seen news reports of

tornadoes and hurricanes and the devastation caused.

'Bloody dangerous if you let one run over you, it could spit a boat of this size out, no problem. But hey, you get used to them in this area and you get used to dealing with them!' Frank was trying to sound self-assured, but even to Caittie now it sounded a repeat of his earlier boastful self. 'By the way, could you tell Michael I'll need him at eleven for a couple of hours to take over here, then if you could do from one to three, I'll be back for the final approach. It's nothing to worry about, I'll do the change-over and show each of you what to do and the heading!' Caittie nodded and went below to find Michael. Under the noise of the boat, he proceeded to tell her what had been happening.

'The men kept tabs on the secret service personnel who showed up at the mall, while Charlie watched the single access road to the peninsular at Cap's Place. According to the second team, a car had pulled up and talked to the secret service men outside the mall, but the driver never got out, so we've got no description beyond middle-aged male. However, a car of the same make was spotted near the peninsular during our meeting with Frank. In short, it's possible that Frank is being followed. It's also possible that he's *having* himself followed.'

Caittie struggled with this. 'But is he with us or not?'

'To be honest, I just don't know. He didn't pick up the note himself, so we know he's not working alone.'

'But we have no other choice other than to trust him!'

'Wrong, Caittie! There's trust and trust. Don't tell him a syllable more than he needs to know! But in one respect, our hand is being forced. Costas told me that Sharon's false identity has been traced to you, so our time is running out even faster than I thought it was.'

'You mean they've tracked my flight?'

'If they haven't, then they soon will. But that's not all. Soon there'll be police bulletins to trace you – perhaps even a reward.'

'But why?'

Michael's warm hand gripped hers.

'For conspiracy with regard to Sharon's murder.'

She smothered a half-scream. 'How?'

'He was your boyfriend and you travelled on Sharon's papers. It makes sense. But don't worry, there's no possible way they could make it stick. It just – well, it just looks bad, that's all.'

'So *that's* why our luggage is here.'

'Of course. Frank could drop us off at Bermuda with samples of the bones and make his own escape. After all, you're the archaeologist and he would have to trust you on the best way to bring about exposure of the truth.'

Caittie fought back a rising panic.

'But how can we possibly get back without being discovered?'

He had not let go of her hand. Now he said, 'Costas can get us to Cuba. From there we can get to back to Crete. There's no extradition from Cuba.'

Finally she said, 'How do we know that we're not being followed now?'

'The radar. And once it's our turn to steer we'll be even surer. Any boat on the radar without overt identification should stick out like a sore thumb.'

'And if someone's waiting for us on Bimini?'

He sought her lips, 'Someone already is. Half my men are there. Don't you trust me?'

Her eyes gave him his answer, and he kissed her again, with still more intensity.

'I wish it was only us,' she said at last.

'Well, it isn't. And until we know for sure what was happening, it's better not to confront Frank with anything.'

'Of course not.'

Frank's instructions on the headings and checking the weather reports were pretty clear. Both Michael and Caittie kept a careful eye for any blip on the radar, but there was no sign of any following vessel. While Frank was steering, Caittie found it hard to sleep, set with a mixture of anxiety and excitement, managing a series of restless naps. Once Michael took over, Frank went into the cabin to sleep, but Caittie was determined to be on the galley bench in case of any problem. Her anxiety wasn't helped by Michael's constant fiddling with the radio as he tried to listen in on other traffic. Its pulsing whine grated, seemingly bouncing straight off the clear night sky.

Caittie's own stint at the helm was a new strange experience, especially in the dark. The stars were shining so brightly that she could pick out reflections on the smoother waves that attempted to echo the steely mood of the moon and the fainter glint of stars. Frank had explained that the Gulf Stream threw up the water spouts and sudden storms, which was why he had chosen their times when all should be quiet, and it was. The boat's engines fell into a rhythmic hum and the emptiness of the sea lent the scene a tranquillity at odds with her nerves. Strangely awake and staring into space, she found herself praying that tomorrow she would be able to take that next step and show the world that her father's sacrifice, Sharon's and the others' had been worthwhile.

By half-three, Frank was back on deck.

'All right, skipper?' he asked Caittie lightly. 'Then just let me check the dinghy.'

Then he untied the small fibreglass dinghy that was tied down across the backboard. With Michael's help, Frank launched it over the back and scrambled in with an outboard motor previously stored at the back of the deck. The dinghy bobbed around riskily as the wake tossed it on a short line. Frank then climbed back to join Caittie at the helm.

'Right, now we have a choice. We can go into Brown Cay – as near as we dare – with the boat and then weave our way through the reefs with the dinghy. Alternatively – and it *will* take a bit longer – we can head into the harbour at Ocean Cay and then take the dinghy across the gap. If we head straight there we should be there before first light and can anchor well away or else wait until daybreak.'

'Why's that?' asked Michael keenly.

'Simple, we can't risk taking damage on the reef. Ocean Cay is a man-made island, and is generally pretty empty this time of year, thanks to the heat and bad weather. They still use it for mining but for those reasons don't operate all year. For me, this is a better bet, as it will get us there for daylight anyway and no matter what weather blows up we know the boat is fairly safe.' Frank stopped, looking for response.

'What happens if Ocean Cay's pit is still working?' asked Caittie.

'If there is anyone there, it'll only be maintenance and they won't be staying up. Far more likely they'll stay on one of the bigger Cays and motor in. I can leave a note on the boat with some excuse, like a damaged rudder or a problem, as it's not uncommon for people to pull into the first harbour they can when that happens.'

Caittie couldn't imagine how even Michael could oppose Frank's advice without the benefit of local sailing knowledge. She said, 'Right, I vote for Ocean Cay.'

Michael shot her a look, but calmly said, 'OK, but can we look at the chart first?' This pleased Frank, who promptly fetched a chart for Michael before taking over the helm.

Michael took the map below stairs to get better light. Upon Caittie's following, he muttered to her, 'Frank knows too much. I thought we agreed that everything was meant to be on a strictly need-to-know basis.'

'I never told him about it being the second quay from the end.'

'Then how could he *know*?'

'Well, if you look at the map, it does seem the most plausible.' There was Brown Cay, the second from the famous tip, Bleak Cay. The reef from which the islands were formed was evident at least forty miles along the Bimini chain. It seemed a reasonable enough distance to cross between any two in the dinghy, assuming they kept to shallow calmer waters.

'OK,' said Michael, 'I think you're right. But I still think it would be better to wait and question Frank when we reach Brown Cay.'

'Absolutely!'

He caught Caittie to him and kissed her urgently, until she felt boneless with desire. But after a long moment she whispered, 'What if Frank suspects?'

'I don't care,' he flashed back, but reluctantly released her all the same.

Within the hour they entered Ocean Cay harbour, under their own small and rather spooky floodlights, in what was otherwise near-total darkness. The place was as deserted as Frank had described, with the feel of a ghost town. They both started helping Frank fill the dinghy with supplies. Besides the digging tools, some food and plenty of water, he also threw in an inflatable smaller dinghy wrapped up in a small, deflated bundle.

By the time they were all set, it had gone six and the first hints of rosy sunlight were just breaching the edge of the horizon. With the light beckoning, they all squeezed into the dinghy and set off.

The waters seemed almost eerily calm and close to the reef almost smooth. This was lucky, as three people plus supplies made the dinghy sit low in the water and Caittie found the odd splash of spray that came over the front of the bow almost too refreshing for this time of the morning, especially combined with a lack of sleep.

The little outboard buzzed away, at first appearing to make little or no headway, but suddenly as they approached Brown Cay the land seemed to rise up to meet them. Frank cut out the engine and tilted the craft at an angle as they approached and, just as the dinghy brushed the sand, he jumped out into the water and grabbed a rope to pull it on shore. Caittie and Michael followed, uniting to help out on the opposite side.

'If we're going to leave the boat, we need to make sure it's past any tide line,' Frank ordered, 'If we don't, it might not be here once we get back!' With that incentive, they hoisted it a good twenty feet past the debris line. Then Caittie and Michael each began to load themselves down with tools and supplies, surprised to see Frank still wrestling with the spare dinghy.

'Come on, Frank, let's get moving,' Caittie said lightly, trying to make it look natural, as Michael appeared itching to quiz him.

'It's not good practice to leave both boats together!' Frank's words were muffled with his back to them, but as he finished the words he swung the inflatable pack round his body and threw it further onto the beach. Continuing for a few seconds to fiddle with more things in the dinghy, he eventually turned and walked towards them. When Caittie saw what he was carrying her heart stopped.

'What the hell are you carrying a gun out here for?' spat out Michael, but Frank only smiled.

'Why do you think?' Frank knew he was in control and the slowness of his words said it all.

'Bastard! I checked you over before we left!'

'Perhaps you omitted the inflatable?' inquired Frank, suddenly sounding more British. 'Or did you really think I was really going to wait around for fifteen years just to be your errand boy again?'

Michael breathed, 'It makes sense now, that was your car at the mall – and your car at Cap's Place!'

'What do you mean?' asked Caittie.

'And it was also Frank talking to the secret service at the mall.'

She realised it all, and bit her lip.

Michael continued, 'And the reason he wasn't followed – because it was his secret service car he was driving!' To Frank he added contemptuously, 'CIA or FBI?'

'Neither. Believe me, I told them to lay off this, but, as usual, nobody listened!' And with this, Frank pulled out a revolver and another, smaller pistol from inside his shirt – with one in each hand he pointed one at each of them, evenly, accurately. But Michael retorted, still irritated.

'So the post box belongs to the secret service, that's how you got back to us so quickly!'

Frank scowled. 'Hey, that box was mine for years before it found a better use. The janitor there's my cousin and I got him to set it up for me. Basically anything posted in that box can be retrieved in the janitor's room, at any time. As for the reason I got there so fast, well I luckily wasn't on a diving expedition, so I had nothing better to do that to wait for little Caittie here. In other words, I was just waiting to find out where the bones are!' Frank gave Caittie a knowing smile, which turned her stomach.

'But why bother with us, Frank, why when all you had to do was lie low?' Michael was still trying to draw him in.

'Because I'd got no other choice, fool! They were on to me the minute we first turned up at the Russian sub site asking questions! First, my brother was carpeted, because the supposedly safe coordinates had been breached. He was in trouble, big time, and as things stood even a liability, unless we were all eliminated. But he convinced his superiors that if they recruited me then they'd stand a better chance of clearing up this mess. Which was just fine by me because I got a well-paid job instead of a grubby old coffin.' The smugness on Frank's face infuriated Michael but Caittie's attention was caught.

'What do you mean, this mess? Does that mean there are other messes besides this one?'

'You still don't realise what you're into here!' Frank said contemptuously, but his guns never wavered. 'What we need to know now is where the bones are buried and that's what dear little Caittie here is going to tell me.'

'I'm not telling you anything until I know what this is really all about!' Caittie had already suspected that the location was now the only thing keeping them alive – for the moment.

'Jeez, what is it with your family?' Frank complained, though his hands never wavered. 'But at least this time I have the right cay, so if you don't tell me, we will just have a better reason to pull this part of the island apart.'

'*Her family!* Does that mean you killed her father as well as poor old George then?' Michael interrupted keenly.

Frank laughed, but his gaze never left Michael's.

'Oh dear me, no, no, no, not George! I couldn't be in two places at once, could I? I was busy trying to intercept her father.'

'And by intercept, you mean –' Caittie whispered.

Frank whined, 'That was his own fault! He wouldn't tell me the location either, so he left me no choice other than to make sure he didn't keep looking. After all, I had to assume that it wouldn't have stayed hidden forever, especially once I'd learned that he'd left a trail for others to follow!' Frank looked straight at Caittie. 'Everyone had to agree that this was most likely to include his dear little Caittie. Even if we couldn't break the information out of your father, all we had to do was to wait for you to track Michael down. And a long wait it's been, not easy keeping track of either of you! After all, we had to make sure we kept the pressure on, and to make dead sure that this mystery remains just that – a mystery.'

Michael jeered, 'So you finally found your true vocation, didn't you? Doing somebody else's dirty murders, without any real clue about what you are doing!'

'I still know a lot more than *you!*' said Frank hotly, but Michael only said contemptuously, 'Sorry, my mistake, you never were anybody in the first place, other than an egotistical little runt sucking up crumbs from your brother's table!'

Caittie thought, he's deliberately baiting Frank, and noted his nervous energy, suggesting that he was only waiting for an opportunity. Michael's hand nearest to hers was clenched tight with sand.

'Don't you dare to try to lecture me, you sadistic pervert!' Frank spat. 'You're just thinking that this is some trivial rubbish about time shifting and to that degree you're right. But you haven't begun to imagine what such a discovery might *mean!* We've had experts working for decades on this and we still don't know what it means, but what we *do* know is that all the governments involved are conspiring to make sure that – whatever it is – it's kept secret. Can you imagine the panic your random time shift theory would cause the general public? What government would want that? Why do you think they refuse to confirm UFOs?'

'I don't know,' said Michael, flatly. 'You tell me.'

'Because, whatever they might *look like* they aren't alien vessels. They're earth-bound vessels shifted in time, mostly from the future, and believe me, the extreme future can look pretty alien. But that's all we can do, as we go round tracking down the evidence, because mankind has no other explanation.'

Caittie said blankly, 'You mean, you destroy them?'

'Not any longer,' Frank told her. 'Of course, in the early years they were pretty much demolished on the spot. But nowadays any discovery is dragged or lured away to Area 51 and investigated. And in recent years DNA testing of samples of creatures previously thought of as aliens have in fact confirmed the samples as humans from the far future instead.'

'That's amazing!' said Caittie, and he flashed her a moody glare.

'Right. So you see rather than being some "nobody", you're looking at one of the few people –'

'Or agents,' put in Michael.

'– who actually know the whole story, or most of it. In other words, I've got the job of clearing up the messes of the past, at least until the powers that be decide it's time to confess to whatever energy force is causing this. The problem is, no one seems anywhere near to understanding it fully. Which may just be where your centuries-old bones come in.'

'Energy force,' murmured Michael. Caittie thought, *is he trying to tell me something?*

Frank said bluntly, 'So, come on then, you two, if you're so blinking clever, tell me how this energy beam works then? Tell me where it comes from and what it's for?' In the face of their stillness, he smirked, 'Exactly. Then how do you expect the governments to tell people what's happening? But we've wasted enough time here.' Frank checked his watch, as if he had been waiting for a certain length of time, a time that would soon be up.

For Caittie, having done her research before she left, it made some sense. It roused more questions than she had previously imagined, but there was no use considering such things when someone was pointing a loaded gun at you. All she could do was to pray that she'd be allowed a chance to be part of the answer – and that there could be a way allowing others to learn the truth.

After consulting his watch again, Frank said roughly, 'OK, joke-time is up. Now it's just a matter of deciding which of you will squeal the most appealingly while the other one dies.'

'I don't get it,' said Michael, 'You've got two guns there.'

'Exactly. Precisely. I have a standard revolver and a poison-dart gun, and in here –' Frank nodded towards his shirt pocket, 'is the only known antidote to its poison. Although the person darted will black out in a few seconds, there's still a few minutes left to administer the antidote. So, the question I keep coming back to is this: did little Caittie tell dear Michael the location while making love – or not?'

They were both completely still, determined not to assist him, though Caittie flushed hotly.

Frank continued to muse, 'It would probably make more sense to shoot Michael, if Caittie's the only one who knows. However Caittie, despite shagging him stupid, still might not have trusted him enough to tell him the whole truth – you see, my dear, if I could only be *sure* that you'd shared this information then I know Michael's gallantry would tell me rather than see *yet another girlfriend* die at his expense.'

Caittie sensed Michael quivering with restrained anger, his face as rigid as if primed to explode.

Suddenly someone cried out from down the beach – in what language, Caittie wasn't sure. For the briefest millisecond, Frank half-turned, which was enough for Michael to lunge forward, tossing the sand hard into Frank's face while simultaneously drawing a heavy knife from beneath his right trouser-leg. A shot spat out blackly as Frank reeled back. But by the time Michael landed on him with the intensity of his full weight and power, the two had become a wild mix of limbs. Caittie watched in an agony of fear as a gun went off and both men hit the ground, wrestling furiously. She spotted a dark splat of blood on Michael's side where a bullet had entered, but before she could move something else shocked her into a renewed surge of panic. A sharp involuntary 'Ouch!' and a glistening black dart coursing into her leg, injecting a red-brown liquid inside her veins. Numbness swept through her, then everything went black.

29

The written word

At last Peter said, 'Now, before I give you the information you need, we have to discuss the problems with the written word itself.'

'What do you mean?'

'I'm talking about interpretation.'

'Right, yes.'

'While the other most crucial thing you must try and do, besides of course pass on the information, is to avoid and – if possible – negate the fascination mankind possesses with self-importance.'

Andrew said, 'Fine, great, but how can I be supposed to negate something embedded into the very nature of man?'

'I know what you mean, and it feels very annoying that I have to deal with these failures, even though various tools and guidance have been laid down precisely to avoid such a circumstance,' Peter paused and calmed down, saying, 'And yet this trait in mankind is deliberate. Only by learning how to behave, and only by finding the integrity to adjust their behaviour in the face of changing circumstance, can any person be judged to pass the test.'

'What test? Do you mean, the test to meet God?' asked Andrew, but Peter overruled the question, saying, 'There's no point in discussing the detail of these requirements since they're pretty universal across scriptures of all origins as well as perfectly commonplace within the psychology of your age. What I want to get across is this: the most problematic aspect of mankind's self importance is its tendency to hide the truth from itself, as you know better than most.'

Andrew said, 'Absolutely.'

'This is not a new phenomenon, as it has happened in every religion. You'll have noticed that almost none of the great prophets wrote for themselves, and that the recordings of their lives were only done after their lifetime – sometimes decades after! This was deliberate, based upon the predictive nature of this trait. As any history or philosophy is translated, it will always be viewed through the lens of the needs and desires of people at that time. Mankind will draw every variety of conclusions based on what they long to find.'

'You mean, self-interest takes over,' observed Andrew.

'Exactly. For many centuries this was reckoned a beneficial element in controlling mankind's progress, in that the greater truths, without sufficient science to understand them, simply end in confusion. Yet there are certainly different points in history, points when it becomes prudent to reveal more of the truth or times to instead refocus on a deeper understanding and trust in mankind's ability to accept a new level of science.'

'You mean, the coming of Christ.'

Peter threw him an approving glance.

'In the coming of Christ and Muhammad we had both these things coinciding.'

It was a hammer of an explanation, ending with two names that couldn't possibly be advocated side by side. For a moment Andrew was too winded to speak, then he said, 'Christ – and Muhammad? But surely one must be right and the other wrong?'

Peter said, with just a touch of impatience, 'Andrew, none operating in peace should clash with each other. Naturally, it was *expected* that they would clash, thanks to the deep gaps in the information supplied on either side. But these gaps are crucial – these are the gaps where the truth can come in! These gaps are there for mankind to work out how to fill, with positives or negatives, good or evil. If every detail was given, it might perhaps prevent appalling wars and misunderstandings, but it would undermine the most essential element – every individual's personal free will!'

Andrew couldn't help murmuring, 'That's going to be an easy sell, isn't it! Hey, Andrew why don't you go out and have a go at overturning a thousand years of hatred?'

'Don't worry, you may with luck make some ground toward this goal, but it will certainly take more than any one person's efforts to succeed! Trust me, and trust God. When I give you the information identifying the true nature of these relationships it will all begin to make sense.'

Peter waited, and Andrew nodded, as if to say, carry on.

'Good. So let's get back to the problems existing with the written word in general. Take the word – any Holy word – literally, and you risk taking in not the realities but also the maladjustments, the misinterpretations – even the mistakes! These works may be God-*inspired*, but God *wrote* none of them, people did. Then there's the still greater risk of taking in words of devilment from misguided souls, no matter how devout their intentions appear to themselves. The requirement to follow words, in short, has far more to do with the convenience of whatever religious establishment is concerned than with God's purpose.'

'I believe you.'

'Of course you do – you know, at least as well as I, that the same self-importance returns with these splits, as each branch of whatever religion it might be competes against the other branches for some spurious supremacy. Again, often under the pretence of doing God's work – but when you consider that most of the larger ones are based on the same god, it's just wildly absurd!'

Andrew said, wistfully, 'And you're sure it's the same god, are you?'

Peter said, his face glowing, 'I am, because I know Him, which one day you will do also. But how anyone can justify killing those who believe in the same god as they do, just because they see Him differently, still baffles me! Man's own need for self-importance has divorced them from any concept of God's wishes. This leads to mankind's most horrific atrocities.'

'Not to mention being used by intelligent atheists as an argument against religion,' Andrew agreed. 'But let's accept that your average person, in the round, is a big-headed prat who enjoys a fight and whose attempts to justify justice make mankind into a bit of a mess. Now don't get me wrong, I'm not *denying* that mankind, and womankind too, is a bit of a mess, but what I'd like to know is why God, with all His overarching wisdom and unlimited power, doesn't just get His hands dirty and sort them out?' It was a question Andrew had heard a thousand times before – if there is a god why does he not stop every bad thing from happening? He had a chance in a million to ask someone who ought to know and he couldn't resist.

Peter was unimpressed. 'But that's the last thing that's needed! Free will means that people must endure most of the chaos that they – or others, or even nature itself – creates. Both good and bad occur in the laws of adversity, but it's mankind's predictable failures and diversions from any true path that creates a large part of the adversity people are obliged to overcome.'

'But where's God in all this?' demanded Andrew, 'Is He just sitting back with His popcorn and watching the show?'

'God's power can only ever redress this balance, not prevent it. To prevent it would be, would be –'

'To wreck the game!' Andrew interrupted.

Peter said irritably, 'I understand you, of course, which is probably why you were sent to *me*, and not to another. Yet none can hope to leave evil behind by ignoring it – integrity is strengthened only by facing it. What you are – at least what I truly hope you are – about to undertake is the conveying of a truth that shows mankind's real position in God's plan of creation, which will entail getting people to lose the passionate self-importance they're addicted to.'

Andrew said, 'Before we go any further, could we just clarify this self-importance thing? I've often thought of lacking sufficient ego as a deliberate stance, in order to avoid having too much pride. Yet it seems as if the ego itself is deluding people into believing whatever they're doing is right.'

'Both of these notions are partly true, but it's enough to understand that your mission is to attempt to undo the power of the *collective* ego. When like minds congregate, each feeds off the other, which is how belief systems become inter-connected, as with Buddhism. Even modern psychology can give the same analysis, even if only in a stale and directionless way. Your message is to those who can see the difference and still find their way to collaboration, as the new information will in time make that path easier to see.'

Andrew said doubtfully, 'I still doubt that I'm up to it. But surely this isn't my only job?'

'You'll see as you explore the problems how many well-intentioned messages, in a later time and place became distorted and misused.'

'By atheists, you mean.'

'Certainly such people will often start off by drawing on any convenient confusion within religion and then extrapolating into a peculiarly blinkered form of science. And it's also true that, once entrenched in the wrong direction, their self-importance won't allow them to concede any argument, however cogent, for it becomes a matter of losing face.'

Andrew was about to agree, but Peter was not to be stopped.

'Yet, within the so-called churches, it's even worse! All too often, once mankind has successfully distorted a religion, they'll demand of its converts a continual determination to pressure others to believe exactly as *they* believe! This can even end in violence. Sometimes both believers and non-believers will demand that all believes as they believe. This is often because, somewhere in the purity of their original intention, they might recognise that their argument is incomplete or has been diverted from its true path. Their desperation causes them to cover this up by converting others and by justifying their position. I warn you: don't get drawn into their arguments. They can distort truth itself simply because they're compelled to have the last word!'

'So how would you propose my tackling an atheist or a zealot, if not to mess with the detail?' The prospect of reasoning without argument was still hard for Andrew to consider, especially since he loved a good argument. But Peter was adamant.

'Andrew, even the most ardent atheist secretly longs for proof, while in their petulance he defies his Maker. In such a position, I would ask whether a child should demand of its parents to prove their parenthood before believing in it? Isn't the actual growing up in that family enough proof, whoever the father might have been? And so, though I have yet to explain the Laws of Adversity, the atheist will use all imperfect things as triumphant evidence that a perfect god cannot exist, while contriving to ignore any evidence that religion has been tampered with by man. Some will even disregard all evidence of free will, deducing that if man himself is by God's own design, that any flaw in man must in turn be God's personal failure.'

'I know what you mean,' said Andrew. 'It's as a child might tell its father "My world is imperfect, my feelings are often wounded, therefore as a father you must be rubbish!" They assume that God's being all-powerful should make everything perfect.'

'Precisely, yet by ignoring mankind's own powerful role in history, they increasingly gradually distort the facts away from the entire integrity of God. Then, as if by magic, they will end by concluding God's non-existence on bizarre criteria set by man himself in the first place.'

Suddenly Peter got up and walked towards the door, while Andrew noticed, this time without surprise, that he now needed to stoop to get under the frame.

'I'm sorry, but I'm being called. I must leave you to think a short while,' he said, and then he was gone.

30

Wrong place, wrong time

The numbness spread through Caittie's brain, leaving a gaping hole where thoughts used to be. The last remnant of physical consciousness seemed crushed groundwards. The scudding instance of pain, so heavy at first, rebounded into weightlessness, while – for a moment – time and space alike failed to exist. Then, as if arising from the depths, her limbs tingled, as if her body had unfinished action left inside. Shock, panic and nervous energy coalesced, while something between a gasp and a cough forced her eyelids open. Squinting in the glaring brightness, it was surprising to realise the light came from an artificial source, rather than the bleached sunlight of Bimini, while at her feet curved the arched frame of an old-fashioned hospital-type bed, surrounded by whitewashed walls.

In front of her was a wooden chair, where a petite, silver-haired woman in a white uniform was sitting strictly upright. Her hospital-styled uniform tunic was faded but starched. The room was almost small enough to have been on a boat, but there was no movement from the sea or sound from any engines.

'Caitlin, welcome! It's good to have you with us!' she said, but Caittie was all defiance.

'I'm not telling you the location,' she warned. 'Not you and not anyone!'

'Whatever you're seeking is of no interest to me.'

'Then what am I doing here? Why didn't you just let me die?' Caittie watched as the woman considered, but couldn't help adding: 'And Michael, is he all right?'

'They say he is recovering. The shot missed all the crucial organs.'

'Then –' Caittie paused, doubtfully, her colour rising. She said hesitantly, 'Then, can – then may I see him?'

The woman shook her head. 'I'm afraid you'll just have to regard that chapter as finished.'

'What chapter? What do you mean, finished? Who *are* you?'

The little woman's eyes blazed coldly, flagrantly blue. 'It doesn't matter who I am. All I need from you is confirmation that you understand what it was that you asked for.'

'What do you mean?' Caittie was very confused now. She had always anticipated being interrogated, but what perverse form of torture would give you what you asked for?

'Didn't you change the course of your life and go in quest of a truth that your father had also searched for? Please, answer freely! You have nothing to fear!'

Caittie said faintly, 'How could I not be afraid? Frank was determined to kill us, and I felt... and I felt... My leg...'

'And didn't you spend that moment praying that you might be involved in the delivering of truth?'

Caittie felt hot and cold, it was ridiculous, how she possibly could know such a thing? Was she a witch, or an angel, with those opaque eyes? (Did she, Caittie, even believe in witches?). And yet, if she knew a prayer in her head on a remote island, never uttered to a living soul, and never shared, except of course with God.

At last, she said, with an effort, 'Yes, but that was inside my head. Nobody knew! Who *are* you?' Because she seemed an unlikely angel, in her scrunched hospital uniform with her thin, worn face.

'That doesn't matter. What I'm asking is far more important. If given the chance, Caitlin – Caittie – would you hope to grow in the new integrity and faith you've found?'

But Caittie only looked wildly at the bleached walls, the anonymous atmosphere.

'Is this a trick? Drugs – hypnosis? At any rate, something or someone's got the information out of me!'

'I assure you –'

'If it's not a trick, then I'll believe you when I can see Michael – or when you convince me why I can't see him!'

The little woman's eyes softened. Finally she said, very quietly, 'Because he couldn't save you – his struggle with Frank took too long. The pouch of antidotes was crushed in the struggle. You died on that beach, at Bimini, within only a few hundred metres of what your father too died trying to protect.'

Caittie swayed, and, had she been standing up, would have fallen. Dead! How could she be dead? Everything she'd been thinking had just shivered into nothingness. Would she never see Michael again?

And her father: could he be here? Her eyes darted around the room stupidly, returning at last to the tranquil countenance of the azure-eyed, silver-haired woman.

'You mean, the dart –'

'I'm afraid so,' said the woman, very gently.

The shock whipped through her entire body. Surely this must be a dream? It took only a few seconds, but it seemed like decades as Caittie struggled with accepting it all. Her father... Michael... her sorrow, her failure, her hurt pride, and how utterly embarrassing after all along her best attempts, to have fallen headlong into Frank's trap – but how much more she longed for the glint of Michael's eyes, the grasp of his warm hand!

In the end she said, 'But what can I do?' They were half-hearted words encumbered by failure.

'You mean, you're willing to help in order to see justice done?'

Caittie looked up, suddenly hopeful, 'You don't mean – I could go back? But what about my father?'

'Eventually, dear one, you'll see everyone you ever loved. That much I can promise you.'

Tears rushed to Caittie's eyes – tears of gratitude. At any rate, all she could do was her best. But she was touched by how this woman's expressing faith in her.

'I'll do whatever you ask – if I can! If I'm good enough, that is.'

'Don't worry, you won't be thrown into leadership! Instead yours will be a journey of learning, assisting and teaching. In a few minutes someone will collect you and take you to meet the others selected for the task, where all will be explained.' The woman stood up – how tall she seemed, suddenly! – and, touching Caittie's hand, she said simply, 'Thank you. Wait here a while and rest if you can.'

Caittie wanted to return the woman's warmth but fear stifled her. She was a pawn now being put back on the board, though willingly enough – yet how could she cope with turning yet another corner? But this was no ordinary corner – death redefined as leaving another life behind.

The woman left through the now-illuminated door. The minute she had gone beyond Caittie's sight she became Peter again, with Peter's whipping stride and powerful shape – only the eyes remained the same.

31

Perception of history

As soon as Peter had left the room, Andrew flopped back onto the bed as if released by inner elastic. Paradoxically, for the first time he felt almost as if he could relax. But how crazy could *that* be, in a surreal illusion of a nightmare that was rapidly becoming a living reality? He seemed totally at peace, until he realised that whatever Peter had so far put him through was likely to be a mere bagatelle compared to whatever was to come. His eyes, having closed themselves, flashed open – curtains drawn back by his anxiety.

Andrew felt as if he was hanging desperately onto consciousness, recalling that the last such time he had been confronted by the strange visions of the shepherd, visions so confusing as to overload his brain. Then, as obscure as it seemed, he found himself forming strange connections between them. He struggled to keep his eyes open, determined to be ready for Peter's return and not be weighed down with more confusion. He blinked again, forcing his head up, but with his focus reasserted he felt shaken to see Peter already quietly sitting behind the desk, exactly as if he had been waiting for him for some time. Yet – surely – he hadn't been gone longer than a few moments?

'You looked shocked, Andrew.'

'Well, I'm surprised. You said there was something to do.'

'Ah, I understand. You had a short nap, but don't worry, for here time is not necessarily chronological. However, its best that we don't go into that, as it borders on areas that would be dangerous to know.'

Andrew swallowed his questions, and waited expectantly, noticing Peter's purposeful fidgeting, as characteristic as a fingerprint. He imagined Peter on the mountain, edgily questioning Jesus. For surely, despite his living in a spiritual world, he still carried with him his own earthly mannerisms. Andrew found this suddenly endearing, giving him a real sense of affinity with the angel, along with the first thrill at having been chosen, as Peter himself had once been chosen. Chosen apparently because he had a foundation of thinking beyond earthly conceptions – he could only just hope he had the ability to learn to deal with the rest.

'Andrew, I'm about to take you through the history of the world from a new perspective – God's. You might at various points want to know more, but this isn't about detail, it's about reasoning. Just as several paintings might appear to an untutored eye to be the same, it's about identifying the original. The complication here is that the originator of all things chose to allow these forgeries to exist, until their true purpose could be safely explained. Is this clear?'

Andrew nodded.

Peter replied, 'This is also my last session with you, following which you'll leave this room and be taken to an anteroom to meet other souls. Together with them you will be given the directions." Peter could see Andrew shifting on his seat with his hands tucked under his legs in an attempt to hide his almost childlike expectation.

'This is best done in blocks of history, focusing our consideration on the key points where mankind's version differs from God's intention. I can then give a general outline of events in between and focus on the differences at these junctions. Unfortunately the first chunk covers the period where mankind will always struggle, as it covers everything up until Adam and Eve.'

'Don't you mean the concept depicted as Adam and Eve?'

'No. I mean Adam and Eve.'

Andrew's head felt swimmy again.

'I hope you are not going to try telling me the earth was made in six days and everyone on earth is descended from these two people?'

'No, I'm not – but just a few slight changes to that sentence and it would be so close to the truth! You must recall that many Biblical texts have been adjusted over time. And then with several versions available people will inevitably select the one that best suits their immediate purpose, rather than the version closest to the reality. The vocabularies available were also very limited, with the same word often having several different meanings. The scribes that recorded these texts had to simplify the science they did not understand, so that it would not frighten the masses or deter the chances for belief.

'Genesis is a good example of a truth simplified by mankind so that the rulers of the day could explain the inexplicable. On the other hand, God might well be tempted to ask exactly how many prophets and sons He would have to send to earth, before people could take onboard his intent rather than the literal text! So, let's start with the creation of earth in seven days.'

'In SEVEN days? To be honest, I think most people have worked out that it is some kind of metaphor, because science has destroyed any literal meaning.'

Peter said testily, 'That's the whole point of this process! Faith and belief have to be rooted in truth, just as science has.'

'But surely it is going to be complicated to change minds now, with all the science available?'

'The truth is often simpler than that. Sometimes things seem cryptic, simply because of all the many overlaid distortions have to be sifted through. Any scholar that ignores the history of the early Bible being written by writers of a monotheistic society, struggling against many surrounding polytheistic peoples, does no justice to the psychology and intelligence of the authors.'

'Right, that makes sense.'

'Good. The first thing in Genesis is that the seven days were just that. The difference is that the godly term used was meant, not as a 'day' but as a 'visit' – while the vast expanses between the visits no man could or even wished to explain. There were actually more visits than the first six of creation, but simplicity was key in these early years.'

'I know you said there is no proof for such things, but how are people supposed to differentiate between the scientific claims on creation with what you're suggesting?'

'God is not claiming creation as it is written, Andrew. Selected highlights of any interview can change the whole meaning – that's how newspaper editors sell papers. These early texts certainly sold papers, but what God brought to His earth – the earth he spun out of the spheres in the first place – was evolution. God's visits established a process that would culminate in a diversity that only evolution could bring – a diversity that is as essential to heaven. Earth you must realise is just a part of God's plan.'

'But evolution is what atheists use to prove the non-existence of God!'

'Ironic, isn't it? Even theologians have concluded that evolution must fit in with scripture somehow, but their dogged insistence on immovable text won't let them see the full picture. This focus of theirs has been about directing all religious events as if they are just about mankind. God's agenda is greater than that.'

'Well, go on! I'm desperate to know. What IS His agenda, then?'

'What do you think?'

'You're sounding like a psychiatrist again,' Andrew complained. 'I want to *know*!'

'All right, what were you created for, do you think?'

'To worship God?'

Peter said, in annoyance, 'Do people really believe that all this effort and trauma was just to create souls to worship Him? No wonder people turn away and find reasons to disbelieve! God already has worshippers and if that were all he wanted, there would be far easier ways of obtaining them. There are good examples of this in Revelations and many parts of scripture where God already has beings from different worlds – individuals that already have the ability and life experience, souls fit for heaven.'

Andrew said slowly, 'So, evolution, set in motion by God, creates the species that can carry such souls in a chasm of time long enough to let those souls develop.'

'Good!'

'But, accepting that people can in fact become "fit for heaven", as you put it, still every faith has a different slant on it, such as accepting Christ and repenting one's misdeeds, or something similar. How do these differences relate to what you're saying?'

'There are many gates to heaven, Andrew! Whether through Christ, Muhammad or any other godly doctrine, there is a clear path towards the quality of the soul. You'll find out how these all came about and relate to each other, but in every scripture there is always this first step toward God. Just as, in all religions there are those that wear the badge, but do not take it into their heart, reasoning often that the same first step is enough. If someone doesn't believe in God and cannot find room in your heart for Him, then what point is there in letting such a person go to heaven?'

'That rules out such a lot of people!'

'The people have the choice to rule themselves out.'

'It is not their fault, surely, with so much disinformation about?'

'It's not about blame or fault, but the desire to grow, while disinformation can only be corrected by such persons that can see through it while sharing their foundation in God. This is why you must convey everything I'm telling you. Only when people see that this whole process of evolution was to select a species that could have such a journey with God, will many more take it seriously.'

'I hope so,' said Andrew, rather doubtfully.

'Evolution is what God created – meaning periodic visits to modify the environment such as to be suitable for a being with a soul. Initially it was about creating variety and then selecting from it. God needs that new variety, new abilities and moreover different mortal life experience. Only from such variety in society can you gain any sense of eternal pleasure. Imagine a heaven full of perfect identical beings living and having only experienced sameness! God has the power to make them, but the result would be a society of rigidity rather than of one to nurture intelligence and pleasure. Evolution is the key and when God realised prehistoric man had finally evolved the potential to maintain a soul, they were chosen for that task. I know mankind has recorded in Genesis that they were made in the image of God, but that again is man's self-importance twisting the truth. Man evolved under the guidance of God and when chosen was sub-genetically altered to contain a soul. This soul is the basis and context of being in the image of God, not our appearance in the mirror.'

'No disrespect,' said Andrew thoughtfully, 'but slipping in terms like "sub-genetically altered" might confuse a lot of people, including me.'

Peter agreed, 'I cannot tell you exactly how it works, because that would uncover the science before its time. However, assuming you can accept this principle, let's continue with the formation of a being with a soul and in biblical terms that would bring us to the period just before the Garden of Eden.'

'I'm hugely looking forward to hearing you explaining this one.'

'It's as I said in the beginning, it's true but not as mankind conceives it. Even now, in the light of your science, it will not be easily palatable to most human minds. In addition, as is obvious in the early texts not everything seemed to have worked out according to God's plan, but there is a lot from these early events that are about balance and the Laws of Adversity. This is also why God may seem angry at times.'

'Waxed wroth, you mean. He did that a good deal.'

'Don't believe everything from mortal pens! However, be assured that God's power means that in time events will transpire exactly as planned. Now, every account of heaven gives descriptions of creatures beyond earthly experience. Perhaps this self-importance issue confuses mankind, in that they might not be first and foremost, but they are nonetheless chosen. All we need to grasp now is that they exist and that some were chosen to help God with such work as adapting mankind on earth. So at this period of testing, God brought those generically described as angels to earth and even cherubim and seraphim. Each of these helpers was given an area to administer. They were here to test the modifications of mankind's soul and to develop the process for future alterations.'

'It sounds like a laboratory. So without any scientific proof I have to convince people that God is responsible for evolution?'

'Andrew, investigate the whole process of evolution and you'll see so many gaps – enough to defy any statistical likelihood! Doubters hang onto the theory that Earth is the almost impossible freak event in the universe, rather than admit to the prospect it was likely a planned sequence of interventions by an outside force.'

'I don't wish to be critical, I worry that lots of people are going to be uncomfortable with this, I mean, angels...'

Peter was annoyed.

'How long must we wait for people to come to terms with the reality of these circumstances and the real purpose of human existence? This is about reconciling history, science and religion and dispelling the convenience originally assigning many of these events to pagan misconceptions. I understand this confusion, for I too had trouble understanding, from having giving my life to Christ in a world surrounded by seemingly pagan or mistaken worship. But the main issue for people to grasp is that not all pagan deities are man made invention, but most of them have an angelic origin from the depths of history.'

'You mean, Zeus was an angel?'

'As were all the Greek gods, which later became the Roman ones and spawned so many myths and legends from all corners of the earth! All this shouldn't seem so strange once you compare the depicted and similar abilities of angels to those of some of the assumed pagan Gods. Why, mankind recorded them as pagan is another subject, but you will see this initial period of the cherubim and seraphim mentioned in the traditional translations of the Bible, even if it has been edited out of late. There is also the fleeting reference to the time when giants walked the earth. We can also see it recorded that these angels came to adore the beauty that was now beginning to exist in mankind, taking some to their side and having children by them. The power of these angels obviously was passed down in some part to these children and many of them and their descendants are what you know as the legends and great ones of old. Again, you will see this depicted in some way, albeit vaguely, in other religious scriptures.'

'I'm no expert on other religion's scriptures.'

'No, but you can see that the reality of these early days couldn't be given in any detail because it would have undermined the process. You can see why it was deliberately hidden. You see, these angels were tasked with creating centres across the world to control this adaptation of the species – one in particular you would know better as Atlantis.'

'Which existed?'

'Which existed, but was turned into mythology when Atlantis and its satellites had passed their usefulness. There were of course many Atlantis-type centres set up and folklore has many theories of their locations: Spain, Egypt, Japan, Turkey, Crete, the West Indies, South America, India and many more. They are mostly true and the pyramid structure commonly at the centre of many of them has been copied by many civilisations thereafter. This shape enables a large structure to be defended and guarded by just a few. These centres spread ever outwards, each creating ever new layers of defences. One of the key elements here is that each centre allowed different specialist testing in isolation from the others.'

Andrew was unconvinced. 'This testing thing is not going to go down well, let alone convincing anyone that such myths are some kind of truth. Surely there's some proof somewhere that can back it up.'

'Proof in evolution comes from taking these oddities of information, just as Darwin did with the origin of species and creating a new truth as the pieces of jigsaw create a clearer picture. Each one on their own is meaningless until they complete an undeniable reasoning. Juxtapose the information I give you against mankind's previous assumptions and then see which has structure. Take something as monumental as the Egyptian pyramids, a wonder of illogical effort and proportion, until you realise they were just copies of the original Atlantian central structure and its religiously significance to God. So my advice is, just let the facts come to you and it will form a more plausible picture, even if uncomfortable in places.

'Let's get back to how this comes toward Adam and Eve. Are they the first two people on earth? No! Are they the first two people of the Jewish nation? Yes! It should be no surprise that if the account of creation is written by the Jews then these two will appear as the first. Why were they placed in the Garden of Eden? Simply because even your current science has worked out that under any such introduction or testing, there has to be a control group. They are isolated and controlled directly by God, until the process is proven. The position of the Jewish one to the east of the scribes then creates the Egyptian recognition of God in such close regular proximity. This is a basic error in translation from archaeologists, as these ancient tribes did not worship the sun as a god, but rather they worshipped a god that appeared often as a sun. Then of course, without any greater understanding there would be an inevitable confusion between the two. Moses and the burning bush is a good later recorded example of this. The bright burning object to people of this time would naturally be related to the sun. That of course brings us to –'

'The serpent!'

'These partial or prototype souls were of course put to work to help in the fabric of these new colonies, but with all such things many escaped. That itself was not a problem, as it was almost desired, but one was not supposed to break into Eden – though one did! They were the slime that crawled over the earth, but unfortunately lacked much of the moral reasoning tools required for the long-term destiny of mankind. Hence their description as being the serpent and truth is easily disguised in poetic translation. Anyway, it was one such creature that found its way into Eden. Only this serpent had a quest for finding why he existed as he did. He was in search of answers.'

'I am rather glad you are not asking me to convince people an actual snake talked, as I could never relate to that!' joked Andrew.

'And this is about leaving behind the surreal confusions the scribes of the past had to use. So as we come to Adam and Eve in the garden, with this serpent doing some occasional trespass. I expect you, like most in the modern educated world, are still holding onto some fairytale picture to depict these events – or some great parable or metaphor.'

'Pretty much – until just now, that would describe my ideas exactly.'

Peter said, 'Such are the problems of the written word. The picture is drawn of a man and a woman standing around naked, eating fruit from a tree. So it is not that they eat fruit of the tree, but the word originally used meant eat as in consumed. Eden was the control, perhaps to be kept pure and educated, in case other testing did not prove satisfactory. You see, the fruit of the tree was not that of the edible variety, but what is well known in the modern world as paper, some might say the greatest fruit any tree has ever provided. Quite simply, God created a library of information for Adam and Eve to eventually learn and draw on. This knowledge was to be extended by their own recordings on paper as they prospered.'

'So they were scholars?'

'For their time, very advanced scholars indeed. Yet, as with children, certain truths you withhold until they mature, because such information can corrupt their development. Such knowledge was what the serpent enticed them to read, thus breaking God's trust in them. The ideal of Eden needed that ideal of innocence, unity and obedience kept unsullied until it was ready for the whole truth. Once lost, the pair had to join the rest of mankind by evolving under the process of reincarnation. They were expelled from an eden of ignorance into a world of sorrow.'

Andrew said, 'Hang on, you just mention "reincarnation" when to most of the modern world it is at best wishful thinking and contrary to most modern beliefs of going straight to heaven! Do you mean that reincarnation was the known tool of God at this time or the hidden process?'

'Why do you think reincarnation was an adopted belief in all corners of the world years ago? Moreover, history will show that so many unconnected tribes adopted it within their beliefs and some beliefs still do. You may be confused because in your world this changed with the advent of Christianity, but this doesn't preclude the use of reincarnation where needed. This is about people choosing a path toward Him – or not as the case may be.'

Andrew retorted, 'Of course I'm confused! If you mean to say that reincarnation existed, then surely everything changes. Instead of one chance per person, there might be millions of chances!'

'If this does not make sense, track the ages of the descendents of Adam and Eve and see their ages fall by half each time their genes are diluted. And then, if Adam and Eve were the only two people on earth, as it is written, whom did their sons mate with? How could anyone explain the existence of such women without giving some detail about those that had spread from the Atlantis-type centres and satellites?'

'It's been a problem for a lot of literal-minded Christians, I admit,' said Andrew.

'The next problem we have is the consequence of forbidden knowledge. The library in Eden not only contained the lust, desires and other forms of testing that existed in the other centres, it also contained the original plan to test the sons of Adam and select the best and discard the least. The knowledge of this plan was passed onto Cain and Abel. What they didn't know was that, in expelling them from Eden, God had abandoned the need for such refining and testing, but they couldn't know this as he couldn't confide in them. From this confusion came the murder of Abel, as Cain saw it as his only path to survival.'

'But wait – if God was aware of this problem, why didn't he stop this murder? I mean, he could have intervened without divulging any more than he needed to and protect these first few precious lives even if they had been released into the world.'

'Why stop any murder? You cannot get evolution if you interfere with the result. Once the controlled environment of Eden was abandoned, evolution had to be set free. As you will see throughout history, just as here, God will more often than not let mankind lay bare the results of their disobedience.'

I don't know, thought Andrew, it all seems vaguely unkind to me.

'So let's look at the next block of time, approximately 4000 to 2500 B.C. It appears all chaos and confusion, although a small part is partially recorded in the Bible, but the larger part of history has been removed. The spread of people over this time starts to undermine the very concept of the centres, as the duties of angels were altered. It also marks a process of expansion and migration, bringing an innate conflict of authority.'

'Hang on,' said Andrew, 'Can I ask a question about the soul? I sort of take mine for granted and it would be a lot easier making sense of all this if I had some idea of what the testing was based on. After all, if this was a jigsaw then the soul *has* to be the key piece!'

'That's difficult – without giving away the science, that is,' said Peter dubiously.

'You mentioned sub-genetic modification in passing.'

Peter considered, and then said, 'Just to say that, as much as genetics define the individual, there's another layer. You understand that in an atom the electron isn't just something spinning round a nucleus but instead an energy field, a pulsating wave form?'

'I've seen a few TV programmes, but even so, each scientist seems to take a slightly different view.'

'Then you'll probably appreciate that humans have barely scratched the surface of the complexities involved. Just as a radio wave can hold the digital information imposed upon it, so energy waves within atoms can hold information. This is pure energy – a memory layer existing within and upon the physical, programmable before birth and recoverable at death.'

Andrew felt a little shiver of excitement. 'You mean our souls.'

'Exactly. Unfortunately, they're also prone to interference by other forces, being bound by the same laws of energy. You see how crucial emotional energy is! What you may find more difficult to accept is that these laws aren't fixed in time. At death, any of these corruptions can cause the energies of the soul being lost into what humans call the supernatural.'

'So ghosts are actually some energy force bouncing around aimlessly forever?'

'Yes and no! They're dealt with in good time. To explain further would be to take you too far beyond Einstein, but basically, mankind expends so much effort trying to misuse the energy within an atom, but with too little regard as to where it comes from! They've worked out the possibility that space isn't really nothingness but it will still be a long time before they understand that the space between the electron field and the nucleus is much more than simply space. It still confuses people that they know an atom is moving, but when they look at it, it appears to be standing still. Think of a spinning wheel – you know it is going round, but at certain speeds it appears still. Shouldn't this make it obvious that there's some crossover of energy and time within an atom?'

'Yes, but hang on, scientists are making new breakthroughs on this technology every day! Isn't that a problem?'

'Frankly, I think we can safely leave the timing of Judgment Day to the Lord!'

'But if people continue digging into science, isn't there a chance they'll bring about Armageddon?'

'If you're asking whether mankind can bring about the Armageddon, the answer is yes, of course. Whether it is a major event in adversity or complete Armageddon is simply a matter of degree.'

Easy for him to talk, thought Andrew, he can't be involved – but then, perhaps, neither can I. What a strange thought that was! He said, 'OK, we have the soul, programmable and recoverable, but how does this fit with reincarnation?'

'Just as in the atomic world particles have neither eyes nor ears, all such movements are recorded in the memory layer, a mirrored storage of all brain functions, as forms of energy. It's the combinations in the brain that make all this encoding and recovery possible. We could talk about how the fringes of this process show themselves in the theories of particle physics, but it isn't strictly necessary. You're looking puzzled.'

'I suppose it'll take a little time to sink in,' said Andrew dubiously.

'Exactly. Just as when you were a boy it was hard to get a clear line for a simple phonecall, you now accept masses of digital information down that very same line. Imagine trying to explain such theories to someone in a time before electricity was a commonly used or known form of energy – let alone transferring that same technology to light!'

'So the soul is an energy force.'

Peter nodded. 'And thus indestructible, with each memory stored both at the physical level and the metaphysical level. Therefore it can be changed, on very rare spiritual occasions, but is easiest to implant early on when the chip is blank. As you might expect with any such process, occasional errors occur, creating the phenomenon of passed-life experiences, as I mentioned before. But is this surprising? People are still battling with similar dysfunctions in computer software – imagine a level existing as low as the background noise of the universe! Someone in your own lifetime, Professor Stephenson, made many recordings of passed lives containing facts simply not possible for any one person to have. How easy it is for mankind to dismiss this as fantasy, simply because they've got no logical explanation!'

'There's something comforting about logic,' argued Andrew, but Peter dismissed this with a wave of his hand. 'I hope by now you're coming to realise that, as the brain functions, memories are copied into the soul. In your case, the shell of the person you were still exists in your own body for convenience's sake, for the body and soul are normally separated at death.'

'What happens to it?'

'To the body? Normally, it would be used in the reincarnation process. A heavenly body is only given at the conclusion of the testing as I told you earlier, otherwise the soul will be passed onto its next human life, for its next phase of testing – or, in special cases, held back.'

'Why held back?' asked Andrew. 'After all, I thought adversity was set to run its course.'

'To a large degree it is, but it's still essential to obtain the balance and direction of adversity. Just as nature requires balance, there remain counterbalances within any evolutionary process, especially within species. It's all about the final goal and not completely controlling every detail.'

'Right, I think I see. The balance could only be obtained if there was a method of injecting positive and negative, good and evil forces. But the question is how will this balance shift towards the end of the process?'

Peter lifted an eyebrow.

'Its part of the journey to try and work it out, you'll get no assistance from me! However, rather than get distracted, it would be more helpful to return to 4000 to 2500 B.C and to the descendents of Adam. The mayhem that existed for them is recorded in the Bible, but it fails to tell the whole truth. Certainly the first souls were selected for heaven, but on earth interbreeding, expansion, political squabbles, plus overt aggression from those outside the test centres, soon made angelic control unviable. Reincarnation and selection alone enabled a soul to gain enough emotional experience to fit them for heaven, albeit over several lives.'

'This selection process…' said Andrew, and hesitated.

Peter smiled thinly. 'You want to know how it's done?'

'Doesn't everyone?'

'In principle, no more than you see in every culture. As for the transportation of the integral soul, that's only an extension of the vision we discussed before – the soul as an energy form, dispatched as a beam of energy. It'll probably be hard for you – as for so many before you – to accept that your entire being could be reduced to mere data, but this is science capable of distinguishing between life and information. Just because the knowledge mankind even now transmits has no life force within it doesn't mean it doesn't exist! These earliest transmissions are clearly depicted in such structures as the Egyptian pyramids.'

'I'd thought that those represented the Atlantis-type centres,' objected Andrew, although Peter paid no attention.

'And the central pyramid symbolised the soul's departure – although this was reserved only for the elite. The secret hole running from the central chamber to the outside copied the line of the principal transmission beams. They had already – even back then – worked out that the energy beam was aimed toward a certain star constellation. If you take measurements, you'll notice that the holes point in different directions as the constellation moves its own position.'

Andrew marvelled, 'So even astronomy...'

'Yes, but don't leap to conclusions because, although the principle may work, you already know that things can bend in both time and direction.'

'You said that earlier, but what happens now?'

'Now we need to focus on the 2500 B.C. point, when everything starts to move. The control centre areas are no longer viable amid the growing chaos. God, having watched evolution unfurl, had – despite many dashed hopes – finally discovered Adam's worthiest descendants and moved instantly to save Noah and family from what was to come. This same event also happened in a different way in other centres in the world, in a process that could be described as a selective culling.'

Andrew was appalled. 'You cull animals – if absolutely necessary, that is. You don't cull people!'

Peter stated, 'The flood was a needed adjustment to the direction of evolution. If all this sounds a bit fanciful – because, after all, records no longer exist – then just look at different religions across the world, both past and present. There you'll see a common thread, a common path to enlightenment, despite espousing slightly different methods and messages. The records for many of the centres were often scarce, simply because structure under angelic jurisdiction was different.'

'So God sent the great flood and culled all the people,' said Andrew, disgusted.

'Not quite all,' Peter reproved him, 'and there was no choice. On the one hand, there were human centres outstripping angelic control, and on the other new cities were being built with no guidance at all. All this, with God knowing that humanity's scientific awareness could only grow and that He had to act before there was any possibility of the old centres being breached.'

'But if souls were transmitted from these centres, wouldn't an almost total wipeout destroy God's very objective, as with the dinosaurs?'

'When God selected Noah, it was on the basis that a new transmission system had to be set up and tested. The earliest soul transmissions from the pyramids were always worrying, but there was no point deploying the ultimate technology until it unquestionably fitted with the evolutionary process. That new system, to describe it simply, moves in energy, type and time. This makes it almost invisible to man, despite the fact that such concentrated energy transmissions can still have disturbing results.'

'What, more culling?' demanded Andrew sarcastically.

'Unfortunately, the transmission beam that sends souls to heaven has to function on a certain alignment. We do everything we can to avoid accidents, if anyone in real time ventures into it, but, once set in motion they can be dragged across time itself. You'd have heard of one such place as the "Bermuda triangle", which, not coincidentally, is where the old angelic centre used to be. Because of that–'

'You mean, the Bermuda triangle spins people into another time?'

'Because of that,' said Peter evenly, 'in order to get back to Noah's own time, God enacted a simple plan. All the angels were recalled and advised about the way forward. Noah had already built his ark and collected the animals as instructed, simply because God – as with Eden – needed a control, as well as to ensure that any imbalance could be restored quickly by clone-type reproduction. As you probably appreciate, similar plans were established at different points throughout the world. But with free will, it's difficult – not to say impossible – to ensure an immediate new balance in the Laws of Adversity. So once the angels were recalled and the ark deployed, every angelic centre on earth was destroyed, in Bimini as elsewhere.'

'And God's purpose?'

'To remove all trace of His early work on earth, a monumental destruction had to occur, creating earthquakes and tsunamis across the world. One sub-continent collapsed entirely under the weight of gigantic waves, while sea and coastal centres sent huge plumes of cloud and water upwards into the air, creating storms and rainfall for weeks without cessation. Unsurprisingly, the uninitiated recorded this rainfall and flood as mere cause and effect, in the absence of the real explanation.'

'They probably just didn't like being culled,' muttered Andrew, 'But then what happened?'

'The angels had two main tasks: to remove any remaining signs of the previous angelic centres and to deal with any survivors not actually born of Noah. After all, this process was all about restoring some measure of control over the most tempestuous planet. Yet, you'll note, even here, that those great minds yet to come, such as Confucius, always claimed that his teachings came not from him, but from the great ancients – the angels. Yet this was now a phasing-out period for the angels, as they had been told something of our Lord's future plans.'

Andrew sighed. 'So you're saying that all of God's previous creations were destroyed with Noah's version of Earth, making the pyramids and other historic wonders around the world the feeblest, merest copies of what had existed before?'

Peter was pleased. 'Exactly. It's what mankind is best at – copying! It started with men rebuilding the pyramids in Egypt, in emulation of those lost angels they themselves revered as gods. In South America, one can easily observe the same. In areas where sufficient materials or knowledge was lacking, they just presented the image in forms such as burial mounds.'

'But surely that was man's imagination at work!'

Peter said, ironically, 'Sorry! All remaining copies of the original possess an underlying theme. This was indistinguishable mimicking of the lost angels, and – incidentally – why many early civilizations fell into the same pattern of assuming their rulers would become Gods. It's no coincidence that the Bible depicts the great flood and science dates the first pyramids at approximately the same point in time. Stonehenge and all the rest all followed within the next couple of hundred years.'

'So everything before the flood was destroyed and everything left behind dates after it. But why hasn't everyone spotted this already?'

'Not quite everything dates after it, but certainly everything *relevant*! And don't be too amazed at the lack of academic perception, the scholars aren't necessarily to blame. So much information was removed that there's no longer enough collaborative evidence to support the reality – apart from the Bible, which was taken as a symbolic or metaphorical event.'

'Now from this point, we enter the period 2500 B.C. to about 500 B.C. I select 500 B.C. not simply for convenience, but because at this time several important things happened. First we have Noah's descendents expanding across the globe. You'll also note, as this process cascades, Hindu religious records notes the arrival of migrants from the west.'

'Frankly, I couldn't have put a date on it.'

'It doesn't matter. What does matter is that Hindu tradition reconstructed their religion from the remnants of the old centre's teachings. Once the Asian college of angels was formed, the more they tried to intervene, the more their previous demi-god status interrupted the array of gods they now worship.'

'Not a bad life, that of a demi-god,' observed Andrew.

'Possibly not. Yet parallel to this we can traipse cheerfully through the Bible with Abraham, Jacob, Moses, without any real mention of Satan until David.'

'Do you mean that Satan actually exists?'

Peter said crisply, 'Of course he exists! I've explained the serpent and how – to that end – most of mankind's links to Satan have been misconstrued.'

'What, you mean that Satan is a well-meaning type of fellow?' But Peter was unimpressed.

'Most of these rare early references between God and Satan are in essence collusion. It's with this new agenda that Man is led to cast Satan in a far more severe role, despite the truth that Satan was simply the angel appointed by God to assist in the management of Hell and the processing of souls.'

'Poor thing,' said Andrew, with irony.

'Indeed,' responded Peter, with no irony at all. 'The first reason was to contain those not wanted on earth and thereby control the level of adversity. This was what I previously termed "the holding back". Satan controls this section of Hell. Satan is also responsible for controlling those evil spirits placed into the realm of adversity and taxed with collecting them. It's also in this role during this period that he was also given access to all areas of Earth and can be seen in interventions as bizarre as those of Eastern Mysticism as they tried to hang onto the old style of what they thought of as God's truth.'

'I bet he had a whale of a time,' said Andrew.

'I have no information on that point. However, his causing

destruction, confusion or dissention was adopted as the destroyer Shiva, for if you have ever seen a picture it can be no coincidence that Shiva and Satan are both often depicted as holding tridents.'

'Yes,' said Andrew doubtfully, 'But Neptune... or perhaps he was a prototype?'

'Exactly. Therefore, this adoption of the role in general of Satan and his little helpers is not merely to cause chaos, but also to control certain aspects that would otherwise be randomly abused. *Now* they may seem to run amok, but it's only to avoid tapping into the old-style connections to God by utilising the soul, apart from the body, through meditation or drugs.'

'I don't quite get what you mean by an old-style connection. Also, what has that to do with meditation? What's so bad about meditation?'

'Prayer, meditation and the Holy Spirit have a complex interconnectivity.'

'Go on,' urged Andrew, but there was a shadow across Peter's old-young face.

He said, 'Just as in the period of which we speak, a few people found that they could take a few practices from the old centres and misuse them. Especially since the new gateway opened by Jesus can be so easily abused. Whether unwittingly from the old practices or deliberately in more recent times, adversity must be set in the path of corruption. And, much as people long to seek Nirvana, Satan will ensure they will often find demons instead.'

'I thought you seemed vaguely sympathetic to Satan.'

'Well, anyone looking to control lost souls, especially in the balance of adversity, is bound to get a bad press. Yes, Satan is in some sense in control of sin, but good can't exist in the utter absence of evil. Satan's unfortunate image was inevitable – especially as earth-bound authorities play on such fear to enforce social control.'

'Surely there could have been better ways?'

'No. Once Satan questioned humanity deserving their souls, there could be no other way to separate good and evil. And who better to be given the free will to test it, albeit under the terms of the Laws of Adversity?'

'I see what you're getting at, but I hope it's possible to keep a clear head, in the face of a couple of thousand years of propaganda and a film industry intent on inventing every kind of monster to feed our fascination.'

Peter considered answering this, but instead went on. 'You know of course how Israel as a nation formed, grew and prospered. This sequence is well recorded, along with the ravages predictably visited upon. Yet who knows what would have happened if the Jews had stayed resolute towards the spirit of God, rather than placing man to the fore, elevating the human and creating vain rabbinic teaching? Much of this type of change is documented within Greek mythology. In the eastern region, the Hindu religion had also gone from growing strength to losing its way and message, as its practitioners became consumed by mortal ambition.'

'Though I still think of the Hindus as less materialistic.'

'Not necessarily. In the end, God knew that He would need to prepare the ground for a different way. It was therefore necessary to withdraw the angels from control and allow mankind more self-autonomy, with just minor adjustments from afar. This is also why Satan, sometimes called Hades, became more prominent. The change from a more background role to a forefront image is increasingly obvious as scholars and scribes mention him more. This understanding of man's growing sinfulness still exists, though societies are now such, that interference is no longer required. Angelic adjustments become rare, generally in response to faith or personal appeal to God.'

Andrew said, 'So the power exists for God to change anything, but –'

'But for Him to use it would be pointless, especially if you recall that this is an evolutionary process. One accepts that evolution will cause deviation and the art of God is to allow it, but with the long-term furthering of faith being the ultimate goal, even if things appear to be heading appallingly off-course. Consider it as a pendulum that will tend to swing and adjust rather than to halt altogether.

'Around 600 B.C., Rome started to become a power that would eventually take over from the empires of Persia and Greece. Around that part of the world, belief in angels remained, even if their actual interference had become limited. This fading of faith in the angels, as the mythological gods, is essential for the uptake of the future basis of faith. Already the Jews are suffering from their abandonment of the realm of judges and have begun their cycles of captivity and turbulence.'

'Why couldn't they succeed, like the Romans did?'

'Because had Israel been powerful and successful, the new way forward would never have made an impact! The people who flocked to hear Jesus would have dismissed him, convinced that their success would have been proof of their godliness and that they had no need for any new message. But this is just one side of the story. The east had developed similar feudal problems, but with the added prospect and problem that Hinduism and its allies was growing in strength to become a large force.

'In the East, there was an added problem with the enlightenment of the soul gradually taking a more prominent role than actual faith in God. In some places, reincarnation was now also being confused with man-made adaptations. Despite all these issues, it had to remain for the majority that each faith was the only faith, so that it would focus their effort on doing their best within each existence. So rather than make corrections, it was more useful to retain such faiths as Hinduism, but to divide and confuse them further by introducing several splits from the basic Hindu concepts. It is sort of one of the heavenly jokes that man considers himself so clever, but has hardly ever questioned such illogical periods of history as the single fifty-year span when Buddhism, Taoism and Confucianism were all established!'

'I accept that the odds that three such minds would form religions or even exist within one such period have to be considered remote.'

'This tripartite whole process rooted out the odd remnants of teachings from the old Atlantis centres. It doesn't invalidate any of them, for each was a prophet, whether knowingly or not, part of God's enlightenment. They were left to germinate a couple of hundred years until like fruit the information became ripe to be plucked. We also have to take in the advent of the phenomenon that the west has come to know as Socrates. Although his depth of thinking could be compared in some way to Confucius', his purpose lay in a different direction. There was turmoil and wars flaring out across Europe and the Middle East, as man tried to fill the void left when the angels withdrew. But meanwhile, Socrates was guided to put the pieces together and work out the old teachings. Surrounded by people deploying falsehoods symbolically attached to pagan gods, what alternative did he have other than to question and challenge? Jesus was yet to come. And for questioning and challenging alone he was sentenced to death.'

Andrew used the ensuing pause. 'You said needed of him, as if in this special purpose Socrates was "guided". It seems a strange word to choose.'

'In the east, the uptake of the three new enlightenment religious teachings had caused division, allowing each to be weakened sufficiently. But in both east and west, bits of information from the past angelic centres would be at risk of falling into the wrong hands. Socrates was needed to start a chain of philosophical thinking in the west as in the east, but without the formation of any large-scale religious following. However, the most significant things for you to be concerned with came from his students – most notably Aristotle and Plato.'

'It's been decades since I read anything about either of them.'

'That doesn't matter. Plato took on the work of Socrates and laid down the mysteries of Atlantis, but in a way that ensured that he did not suffer the same fate. This had to be there as a path to the truth for you and others to follow, even this jigsaw needed enough pieces left in place to make a picture. His use of mythology was perfect, as it teased at the truth without alerting those obsessed with self. But simultaneously a second event was happening, thanks to Aristotle. The most pressing issue here was the greater plan to remove the obvious evidence that existed in the old inscribed records, especially those in the east. The possibility of their falling into unscrupulous hands constantly increased, with growing travel and communication. So what better way than take the successful policies from the west and use them to destroy those remnants of information left in the east?'

'Philosophically or by conquest?'

'Both – though the conquest was by proxy. Aristotle's increasing prominence gave him the tutorage of Alexander the Great, son of the Greek's King Philip II. You must understand here that, with the withdrawal of the angels, God now could only exact change by manipulating man. Open interference would give away everything. Yet eventually – once people were capable of putting the fragments together – the goal was that they should be prepared to cope with such knowledge. That time, Andrew, has arrived, and delivering this information is the task you've agreed to be part of.' Peter stopped and looked, waiting for a few seconds to pass.

Andrew felt a little thrill, whether of fear or excitement – or both – he could hardly have said.

'I understand – I hope – what you're telling me, so far. But how did the great philosophers know what to do, as the angels had effectively withdrawn from the field?' Andrew was going to add more to his question, but Peter raised his hand.

'The short answer is divine guidance, but history recorded it as myth and legend. You see that the guidance of Aristotle and Alexander is one of the last deeds done by the chief angel of the European college, known as Zeus, though this isn't his real name. When Alexander was ready, Zeus confided to him the quest that he was commanded to do.'

'What, through a dream?'

'As a young man, Alexander often clashed with his father and had taken to hiding for periods in local caves until his father's annoyance blew over. It was on one of these occasions when Zeus instructed Alexander – and, incidentally, where a few of his close friends were witnesses. These few friends have confounded historians ever since, as their undying loyalty to Alexander was such as to defy rational explanation. It was however this witnessing and their oath to the angel Zeus that made them so loyal.'

'It makes sense.'

'I'm glad to hear you say so – and with reason! For not only did Zeus promise to guide the young Alexander, but the prince was promised that he would be considered as the adopted son of Zeus. This symbolic offer was strictly conditional, on the basis that such a pact remained secret and conducted with honour. Alexander was given his chance, but never told how it would end. Here in the midst of our discussions – as perhaps you might have realised already – you are yourself within just such a process. And, just as Alexander was, you will be told things that you must judge when to tell others – if ever!' Peter looked at Andrew with a heavy seriousness that he hadn't shown before.

Andrew was startled. 'How am I supposed to know who to trust?'

'If you start to use the information for yourself, it loses its power. Then not to speak might not push you to into battle, but you could easily endanger both yourself and those around you.'

'That sounds like a threat.'

'A threat – or a challenge, the difference lies only in semantics! You'll see as you look at the events around Alexander how he started well, but his later conduct fell well short of the integrity expected if he was to aspire to the privileged position promised to him.

'In short, Alexander took the throne at a very early age, following his father's assassination. Only mankind could conceive a situation whereby a fellow hardly out of his teens could conquer much of the known world in just seven years without divine help – help which Alexander naturally had, of course. The logistics alone are so preposterous as to be considered realistic only from the safe distance of tens of centuries – or in the mind of a child.'

'I think every schoolchild admires Alexander.'

'That's no excuse! Take the last battle against Darius III, for example, king of the Persian Empire. There he commanded fifty thousand troops against a well-equipped force of a quarter of a million. Certainly, he had a mind inspired by Aristotle, combined with a working knowledge of Greek warfare, but his achievements wildly surpassed that advantage. The truth is that the primitive supply lines and huge manpower needed made his task humanly impossible – but nothing is too difficult for God.'

'Why was he so favoured?' asked Andrew, beginning to resent the way his former favourite was being diminished.

'Because his task was to collect historical documents. His messengers were sent to even the most remote places to demand all such documents and artefacts in return for peace, while his reputation was fearsome enough for most to capitulate without a struggle. From his first conquest, Alexander set a precedent, often confounding his allies by offering such deals to those lying in the path of his armies. As long as they surrendered their documents and paid Alexander due tribute, he was perfectly willing to reappoint the ruler as his satrap, or governor – not an unattractive option, given the likely consequences of resistance. Zeus had advised him to do this as he proceeded into Asia, so that the fear of his reputation would deliver these objectives with minimal loss of life.'

'I'm not surprised they gave in, all the same,' said Andrew. 'Most rulers would surrender old documents in return for their power and wealth.'

'And some were consoled by the prospect that Alexander was collecting the information rather than destroying it. Modern scholars have long sought the hidden libraries of Alexander, but they've never been found. Throughout history, Alexander's thirst for information on local religions was reported as an incidental side issue – even a hobby – of Alexander's, rather than what it really was – the main point! Yet even today, people miss the relevance of Alexander's eager fascination with the beliefs of every country he vanquished. For example, he went to great lengths to be the first to get the Jewish biblical texts translated into Greek. Scholars have often noted how this enabled the fledging Christian church to spread, but they rarely connect it to other acts of Alexander. Another crucial condition was that, if Alexander was to die in battle, all the ancient documents should be destroyed. Thus, with the messy bits tidied up, God had achieved what was required toward the new dawn of spiritual history.'

Andrew said, 'But what about Alexander himself, as a person?'

He rather expected to be ignored, but Peter took him seriously.

'You might well wonder. Such success took its toll on such a young man, especially a young man with so many nations under his control. Many had started to treat him as a god himself, as they still followed the old practices. One of the reasons he chose Alexandria as the safest place for his greatest library was because Egypt still retained the practice of worshipping their leaders as gods. Yet this act, intended simply to frighten the populace into respecting his precious library, got out of hand. Being still human, Alexander made the signal mistake of ignoring the divine conditions initially laid upon him. Being worshipped, along with the belief he would eventually become part of the angelic hierarchy tempted him into defying God.'

'You mean, he began to believe he was some kind of god?'

'No, but he dared to pronounce before time that he was the son of Zeus. He was struck down with illness, dying within days, simply because he had said that which he was forbidden to say.'

'Is that then the choice you are giving me? I'm somehow to use this information – whatever information I'm given – with integrity or be struck down too?'

'Let's just say that, by entrusting you with the mission, we understand what that will mean. Although lacking guidance may be difficult, you must keep true to your faith. If you do this, Andrew, you can't fail. And if you can't, if you lose control of the information given to you, then adversity will redress the balance. Just as Alexander's death was rendered necessary before he could create an empire so established it could be misused by any successor.'

Andrew joked, 'I suppose I haven't got much to lose. After all, I've died already!'

'So had Alexander, several times, in fact. Yet even in his

comparative failure, he did much and was greatly revered. Ptolemy, one of his earliest and closest aides, with him at the time of Zeus's visit and previously governor of Egypt, took control of that area and pronounced himself Pharaoh. He then launched a mission to recover Alexander's body and have it reburied in Egypt. Such a risk – and such an expense – was born not from need, but from knowledge of the divine connection.'

'But did –'

Peter interrupted briskly, leaving Andrew with questions still burning. 'I think that's enough about Alexander. The next three hundred years with their chaos and wars eventually ended with Roman dominance in both Europe and the Middle East. God's plan remained set and it's not surprising then that He occasionally shared parts with His prophets, various sons of Noah. So here and there we see the repetition of great truths emerging through prophets. It has been God's choice throughout to impart the truth in such a way that each individual has the option to choose the truth – or not.'

'And if they never heard?' asked Andrew curiously.

'For a man to stand at judgement saying, "I never heard", is the same as saying, "My soul is unready for heaven." If man looks with an earthly eye he will see only with an earthly eye. Only when – as I hope you have grasped, Andrew – man looks from the soul within, is it possible to see past the confusion.'

Andrew longed to ask if he was reckoned to have done this, as it seemed to him as if his entire life had been composed of confusion, but he didn't dare to interrupt again. Peter said, 'So the ground was prepared for the coming of Our Lord. The most successful areas of the world had now worked out that they needed social order and that the individual was coming to perceive the need for enlightenment. Some still hung onto their worship of the mythological gods, as the angels were still revered, even if they had all but vanished, but most of Roman society filled the void by elevating man himself. The lesson from this is that both society and enlightenment, if not routed towards God, are destined to failure.'

'Of course,' said Andrew.

'There are many other things that happened before Jesus came to prepare the pathway to his Father for the masses. However, it's not my intention to cover every detail here, but instead to set before you the real history besetting mankind, not the history it so passionately hangs on to. By now I hope you'll credit God with the power to enable a genetic virgin birth.'

'Naturally.'

'And the Prince of Peace was born. I won't go into the teachings of Jesus, as they're surprisingly well recorded, if often misused. As much as some might think this new covenant replaced all others, it was in fact a new, clearer, additional gateway.'

'You mean, there were still several ways to be acceptable to God.'

'Yes. One of the most important indicators was given when Jesus preached at the Sermon on the Mount. He made it clear that all will be judged as they themselves judged. Now in every religion proceeding Jesus, there existed the possibility of some souls evolving into qualification for heaven. Even after Jesus, if any other religion is chosen, its adherent can still qualify for heaven, assuming they avoid man-made derivatives or false paths. It's perfectly possible – it's just very much harder.'

'Which is why very simple people can find faith easier?'

'Of course. Those who look from a clear soul will see more clearly, and will more naturally avoid unnecessary hatred and violence. For the learned it can be harder, partly because original teachings are rarely recorded accurately. With so many splits and mistranslations, it's unavoidable that false prophecies were concocted to fill the gaps. But then this is also an issue for the way the Bible was constructed – not to mention the latter-day distortions of Islam. Still, despite these confusions, there is a clear context towards the evolution of the soul. The truth remains within the texts, but not all within the texts is true.'

'That explains quite a lot,' said Andrew.

'If any part of this still sounds circumstantial, then ask yourself why, from many religions, there's so little written evidence? The detailed text of the Bible stands out in this. There are fragments within such faiths as Hinduism, but the Vedas texts are mere remnants. Even the theory that great philosophers refused to have their teachings written down so they couldn't be misinterpreted fails to explain this oddity. The truth is, throughout history, men have edited manuscripts to better suit their own purposes. This has always been apparent to God, hence the simplicity of the Ten Commandments.'

'Sorry Peter, but may I ask a question?'

'You may, but not yet. The Holy Spirit enables someone to sin and still find enlightenment of the soul and forgiveness from God within a single lifetime. It's a true alternative to reincarnation, to an endless recapitulation of trial and error. As long as one can prove true contrition and true belief, they can progress to heaven. This is the new gateway. Which is not to say God would fail to honour any covenant from alternative religious doctrines, whether from the old angelic colleges or those branching off from the mainstream – but it would probably take several lifetimes.'

'So what Jesus refers to when he says the "only" way is through him –'

'Is a mild case of misreporting. Under the old ways, the rate of return was dispiritingly low and few could ever hope to aspire to heaven. But through Jesus, the Holy Spirit enables all who truly long to seek it to be fulfilled.'

'But is this the same process for the same heaven and for the same God?'

'Yes. No matter how good a person you are, you can't proceed to heaven unless you first submit your soul to God. So if you like, it was the ability to experience the many tests that lead one to enlightenment within a single lifetime.'

'Why didn't Jesus make this clear?'

'It wasn't for Him to try and explain the difference between the different gateways, for He came to deliver the new way.'

'And I suppose Paul was also sometimes misreported, for example, about women?'

Peter smiled. 'Correct. Within the teachings of Jesus, but withheld from the mainstream recorded history, is that this new covenant includes a new covenant toward women, which the disciples decided to suppress. Yet it was some 300 years before Rome adopted Christianity and some further 300 before it was determined what exactly should be included in the Bible. Unfortunately, if predictably, the men concerned ignored the opportunity to overturn the misogyny that kept women as a class below.

'The subsequent selection of the books of the Bible, so as to ignore any reference toward a new equality for women, had several consequences. The part women played around Jesus and his treatment of them is only selectively recorded and many other references are missing. In later years, scholars have unwound these contradictions and in recent times society has caught up. Such things can only delay God's intention, it will not prevent it – and nor did the attitude of the Pharisees.

'As so often, it will be asked, why did God allow such things to happen? The answer is that God freely gives opportunities for mankind to grow, but generally the choices they make often merely prove that more lessons are needed. And after Jesus, of course, the world saw a new religion born and a new balance of adversity.'

'Islam.'

'The angel Gabriel came to Muhammad, sent to give the world Islam. A people born from the chosen tribe were empowered by these new teachings, although beset with ambiguity – and thus subject to many different splits. The irony of Islam is that it contains the perfect seed for the foundation of sexual equality and peace, but simultaneously sufficient lack of clarity for it to be horrifically distorted. And of course adherents are supposed to defend Islam, even to fight for it – but only within the context of peace, by bringing all religions under one brotherhood. It is always wrong to set one of God's religions against another! I can tell you this, also – no person can hope for heaven if they fight for their branch of religion with hatred and vengeance in their souls, as some parts of Islam have been warped. And not only Islam either.'

'May I ask something else?'

'Of course.'

'Why introduce Islam at all, if it only muddied the waters?'

'Islam was created so that man had the option of taking belief to the higher moral ground that it theoretically contains, thereby forcing the Christian church to correct its own appalling distortions. It also answered the Zoroastrian problem in the area, as Islam gave a stark contrast to Christianity, as opposed to any that might confuse the issue when preaching from ancient sources and sounding too similar. The fact that many have chosen Islam to advance bigotry and suppression comes from men's stubbornness in choosing the wrong path within both religions – or, I may say, all religions.

'All I have told you here is known, though misinterpreted and misrepresented by men. Mankind cannot resist these false assumptions, as his thirst for knowledge and his innate impatience distorts all he doesn't know into what he longs to imagine. If you choose to research, you'll wind up with the works of Edgar Cayce, Churchwarden and Blavatsky, among many others. You'll observe them grasping some elements of the truth, or through science – even archaeology – trying to piece some of the puzzle pieces together.

These scholars failed because they couldn't bear to wait to find the whole truth. That's the frustration of having a part of the truth – it wasn't long before each gave into the temptation to push too wildly into the unknown, as their followers demanded more answers than they could supply. Rather than be seen *not* to know, they used guesswork to patch up their own self-esteem.'

'And yet they were great men.'

'They were gifted people,' Peter corrected him, 'regretfully, not great. So now, my friend, we're back where we started, with the tendency of people to invent answers. Each generation seems intent on proving the previous ones foolish in their assumptions or beliefs, yet all their new knowledge manages to leave history completely disjointed – even to disjoint history! What I've given you here is the outline of how history is a constant flow of cause and effect, while historians still imagine that a whole civilisation can become deluded into adopting strange or fanciful religious practices. They don't want to see the causes that created such beliefs, preferring to rejoice in their seeming superiority to those peoples who preceded them. What these texts – the texts you will be given – are to do is put an end to this practice.'

For the first time, Andrew saw Peter's hazel eyes firing with the look that must have been there when he first left his fishing boats to follow Jesus. He longed to speak, if only to say, 'Me? I can't do anything of the sort! I'm no historian, and certainly no orator. I'm just a normal, middle-class person who lives in Surrey with his wife and his teenagers and – when the weather is fine – sometimes skips church. I doubt I could even understand any texts you might give me!' But awe kept him silent, for Peter in full flow was unstoppable.

'History shall be seen in its true flowing state at last! As for you, you were chosen because you have searched and waited, without arrogance, with sound judgement, and because you have been faithful. You also have an intuitive understanding of emotional energy. So from here I will take you the final room, where you'll learn more.'

Andrew sat back with a deep breath as Peter came to (what seemed to him at least) an abrupt conclusion. So much of the information challenged what he thought he understood and yet didn't. The result left him trying to clear the fuzziness of these conflicts swirling in his head.

'Peter, can you clear up a couple of things first?'

'I expect some issues will need further explanation. Some, however, must be left incomplete – only because they will make more sense when the final stage of explanation is given – to you and the others.'

He was relieved to hear about the others. Probably, he thought, with a sudden surge of hope, I'm one of many.

'So am I right in assuming that my task is to convince people that history should show there is and can be only one God and that God has been behind all the major religions? Probably my mind is simply clouded with prejudice, but it's just a very hard concept to take in – or to impart, for that matter.'

'Andrew, *all* religions think their god is the only one. Would it be logical that all the others are wrong and Christians alone in the right?'

'No, I accept that.'

'And is it hugely likely that numerous almighty powers would coexist in competition with each other, quibbling over the spoils of mankind?'

'Not particularly.'

'I would suggest that the most probable option would be for the existence of one god – albeit one god viewed differently from different cultures and perspectives. What I've given you – and what I'll give you – is the missing perspectives in how all these different views were created and the circumstances behind their creation. How history has had to be managed to create the new way forward. Remember that mankind's self-importance means he will hold fast to his religion and its own version of history above any other, thereby blinding himself to the connections between them all. After all, isn't it a human trait to see what they want to see, rather than what exists?'

'Yes, but just to be sure, does it mean that people who don't believe in *any* god are doomed?'

'"Doomed" is a harsh word. God might still use such a person to face adversity, though whether the outcome involved actual enlightenment would depend upon the circumstances. But you may be sure that such every person will face one lifetime of adversity after another if they aren't prepared to find God. By the time we've finished, you'll understand the Laws of Adversity and how they're used in helping the development of souls going to heaven.'

'So all things and all people are part of a sort of huge test to help us learn what we need for heaven?'

'Simple, isn't it? Just like many great truths. Because there are only two options, in reality – either there is one God, creator of the soul that gives mankind hope towards passage to heaven, or else the world and everything within it is merely a gigantic freakish accident, temporal, purposeless – finite. It's a general human need to have proof as well as answers. The main problem here is that you, as others, long for the proof of the spiritual realm in terms of the physical realm, and this cannot be until the end of all things.'

Andrew took a deep breath.

'In that case, I have nothing left to ask – or say, except to thank you for all your time and patience with my stupidity and foolishness.' He rose and offered Peter his hand, to which Peter grabbed warmly with both of his – but only for a flashing instant, in consideration of Andrew.

The angel's hands were burning.

32

The Mission

A strange dizziness followed the release of his hands, which retained a pattern of heat from Peter's. Andrew looked almost fearfully up, and was relieved to see Peter looking exactly as quizzical as usual.

'My friend, I must now ask you to follow me.' Peter moved to the door, which flickered opened as he neared it. Andrew felt almost giddy in the sudden realisation that it was now time to leave. Glancing round as if to gather his possessions, he realised that it contained nothing of his. Yet these surroundings, though strange to him, had grown familiar, almost comfortable, and he seemed almost reluctant to leave them – though he recognised that there was no logic in staying there, other than his own fear of what was to come.

The door ahead of him the same door he had so longed to open when he had recovered consciousness. How strange it was, to finally step through it, into a wider brightness (to which his eyes took a moment to adjust). Following Peter, he found himself entering a blur of tunnels. They were plain tunnels, smooth and white, cornerless, seemingly tapering, but always staying the same size. Perhaps they were flying – but he felt no rush of air. His eyes clung to the folds of Peter's clothes before him. Suddenly the light changed – he still couldn't see clearly, but a still more feverish brightness was certainly emerging ahead. Although "his" room in comparison had been dim, the brightness of the tunnels was certainly surpassed by what lay ahead – could it be? Was it possible? Andrew's heart sped, recalling various stories of near-death experiences – tunnels, light… then they emerged through the end of a tunnel into a large open space. As Peter slowed and paused, Andrew took the chance to stand aside and have a quick glance around.

The vast enclosed area was shaped and arranged like a strange gigantic auditorium. The whole floor sloped down in a concave arc towards a raised platform at the lowest central point. It had to be at least several times the size of a football pitch, wildly bright, as the walls and ceiling glowed with a strange and radiant incandescence. Still brighter were two jewelled large doors, much larger than those to his room, positioned either side of the central platform. Even from the far distance, Andrew could see that the platform was adorned with an elaborate lectern, representing eagles, set in gold, and inlaid with green and blue precious stones.

Just as Peter turned and beckoned him to follow, Andrew noticed several ordinary-looking people entering through the doorway to the left of the lectern. It seemed years – decades! – since he had seen anyone apart from the angel. He longed to ask Peter who they were, but Peter was on the move again. As he saw them leave, he felt lonely again, a painful few seconds until Peter moved towards the same door.

The excitement of getting closer to his "task" – the curiosity aroused by these strangers – an urge to be among fellow humans again. All these combined with his fear being overpowered by what he was expected to do. His heart hammered at him relentlessly, it was dogged proof at least that some part of him was still alive.

Caittie was lagging behind the others. As instructed, she had been collected into a group of about a dozen people. They were all strangers to her, and one of them was a shaven-head, orange-clad Buddhist monk, yet all looked equally lost – and at least equally nervous, which felt vaguely reassuring, although any reassurance was clouded by her sense of failure.

Caittie stubbornly attempted to tell herself that she hadn't failed, that she'd in death only proven her father to be right, and on the trail of something critically important, crucially worthwhile. She tried to imagine too, that her own sacrifice might enable someone else to find a way, though having kept her own investigations secret made it difficult to see how anyone would be any the wiser.

Except for Michael, of course. She had visions of Michael, too – horrific visions of his falling after the shot, bleeding to death on the spot, or saved, captured, even freed on condition that he never pass on all they'd discovered. Her feeling for Michael had simultaneously deepened and weakened – she found it possible to think of him sexually – for whatever reason – yet her *feeling* for him was stronger than ever. Yet if he too was dead... for the thousandth time, she upbraided herself for leaving no 'box' or trail of her own. Though, if so, to whom could she have left it? Who did she truly trust – or even love?

Another failure, she thought, humiliated. Guilt flooded her, not only for having failed, but – still worse – for having involved and endangered innocent people. Nor could she shake off her own sense of disappointment, in Frank himself and in the truth that he had defeated them.

Yet through all the heavy burden of pain shone the light of the strange lady's words, especially being Peter so disguised, that she would be included in some way in something connected to it! But how could that be, if she was dead? There were times when she half-determined that Peter was a devil, teasing her with hope when hope, as well as Michael was almost certainly dead. Although she didn't feel dead, and, after all, she was walking. And there was a stubbornness in her that didn't *feel* finished, somehow.

Mixed up with her sorrow was the realisation that she half-wanted to punish herself for the years of resentment she had clung to towards her father. Part of her believed that whatever fate had in store for her, it couldn't be as bad as she deserved.

The other people walking with her had been of little interest, once she had stopped, breath caught, looking for anyone she knew. And they had been walking – if it was walking, it didn't *feel* like walking – for so long that she was surprised when they emerged from the tunnels along the edge of a huge auditorium. In the corner of this large space they were heading towards a large podium, decorated with elaborately gilded birds of prey, about halfway along the lower wall. The others were disappearing into a doorway further ahead as the numbers in front of her diminished. Caittie was suddenly conscious of a collective feeling of trepidation. She caught the eye of an older woman, who attempted a crinkle-eyed smile, which Caittie was too nervous to return.

Glancing up at that moment, she noticed a couple of other people over at the far end were moving towards them. Following them into the room she faced a set of chairs in neat rows strategically placed with a generous space around them. The chairs, which had a peculiarly opaque quality, like softened marble, all faced away from the door, so apart from the group she entered with, she could only see the backs of those already seated. Ushered into the back row, she felt vaguely glad to be sitting next to the woman who had noticed her, in the next to last seat. With a shock of recognition – but what else could she had supposed? – she recognised her name inscribed into the back of the stone of her seat, and an envelope – if there could be an envelope with no obvious means of opening it – on top of it.

Nobody spoke, although there was an indescribably beautiful thread of music running through the room. The wall in front of them was far brighter than the others and the angels who had collected them were standing quietly to one side: she noticed one with a great Roman nose and another, despite her black complexion, with eloquent green eyes.

Caittie found herself recalling the strange interview she had had with Peter, in which he referred to her prayers. All that Peter had said had seemed dreamlike, except when he had made it clear that she would be part of some team, set on a task of divulging something of what she had discovered. In her depressed state of mind, she doubted that she could help anybody, as all she had done was to take on her father's obsession and succeed in making others suffer. Equally, if this *was* death, surely she would be punished a thousand times for deluding herself and getting Sharon killed? How could she – or anyone – ever atone for her level of stupidity and arrogance? Despite the luminosity of the room, in the absence of answers, her mind felt as if it was drowning her in its dark unstoppable waves.

Andrew followed Peter through the door, whereupon the angel said something to a colleague in an undertone. Seeing Andrew hesitate, Peter rather impatiently indicated the last remaining empty chair at the back row of the audience, before moving towards a group of angels standing at the side. Once Andrew had taken his seat, the rectangular block of thirty or forty chairs were all filled. It struck him that no one was talking or gazing around – they all sat resolutely or pensively staring towards the front. He moved round the back of his chair, noticing a smooth, pulsating envelope-shaped object on the seat. He stopped at the side, bending to pick up the envelope – it had his name on it – and stopping to look down the row of faces. He noticed first the woman beside him, her pale, wistful face, her almost trance-like gaze. He would guess she was in her late twenties, but her expression gave the impression of youth, as if some childlike fear engulfed her.

Caittie noticed the last person arriving as he moved into the place beside her. She felt unable to greet him, though he wasn't intimidating – a slim, hesitant, mild-looking fellow in his forties. She turned her head slightly, and as she did, he smiled warmly at her, though she couldn't quite return it.

It was clear to Andrew that the girl was troubled, though whatever nerves he'd felt himself had swerved to adrenalin, giving his body a renewed sense of energy. He noticed that the girl had imprisoned her hands to between her legs as if to disguise their fidgeting. He glanced towards Peter, but Peter was immobile, lips moving – praying? – and in the end Andrew put his hand on hers and whispered, 'Don't worry. You'll be all right.'

That this stranger, almost old enough to be her father, had touched her hands felt oddly comforting, his warmth just thawed her chill of fear. If this man wasn't frightened then why should she be? He moved to withdraw his hand just as she squeezed it – a lifeline. There could be no resisting such a silent plea. As the seconds ticked past, her mind switched its fretting to why she was holding the hand of this stranger, but it still felt safer holding on than letting go.

Finally Peter and the others stood up as a new angel materialised and stood at the centre of the podium. He was almost as tall as Peter and looked very much older – how, Andrew could not have said, but his movements gave an impression of gravity and weight besides which Peter seemed almost impulsive.

'Welcome.' The older angel stretched out his arms as if to include all. There was a collective sigh as he scrutinised her face – though Caittie didn't suspect it, each person in the room felt exactly the same sense of scrutiny. For his own part, Andrew felt a shock of recognition, as if he had always known the angel, but instantly realised that this was some power far harder to explain.

The man continued. 'Some of you now fear the worst, but this process or task you are about to enter, although difficult, will bring you reward worthy of your effort. The situation is as follows: you have all failed in some way and instead of the usual corrections, we have selected you all to be part of a very special task.'

A ripple – was it surprise? Relief? – shivered through the audience. The angel continued, 'This may shock those of you that have not been told a great deal during your interviews. However, just so there is no more confusion, this place you have been brought to is the double gateway – the gateway to Heaven and to Hell.'

At the back, Andrew could clearly see many heads turning. The girl beside him was gripping his hand almost painfully, but he didn't want to offend her by moving it away.

The man continued, 'This actual centre is really more of a link, a place outside all other places. This is not where you will someday receive God's judgment, and nor will you be honoured by seeing Him – not yet. Instead, you will each be given a new life, a second chance, which will include retention of this information in the depths of your souls. The reason I'm telling you this is because we wish you to retain key triggers that will focus you, back on earth, towards your objective. You will retain enough from here to commit to the task, but in most cases you will not even remember this place.'

He paused and checked round the room as if to ensure himself of everyone's attention. 'Just so you get a picture of how this will operate, will all those who have heard about the Laws of Adversity in their briefing please raise your hand?'

After a moment, Andrew did. He doubted that he understood the Laws of Adversity, but he still had Peter's riddles running round his head and he had assuredly mentioned them. From his position, he had the advantage of being able to see the whole room of people. It was clear that only one from each row put up their hand. It struck Andrew seeing a glimpse of their faces for the first time that they were all different colours and types of people.

'Thank you,' said the leader. 'You have been chosen as leaders or instigators within your field, time or religious division. The others in your row will be your helpers or new leaders to take on the work, as this will be a process that in some instances will take more than one lifetime. And now, will each of you instructed in the real history of the world, as opposed to earthly perception, now indicate this please?'

Andrew had no doubt at all about acknowledging this. The more he thought of all that Peter had said, the more life, earth and history made sense. His hand went up boldly – at least at first. Yet as he glanced around, something seemed wrong. The people in front of him were still looking up and down. Slowly some started to turn round as they realised that no one in their own row had put up their hand. As they turned and looked, one by one they focused on Andrew, as his was the only hand raised. Andrew did not know whether to be excited or embarrassed as eventually the entire block of people were looking at him – the girl, embarrassed to be holding his other hand, had already released his. Finally, he slowly lowered his hand.

The man at the front continued, 'This is Andrew. Remember him. Now, no matter whether you have been selected as preachers, helpers or supporters, you will need the support of each other. This is not about divine intervention, but about achieving a change of emphasis within the new covenant. You have just seen that only one of you – that is, Andrew – has been given the answers to both questions and for this purpose he will be the trigger to the process.

'If this seems an impossible task for so few, please remember you are only the core group. As needed, other helpers will follow.

'More importantly, at times you may face rudeness, derision and persecution, but there is no question that, if you are faithful, you will overcome all resistance, even from those who see the truth as a threat. The key to this task will be the words "Paradox Lost", as this is removal of the first paradox relating to faith in our God. Back on Earth, when confronted with these words, you'll know what to do. And now, I'd like you all to release the messages left on your seats. These give an indication of where and how you will be replaced back into earthly life.'

Andrew held his envelope, on which bold type suddenly surfaced. At the top was – *Reinstatement* – and then below – *asleep, heart attack revoked.* The moment he finished reading it the envelope disintegrated inside his fingers. He couldn't help noticing that the girl had been much slower. In bold type she had – *Reborn* – but the text below was several lines and difficult to read from an angle. He could only make out, *Died in 1990. To be reborn…* after which the words curled in a rosy haze and dematerialised. Everyone around them seemed to be drawing breath and taking in what they had read. The messages left a pleasant smell – similar to mown grass – upon the air.

Although to Andrew his own death still seemed surreal, it seemed an even stranger notion that God was planning to undo it. Then his mind remained perplexed at his accidental view of his neighbour's instructions. How could they both be sitting here, yet she at least was to be reborn? He thought that her profile looked clear and less troubled, as if a weight had been lifted and she was no longer trembling.

Although he could still hear Peter's words resounding in his head about time, he still felt puzzled. It had seemed possible to envisage theoretical time differences while he was still alive, but having met and even made physical contact with someone who

266

would be placed spuriously in time was a whole new challenge.

As if this thought was general, the angel said, 'Don't worry if anything still seems a bit vague. The crucial point is that you've all been selected to set a new approach to Our Lord. If you feel unworthy, don't worry because you'll be given the necessary tools in your new life as Moses was. The information we give you won't be instantly available to you, but will instead be triggered by the publishing of a book called *Paradox Lost*. In addition, in your new life, you might not necessarily directly recognise each other, but that doesn't mean you'll be alone.

'Now I need to clarify some basic elements of the mission, which is to spread a new understanding within all faiths. We're not intending to start a new religion – nor to further split those religions already established. Instead, it's your task to work within all religions – in fact, you've been specifically chosen to make an impact in the widest possible number of beliefs. It will be your task to educate all those in authority, whether in a faith or a non-believer, that there is only one God, but there are many paths leading to Him.

'Remember, if any of you even attempted to raise a weapon in the name of conversion – as has always been the case – you do so from the standpoint of earthly corruption rather than divine guidance. Christians have killed non-Christians in the past because they failed to understand the old covenants. Muslims have murdered – and all because a tiny minority deliberately refuse to understand what Islam means.

'In fact, what we require is the foresight of Muhammad when he was first visited by Christians. He invited them to worship in his Mosque, understanding perfectly that they had a different way of praying, but understanding too that different methods of worship should never limit access to a true place of worship.

'If any of you are worried that such tolerance might undermine your own faith, then you're praying to protocol, not to God. You've been given a message of unification and resolution – the single sacred origin of every faith. It has taken 2,000 years for even a handful of religious leaders to come to realise that their previous attitudes only lead to mutual destruction – yet even some of these fail to concede the greater purpose they need to find. This is your purpose and your mission.

267

'Many of you might still be wondering "Why me?" I know most of you have had discussions about this already. For those still doubtful, this is not about perfection. We have chosen people from all walks of life, none perfect, but all honest in striving. God did not choose perfect tools. If this message was delivered by another Christ or a divine messenger, we would only run the risk of starting yet another branch of worship.

'But don't be afraid, for many people of good will only go along with mankind's confusion in the absence of an alternative. You will find many ready to help you.

'Your goal is to ensure that in time people will no longer see themselves as Christian, Muslim, Hindu and so on. Not that they'll be expected to abandon the traditional roots of their religion – no, they'll refer to themselves as Yahwehian through Christ, Yahwehian through Muhammad, Yahwehian through the ancients or Yahwehian through some other Godly path or belief. Religion will be the expression of unity, as opposed to ignorance and enmity.'

Caittie's head ached as the deluge of words almost overcame her ability to take them in, as she couldn't seem to connect the "task" with either her father's dreams or her own longings. She couldn't get past the feeling that it *should* have been her father, how he would have loved to be involved in this! She even caught her breath once, when she imagined that she saw him a few rows in front – a man of his build and posture, but with quite a different profile.

But then her father had never had time for God. She would have given anything to have a supportive word from him before going back – just a hug would have meant everything! Yet the man next to her had given a kind word, perhaps he would make sense of her instructions and make the unbearable bearable. The angel at the front paused and changed tone, which startled Caittie from her musings.

'Now I must ask Peter to take Andrew and set him on his way to write *Paradox Lost*. You must all leave in relevant order so that there's no possibility any one of you can guess the future of another.' The man at the front then stood aside, as if disengaging himself temporarily from the audience.

Peter moved towards Andrew, his face very serious, and seeing him approach Andrew rose, half-reluctant, half-nervous. At the same moment he noticed the girl looking at him intently, and hesitated, longing to say something helpful, but only managing a reassuring smile.

He followed Peter along the side of the room toward the front. They were heading towards a small doorway on the opposite side, Peter leading, and Andrew, as before, training his attention on the folds of his tunic. At the entrance, Peter put his hands on Andrew's shoulders (which heated instantly) to indicate that he should go first. Behind them they left the music and the light.

The doorway led into a tunnel, faint fragments of the other angel's voice echoing round Andrew's head. He hoped that Peter would tell him where to go, but there was no noise from the angel, and turning to ask, Andrew discovered he seemed to be alone. In fact, there was nothing but a silver-grey soundless fog surrounding him on every side. He refused to panic, knowing that it was meant to be. When he realised he might be surrounded by any of the others in the mist, he even half-chuckled.

Suddenly, his chuckling turned to choking. He was gasping for breath, but his lungs seemed dysfunctional. The miasma surrounding him suddenly tingled on his skin and eyes. He was lying, yet spinning, gravity deserting him, sickening his senses. His eyes tried to focus on what was now a narrowing blur. Then, just as suddenly his heart, which had at first felt constricted, squeezed as by a giant snake, as suddenly swelled open, and suddenly he was hearing again.

He was on his own sofa, in front of the TV. His son's words bounced off his ears in a barrage of friendly ridicule. Such banality felt incompatible with Peter's heat still warm on his shoulder. He stood up, his legs woolly.

'You all right, darling?' came from his wife, absently, but he had no words for her either, not just then, with the dust of heaven still clinging to him. Andrew turned to leave the lounge, reborn and changed forever.

Epilogue

Since writing this book, man has witnessed the possibility of matter traveling beyond the speed of light. This has been evident to me for some time, for when I applied logic equations onto quantum physics (equations developed to calculate the effects of emotional energy and is a subject based on real events), it made it a certainty. I chose not include any detailed arguments relating this to the time shift theory, for without proof it was best left as fiction. It would also draw the book into the same technical explanations toward the mysterious 21g weight loss suffered by the body at the point of death.